D0447020

She whipped open her front door and stopped short.

The lanky silhouette of the *Capricious*'s Captain Cordell Lamarr filled her stoop. The artificial light of Gantry Station's day cycle wreathed his dark brown skin with a yellow halo, blinding her hungover eyes and blocking her view of his expression. Was he angry? She didn't wait to find out.

"Hey, Bootsie," was all he got to say before she rushed forward and sunk a kick so hard into his groin he came off the ground.

She considered shoving him over the railing, but it was ten stories to the ground, and she owed him for old times' sake. Instead, she knocked his forehead against the rail as he doubled over, then she muscled past.

She couldn't tell if he swore or choked on his own spit, but it didn't matter. She'd put him down, and she'd be far away by the time he got back up.

A
BIG SHIP
AT THE
EDGE
OF THE
UNIVERSE

The Salvagers: Book One

ALEX WHITE

www.orbitbooks.net

This book is a work of fiction. Names, characters, places, and incidents are the product of the author's imagination or are used fictitiously. Any resemblance to actual events, locales, or persons, living or dead, is coincidental.

Copyright © 2018 by Alex White
Excerpt from *A Bad Deal for the Whole Galaxy* copyright © 2018 by Alex White
Excerpt from *Adrift* copyright © 2018 by Rob Boffard

Author photograph by Rebecca Winks
Cover design by Lisa Marie Pompilio
Cover images by Shutterstock
Cover copyright © 2018 by Hachette Book Group, Inc.

Hachette Book Group supports the right to free expression and the value of copyright. The purpose of copyright is to encourage writers and artists to produce the creative works that enrich our culture.

The scanning, uploading, and distribution of this book without permission is a theft of the author's intellectual property. If you would like permission to use material from the book (other than for review purposes), please contact permissions@hbgusa.com. Thank you for your support of the author's rights.

Orbit
Hachette Book Group
1290 Avenue of the Americas
New York, NY 10104
orbitbooks.net

First Edition: June 2018

Orbit is an imprint of Hachette Book Group.
The Orbit name and logo are trademarks of Little, Brown Book Group Limited.

The publisher is not responsible for websites (or their content) that are not owned by the publisher.

The Hachette Speakers Bureau provides a wide range of authors for speaking events. To find out more, go to www.hachettespeakersbureau.com or call (866) 376-6591.

Library of Congress Cataloging-in-Publication Data:
Names: White, Alex (Novelist), author.
Title: A big ship at the edge of the universe / Alex White.
Description: First edition. | New York : Orbit, 2018. | Series: The salvagers; 1
Identifiers: LCCN 2018003063| ISBN 9780316412063 (softcover) | ISBN 9780316412087 (ebook)
Subjects: LCSH: Space ships—Fiction. | BISAC: FICTION / Science Fiction / Adventure. |
    FICTION / Science Fiction / Space Opera. | GSAFD: Adventure fiction. | Science fiction.
Classification: LCC PS3623.H5687 B54 2018 | DDC 813/.6—dc23
LC record available at https://lccn.loc.gov/2018003063

ISBNs: 978-0-316-41206-3 (trade paperback), 978-0-316-41208-7 (ebook)

Printed in the United States of America

LSC-C

Printing 7, 2022

For Craig, and all the other adventurers
who never made it home.

Chapter One

D.N.F.

The straight opened before the two race cars: an oily river, speckled yellow by the evening sun. They shot down the tarmac in succession like sapphire fish, streamers of wild magic billowing from their exhausts. They roared toward the turn, precision movements bringing them within centimeters of one another.

The following car veered to the inside. The leader attempted the same.

Their tires only touched for a moment. They interlocked, and sheer torque threw the leader into the air. Jagged chunks of duraplast glittered in the dusk as the follower's car passed underneath, unharmed but for a fractured front wing. The lead race car came down hard, twisting eruptions of elemental magic spewing from its wounded power unit. One of its tires exploded into a hail of spinning cords, whipping the road.

In the background, the other blue car slipped away down the chicane—Nilah's car.

The replay lost focus and reset.

The crash played out again and again on the holoprojection in front of them, and Nilah Brio tried not to sigh. She had seen plenty of wrecks before and caused more than her share of them.

"Crashes happen," she said.

"Not when the cars are on the same bloody team, Nilah!"

Claire Asby, the Lang Autosport team principal, stood at her mahogany desk, hands folded behind her back. The office looked less like the sort of ultramodern workspace Nilah had seen on other teams and more like one of the mansions of Origin, replete with antique furniture, incandescent lighting, stuffed big-game heads (which Nilah hated), and gargantuan landscapes from planets she had never seen. She supposed the decor favored a pale woman like Claire, but it did nothing for Nilah's dark brown complexion. The office didn't have any of the bright, human-centric design and ergonomic beauty of her home, but team bosses had to be forgiven their eccentricities—especially when that boss had led them to as many victories as Claire had.

Her teammate, Kristof Kater, chuckled and rocked back on his heels. Nilah rolled her eyes at the pretty boy's pleasure. They should've been checking in with the pit crews, not wasting precious time at a last-minute dressing down.

The cars hovering over Claire's desk reset and moved through their slow-motion calamity. Claire had already made them watch the footage a few dozen times after the incident: Nilah's car dove for the inside and Kristof moved to block. The incident had cost her half her front wing, but Kristof's track weekend had ended right there.

"I want you both to run a clean race today. I am begging you to bring those cars home intact at all costs."

Nilah shrugged and smiled. "That'll be fine, provided Kristof follows a decent racing line."

"We were racing! I made a legal play and the stewards sided with me!"

Nilah loved riling him up; it was far too easy. "You were slow, and you got what you deserved: a broken axle and a bucket of tears. I got a five-second penalty"—she winked before continuing—"which cut into my thirty-three-second win considerably."

Claire rubbed the bridge of her nose. "Please stop acting like children. Just get out there and do your jobs."

Nilah held back another jab; it wouldn't do to piss off the team boss right before a drive. Her job was to win races, not meetings. Silently she and Kristof made their way to the door, and he flung it open in a rare display of petulance. She hadn't seen him so angry in months, and she reveled in it. After all, a frazzled teammate posed no threat to her championship standings.

They made their way through the halls from Claire's exotic wood paneling to the bright white and anodized blues of Lang Autosport's portable palace. Crew and support staff rushed to and fro, barely acknowledging the racers as they moved through the crowds. Kristof was stopped by his sports psychologist, and Nilah muscled past them both as she stepped out into the dry heat of Gantry Station's Galica Speedway.

Nilah had fired her own psychologist when she'd taken the lead in this year's Driver's Crown.

She crossed onto the busy parking lot, surrounded by the bustle of scooter bots and crews from a dozen teams. The bracing rattle of air hammers and the roar of distant crowds in the grandstands were all the therapy she'd need to win. The Driver's Crown was so close—she could clinch it in two races, especially if Kristof went flying off the track again.

"Do you think this is a game?" Claire's voice startled her. She'd come jogging up from behind, a dozen infograms swimming around her head, blinking with reports on track conditions and pit strategy.

"Do I think racing is a game? I believe that's the very definition of sport."

Claire's vinegar scowl was considerably less entertaining than Kristof's anger. Nilah had been racing for Claire since the junior leagues. She'd probably spent more of her teenage years with her principal than her own parents. She didn't want to disappoint Claire, but she wouldn't be cowed, either. In truth, the incident galled her—the crash was nothing more than a callow attempt by Kristof to hold her off for another lap. If she'd lost the podium, she would've called for his head, but he got what he deserved.

They were a dysfunctional family. Nilah and Kristof had been racing together since childhood, and she could remember plenty of happy days trackside with him. She'd been ecstatic when they both joined Lang; it felt like a sign that they were destined to win.

But there could be only one Driver's Crown, and they'd learned the hard way the word "team" meant nothing among the strongest drivers in the Pan-Galactic Racing Federation. Her friendship with Kristof was long dead. At least her fondness for Claire had survived the transition.

"If you play dirty with him today, I'll have no choice but to create some consequences," said Claire, struggling to keep up with Nilah in heels.

Oh, please. Nilah rounded the corner of the pit lane and marched straight through the center of the racing complex, past the offices of the race director and news teams. She glanced back at Claire, who, for all her posturing, couldn't hide her worry.

"I never play dirty. I win because I'm better," said Nilah. "I'm not sure what your problem is."

"That's not the point. You watch for him today, and mind yourself. This isn't any old track."

Nilah got to the pit wall and pushed through the gate onto the starting grid. The familiar grip of race-graded asphalt on her shoes sent a spark of pleasure up her spine. "Oh, I know all about Galica."

The track sprawled before Nilah: a classic, a legend, a warrior's track that had tested the mettle of racers for a hundred years. It showed its age in the narrow roadways, rendering overtaking difficult and resulting in wrecks and safety cars—and increased race time. Because of its starside position on Gantry Station, ambient temperatures could turn sweltering. Those factors together meant she'd spend the next two hours slow-roasting in her cockpit at three hundred kilometers per hour, making thousands of split-second, high-stakes decisions.

This year brought a new third sector with more intricate corners and a tricky elevation change. It was an unopened present, a new toy to play with. Nilah longed to be on the grid already.

If she took the podium here, the rest of the season would be an easy downhill battle. There were a few more races, but the smart money knew this was the only one that mattered. The harmonic chimes of StarSport FN's jingle filled the stadium, the unofficial sign that the race was about to get underway.

She headed for the cockpit of her pearlescent-blue car. Claire fell in behind her, rattling off some figures about Nilah's chances that were supposed to scare her into behaving.

"Remember your contract," said Claire as the pit crew boosted Nilah into her car. "Do what you must to take gold, but any scratch you put on Kristof is going to take a million off your check. I mean it this time."

"Good thing I'm getting twenty mil more than him, then. More scratches for me!" Nilah pulled on her helmet. "You keep Kristof out of my way, and I'll keep his precious car intact."

She flipped down her visor and traced her mechanist's mark across the confined space, whispering light flowing from her fingertips. Once her spell cemented in place, she wrapped her fingers around the wheel. The system read out the stats of her sigil: good V's, not great on the Xi, but a healthy cast.

Her magic flowed into the car, sliding around the finely tuned ports, wending through channels to latch onto gears. Through the power of her mechanist's mark, she felt the grip of the tires and spring of the rods as though they were her own legs and feet. She joined with the central computer of her car, gaining psychic access to radio, actuation, and telemetry. The Lang Hyper 8, a motorsport classic, had achieved phenomenal performance all season in Nilah's hands.

Her psychic connection to the computer stabilized, and she searched the radio channels for her engineer, Ash. They ran through the checklist: power, fuel flow, sigil circuits, eidolon core. Nilah felt through each part with her magic, ensuring all functioned properly. Finally, she landed on the clunky Arclight Booster.

It was an awful little PGRF-required piece of tech, with high output but terrible efficiency. Nilah's mechanist side absolutely despised the magic-belching beast. It was as ugly and inelegant as it was expensive. Some fans claimed to like the little light show when it boosted drivers up the straights, but it was less than perfect, and anything less than perfect had to go.

"Let's start her up, Nilah."

"Roger that."

Every time that car thrummed to life, Nilah fell in love all over again. She adored the Hyper 8 in spite of the stonking flaw on his backside. Her grip tightened about the wheel and she took a deep breath.

The lights signaled a formation lap and the cars took off, weaving across the tarmac to keep the heat in their tires. They slipped around the track in slow motion, and Nilah's eyes traveled the third sector. She would crush this new track design. At the end of the formation lap, she pulled into her grid space, the scents of hot rubber and oil smoke sweet in her nose.

Game time.

The pole's leftmost set of lights came on: five seconds until the last light.

Three cars ahead of her, eighteen behind: Kristof in first, then the two Makina drivers, Bonnie and Jin. Nilah stared down the Makina R-27s, their metallic livery a blazing crimson.

The next pair of lights ignited: four seconds.

The other drivers revved their engines, feeling the tuning of their cars. Nilah echoed their rumbling engines with a shout of her own and gave a heated sigh, savoring the fire in her belly.

Three seconds.

Don't think. Just see.

The last light came on, signaling the director was ready to start the race.

Now, it was all about reflexes. All the engines fell to near silence.

One second.

The lights clicked off.

Banshee wails filled the air as the cars' power units screamed to life. Nilah roared forward, her eyes darting over the competition. Who was it going to be? Bonnie lagged by just a hair, and Jin made a picture-perfect launch, surging up beside Kristof. Nilah wanted to make a dive for it but found herself forced in behind the two lead drivers.

They shot down the straight toward turn one, a double apex. Turn one was always the most dangerous, because the idiots fighting for the inside were most likely to brake too late. She swept out for a perfect parabola, hoping not to see some fool about to crash into her.

The back of the pack was brought up by slow, pathetic Cyril Clowe. He would be her barometer of race success. If she could lap him in a third of the race, it would be a perfect run.

"Tell race control I'm lapping Clowe in twenty-five," Nilah grunted, straining against the g-force of her own acceleration. "I want those blue flags ready."

"He might not like that."

"If he tries anything, I'll leave him pasted to the tarmac."

"You're still in the pack," came Ash's response. "Focus on the race."

Got ten seconds on the Arclight. Four-car gap to Jin. Turn three is coming up too fast.

Bonnie Hayes loomed large in the rearview, dodging left and right along the straight. The telltale flash of an Arclight Booster erupted on the right side, and Bonnie shot forward toward the turn. Nilah made no moves to block, and the R-27 overtook her. It'd been a foolish ploy, and faced with too much speed, Bonnie needed to brake too hard. She'd flat-spot her tires.

Right on cue, brake dust and polymer smoke erupted from Bonnie's wheels, and Nilah danced to the outside, sliding within mere inches of the crimson paint. Nilah popped through the gears and the car thrummed with her magic, rewarding her with a pristine turn. The rest of the pack was not so lucky.

Shredded fibron and elemental magic filled Nilah's rearview as the cars piled up into turn three like an avalanche. She had to keep her eyes on the track, but she spotted Guillaume's, Anantha's, and Bonnie's cars in the wreck.

"Nicely done," said Ash.

"All in a day's work, babes."

Nilah weaved through the next five turns, taking them exactly as practiced. Her car was water, flowing through the track along the swiftest route. However, Kristof and Jin weren't making things easy for her. She watched with hawkish intent and prayed for a slip, a momentary lockup, or anything less than the perfect combination of gear shifts.

Thirty degrees right, shift up two, boost... boost. Follow your prey until it makes a mistake.

Nilah's earpiece chirped as Ash said, "Kater's side of the garage just went crazy. He just edged Jin off the road and picked up half a second in sector one."

She grimaced. "Half a second?"

"Yeah. It's going to be a long battle, I'm afraid."

Her magic reached into the gearbox, tuning it for low revs. "Not at all. He's gambling. Watch what happens next."

She kept her focus on the track, reciting her practiced motions with little variance. The crowd might be thrilled by a half-second purple sector, but she knew to keep it even. With the increased tire wear, his car would become unpredictable.

"Kristof is in the run-off! Repeat: He's out in the kitty litter," came Ash.

"Well, that was quick."

She crested the hill to find her teammate's car spinning into the gravel along the run of the curve. She only hazarded a minor glance before continuing on.

"Switch to strat one," said Ash, barely able to contain herself. "Push! Push!"

"Tell Clowe he's mine in ten laps."

Nilah sliced through the chicane, screaming out of the turn with her booster aflame. She was a polychromatic comet, completely in her element. This race would be her masterpiece. She held the record for the most poles for her age, and she was about to get it for the most overtakes.

The next nine laps went well. Nilah handily widened the gap between herself and Kristof to over ten seconds. She sensed fraying in her tires, but she couldn't pit just yet. If she did, she'd never catch Clowe by the end of the race. His fiery orange livery flashed at every turn, tantalizingly close to overtake range.

"Put out the blue flags. I'm on Cyril."

"Roger that," said Ash. "Race control, requesting blue flags for Cyril Clowe."

His Arclight flashed as he burned it out along the straightaway, and she glided through the rippling sparks. The booster was a piece of garbage, but it had its uses, and Clowe didn't understand any of them. He wasn't even trying anymore, just blowing through his boost at random times. What was the point?

Nilah cycled through her radio frequencies until she found Cyril's. Best to tease him a bit for the viewers at home. "Okay, Cyril, a lesson: use the booster to make the car go faster."

He snorted on his end. "Go to hell, Nilah."

"Being stuck behind your slow ass is as close as I've gotten."

"Get used to it," he snapped, his whiny voice grating on her ears. "I'm not letting you past."

She downshifted, her transmission roaring like a tiger. "I hope you're ready to get flattened then."

Galica's iconic Paige Tunnel loomed large ahead, with its blazing row of lights and disorienting reflective tiles. Most racers would avoid an overtake there, but Nilah had been given an opportunity, and she wouldn't squander it. The outside stadium vanished as she slipped into the tunnel, hot on the Hambley's wing.

She fired her booster, and as she came alongside Clowe, the world's colors began to melt from their surfaces, leaving only drab black and white. Her car stopped altogether—gone from almost two hundred kilometers per hour to zero in the blink of an eye.

Nilah's head darkened with a realization: she was caught in someone's spell as surely as a fly in a spiderweb.

The force of such a stop should have powdered her bones and liquefied her internal organs instantly, but she felt no change in her body, save that she could barely breathe.

The world had taken on a deathly shade. The body of the Hyper 8, normally a lovely blue, had become an ashen gray. The fluorescent magenta accents along her white jumpsuit had also faded, and all had taken on a blurry, shifting turbulence.

Her neck wouldn't move, so she couldn't look around. Her

fingers barely worked. She connected her mind to the transmission, but it wouldn't shift. The revs were frozen in place in the high twenty thousands, but she sensed no movement in the drive shaft.

All this prompted a silent, slow-motion scream. The longer she wailed, the more her voice came back. She flexed her fingers as hard as they'd go through the syrupy air. With each tiny movement, a small amount of color returned, though she couldn't be sure if she was breaking out of the spell—or into it.

"Nilah, is that you?" grunted Cyril. She'd almost forgotten about the Hambley driver next to her. All the oranges and yellows on his jumpsuit and helmet stood out like blazing bonfires, and she wondered if that's why he could move. But his car was the same gray as everything else, and he struggled, unsuccessfully, to unbuckle. Was Nilah on the cusp of the magic's effects?

"What…" she forced herself to say, but pushing the air out was too much.

"Oh god, we're caught in her spell!"

Whose spell, you git? "Stay…calm…"

She couldn't reassure him, and just trying to breathe was taxing enough. If someone was fixing the race, there'd be hell to pay. Sure, everyone had spells, but only a fool would dare cast one into a PGRF speedway to cheat. A cadre of wizards stood at the ready for just such an event, and any second, the dispersers would come online and knock this whole spiderweb down.

In the frozen world, an inky blob moved at the end of the tunnel. A creature came crawling along the ceiling, its black mass of tattered fabric writhing like tentacles as it skittered across the tiles. It moved easily from one perch to the next, silently capering overhead before dropping down in front of the two frozen cars.

Cyril screamed. She couldn't blame him.

The creature stood upright, and Nilah realized that it was human. Its hood swept away, revealing a brass mask with a cutaway that exposed thin, angry lips on a sallow chin. Metachroic lenses peppered the exterior of the mask, and Nilah instantly recognized their purpose—to see in all directions. Mechanists had always talked about creating such a device, but no one had ever been able to move for very long while wearing one; it was too disorienting.

The creature put one slender boot on Cyril's car, then another as it inexorably clambered up the car's body. It stopped in front of Cyril and tapped the helmet on his trembling head with a long, metallic finger.

Where are the bloody dispersers?

Cyril's terrified voice huffed over the radio. "Mother, please..."

Mother? Cyril's mother? No; Nilah had met Missus Clowe at the previous year's winner's party. She was a dull woman, like her loser son. Nilah took a closer look at the wrinkled sneer poking out from under the mask.

Her voice was a slithering rasp. "Where did you get that map, Cyril?"

"Please. I wasn't trying to double-cross anyone. I just thought I could make a little money on the side."

Mother crouched and ran her metal-encased fingers around the back of his helmet. "There is no 'on the side,' Cyril. We are everywhere. Even when you think you are untouchable, we can pluck you from this universe."

Nilah strained harder against her arcane chains, pulling more color into her body, desperate to get free. She was accustomed to being able to outrun anything, to absolute speed. Panic set in.

"You need me to finish this race!" he protested.

"We don't *need* anything from you. You were lucky enough to be chosen, and there will always be others. Tell me where you got the map."

"You're just going to kill me if I tell you."

Nilah's eyes narrowed, and she forced herself to focus in spite of her crawling fear. Kill him? What the devil was Cyril into?

Mother's metal fingers clacked, tightening across his helmet. "It's of very little consequence to me. I've been told to kill you if you won't talk. That was my only order. If you tell me, it's my discretion whether you live or die."

Cyril whimpered. "Boots...er...Elizabeth Elsworth. I was looking for...I wanted to know what you were doing, and she...she knew something. She said she could find the *Harrow*."

Nilah's gaze shifted to Mother, the racer's eye movements sluggish and sleepy despite her terror. *Elizabeth Elsworth?* Where had Nilah heard that name before? She had the faintest feeling that it'd come from the Link, maybe a show or a news piece. Movement in the periphery interrupted her thoughts.

The ghastly woman swept an arm back, fabric tatters falling away to reveal an armored exoskeleton encrusted with servomotors and glowing sigils. Mother brought her fist down across Cyril's helmet, crushing it inward with a sickening crack.

Nilah would've begun hyperventilating, if she could breathe. This couldn't be happening. Even with the best military-grade suits, there was no way this woman could've broken Cyril's helmet with a mere fist. His protective gear could withstand a direct impact at three hundred kilometers per hour. Nilah couldn't see what was left of his head, but blood oozed between the cracked plastic like the yolk of an egg.

Just stay still. Maybe you can fade into the background. Maybe you can—

"And now for you," said Mother, stepping onto the fibron body of Nilah's car. Of course she had spotted Nilah moving in that helmet of hers. "I think my spell didn't completely affect you, did it? It's so difficult with these fast-moving targets."

Mother's armored boots rested at the edge of Nilah's cockpit, and mechanical, prehensile toes wrapped around the lip of the car. Nilah forced her neck to crane upward through frozen time to look at Mother's many eyes.

"Dear lamb, I am so sorry you saw that. I hate to be so harsh," she sighed, placing her bloody palm against Nilah's silver helmet, "but this is for the best. Even if you got away, you'd have nowhere to run. We own everything."

Please, please, please, dispersers... Nilah's eyes widened. She wasn't going to die like this. Not like Cyril. *Think. Think.*

"I want you to relax, my sweet. The journos are going to tell a beautiful story of your heroic crash with that fool." She gestured to Cyril as she said this. "You'll be remembered as the champion that could've been."

Dispersers scramble spells with arcane power. They feed into the glyph until it's over capacity. Nilah spread her magic over the car, looking for anything she could use to fire a pulse of magic: the power unit—drive shaft locked, the energy recovery system—too weak, her ejection cylinder—lockbolts unresponsive...then she remembered the Arclight Booster. She reached into it with her psychic connection, finding the arcane linkages foggy and dim. Something about the way this spell shut down movement even muddled her mechanist's art. She latched on to the booster, knowing the effect would be unpredictable, but it was Nilah's only chance. She tripped the magical switch to fire the system.

Nothing. Mother wrapped her steely hands around Nilah's helmet.

"I should twist instead of smash, shouldn't I?" whispered the old woman. "Pretty girls should have pretty corpses."

Nilah connected the breaker again, and the slow puff of arcane plumes sighed from the Arclight. It didn't want to start in this magical haze, but it was her only plan. She gave the switch one last snap.

The push of magical flame tore at the gray, hazy shroud over the world, pulling it away. An array of coruscating starbursts surged through the surface, and Nilah was momentarily blinded as everything returned to normal. The return of momentum flung Mother from the car, and Nilah was slammed back into her seat.

Faster and faster her car went, until Nilah wasn't even sure the tires were touching the road. Mother's spell twisted around the Arclight's, intermingling, destabilizing, twisting space and time in ways Nilah never could've predicted. It was dangerous to mix unknown magics—and often deadly.

She recognized this effect, though—it was the same as when she passed through a jump gate. She was teleporting.

A flash of light and she became weightless. At least she could breathe again.

She locked onto the sight of a large, windowless building, but there was something wrong with it. It shouldn't have been upside down as it was, nor should it have been spinning like that. Her car was in free fall. Then she slammed into a wall, her survival shell enveloping her as she blew through wreckage like a cannonball.

Her stomach churned with each flip, but this was far from her first crash. She relaxed and let her shell come to a halt, wedged in a half-blasted wall. Her fuel system exploded, spraying elemental energies in all directions. Fire, ice, and gusts of catalyzed gasses swirled outside the racer's shell.

The suppressor fired, and Nilah's bound limbs came free. A harsh, acrid mist filled the air as the phantoplasm caking Nilah's body melted into the magic-numbing indolence gasses. Gale-force winds and white-hot flames snuffed in the blink of an eye. The sense of her surrounding energies faded away, a sudden silence in her mind.

Her disconnection from magic was always the worst part about a crash. The indolence system was only temporary, but there was always the fear: that she'd become one of those dull-fingered wretches. She screwed her eyes shut and shook her head, willing her mechanist's magic back.

It appeared on the periphery as a pinhole of light—a tiny, bright sensation in a sea of gray. She willed it wider, bringing more light and warmth into her body until she overflowed with her own magic. Relief covered her like a hot blanket, and her shoulders fell.

But what had just murdered Cyril? Mother had smashed his head open without so much as a second thought. And Mother would know exactly who she was—Nilah's name was painted on every surface of the Lang Hyper 8. What if she came back?

The damaged floor gave way, and she flailed through the darkness, bouncing down what had to be a mountain of cardboard boxes. She came to a stop and opened her eyes to look around.

She'd landed in a warehouse somewhere she didn't recognize. Nilah knew every inch of the Galica Speedway—she'd been coming to PGRF races there since she was a little girl, and this warehouse didn't mesh with any of her memories. She pulled off her helmet and listened for sirens, for the banshee wail of race cars, for the roar of the crowd, but all she could hear was silence.

Chapter Two

Memory and Debt

Rule number one when crafting a compelling salvage map: magic must always be the point. Of the almost fifty legends Boots had cobbled together and put out for sale that year, thirty-two of them had been focused on the arcane. Star charts for ancient artifacts or sites of incredible spiritual energy commanded a high price, bringing in almost a week's worth of living expenses apiece. Treasure hunters would scramble to snatch them up far more often than the charts for mundane prizes. Maybe it was because no one knew the limits of what magic could do. Maybe everyone fancied themselves grand magi in the making.

Elizabeth "Boots" Elsworth had a pedigree. Once in her past, she'd been right about a treasure. Even after all this time, that was still worth something.

Boots thought on this as she looked over the ephemeral screen that contained her bank account information. She wasn't broke. Broke would've been good—comforting, even. She was less than broke, and soon, debtors would come calling.

"You have some new messages," Kin's tinny voice echoed through Boots's firetrap studio apartment.

She pushed the projected screen away, where it wafted into nothingness, then stretched as she made her way across the room, a new pop in her shoulder the latest in a host of recent bony creaks. Her gait had a drunken limp this morning, and she supposed she shouldn't have tied on her sixth glass the previous night.

Rule number two: a good legend is a fluffy story wrapped around a piece of hard evidence.

Boxes of binders leaned on shelves of books, which were piled atop towers of sheaves. Loose leaves stuck out from every edge, and hundreds if not thousands of scroll tubes stood precariously on top like crenellations on her makeshift fortresses.

Of all the people on Gantry Station, she imagined she had the most paper at any one time. The rubes loved paper, and the older the print, the more true something became—even if it was just a census chart or loose page from a catalog. She told herself she read the papers to craft legends, but she couldn't deny that part of her hoped to find another truth.

She bought the pages where she could, particularly favoring anything from Origin, but she couldn't afford first editions—only copies. As long as she could point to some shred of hard copy as evidence, her customers would happily snap up a star chart for a few thousand argents. After operating expenses, archival purchases, paid searches, and maintaining her office lease, that didn't leave much.

"It looks as though you might have some new clients," said Kin.

She scoffed at the word "client." There was nothing reputable about her remaining fans. They were fools at best and insane at worst. Still, if they wanted to show up and buy star charts, she'd make sure there were a few for sale.

Safely arriving at the dispenser, she dropped a cube of coffee into a mug and filled it with hot water. "Just read the messages."

"Sure thing, Lizzie."

She gingerly took a sip, waking up a tiny bit of her whiskeyed brain. Kin began to read: the landlord had no intention of fixing her lock and suggested she buy her own (no cash). Some guy named Cameron wanted to partner up for a salvage run (probably a scam). Her neighbor Arty wanted her to stop slamming her door if she was going to be out late drinking (nope, not happening). There were an additional eight messages from various conspiracy theorist whackadoos who saw her ads but couldn't afford her products.

"Oh boy," Kin sighed. "Let's just skip this one."

"Let's not," said Boots. "What is it?"

"Voice message. Death threat from Rocco."

"So? I get those all the time. Play it."

"Lizzie, I don't think—"

She rolled her eyes. "I said play it, Kin!"

After a short hiss, the message began. Rocco's voice had a musical quality—like an accordion being kicked down some stairs. Boots winced as he barked the first sentence: "Boots, I been using your maps for years. I believed in you. But this is the fifth run with no treasure, you short, ugly, double-crossing, sparkless, dull-fingered—"

And that was all Boots heard before her cottony skull awoke to a new fire. Her nostrils flared, but she managed to stop herself from smashing her mug into the floor.

One in five million people: those were the odds of being born without magic—arcana dystocia. Most people would never meet a spell-less person, yet everyone had a word for her condition—"dull-fingers," "nulls." "Sparkless" was a particular favorite, because she didn't have a cardioid like every other human. It was a tiny little nub of an organ nestled next to the amygdala—but it left a big hole in Boots's life. Without it, she'd never spark her fingers to cast a spell.

"Stop the message, Kin." And Rocco was silenced.

"Dull-fingered?" Had she heard right? There was no way Rocco

19

would've said that to her face without a broken nose. She hadn't been called dull in a few years, and the last fellow who said that had ended up in a cast.

"That cocky scribbler..." She set her coffee down. "What was the last thing I sold Rocco?"

"He got coordinates for the Connick Cargo—a shipment of crystals lost in the—"

She waved the computer off like an unpleasant smell. "Yeah, I remember now. Shoot those coordinates over to Vargas and tell him where his old partner is."

"He'll want to know the reason for your betrayal."

"Tell Vargas that punk called me dull. No point mincing words."

"This might result in Rocco's death. Those coordinates are a long way from a jump portal. Vargas will get there long before Rocco can escape."

She picked up her mug and took a warm swig. "Wages of sin, I guess. I'll show you 'dull-fingered,' you supremacist piece of..."

Rule number three is the most important one. A great legend always happens in the middle of nowhere. Rocco wouldn't be getting away from his past this time. That system was a big one, but there weren't many places to hide from a good scanner.

"It's done," Kin sighed.

Boots felt better already. "Great. Next message."

"This one is from the... Asselion Group."

Boots winced whenever he mispronounced things. On a good day, she could pretend he was still alive. Kinnard, the AI assistant, was constructed from her memories of the real Kinnard, who'd fought alongside her in the Famine War... and a pale imitation. When she'd bought his voice from the mnemonimancer, she didn't know the word "Acclion," so neither did he.

"That's pronounced 'Ack-lion.' It's the leasing company," she said.

"Roger that. It's in regard to your office on their premises."

"Read it."

"Ms. Elsworth, hello. This is Sondra Kohan from the Acclion Group, contacting you in reference to claim number 4506J-00349, the fire at our Cresting Flows location. The fire marshal's investigation revealed that the flames started outside your office. They believe it's an arson case. Arcane explosives were involved, and there was a distinct resonance.

My questions at this point are myriad, as I'm sure you can imagine. Of course, our concern for your safety is paramount, so we hope you will not attempt to visit the remains of your office for the time being. If this was an attempt on your life, it would be dangerous for you and others around you to be here. All future correspondence will be remote.

As this is an arson case, it's your liability. This is clearly stipulated by the leasing agreement, and we are not responsible for any loss of property. I've sent the contact information for our general counsel to your assistant. Per the terms of our contract, please contact us with any developments law enforcement has regarding your investigation."

That office contained half of her archives—the good half she used during meetings with hopeful salvage captains. Those archives weren't officially appraised, but she'd sunk a sizable portion of her savings into them. Her office was her taxable business front, and she'd hoped to convert part of it to a realty later so she could draw a more stable income.

But now it was up in smoke, and they weren't going to replace her papers.

Boots spat into her trash can. "So much for going legit."

"You want me to read you the contact info?"

"Nah. Screw them. That bloodsucker can call me if she wants me. Any theories on who toasted my office?"

"I wouldn't want to speculate." That was Kin's code for "not in my memory banks."

"What other messages do we have? Anything?" Boots tossed her mug into the dishwasher.

"Let's see...here we are. It's from the dockmaster."

After a beep, she removed her mug and put it back on the countertop. No point putting it away when she was just going to use it again at lunch. "The dockmaster?"

"You put out a watch on the *Capricious*, in case it came into the station."

Her stomach dropped. "And?"

"Looks like it docked six hours ago. Second time this week, in fact. He says he's sorry for not telling you sooner. It slipped his mind."

"Oh no. Kin, eject your core. We've got to go."

"I was about to order some breakfast for—"

"Now, Kin!"

She scrambled over her couch to get to the dresser, where she tore into her drawers. She located a duffel and began stuffing her clothes into it as quickly as possible. Pants, shirts, and undergarments went in first, then she dug out the case for her old slinger. Boots popped the latches and looked inside at the dusty weapon—an ancient Carrington 23. She had scarcely fired it since the war, and she hadn't been a crack shot even then. It had a few cartridges, each aglow with the orange light of a fire spell. Maybe she couldn't carve a glyph, but even a dull-finger could pull a trigger.

She slapped the case shut and threw it in the duffel, then dashed to the wall panel where Kin's crystalline core had begun to slide out of the edifice.

"Where are we going?" asked Kin.

"Away." It was the truth, because she had no idea. "Get me a ticket on the first ship leaving the system."

"You have no money, Lizzie."

"So? You're a military-grade AI! Make one for me!"

"Roger that. This will require several hours, and there is a high chance of alerting the authorities." Kin was an ace code breaker, but he wasn't exactly subtle inside a database. His attacks were brute force and left lots of evidence. "You're likely to be arrested."

"Forget it," she growled.

She could've snapped that dockmaster's neck for his failure to alert her. Those idiots on the *Capricious* were the last people in the galaxy she wanted to see after what she'd done to them. Yanking Kin out of the wall, she shoved the cube into the duffel and zipped it shut.

She whipped open her front door and stopped short.

The lanky silhouette of the *Capricious*'s Captain Cordell Lamarr filled her stoop. The artificial light of Gantry Station's day cycle wreathed his dark brown skin with a yellow halo, blinding her hungover eyes and blocking her view of his expression. Was he angry? She didn't wait to find out.

"Hey, Bootsie," was all he got to say before she rushed forward and sunk a kick so hard into his groin he came off the ground.

She considered shoving him over the railing, but it was ten stories to the street, and she owed him for old times' sake. Instead, she knocked his forehead against the rail as he doubled over, then she muscled past.

She couldn't tell if he swore or choked on his own spit, but it didn't matter. She'd put him down, and she'd be far away by the time he got back up.

She couldn't take the stairs down. They'd be waiting. She could try to make the one-and-a-half-meter jump to the next building— it was only certain death if she fell. Boots took one more look at Cordell and vaulted the rail, launching across the small gap between the two buildings to land on the roof of Skylane Apartments. She rolled, but her knee responded with searing pain. Cordell bellowed her name somewhere behind her, but she wasn't about to look back. Scrambling to her feet, she limped quickly to the other side of the roof and looked over the ledge.

Boots instantly recognized Orna Sokol, the *Capricious*'s quartermaster, lurking far below. Close-cropped black hair, a scarred face—even outside of her fighting armor, the tall woman couldn't blend into a crowd. Boots searched her memory; Cordell needed six crew for a full complement, and a good captain never went out half-cocked. There'd be others skulking around.

"Boots, get back here!" Cordell shouted from the balcony, a quaver in his voice—not so commanding now. He clutched the railing, pain further contorting his enraged face.

She didn't take the time to respond. Instead, she crossed to the escape ladder, slung a leg over, and slid down. She landed hard, her ankle taking the brunt of the blow. That leg wasn't going to withstand much more punishment, and she'd be buying a healer's mark if she wasn't careful.

The plan had been to kick her way into someone's window and head down through the building's quick chutes, but she spotted an emergency box on the wall. She bashed in the glass and was pleased to find an unused descender, though now the fire alarm clicked on, alerting everyone to the nonexistent distress. Taking the small, crystalline disk in one hand, she mounted the side of the fire escape and leapt into the open air of the alley.

She crushed the fragile crystal, and its gooey magic enfolded her in a gelatinous cocoon. Her container hit the floor of the alley once, then after a big bounce, struck again, splashing open like an egg. She was left dripping wet with phantoplasm, flat on her ass in the middle of a dirty alcove, but at least she'd gotten down quickly.

Once upright, she surveyed her exits. Starward, there were more narrows to dive down and maybe lose her pursuers. Planetwise, she could rush into the public thoroughfare, where she might be able to confuse them.

"Orna!" screamed Cordell, tracing out a glowing glyph with all the speed of a pro. "She jumped! She's in the alley!" He finished his spell and leapt over the edge. A bright blue shield snapped into focus around him and he shattered the pavement where he landed.

Not waiting another minute, Boots took off for the crowded street.

Hundreds of people milled through Gantry's lowtown marketplace, and Boots was happy to see all of them. This was her town, and she knew dozens of places on the other side of the market to hide. Cordell wouldn't shoot into a crowd, and he wouldn't let his subordinates do that, either.

Boots knew a few of the vendors, and as she pushed her way toward safety, she prayed no one would call out to her. She pulled up her collar and kept her head down.

She wasn't often thankful for a short, stocky stature and plain looks, but they came in handy from time to time. In a bland work shirt and worn pants, she looked exactly like everyone else. Cordell's crew would have a tough time locating her from behind, unless they had a mage who could sense her specific life force. She'd only met three of his crew, so who could be sure?

It had been cold-blooded to sell them the map—even Boots had to admit that. But Cordell had so much money from two decades of smuggling, and was it Boots's fault he wanted to believe in old legends? If anything, she was doing him a favor, because someone else might've led him into a trap, ambushed him on the far side of the galaxy and left his poor crew adrift in deep space. Boots didn't have the resources required for an ambush, a starship, weapons, or a crew, but her impulse to spare them surely made her a good person.

She ducked down a side passage and sprinted to the next row over, all the while mulling the situation in her head. She didn't feel bad about screwing over Cordell; he was part of the reason she was a broke liar in the first place. She'd tried to play nice after the war, do the right thing and surrender. Big-shot Arca Defense Force Captain Cordell Lamarr had refused.

She emerged from the passage in front of her favorite bar. A quick flash lit the crowd, and she spun to see a petite woman in a pilot's jumper complete a glyph: she had marksman's magic, which meant she'd never miss her next shot. On instinct, Boots tried to raise her duffel in front of her face, but the pilot leveled her slinger and put a clean shot into Boots's hand. Numbness slithered up Boots's arm and she lost her grip on the bag as a spasm flung it into the crowd of screaming bystanders.

The pilot's aim snapped to Boots's face and both women locked in place.

"Don't even think about it," said the pilot. For such a skinny thing, her voice had a clean edge. She was definitely ex-military. "Paralysis bolt. What do you think happens if this hits your chest?"

Boots slowly raised her nonparalyzed arm as the crowd parted behind her. "Easy, kid."

The pilot's slinger didn't waver in her hand one bit. Boots hadn't seen a marksman mage since the war, and the effect unnerved her.

She cleared her throat. "What do I need to do to make you stop pointing that heater at me?"

The pilot smirked. "We'll ask the captain when he gets—"

A hard tackle from Garda, Boots's regular barman, cut the pilot short. "Run!" he screamed as his two brothers came bursting through the front door. Her eyes darted to the duffel, but Boots did as she was asked, one arm flopping limply at her side.

Garda, a teenager with a hero complex, probably thought he was helping a defenseless older woman out. She'd have to remember to play that up next time she saw him; maybe it was worth a few drinks. Just before she rounded the corner, Boots saw Cordell and Orna descend into the melee with a few other members of the crowd. Silently, she thanked everyone who bought her a tiny sliver of time as she disappeared into the circuitous depths of Gantry Station.

The sign over the Widow's Watch had extinguished long ago, its ephemeral beacon once a rallying point for all the refugees of Clarkesfall, both Arcan and Kandamili.

You don't have to go in. Boots kept telling herself that, but she knew otherwise. She'd lost Kin in the scuffle, and she needed answers, so she came to the only place on Gantry Station she could get them. Boots despised the Watch and its owner, Silas, but he was connected, and he'd helped her out more than a few times. She watched the open door to the bar as though it would come billowing toward her, swallowing her alive. She wouldn't be the first to die in there; there were loads of folks who shot one another inside those walls, or simply dosed themselves into a wakeless sleep.

Get in. Get info. Get out.

She stepped through the doorway and muscled past the junk-strewn alcove.

"Look who it is!" Silas's rickety teeth barely supported the weight of a disgusted grimace. "I thought me and the boys kicked you out last time for fighting."

He gestured to the "boys." Not one of them was under forty. They languished in the darkness of the bar, listless each. They slept in military jackets worn twenty years past their use.

"Maybe you came to make amends . . . or maybe you want to peddle some more of your trash," he added; pretty rich, coming from him. "Some of your junk star charts."

"They're not junk."

"Maybe those charts were good, once. I watched your show. We all did. Cheered for you even, but in the end, you're one of us: destined for the garbage heap."

"Didn't come in here to talk about the show." She scooted to

27

the bar and knocked twice for a drink. "Just want to know a few things."

Boots glanced behind herself. She didn't have time for the posturing and conversation, not with Kin lost and Cordell on her tail. He'd think to look for her here sooner or later, so she needed to get her facts and beat feet.

Silas reached under the counter to find his cheapest rotgut in a scuffed, oily plastic bottle. He made a show of taking a slobbery shot from the mouth before pouring some of it into a dirty tumbler.

She took a long pull of the glass, its burning liquid like sucking an eidolon power crystal. Then she put it down, never breaking eye contact.

"Did Cordell burn down my office?"

"Maybe." He sniffled. "Did you deserve it?"

Boots's scowl could've scorched a lesser man, but Silas barely noticed. "I've done some low things in my time, but of course I didn't deserve it. I had half my assets tied up in there."

"I don't think Cordell put one through your office, but he came in after that. He was asking about you, and of course I told him where you was living."

Her stiff swallow left her coughing like a dying man. "Why would you do that, Sy?"

"I just wanted you two back on the same team is all. Miss the old days."

"Not going to happen. So can you take a guess at the arsonist?"

"I got better than a guess, but you got to pay for that."

"Only if you comp my whiskey."

"Tell you what: it's five hundred for the glass."

She cursed and dug around in her pocket for her paragon crystal—a small, metal box they gave to folks who couldn't trace a glyph for payment. Everyone knew what they looked like, but whenever she pulled hers out, people acted like they'd never seen one before.

Silas smirked. "What happens if you lose that thing? Can I get into your bank accounts?"

It'd happened before. There were plenty of scribblers who'd boost it from someone who couldn't cast. She made a habit to keep the paragon a secret, but once or twice, it hadn't panned out. She'd woken up beaten in an alleyway with a drained bank account. The cops would just tell her she was lucky to be alive.

She tapped it to his cash pad. "Sure. Except you wouldn't be stealing much."

He gave her a hard stare while he waited for the money to clear. Then his look darkened. "You got a bad sort looking for you. This old crone came through the refugee district knocking heads, looking for Arcans. You got to know something about this one: she looked like a walking war crime. Had the kind of cruel gaze I used to see a lot during the last days on Clarkesfall."

Boots suppressed a visible gulp. She knew that look: hungry and brutal.

"She was asking where you lived, and them boys told her where your office was instead. Ain't nobody going to sell out another Fallen, spite of your ways."

Don't call me that. "Ask about anything in particular?"

"Sure. She wanted to know who was peddling info about the *Harrow*."

Boots sucked her teeth. The story of the *Harrow* was a difficult one, and something she'd cobbled together out of a lot of different sources. A simple enough tale: the *Harrow* was a Taitutian conspiracy theory about a legendary warship capable of wiping countries off planets. It supposedly disappeared under spooky circumstances, but the story was all garbage.

The legend had fetched a high price from some creep back in more civilized space. She couldn't remember the fellow's name, but his argents spent just like everyone else's. Kin would know who the buyer was.

Except she'd dropped Kin back in the marketplace.

She had what she needed; time to find a graceful exit to the conversation and go. A flash of light in the dull room caught her eye: a single screen hovering near the back of the room. It was bent and twisted, its magic about to unravel from years of use and no maintenance. Race cars streaked across it, their colorful stripes setting them against the dingy tavern scenery.

"Shame," grunted Silas.

"That so many people watch something so stupid?"

"I'm going to ignore that. A racer died today, first in decades. Cyril Clowe—son of a Fallen."

The screen switched to a distant, blurry shot of a smoking wreck blasting out of a tunnel.

Boots scratched her nose. "Yeah? You know him?"

"Cyril? His daddy was a big muckitymuck after the war. But, uh, nah. I didn't know him."

Boots backed away from the bar, sliding her glass forward as she did. "Then who gives a damn? Boy died driving in circles... but I guess you two are a lot alike."

"How so?"

"You both act like you're going forward, but you only end up where you were." She gave him a mock salute, slapping her heart like the Arcans. "Stay cool, Silas."

Chapter Three

Chicane

Nilah wandered through the warehouse district for the better part of an hour, not stopping to talk to anyone. She didn't like the look of the people there; most of them didn't seem like they wanted to speak with her, and she feared anyone who did. Predatory eyes leered at her from the shadows between buildings, and several times, someone beckoned her to come to them. She wasn't stupid, and she had no intention of winding up in an alley with her throat cut, or worse. Her father had always taught her to avoid the lower districts no matter where she went, and Gantry Station was no exception.

In any civilized area, there would've been cops, or at least private security, but this place was bleak and industrial. She found a public terminal, but some intrepid looters had long since gutted it for parts, and there were no Hansom Consoles to hire a cab to take her back to the track and her team.

Her car's radio and transponder had been destroyed, and she had no personal comm unit with her. She had a Fixer chip, but cashing a million-argent policy to get a ride back to the track was massive overkill. There had to be some other way out.

As she walked, the scene of Clowe's death played out over and over in her mind. Mother's brassy exoskeleton and tattered cape sent shivers up her spine. The sight of Cyril's blood oozing out of his helmet would haunt her dreams forever. But another memory crept in alongside the blood: the panicked mention of the name Elizabeth Elsworth. Where did Nilah know her from?

Nilah mentally checked off the names of the team principals; she would've recognized them instantly. Same with any PGRF officials. She felt 99 percent sure Elsworth wasn't anyone from the world of racing. Perhaps it was banking? Her father's business on Taitu certainly brought Nilah into contact with her fair share of those. Yes, that was it. Elsworth had something to do with investment...but what? Maybe some sort of space travel investment.

Then it clicked: the Link. Elsworth was a treasure hunter who'd had some silly famous show where she went around begging for venture capital: *Searching for Something or Other*...Nilah had only watched a few episodes before checking out. She found the whole process rather degrading and couldn't imagine the sort of person who'd invest in legends and myth. Then again, had to be a sucker for every purpose.

The first episode had taken place on Gantry Station. Could Elizabeth Elsworth actually be here? Nilah could look her up and get some answers for herself, or better yet, have Elsworth arrested and let the police sort it out. It'd be good publicity and perhaps get Claire off her back. She still hadn't located a working terminal, and the locals appeared more menacing the farther she went.

Nilah unzipped her fire suit halfway and tied the sleeves around her waist, leaving her arms bare and maneuverable on the off chance someone tried something. She'd left her helmet with the wreckage, not wanting to draw any more attention than she already had. A set of ocean wave tattoos covered her forearms, dermaluxes shivering with a cold purple light—her fear. Under normal circumstances, she enjoyed brazenly sharing her emotions through her tattoos. Her confidence and anger played well on the track, and the press would crow with delight when Nilah's tattoos flared red, amplified by the translucent cuffs on her racing gloves.

In the back streets of Gantry Station, however, she psychically suppressed the luminescent nanobots, hoping no one saw how nervous she actually was.

Was she headed toward the higher decks, or deeper into the industrial zone? She absentmindedly rubbed her forearm where they'd implanted the Fixer chip, reminding herself that she would be fine, and it would be daft to spend so much money when she could just walk.

The Fixers were the gold standard insurance policy among the galactic elite, and technically illegal. Specializing in protection and extraction, the paramilitary group had rescued people from the icy glaciers of Yearling, protected provincial governors during coups, and even broken their customers out of maximum-security prisons. The chip they'd implanted in Nilah had the strongest shadow marks woven into it, and it was completely undetectable by all but the best scanners. She could always fall back on it if things got dicey.

Heading down a long, dilapidated corridor, she arrived at an open-air cafe and allowed her tattoos to show her relief with flowing golden light. At least, she thought it was a cafe, though they didn't serve anything that she'd consider food. As a Taitutian, she wouldn't touch animal flesh, and her stomach churned from the stench of roasting fat and soot. In the ancient past, it'd been considered imprudent to have a fire on a space station. In the cloying fumes of burning meat, she wished fire was still banned.

Nilah spotted a door marked as the water closet, and she made a beeline for it.

"Paying customers only," came the venomous voice of a greasy-faced blond man. He couldn't have been much older than twenty-five, but his skin had been carved with wrinkles, as though someone had stretched it too hard over his delicate face, then let it snap back.

She inhaled sharply, then immediately regretted it. "Of course. Um, right."

He nodded to her fire suit. "You race?"

She donned her podium smile, the one with which she charmed so many interviewers. "I dabble. Do you have a comm I can use?"

"No, and if you want to use the can, you got to buy something."

"The can? Oh the, ah, the loo. Got it. Maybe I could get directions to—"

"You going to buy something?"

"Ah." She pointed to the mass of brown, stringy meat steaming underneath a heat lamp. "What's that then?"

"Chicken."

She gulped. "All of it? Do you have anything fresher?"

His derisive snort gave her the answer she needed. "What, you want a live one?"

She put a hand on her hip. "I'd prefer something not dead and not sentient."

He smacked the metal trays each with his serving spoon. "Beef, pork, chicken, marpo. That's what I got. You want it?"

"Can't I just give you some money to use the restroom?"

The man scowled. "I look like a beggar to you?"

"No. Of course not. I'll have the beef, please."

He slopped some of the meat onto a plate alongside a roll, then poured a soupy, red sauce over the whole thing. The rising vinegar steam mixed with an undercurrent of hot spices nearly knocked Nilah unconscious. Her dermaluxes flared a bright green to the churning of her stomach, and she didn't bother hiding her displeasure.

He held out his cash pad. "That'll be five."

She signed her glyph, then set her meal down at a table before hurrying to the water closet. She held her breath as she wrenched open the door, expecting his restroom to be nothing more than a horrific wreck. Instead, she found it spotless, with a faint scent of flowers. She spun and looked over the chipped cafe tables, then realized how clean they were as well. Damaged, yes, but free of grime, their remaining paint polished to a spotless shine. His kitchen implements, terrifying though they were, also held no spots or grease.

Nilah briskly strode back to the man with the hunks of flesh. "Did you clean these things?"

He barely looked up from his work, where he carved a large slab of muscle into slices. "Yeah."

"You've got the hotelier's sigil." Cleaning magic was rare, and unemployed cleaning magi were rarer still.

His eyes darted between her and the food. "Yeah."

"Incredible. I've never seen one of you outside of hospital and lab work. We've got two at our factory, but you're a hard lot to find."

He slammed down hard with his knife, shearing through a bone.

She winced, but brought back her smile. "How would you like a job, working for me?"

"Got a job."

"Yes, well I can hardly call this working. You're scarcely using your talents. I've been looking for someone like you for—"

He shook his head. "How would you know? You ain't even tried my beef yet."

"I could pay you a lot of money. Setting animals on fire and chopping them to bits is hardly—"

"Just use the damned bathroom and get out of here."

She held up her hands and backed away. "All right. All right. I can see when I'm not wanted."

She'd always desired a hotelier in her employ, but she didn't have time to convince this one—not with Mother out there somewhere. What an awful shame.

She stepped inside the bathroom, where sparkling walls greeted her, and looked down at the skin tag at the base of her wrist; beneath it lay the Fixer chip. The better part of an hour had passed since she'd disappeared during a live stream. Her father was one of the most well-connected financiers on the richest planet in the galaxy. The Prime Minister was basically her godfather, for god's sake. Surely they'd find her before Mother did.

Don't call the Fixers just yet. Just calm down.

Nilah washed her arms and face in the basin. The clear water had a pleasant, herbal scent, like her father's garden after a rainstorm. It didn't matter what that bloody hotelier thought, he was wasting his talents on culinary catastrophes when he could be working for her. After all this was over, she'd send for him with an offer he couldn't refuse. Nilah pushed open the door to find the cafe had taken on a few more diners since she'd visited the restroom.

"Rough" didn't even begin to describe the fellows in the cafe: three blokes in sweat-stained work clothes, wiry and tense. They eyed her from under ragged thermal hoods, never saying a word to one another. She sat down at her table, keenly aware of all the eyes on her, then glanced at her plate—she wouldn't have touched it even if she ate flesh. But now that these men had been alone with her food, she didn't even like sitting near it.

"You like racing?" said the nearest bloke. He was missing part of his nostril, and Nilah looked away, not wanting to stare. She doubted he had lost it in an accident.

She glanced about for the hotelier, but he was nowhere to be found.

Nilah brushed off her legs. "Um, yes. How did you know?" He nodded to her fire suit, its sleeves still knotted around her waist. Her tattoos went a little green with disgust at his gaze.

"Those are some pretty waves, kid."

The dermaluxes turned an acidic shade in response to his open leering.

She prodded her stringy meat with a fork, scowling at the vinegar sauce. "Thank you. If you don't mind, I'm famished, so I'd, uh…I'd like to tuck in."

"I like racing, too," said Clip-nose. "I was watching the GP today."

This wasn't going to end well. These boys obviously knew who she was, and they were toying with her for some reason. If they wanted trouble, she could be trouble.

She put her fork down, cracked her knuckles, and picked it back up. "Oh? Who's your favorite driver?"

"Cyril Clowe."

His cracked-egg helmet oozed back into Nilah's mind, and she shook the image away.

The men stood up in unison, their chairs scraping against the floor like growling dogs. "You're Nilah Brio," said Clip-nose.

Time to get them riled. Riled men make mistakes.

She took to her feet and actively tuned her dermaluxes to a dim white. "You know my name, but I don't know yours. They probably aren't worth knowing."

"You trying to start a fight with us?" Clip-nose looked to his compatriots and chortled. "We're just a couple of concerned citizens, trying to do right by the law."

She kept a tight grip on her fork, not wanting her anger to show in her posture. "Really? You look like a couple of boys contemplating whether or not they can assault a woman."

"We're just here to collect the bounty."

She couldn't catch her laugh before it escaped her lips. "Bounty? I've been gone for an hour!"

Clip-nose sauntered toward her. "I couldn't believe my luck when I heard you were down here. This little payout is going to set me and my boys up for a good long time. Cops are saying you're dangerous. I think we should test that theory."

It had to be a distraction tactic, some way to get her to go along with them voluntarily. She was the wronged party here; she'd borne witness to a murder and lost out on her championship points.

"Oh, spare me. I've got the fastest reflexes in the PGRF. I don't think beating up a couple of malnourished hicks is going to—"

Clip-nose took a swing so telegraphed he could've sent her an invitation to it. With very little effort, she ducked back and planted the fork in the outside of his bicep. He howled in agony, and she kicked his knee out from under him before guiding his head into the table. On his way down, she jerked the fork back out.

Nilah's father had always insisted that a rich person needed to know self-defense. Kidnapping and extortion were common in many parts of the galaxy, and racers were always touring dangerous places. Nilah silently thanked her lucky stars for such a prudent parent.

She took a step backward and straightened, brandishing the bloody fork. "Who's for seconds?"

The two other men flipped out knives and rushed forward without another word. If they intended to escalate, she'd respond in kind. The ocean waves on her arms pulsated with a strobing, white flash, nanomachines responding to her mechanist's art.

Of all the martial arts Nilah had tried in her life, Flicker was the most potent. It was the art of misdirection, of stunning hits delivered with no defense.

She dodged left, narrowly avoiding the point of a knife before whipping her arm in a wide arc, blinding her opponent with her strobing tattoos. She shut off her right arm tattoos and put a right cross through his jaw, snapping it instantly. When his partner came in from the other side, swiping like crazy, she turned everything on full blast, fanning her arms to create a wall of light.

Then she crushed his balls with a racing boot.

Clip-nose had regained his feet, and No-balls and Jawless were considering a second attack. If she stayed, someone might die, and she didn't feel up to making her first kill that day. Worse still, there was nothing more unpredictable than a desperate man. Nilah cut her losses and ran.

Tunnel after tunnel, corner after corner, she pressed deeper into the guts of Gantry. The situation agitated her, but fleeing wasn't all that difficult; her would-be captors faced massive injuries, and she'd grown used to long-distance runs during training. She lost them within a few blocks and found a large rubbish bin to hide behind.

Perhaps those weren't the only men looking for her, though. She'd have to use her chip after all.

Nilah felt her way up her wrist and found the skin tag. She traced her sigil and focused her mechanist's art into the dormant circuit, forming an ad hoc transmitter core. Then the sting hit. The chip glowed white-hot, cauterizing instantly before healing over with a brassy sheen. Her dermaluxes flashed red, and she bit her lip. The sheen faded to her normal dark skin, concealing the fact that she'd done anything at all. Thankfully, the pain vanished, just as the Fixer doctor said it would. The chip would remain active for a few days, then dissolve into her body.

She sighed as the pain subsided, and her waves faded to a cool daylight. The signal had been sent to the Fixers; they'd follow her beacon and see her out of this situation within the hour. They had agents all over the galaxy, and surely one would be on Gantry Station. Everything would be okay. Nilah kept reminding herself that their work was legendary. Maybe the Fixers could even help her with this Mother character who'd murdered Cyril.

The bounty on her head shocked her. Law enforcement didn't typically put bounties on innocent women. Perhaps they only wanted to make sure someone spotted her quickly. She ached to check the news, but had no comms. She racked her brain, trying to think of something she could hack to get a bit of info. Any network-connected device would do: maybe one of the drones shuttling cargo around, an unguarded temperature sensor or lock on one of the buildings. She was so desperate, she'd consider hacking one of the security dispersers guarding a nearby depot.

Then she remembered: the dispersers back at the racetrack hadn't come to her and Cyril's rescue.

What did that mean? Were the station administrators behind this? Could it be someone on Gantry's board of shareholders? Nilah regretted not paying more attention at the various Gantry parties and press events.

She sat down behind the stinking bin, happy to keep her face hidden for a bit. It had been years since she'd been far from her bodyguards, creature comforts, and money.

"Nilah Brio," came a woman's whisper. "I'm Agent Mikaela Dawsey, from the Fixers. I need you to get up right now and come with me."

Nilah peered around the bin to find a skinny, tanned woman with bright, gold eyes and a comforting smile.

"Oh, thank god."

"We believe there is an active threat on your life. Let's get you onto a transport to Lang's headquarters."

Nilah stood and brushed herself off, then held out her hand. "Chuffed to see you, mate."

The Fixer shook it, then handed her a slinger. "Tuck that in the back of your jumpsuit. We're going to walk straight to the maintenance dock, climb on a ship, and head for the jump gate, all right?"

Nilah wasn't a great shot, but her self-defense training had taught her enough. She tucked the slinger into her waistband. "What kind of hazards are we expecting?"

Mikaela looked her up and down. "Let's just get on with the task at hand, shall we?"

They left Gantry's industrial section with little trouble, emerging into a slightly more populous thoroughfare. Nilah drew lots of stray looks, and Mikaela coached her not to look people in the eye. Distant news screens overhead showed pictures of Cyril's crash, along with old footage of Nilah from last season. Her portrait was captioned: CRIMINAL?

"Didn't you bring a change of clothes for me?" Nilah hissed.

Mikaela shook her head. "Everything is going to be fine, Miss Brio. We're almost to the maintenance dock."

"Okay, but there are a lot of people on this street. Suppose one of these clever boys recognizes me?"

Mikaela shot her a grin. "It's my job to think like that, Miss Brio. If you'll refrain from speaking, it makes you less recognizable."

"Right. I should just shut it."

The Fixer nodded. "Yes, ma'am."

Nilah's Fixer chip itched, its golden threads still transmitting her location to their clandestine headquarters. It made sense, not deactivating the transmitter until she was safe, but it still felt strange to be a beacon.

Her breath caught as she saw the first fluorescent orange sign for the maintenance dock. After such a horrid day, she could only think of a hot bath, so she almost missed it when a gentleman in a heavy coat drew a slinger and pointed it straight at her escort.

Quick as lightning, Mikaela drew her own weapon and hammered shot after shot through the screaming crowd. Each sun-bright needle from her slinger went straight through frightened civilians, even as the man dove out of the way. He rolled across the roadway and came up with a flourish, his gun leveled at Mikaela. The small crowd erupted into screams and scattered as police klaxons sounded through the district.

Nilah's escort wrenched her by the arm, placing the racer solidly between the two shooters. Mikaela's gunmetal was hot against Nilah's temple, and she gasped at its touch. She genuinely wanted to see Mikaela as the good guy in this situation, but there were several uninvolved bystanders bleeding to death on the ground— as well as the nagging problem of the slinger at her temple.

"Dawsey!" screamed the man. "Drop it and you get to live!"

Mikaela snorted, "Not happening."

"You betrayed us. All of you did."

She leveled her gun at him, placing a picture-perfect shot straight through his chest. He rocked back with the impact of the hit and signed out the fatalist's mark. Dawsey put a second shot through his stomach before he fired his slinger, but he got one round off. His magic curved his shot through the air, slicing across Dawsey's head and taking off the top of her skull.

Both shooters toppled, leaving Nilah standing in the middle of the moaning and half-dead. She whipped her slinger from her suit where she'd tucked it and checked its capacity. It was loaded with inert practice rounds, the kind they used to teach disarming techniques. Dawsey had given her a fake. The Fixers had betrayed her.

All thoughts of calling for help from the police fled Nilah's mind. If the Fixers couldn't be trusted, local cops were out of the question.

She rushed to the side of the fallen man and knelt next to him, showing him her weapon. "What's the meaning of this?"

He coughed and sputtered. "Nilah Brio, I'm Agent Goltz. The Fixers...have been compromised." He touched the circuit on Nilah's forearm, and she felt his magic key deactivate the system.

He sputtered blood onto his lips. "If you...If you live through this..."

His eyes rolled back in his head, and he shuddered with violent spasms. His hands thrashed the air as his chest ceased to rise and fall. By some miracle, he returned his focus to her, locking eyes for one more second.

"I hope you get a refund," he croaked.

Nilah stood, a dead Fixer at her feet, with no clues about an escape route and in a city full of police that would probably shoot her the second they saw her. Her mind reeled for things to say, but she could only form one question.

"What?"

Cordell hadn't left Boots's apartment all afternoon, and now the night cycle cloaked the station in darkness. Every hour, Boots would make a pass down the street in front of the building, then duck behind the electrical substation to check on her apartment through binoculars. Most of the time, she found Cordell standing out on the front balcony, a red-hot cigarette flaring in frustration.

It struck her as idiotic of him to stand around outside where he'd obviously be spotted. Maybe he genuinely wanted to talk to her, but that was the problem with other refugees: they always wanted to yammer about the old days. Perhaps he was a distraction, a scarecrow put out so Boots wouldn't see the real threat. He had plenty of crew still unaccounted for that could make Boots's life miserable under the right circumstances.

She thought of the mountain of trouble and restrained a groan. Her arm still wasn't working quite right since she'd been shot with that paralysis bolt, and her knee throbbed something fierce. Boots hadn't seen any evidence of Kin, even after canvassing the bazaar, which meant one of the *Capricious*'s crewmembers had him. She bristled to think of them talking to him. She couldn't explain it, but the idea of her former captain talking to the simulation embarrassed her. When Kinnard was still alive, there had been a close triad of friendship between Cordell, Kinnard, and Boots.

If she wanted Kin back, she was going to have to go in there and take him. She shimmied around the corner and checked the contents of her coat pockets. She'd blown what little cash she had on a veritable arsenal of nonlethal measures: sleepers, trip sticks, knock rounds for her slinger, waspspikes, and three blinders. Even though she'd betrayed them, she was still uncomfortable murdering them outright.

The plan was simple: get Kin, figure out who the crone was (and whether or not she could track Boots across the galaxy), then start a new life far from here. Boots owned a few acres on Hopper's Hope, purchased after the brief success of her show. The land would be more than enough to start that distilling business she'd always wanted—though she couldn't afford the gear just yet. If the crone wasn't a danger, maybe it was time Boots disappeared forever.

As she pondered this, she spotted an odd sight: a familiar-looking woman clad in stained, mismatched clothes made her way up the street toward Boots with a nasty scowl. The woman looked like she'd dug her clothes out of a trash pile or maybe a donation box. At first, Boots thought it was one of the *Capricious*'s crew, finally wise to her location. Then she remembered where she'd seen the woman's face before: the newscasts. This was the wanted race car driver whose face had been plastered all over the skies.

There was a huge bounty on that woman, Nilah... Brioche or something: several million argents. If Boots collected, she'd definitely be able to afford the distillery equipment then. She couldn't believe her luck; of all the people on Gantry Station who could've been nearby, this golden opportunity happened to come wandering up the street.

Maybe whatever deity was out there didn't hate her as much as she thought.

She decided to play it cool and make a capture attempt when Nilah passed. A quick hit with a trip stick and a jab with the sleeper would sort things out.

Except, the racer walked straight at Boots. When her target was four meters away, Boots could see her eyes, intent and furious. Red light spilled from under tattered shirtsleeves. Nilah was only a few paces away now, and closing fast.

Nilah was a hugely popular race car driver with more money than some small colonies, so she couldn't possibly have business with Boots, right? Almost in answer to that question, Nilah drew a slinger and jammed it up under Boots's chin.

"Elizabeth Elsworth?" she hissed.

"I get confused for her all the time," said Boots, raising her hands. "Common mistake."

Nilah narrowed her eyes. "Do I look like a sodding moron?"

"Let's just take it easy with that heater, kid."

She dug the barrel into the soft part of Boots's jawline. "I saw a murder. I crashed my car. I've been chased all day, shot at and used as a human shield, so I'll do whatever I want." Her eyes locked onto Boots's, a burning fire in them.

"Okay. What's the plan, then?" Boots gently lowered her hands to where she had easy access to the sleeper in her coat. Her index and middle fingers brushed the metal cylinder in her pocket, and she gingerly lifted it into her hand. As close as Nilah was, she'd never see it.

"I honestly hadn't thought that far ahead," she hissed, "but you know something and you're coming with me...somewhere. Let's go."

Boots fumbled for the button on the sleeper's long metal tube. It wasn't a complicated device. Just flip aside the switch guard, press it into the other person, and hit the button. But which side was the business end again? If she looked at it, Nilah would get wise and give her an extra hole or two in her head.

"Okay, where are we going? You can't just drag me around like this or the cops are going to be pissed."

Nilah sneered. "All right, well...you can start by going to that alley over there. And then...and then we'll discuss where we're actually going."

It was now or never. Boots jammed the sleeper into Nilah's skinny rib cage and pressed the button, sending a jolt of pure arcane energy through her body. Nilah's face froze, agape with surprise, and purple smoke poured from her open mouth. The poor thing couldn't have weighed more than a hundred pounds, and this sleeper was rated for a full-grown heavy infantryman.

Knee throbbing, Boots eased Nilah's limp body onto the sidewalk. Nilah looked aggressively satisfied, like she'd been hunting a nap, wrestled that nap to the ground, and torn out its throat. Too bad that wouldn't last. When she woke up, she'd have one hell of a headache and her whole mouth would taste like she'd been chewing charcoal, but she'd live.

Boots straightened up and admired her handiwork. Nilah's bounty would bring in more than enough argents to get off this tub.

"Hey, Boots!"

She spun to see who'd called her name: Orna Sokol, quartermaster on the *Capricious*...and the two barrels of her massive shotgun. Boots had just enough time to brace before a double dose of knock rounds put her off her feet and far away from consciousness.

Chapter Four

Capricious Fate

Boots awoke to the thrum of a starship and stinging pain across her face. She reached up to touch her cheek and found a gash, still sticky with blood. She creaked open one eye, only to have the bright lights overhead burn into her retina. She swore and rubbed her eyelids, trying to adjust. At least her arm worked okay.

She wasn't on Gantry Station anymore. Real spacers could always tell when they'd been moved to a smaller craft because the artificial gravity was a little too crisp, like she was being sucked to the ground. She ran her fingers over the floor, noting the diamond deck pattern.

"Oh no."

A pair of shield casters stretched a tangerine force field across the opening of a small prison cell. Sitting up, she blinked until the corridor outside the cell came into focus, and swore.

Painted across the far wall in a drunken hand were the words:

WELCOME ABOARD THE CAPRICIOUS!

Boots had scrawled those words over twenty-two years ago at the start of the Famine War, during her first day on board the ship. The *Capricious* had been assigned to take out a Kandamili troop transport that was operating undercover as a cruise liner in the Arcan stratosphere. Once they got to the liner, it contained its running crew, but no passengers, and certainly no soldiers. Cordell still captured the ship's staff and put them in the brig. His orders to Boots had been, "Make the civvies feel welcome."

The cell contained a bunk, a sink, and a toilet. The beds slid into the wall if need be, so the area could be converted to extra storage. She stood, gingerly pushing past the top bunk so she didn't bump her throbbing skull. Her knee complained, but at least she could put weight on it. Unsteadily, she made her way to the force field to check it out. Once, during the war, they'd captured a cadre of assassins; one of them had escaped and killed one of her crew mates. After that, folks onboard the *Capricious* did a better job with the security holes.

She looked back to the bunks and found the sleeping form of Nilah on top.

"You!" Boots cried, anger burbling through all the burst pipes in her brain.

Nilah shivered, a tank top barely covering her unblemished brown skin. "God, no. Too shouty. Much too shouty." She rubbed her hands over her biceps and a set of ocean wave dermaluxes came to life, a deep red light flowing from them. Boots could never remember the color codes for those stupid tattoos, nor could she understand why kids these days wanted to display their emotions to anyone who'd look. She thought it meant Nilah was in pain—good.

"No. You got us into this, so you're going to get up." Boots stormed over to the top bunk, put both hands on it, and shoved it into the wall compartment, scraping Nilah from her bed. The racer bounced off the frame of the lower bunk and onto the floor.

Nilah's eyes danced with murder and the tattoos flared orange. "How dare you?" Arms flickering, she surged to her feet and delivered Boots a savage uppercut, sending her reeling to catch herself on the sink.

Dazed, Boots tried to puzzle through how a tiny woman had landed such an explosive punch.

Boots's opponent loomed over her, dermaluxes coruscating with menace. Nilah started to open her mouth, but then licked her teeth and grimaced. A bit of purple drool seeped out from the corner of her lips, and the dermaluxes flashed deep forest green. Nilah then unceremoniously vomited purple goop all over the brig floor.

The overwhelming stench nearly cost Boots her lunch, but this wasn't her first rodeo. Back in the war, she'd been on brig duty a few times, and that occasionally meant blood, piss, vomit, and worse. Enemy combatants were rarely good guests, but someone had to clean up after them. Nilah ran out of food and began dry heaving into the diamond deck, tendrils of spittle connecting her to the floor.

Boots was infinitely thankful for the grating in the center of the floor, which took in most of the contents of Nilah's stomach. The last thing they needed was her puke getting on the force field, where it might cook. Boots ran a bit of cold water from the sink in the corner and washed the blood from her mouth, which made her present circumstance marginally more tolerable.

"Okay, kid," grunted Boots. "You're going to have to get a hold of yourself if you ever want to stand back up. Those sleepers aren't a joke."

"Sod off."

"We're trapped here in a bucket of your stomach stew, so I promise you, I'm suffering, too."

Nilah attempted to wither Boots with a look, but gave up on the cause. "Where are we?"

"The *Capricious*. It's a stolen Arcan marauder from Clarkesfall. Went missing after the Famine War."

"That's . . . specific. And how do you know this?"

"I used to serve in the Arcan Defense Force. This was my ship."

"You're a soldier."

"Was. My country lost the war. Then the whole planet died."

"Well, Boots, here's what's going to happen. You're going to negotiate my release, and then I'll have you lot arrested, where you will explain to the police what you know of the murder of Cyril Clowe. Then, while you're in prison, I'm going to sue you and everything you love back into the Stone Age."

Boots laughed. "And what are you going to get from me? I'm worthless."

"I could have your ship."

She shook her head. "You don't want it, honey. Besides, this isn't my ship. In case you didn't notice, we're in here together."

"Ah." Nilah glanced about and took a dry swallow. "I see."

Boots stepped away from the sink. "Come on, kid. Get some of this water and you'll feel better."

Nilah stumbled upright and hobbled to the sink, eyeing Boots suspiciously the whole way. It amazed Boots that this champion race car driver, this fierce fighter, could make a face so like a whiny brat. Nilah gingerly sipped from the faucet, but once the cool water passed her throat, she began to lap hungrily at the spigot.

"Thirsty one, aren't you?"

Nilah straightened with a deeply satisfied gasp. "You don't understand. I was in a race when this all started. I'm light on water. We lose up to two kilos of water over the fifty laps."

"Wow. That's a great story, and highly relevant."

"You asked why I was thirsty."

"Since you like to answer questions, why is there a huge bounty on your head?"

She lifted her nose, conjuring what nobility she could. "Probably because they want me returned soon."

"Is that why they don't care whether you're brought in dead or alive?"

"What?"

Boots laughed and patted Nilah's shoulder as she lumbered to the bottom bunk. "Not really. Just wanted to see the look on your face."

"Is it possible to hate someone you've only just met?"

They wouldn't even be here if the stupid kid hadn't pulled a gun in some ham-fisted kidnapping attempt, so the response came naturally. "Absolutely."

"Good. Now let's focus on getting out of here."

Boots shook her head. "You're wasting your time. Those shield generators are military, as is everything else here."

The racer walked to the orange force field and gently prodded it, enough to get a sizzle, but not enough for a shock. She moved to where the shield abutted the wall and began inspecting the seam. "I'm a mechanist. I can get us out of this."

"Yeah, because no one has ever imprisoned a mechanist before."

"All PGRF mechanists are top-flight, and I'm the galactic points leader by a good stretch. I think you understand what that means."

Boots scoffed. "Can you run a race car on all that hot air?"

"Shut up and help me. What's your glyph anyway? Is it stone? A squat thing like you has got to be a mason. You know, your folk can move metal, too, if you try hard enough."

Boots laid back, propping her hands behind her head. Her shoulders ached like someone had jerked her arms out of socket, but stretching helped. "I'm not helping you."

"I intend to escape, and I demand to know what resources we have at our disposal."

"I don't have a glyph."

"Of course you do," said Nilah. "Don't be stubborn."

"No. I don't have one. I'm numb, dry, whatever. Arcana dystocia."

Nilah's ocean waves became a sunset orange. "Oh, that's right... Now I remember. That was the bloody sob story on your show! I'm screwed! I'm stuck on a ship to god knows where and the only person who can help me is a ruddy d—" She stopped short.

Boots licked her lips, tonguing a split. "Go on and say it."

"Say what?"

"You were going to say 'dull-fingered.' Go on and do it so I can kick your teeth in."

Her tattoos flushed a sea-foam cyan. Was that embarrassment? "It's just a statement of fact. Hardly offensive."

"What I do and don't find offensive isn't your call, kid. Now, I want a few answers out of you. Why were you looking for me?"

Nilah spun out the story of what'd brought her to Boots's street, starting at the Awala GP. It was full of boring sports details and a near-constant flow of statistics, but she eventually came to the part where Mother appeared.

Boots leaned forward. "What'd she look like? Would you call her a crone?"

"I wouldn't say it to her face, but yes. She had a certain crone-like air to her. She was stooped and deadly, like some sort of animal. Had a tattered black cloak and a frightful mask, covered in eyes. It was like she... stopped time."

"People gamble on those races, right? Don't you have, uh, safeguards? Dispersers or something?"

Nilah shook her head. "We do. They're supposed to be ironclad. And our intruder detection is perfect—but the dispersers didn't fire and no one showed up to stop her."

"Why not?"

"I don't know," said Nilah. "I just... That wasn't supposed to be possible. And Cyril kept talking to her like there was this, well, grand conspiracy. Like she had track access."

Boots stroked her chin. "Spry for an old lady?"

"More so than you."

"Hey, I'm on the young side of forty. I don't have to take that."

"She murdered Cyril Clowe by crushing his head through his race helmet. I'm fairly certain she's more lively than the both of us." Nilah leaned back against the wall, folding her arms over herself. "I still can't believe it happened like that."

"That a witch squished his head like a grape?"

"It's the first death we've had on the track in decades, and it's a murder."

"Wow. A guy gets iced and you're crying about a safety record?"

"These things are important to us drivers. We live and breathe track life. Of course, someone like you wouldn't understand."

"You're right. I don't care about your safety crap. So you escaped Mother, then what?"

"I called a Fixer, but she'd been bought off. Another Fixer got into a fight with her, and they... well, they killed each other. I eventually found a public terminal, and luckily for me, I had your name. When you're wealthy, you have access to certain, uh, data services that regular people don't. Strictly precautionary measures against stalkers and the like. I found out where you lived, and I already knew what you looked like from the Link. Then I found you skulking around outside your apartment like a common criminal."

Boots gestured to the whole ship. "I was avoiding these guys."

"What'd you do to them?"

"It's a long story. One that has nothing to do with you."

"Well, here I am, so I expect you to tell me eventually." Nilah approached the force field again and peered into its energies, almost close enough to singe her hair. "This is a basic Atheron Capstone circuit. It's remedial-level mechanism at best."

"Don't go playing with fire, kiddo."

Nilah turned to her and smirked. "I think I know what I'm doing."

The racer traced a large glyph, placed her palm against the wall panel nearest the shield generator, and attempted a psychic connection with the ship. The arcane burst that filled the room sent her sliding across the vomit-slicked grating and into the opposite wall, unconscious again.

Boots gingerly got to her feet and checked Nilah's breathing. Two massive magic shocks in one day couldn't have been good for her little mechanist brain. Satisfied that the racer would live, Boots climbed back into her bunk and lay down. She was going to have a long day ahead of her, and Cordell was a notoriously tough customer.

She didn't have to wait long. The captain's tall shadow darkened her cell within minutes.

"Aw, damn, Boots! What the hell did you two get up to in here?"

"Kid had more than she could handle. She's sleeping it off."

He shut off the force field, the room suddenly darker without its orange light.

"Well come on, girl. Let's chat."

Cordell cut an imposing figure in any clothes, civvy or service. His wardrobe that day was a mash-up of businessman and military surplus garb, but he pulled it off with gusto. Boots, in comparison, still wore her sweaty T-shirt and canvas pants from Gantry, and carried a regrettable stink. She normally wouldn't bother with appearances, but she didn't like her past witnessing how far she'd fallen.

They wound through the corridors of the *Capricious*, and she was struck by how little it had changed, though it was smaller than she remembered.

Cordell had aged well. Up close, his stern features hadn't changed much, but the salty hairs in his natural style lent him a bit of dignity. He'd be attractive, if Boots had cared to pay attention to that sort of thing.

They passed the med bay, and Boots did a double take. In the nest of familiar rooms, it showed the most change. Instead of the traditional single bed and chem station, there were three sleep capsules with nutrition systems and monitors. A well-muscled man in lab gear busied himself near a desk in the back. He looked up and smiled serenely at them, and Boots was struck by the clarity of his golden-brown eyes. Whoever he was, he was cut from better cloth than an average man.

"She's awake," noted the technician, his rich voice filling the bay. "Mostly uninjured, too."

Boots nodded to him. May as well get acquainted with the rest of Cordell's cronies. "I haven't met this one yet, Cordell."

Cordell stopped and gestured to the man in the med bay. "Oh, my mistake. Boots, this is Malik Jan, our ship's doctor."

Malik came to them in the hall and took Boots's hand. His palms were soft and warm, if a little dry. "It's a pleasure. I hope you slept well."

"Great. Now you've met," said Cordell, placing a hand on Boots's shoulder. "Doctor Jan, Boots is a prisoner, and if she tries to escape, you're to shoot her."

Malik looked her in the eyes. "I don't think you'll be a problem, will you?"

She shook her head, and he patted her hand once before returning to work. The whole interaction was unnervingly pleasant, especially from Cordell. He was playing the good guy, which meant he'd squeeze her extra hard when the time came.

"You always recruit your crew from clothing advertisements?" she asked as they headed toward the bow of the ship.

"Yeah. The ugly ones like you get under my skin."

They passed Orna in the hall, wearing her classic brutal expression.

"Guess you're going to have to fire your quartermaster, then."

He paused at the base of the stairs and scowled at her. "You know what's amazing about you, Boots?"

"My endless well of talent?"

"Here you are, trapped in an enemy ship with no hope of escape, and you're finding time to mouth off. Why don't you think about what you're going to tell me when we get to my office, instead of making me want to toss your ass out of the airlock?"

They reached the top of the stairs where Cordell's quarters were nestled. Boots had been up there only twice before: once when she was commissioned, and again when she was kicked off the ship.

"Carry me up here and throw me out? That'd be a waste of a perfectly good kidnapping."

Cordell fixed her with his patented stare. Some captains inspired their cadets to valor. Cordell just made them fear the consequences of failure. He'd flown a lot of so-called suicide missions in the *Capricious* and knew how to make someone snap to. He hammered the door panel, and his quarters opened before them.

Unlike the rest of the ship, the captain's quarters were richly appointed with earthy tones of leather and wood, sun-bright yellows and deep umber. Solid gold accents reflected a haze of sparklamps, which hovered across the ceiling like foam atop a wave. Gently flowing in one corner was the purple planetary sigil of Clarkesfall, with the iconic orange half-moon of Arca blazing over it.

A long panoramic window framed his desk. The writing surface was at least two hundred kilos of sculpted rare wood, perfectly planed with two swept edges. Hundreds of brass struts, straight as lasers, held it in place atop sumptuous carpets. Cordell had modified parts of the *Capricious* in the years after the war, and that desk certainly wasn't military-issue.

In cases across one wall, there were numerous awards and trophies, mementos of actions long forgotten by the rest of the galaxy. They sparkled in the white light of gravity plates. She spotted the slicing curve of his award for valorous action in the Battle of Laconte, and quit gawking. He'd done some amazing things in his time, but he was a fool, too.

He walked around his desk and gestured to the seat opposite.

"I'm going to smoke now," he said.

"I know," she sighed.

He took a cigarette from a long brass case on his desk. Sensing its loss, the case whirred and clicked, rolling another. "How long have we been friends?"

"Would a friend be sitting here as a captive?"

He smiled. "Humor me."

"According to you, since Armistice Day."

He lit the stick, taking a deep drag and exhaling. The haze glittered with tiny vermilion sparkles, the sign of smoke laced with eidolon dust. "That's right. So why did you sell me a fake?"

"Because we're not friends at all. You like jamming yourself into my life, and I saw an opportunity to get some cash."

"You sell maps all the time, Boots. They all fake?"

She shrugged. "Some of them work out, some of them don't. I never asked for this. Old fans of the show keep coming to me to buy, and that means I've got to sell."

He leaned back. "That right? And here I thought we were brothers in arms. I had no idea you were so stone cold."

"I never took your calls. Not once. We've never had a personal visit since the war. You think that makes us friends?"

"Yet you decided to do business with me."

She ruffled her hair. "You show up on the Link looking to buy a map, we're going to do business. I take all comers. Not my fault you're a sucker."

"So none of what you sell is real?"

She sucked her teeth. "Can't be wrong all the time, but that's luck for you. I've had one or two salvagers come back."

"You know what hurt? It wasn't you taking ten grand of my hard-earned money."

"Really? I thought that would sting like a—"

"Hush." He pointed out the window to the stars. "It was you sending my crew somewhere that might get them killed. We almost died."

"Yeah, because you've never done that."

"What's that supposed to mean?"

"Laconte." She said the word without thinking, and it choked her like the clouds of tobacco smoke. Of the original eight crew on the *Capricious*, only Boots and Cordell had survived that day. She knew it was a low blow.

"I didn't get a say in where we went," he said. "I just chose how we did it."

"You chose wrong."

He straightened up, his shoulders squaring to an officer's stature. "You should consider your words."

She steeled herself against his gaze. "You're not my captain. You're just a kidnapper."

"And you're a swindler."

Boots rolled her eyes. "Yeah, well, work is scarce when you've got a dishonorable discharge on your record."

"There was work. You could've stayed on this ship."

She stomped her way upright. "And you could've surrendered him to the authorities like you were ordered to!"

"I had my reasons for keeping him. Wasn't about to hand him off to a bunch of invaders and offworld bankers."

She lowered her voice to imitate his. "'Oh, my side lost the war. I guess I get a free starship!'"

He cocked his head like he was considering something horrid, but then smiled. "I guess I did, didn't I?"

"You Fallen are a bunch of idiots. And in your case, a wanted idiot."

"No one is hunting down Famine War people anymore, Bootsie. Not the Arcan side. Not the Kandamili side. I won."

She rolled her eyes, but he was right. He'd gotten away with a pretty grand theft, all things considered.

"You kept your military AI, Boots. That was government property."

"I bought him from a corrupt official, fair and square. Not my fault you can't play the game."

His smile remained, but it drained from his eyes. Boots saw the man who dropped them into countless combat zones, ferried them across raging spells, and tore apart anything that stood in his way. "You're in hot water, Boots. You're going to find a way to pay us back, or I'm going to take this personally."

And there, out of nowhere, was the squeeze. Her wise comments shriveled in her throat, and she stammered, "We could... I could with my bank account, maybe on... I've got money on Gantry."

"Silas told me you've got land on Hopper's Hope. That ought to about cover it."

His statement knocked the wind from her lungs. That land was the last bit of her wealth from her show, *Finding Hana*, and she couldn't stomach the thought of handing it over. That show had come at too high a price, and that land was precious to her. "No."

"We're going to fly there, head to the notary, and you can sign me the deed." He patted his desk with his free hand, as though it was a purring cat. "I always thought the *Capricious* needed a home base."

"Cordell, you're sitting on more money than you ever saw in your life," said Boots, carefully considering her words. She had to get him off the topic of Hopper's Hope. "That girl down there in the brig with me is—"

"Nilah Brio. Yeah, I don't do bounties, Bootsie. Not tossing her to the wolves like that."

"Oh, so you think she's innocent?"

He took another sparkling drag and shook his head. "It doesn't matter. Orna captured her, not you. That means, whatever we do with her, it doesn't count against your debt." He chortled. "Look at you, acting like you brought her here."

"I did knock her out. We could ransom her. She's PGRF, so you know she has stupid amounts of cash."

"Not happening, Boots. I'm not selling some random girl out to pay your debts. We're going to drop her on Taitu, then we're hitting Hopper's Hope for your land."

Boots clenched her teeth. "You can't have my land, Cordell."

"You got something better?"

Boots thought back to the many games of chance that'd been played on board the ship, of the thousands of argents won and lost at sixteen clouds, at triplets, at knights, and she knew she'd been offered a golden opportunity—Cordell loved to gamble.

"I do, but it's too dangerous," she said.

"Okay, if you're going to sell me some bull, I can send you back to your cell."

Rule number one: magic must always be the point. "You've heard of the *Harrow*?"

"Sure. Every captain knows that one. Shadow tech. Hundred-meter glyphs. Discus warheads that could slice a ship in half. Except, it doesn't exist. If the Taitutians had a cruiser capable of frying a whole city, they'd have used it. For one, they had a treaty with Arca, and you never saw the *Harrow* grace our skies. Kandamil bombed our half of the planet, then their half withered away, and the Taitutians didn't raise a damned finger."

Boots sat back down. "I know where it is."

"Shut up. I've heard more than enough of this."

"Have you? It took me twenty-five tries to find the Chalice of Hana. You know that's true because you watched the show like everyone else. I'm not always wrong, and you know it."

He glared but stood silent.

Rule number two: every legend is a fluffy story wrapped around a piece of hard evidence. "Okay, send me to my cell, but I've got real proof and you've got a ship that can make the journey."

"Like what?"

Boots considered the question. Her miner's account had been incinerated in the office attack, along with all but one of her images of the *Harrow*. Besides, Cordell had probably seen the common conspiracy pictures of the warship floating around the Link.

"I'm waiting," he said.

"My office. It was burned down by a woman calling herself Mother."

"Bull."

"Oh, Mother burned down my office. There were eyewitness accounts. I've got the message from the insurance company where they won't cover the damages."

"Where?"

Boots shrugged. "You already have the record. It's in Kin's memory ban—"

She drew up short. She'd never talked about Kin with anyone, much less a friend from his life.

Cordell reached under his desk and pulled out Kinnard's memory core, brandishing it like a precious stone. "I was a little surprised when I plugged him up. Sounds just like him."

She flushed. "Yeah. The mnemonimancers did a good job."

Cordell tapped a button on his desk, and a receptacle slid open. He gently placed the cube inside, where it slid into a snug fit.

"Hello," came Kinnard's voice over the room's speakers. "I'll be ready in one moment."

"Worth every penny, I'd say," said Cordell. "Nice to hear old Kin again." When Kinnard had booted up, Cordell asked him, "Can you tell us about Boots's office getting toasted?"

"I'm sorry," said Kinnard, "but I don't recognize your voice. You're not an authorized user."

Cordell looked hurt, but quickly stifled it.

"Kin," said Boots, "are you okay? Did they mess with your memory?"

"My cores have not been breached, and my processing power is at one hundred percent," said Kin. "Lizzie, would you like to make this gentleman an authorized user?"

She looked to Cordell, who smirked at the name Lizzie.

"Absolutely not. Can you play back the message from the Acclion Group?"

As Kin read the message, Boots watched the change in Cordell's face. When the words "Arcane explosives were involved, and there was a distinct resonance…" came over the speakers, he looked positively elated.

"Stop the message," said Boots. Better to strike while the iron was hot. "A few weeks ago, I sold the location of the *Harrow* to someone. Kin, who was that?" She started to tell him how she'd pieced the legend together, but thought better of it. Her mother had once told her, "Only liars get too specific."

"Arthur Castor," said Kinnard.

"Do you watch racing?" asked Boots.

Cordell shook his head. He'd taken up a thinker's posture, carefully puffing away on his cigarette.

"Okay, so you may not know this, but Castor is the cousin of

Cyril Clowe, a driver who was murdered yesterday afternoon on the track—right next to Nilah Brio." This was her first outright lie, so she thought it was going pretty well.

Kinnard chimed in. "According to the Link, Arthur Castor is also the name of a prominent Arcan senator."

Cordell set down his cigarette on an ash tray. "If this guy was a senator twenty years ago, that means he'd have to be at least in his fifties or sixties."

Boots's heart jumped. She kicked herself for nailing down too much of the story instead of saying the two men were "connected." "Not necessarily. He could be a second cousin once removed— like a grandfather's cousin maybe."

Cordell grabbed his smoke to take a drag, then reconsidered and stubbed it out. "You're lying."

"Then how do you explain the fact that the same crone hunting me tried to kill Nilah Brio?"

"You're lying about that, too."

Boots raised her hands. "I'm not. Silas told me, right after he said you were looking for me. Frankly, I'm just glad you found me first."

"Right."

"Look," she said, "you don't have to trust me, but you trust Silas, don't you?"

"I do, because Silas still remembers where he comes from. You forgot as soon as you took off the uniform and started up that stupid show."

"It was popular."

"Everyone likes watching an underdog go around begging for money. And Fallen are everyone's favorite losers, aren't they?"

She crossed her arms, vowing not to take that bait. "You can say what you want, but if the *Harrow* is real, it'll have enough eidolon crystal to buy a planet. It'll make your last salvage look like a milk run."

His nostrils flared and his jaw tensed as he took a long, slow breath. "We can check out your lead."

"Great. I can coordinate from Gantry. I still have a lot of contacts in the archives, so—"

"Girl, if you think I'm letting you out of my sight, forget it. You're stuck with us." He tapped the desk, and several sections of the grain pattern lit up under his touch. "Orna."

The quartermaster's voice filled the room. "Yes, Captain?"

"I want you to take Boots here back to the brig. She might be staying with us for a while, so take the long way."

"We're letting her out of the cage, sir?"

Cordell looked Boots over with a smirk. "Maybe. We'll see if she can get that temper under control." When the comm unit went out, he said, "It was always a pleasure to have you on my crew. You used to be such a loyal soldier."

"I was loyal to the ADF. That's why I surrendered when ordered."

"So was I. That's why I never surrendered." He chewed his lip. "I'm cordially inviting you to play cards with us tomorrow."

"I can't buy any stakes."

The door slid open and Orna entered, a massive slinger strapped to her side. She stood behind Boots, waiting patiently for her to rise.

"I can spot you," said Cordell. "Oh, and Boots?"

"What?"

"I've been wanting to ask you this for a few years. On the show, you and Stetson busted your butts trying to get a ship that could make it out to the Chalice. You bowed and scraped for all those investors..."

Boots winced at hearing her old partner's name out loud. "Yeah. We did."

He sniffed and scratched his eyebrow with the thumb of his cigarette hand. "All the while, you could've called on me and the

Capricious to take you anywhere you wanted. You didn't have to lower yourself to show business if you wanted to go hunt treasure—flaunting your old uniform for a sympathy coin. I would've forgiven all those nasty things you said, and you know that."

"Why didn't I?" she asked.

"Yeah. We could've found the Chalice of Hana together."

She very nearly spit on his floor. "Because I'd rather be floating out in space than on this ship again."

He gave a sardonic chuckle. "Yeah, but unlike Stetson, I wouldn't have murdered your crew."

"Not with your own hands, maybe. Never forget Laconte," she said, and Orna elbowed her hard enough to leave her wheezing.

"Get her out of here," said Cordell. "See you at cards."

Chapter Five

The Real Welcome

A t almost two meters tall, Orna Sokol wasn't a woman to mess with. Her bare, muscled shoulders rippled at the edges of her tank top. Black tattoos slithered along her long, sinewy arms, marred in many places by old injuries. Her utilitarian frame matched her onyx hair, which had been clipped short for fighting. Her thick boots thunked on the deck as they walked, and Boots spotted a hidden recess for ejecting spikes on the toes.

Orna's huge slinger had a built-in magnifier that could amplify fire spells to melt steel, suck the air out of a closed room, and generally render everyone a crispy critter. Dozens of scars marred her young face, and her eyes glowed like light through ice crystals. The feature that made her the most terrifying, however, was her battle armor.

Boots had seen hundreds of suits of battle armor during the Famine War capable of multiplying the strength of their wearers, rendering them nigh indestructible. She hadn't, however, seen battle armor that walked around beside its owner, following her every move. Boots had seen the armor at a distance, heard stories about Orna Sokol, but this was her first close encounter.

"What's the point of battle armor if you're not going to ride in it?" asked Boots as they walked through the ship.

"Be quiet," said Orna.

The armor was nearly three meters in height, made of duraplex and regraded steel. It stooped in the hall as it walked beside the pair of women. Serpentine plates covered each section, giving the whole thing a scaly appearance, and its hands ended in terrifying, serrated claws. The system's eidolon crystal core vented glowing energy trails through the backplates, giving it the appearance of having two sets of fiery gills.

Orna wore a silver circlet around her head, and Boots caught snatches of blue light from around its edges. Boots didn't know much about mechanists, but she could guess that was how the quartermaster controlled her armor. Mental control wouldn't have disturbed Boots, but Orna treated the armor like a pet. It tromped along behind the pair of them, polyspectral lenses blinking in curiosity.

Boots glanced back as the armor sampled the air closest to her neck. They both flinched. "Okay, that thing just sniffed me."

Orna didn't bother to look back. "Ranger will do that."

"Ranger? It has a name?"

"All great weapons have names."

"Great weapons don't sniff people."

"Mine do."

Boots thought she placed a bit of a Blixish accent in her escort, but it was hard to tell. The planets were all a mishmash of cultures, so a guess was often wrong. "Where're you from?"

"Nowhere."

"Wow. They got nice weather in Nowhere?"

Orna spun to face her. "You may be a celebrity everywhere else, but not here. I had to write the ration reports. I know how close we came to starving in deep space on your account."

Ranger rested a heavy, sharp claw on Boots's shoulder. Its hiss dripped with malice, like steam through a long steel pipe. Ahead of her, human death. Behind her, a walking blender.

"So, uh, how long have you been with the captain?"

"I've been on this ship since I was a little girl. Came aboard after you deserted the captain."

Orna looked to be in her mid-twenties, so Boots did the math and ignored the jab. "Yeah, so I'm guessing that's about fifteen years?"

"Yes. No more questions about me."

Behind Orna's back, Boots silently mocked the quartermaster's gruff delivery.

Orna paused. "You know I can see everything Ranger sees."

They wound through the ship's foredecks until they came to the bridge. It was precisely as Boots had left it almost twenty years ago, with a fresh coat of paint over all the bits that made it an ADF ship. Unlike Cordell's office, which had essentially been gutted and rebuilt, the bridge was a spotless, frozen set piece from the Famine War. Three terraces, each taller than a large man, housed stations and readouts. Overhead, starlight slipped through a tremendous bubble dome. Boots's favorite shift on the bridge had always been the night cycle, when the lights were dimmed and she was alone with the vastness of space.

She immediately recognized the marksman from the bazaar sitting in the pilot's chair three terraces down. The pilot stood up and ascended the stairs at their entry.

"Aisha," said Orna. "This is Boots Elsworth. You've met."

The pilot smiled and took Boots's hand in both of hers. "Aisha Jan. It is my utmost pleasure. Sorry for shooting you."

Up close, she was far prettier than Boots remembered in the bazaar, with smoky eyes and long brown hair that faded to pink at the tips like some bird of paradise. Triads of tiny gemstones rested on her cheeks, and Boots wondered if they were magical or merely fashionable.

"That's . . . a different greeting than I expected," said Boots.

"Don't get too excited about the politeness," said Orna. "Aisha is just more civilized than I am."

Boots shrugged. "Did you say Jan? Are you related to, uh, what's his name?"

"Malik, the ship's doctor, is my husband."

That explained the freakish good looks. They were two of a kind.

"Been on the ship long?" asked Boots.

"Only for two years. Malik knew Cordell from the ADF. They went to boot camp together."

"But, uh . . ." Boots cocked her head. That couldn't be right, because that would make Malik more than forty years old, and he didn't look a day over thirty.

Sensing her question, Orna said, "Malik has sleep magic. Keeps them young. Case closed. Come on. We've got to go waste everyone else's time."

From the bridge, they went to a small office. Various cables and connectors littered the floor, several of them plugged into a central tower with a twinkling crystal ball at the top. Standing over this tower, fingers splayed across the surface of the sphere, was a thin, middle-aged blond man. His lips were locked in a scowl, even as his eyes flashed in time with the crystal.

Boots recognized the art instantly. Aggregation—the art of arcane data sifting and corroboration—was one of the most sought-after skills in the galaxy, and those possessing it were always well paid.

"Armin," said Orna, "this is Boots. Boots, Armin Vandevere— our first mate."

If he was the first mate, his datamancy must've also made him the mission planner. If that were true, Boots's treasure map had fooled him. In spite of her present situation, pride needled her heart.

"Well, well," he said, his eyes never focusing on her, "looks like the liar walks among us."

She stepped forward and offered a hand, but Orna stepped between them.

"No, thank you," said Armin. "I'm busy."

"I can see where I'm not wanted," said Boots, turning to leave. "Trust me, I don't want to be on this ship any more than you want me here."

The scintillating lights from the crystal rendered Armin's face gaunt. "For what it's worth, I was against kidnapping you."

"Funny story: me too," said Boots.

He craned his head. "We're never going to get back our expeditionary expenses from you, because you'll never be worth three hundred thousand argents. We should have called it a loss. However, the captain demanded satisfaction, so I told him to shoot you on Gantry. It's cheaper than having another mouth to feed."

Boots frowned. "Efficient one, aren't you?"

He blinked, his eyes coming into focus and locking onto hers. "You're not worth the oxygen it'd take to blow you out an airlock. Good day."

Orna guffawed and patted Boots hard on the back. "How about we get out of here and let the nice man work?"

They headed back into the mainline corridor, toward the lift to lower decks.

"Cordell wouldn't shoot me," said Boots.

Orna slapped a palm to the lift door, and it slid open. "No, but I would. Let's get you fed and back to your hole."

Boots shuffled into the lift; then Orna and Ranger ducked in behind her. They didn't face the door, like sane people do, but scowled at Boots the whole time—insofar as a robot could scowl.

"We should've taken the stairs," said Orna, resting her hands on her hips.

"You don't look like you need the exercise."

"It's the only place on the ship with no cameras."

The lift moved beneath their feet, and Boots's stomach dropped. Platforms on smaller military ships didn't use motors, but very small changes to the artificial gravity. In her ADF days, the soldiers would say "lightfoot" to go up and "heavyfoot" to go down. They had all kinds of strange phrases like that: inksticks instead of pens, zipperjocks instead of cargo pilots.

The door slid open to reveal the mess, and Boots gasped. The place had been a large dining area for up to ten people during Boots's time in the service. There was no cook to speak of, just a person in charge of invigorating the rations. Tear open a pack, throw it in the radiator, and watch your meal writhe around until it became the high-carb, high-fat diet soldiers loved.

Now sunboxes wreathed the mess, where all species of plants grew under the light of accelerators. They waved in their cages, bent and twisted with swift growth as they reached toward the lamps. Accelerators were generally considered unsafe aboard combat vessels, because a stray round could cause a leak. Humans hit by their rays often developed nasty tumors or splintered bones. The Kandamili Military Special Service had gotten busted after the war for using the lamps as torture devices.

Cordell had added a kitchen, removing the old radiator in favor of a top-of-the-line range of appliances more appropriate to a yacht or luxury liner. The table running through the center was the same one from Boots's time, but polished and repainted across the surface with a shining enamel the color of the half-moon of Arca.

Music blared through the kitchen, a classic Kandamili tune from Boots's homeworld, and an older man came dancing out of the pantry, three huge silver bowls in hand. He slung the bowls onto the countertop with a flourish and ripped off their wraps, spinning once to chuck the balled-up plastic into the cycler. Still oblivious to Orna and Boots, he wheeled about, clapping his hands and gyrating. The guy had moves.

"Didier!" bellowed Orna, and he turned to see them, a bright smile on his face.

He shimmied around the table, clapping in time to the music before striking a pose, his hand extended. "Didier Thomasi, cook."

He had silver hair, worn in a swept-back style that Boots hadn't seen since she was a little girl. Freckled cheeks led to friendly eyes nestled in the cliff of a bushy brow. A broad, curled mustache alighted on a stiff upper lip, as though the man was in a continuous state of sniffing the air around him. He had a few muscles, which stood in opposition to his pot belly, but Boots guessed he could fight like the rest of them. He was Boots's kind of guy: lumpy, a little goofy, with muscles in all the right places.

Finally, a decent human being on this ship. She tried not to blush as she shook his cracked and calloused fingers. He had a chef's grip, firm and thorough.

"Elizabeth Elsworth, prisoner."

"That's cool, man! How long have you been a prisoner?"

"Today is my first day."

He sized her up, grinning like a happy cat. "I bet you'll be good at it. You know the problem with prisoners?"

She shook her head.

"They should really be called 'prisonees,' don't you think?"

Okay, so he's crazy. The looks make up for it. She nodded politely, glancing back to see Orna roll her eyes. Boots opened her mouth to respond, but Didier silenced her with a finger.

"I was in the middle of something when you came in," he said, tracing a green glyph in the air. It looked like the usurer's mark, which could transfer life force from one vessel to another, but not quite.

Usurers were able to heal all wounds at great cost to themselves. The practiced ones learned to take life force from plants and animals, acting as a conduit between the wounded and the soon-to-be victim. They often lived for hundreds of years, became the wealthiest doctors, or on some planets, started cults.

But if Didier was a usurer, he'd be the ship's doctor. For that matter, what was Malik's power again? Sleep?

"I bet you're wondering," he began, peering through the sunboxes, "what that mark was..." He opened one up and snatched a series of grasses from the soil lightning-fast. Boots couldn't believe her eyes as she watched him go from box to box, sticking his hand directly into accelerator rays. It certainly explained his calloused fingers.

"Don't you dare bother him about that sigil," whispered Orna.

"Why would I?" she whispered back.

Once he'd gathered a bounty of tender vegetables and herbs, each kissed by perfect health, he returned to them. "I've got a malformed mark."

Boots flushed. She hadn't meant to stare, certainly not if he had problems. She'd never appreciated anyone prying into her arcana dystocia, and wouldn't dream of putting that on someone else.

And, for the first time in many years, something about it made her feel less alone. A wellspring of conflicting thoughts roiled through her head as she tried to think of what to say. "I don't, uh... I mean—"

He waved off her grimace. "Oh, you're worrying too much. I can still cast, but I can only sense life. Can't move it around. You can imagine how disappointed my folks were, man. Thought they were going to get a doctor and got a gardener instead!"

His immediate honesty kept her on her back foot. "I, uh, didn't mean to dredge up bad memories."

He winked at her. "It's only a bad memory if I wanted to be a doctor."

She feigned a stretch, sneaking another peek at his body as she did. "Well, I'd best get back to languishing in my cell. I think Sokol here is going to murder me if I hang around any longer."

Orna idly inspected her fingernails. "Haven't stopped thinking about it since you opened your mouth."

She bid the cook goodbye before stepping out of the mess and into the cargo hangar. Boots's jaw hit the floor.

Suspended from scaffolding, in pristine condition, was her old fighter: a 2870 edition Midnight Runner with the X-20 strike package. Not hers specifically, because that one had been blown to pieces. Most of it had probably burned up in Clarkesfall's dead atmosphere.

The twenty had a first-in-class cockpit with rock-solid telemetry, engagement planning, and comms. Her old twenty had even been able to pick up ground signals when Kinnard—

She jammed her hands in her pockets. "Whose is that?"

"Mine," said Orna. "I don't need him much, but we like to keep him around. The thing is a relic."

"Holy cats; I take back half of what I said about you, Sokol."

Boots looked around the cargo bay, finding the place littered with spare cores, cabling, tools, and all manner of containers. Someone didn't know how to put away her toys. "Did you restore all that by yourself?"

"Yeah. Got him in perfect working condition, just like he'd rolled off the line yesterday."

"May I, uh..."

Orna regarded her for a long moment, her icy eyes unreadable. Without warning, Ranger surged forward and swept Boots off her feet. Its arms were rough, and might leave a few more bruises to go with her current ones. She was about to complain when the armor leapt, rocketing them up the scaffolding to rest at the boarding ramp. It gently placed her on the catwalk.

The cockpit hung open before her, its familiar pilot's seat scuffed in unfamiliar places. A sharp sting of nostalgia struck the strength from Boots's legs as she approached. The last time she'd flown, she'd been blown from the skies. Her eyes darted to the twin thrusters, where her call sign would've been painted, but she found nothing.

She peeked under the raised windscreen and found the consoles operating in standby power. It had a charged eidolon core, and probably could've scrambled at any second.

"Did you upgrade the power plant?" she called down. "These twenties are finicky."

"No," said Ranger, in Orna's voice. "All parts are factory originals from various vessels. The systems are one hundred percent Synotix and RVC."

"Rook Velocity hasn't been around for years! How did you get them?"

"There are a lot of graveyards on Clarkesfall. Salvage ops." Ranger clanged over to where she stood and offered a hand. "Are we done?" Orna asked.

Sighing, Boots took the creature's claw. She wrapped her arms around it and braced—the bot was far from gentle. Ranger marched to the edge and jumped off, buffering his fall with the thwomp of descender boots. Safely on the ground, Boots loosened her grip and climbed off, careful not to slip on the residue of phantoplasm now coating the floor.

"Why'd you restore this thing?"

"We occasionally need short-ranged engagement capability. The captain and I partnered on the cost."

Boots chuckled. "Sure, but there are cheaper ships if that's what you want…and I'm guessing you're a mechanist, so you can find better quality. Lots of civvy crews have—"

"I used to see them flying by when I was…" Orna's eyes rose to the rafters like it was an open sky.

"When you were a kid?"

Orna glared. The MRX-20 was the standard fighter of the ADF. So she'd lived on Clarkesfall as a child, in Arca no less. Boots had seen a lot of kids bear the unfair costs of global total war, and could only imagine what that did to Orna.

Orna crossed her arms. "The captain thought the Midnight Runner was the best option."

More of Cordell's obnoxious nostalgia. Boots chortled. "Well, yeah, but your captain is a sentimental sucker. Otherwise, I wouldn't be on your ship, would I?"

That wisecrack was the wrong move. The second Boots insulted Cordell, Orna iced up colder than a comet. Every muscle in her exposed arms tensed like she was going to tear off Boots's head with her bare hands.

"Back to your bunk," said Orna, her voice surprisingly emotionless.

To Boots's dismay, Orna led her toward the stairs, Ranger following shortly behind. The quartermaster opened the door for her captive, and Boots stared into the dim illumination of the metal stairwell. It yawned before her, and she couldn't help remembering what Orna had said about there being no cameras in there. She wouldn't take her on a tour of the ship just to kill her, would she?

As soon as the door shut behind them, Ranger hoisted Boots by the collar and slammed her into the steel bulkhead like a rag doll. Lights flashed behind her eyes as the battle armor pinned her by the neck with its forearm. Orna leaned against the railing, chuckling as she drew her high-caliber slinger from its holster at her belt.

Apparently murder was the plan after all.

"What—" *are you doing?* were the words Boots meant to say, but they caught in her pinched windpipe.

"Good boy, Ranger," Orna said. She sidled alongside Boots, placing the slinger's barrel to her temple. "I made a new round, and I've been thinking of testing it out. I call it shadowflash; as in, there's a flash, and all that's left is a shadow."

Shouldn't it be flashshadow, then? Boots cursed herself for thinking that instead of looking for a way out.

With her free hand, Orna stroked Ranger's backplates. "What do you think, boy? If she tried to attack one of us, how would she catch a slinger spell?" She adjusted the barrel's angle so she could paint Boots across the stairs themselves. "Maybe she ran up that way, trying to get to the bridge?" Orna moved to the other side, jamming the barrel into Boots's ear. "Or maybe she tried to make a break for her old Midnight Runner. That seems more plausible."

"The... captain..." Boots coughed.

"Would never know. I think he was torn between killing you and this idiot plan. I'm the quartermaster, and I decide what's on this ship."

She locked back the hammer, and the slinger emitted a high-pitched whine that rose until it disappeared out of human hearing. Ranger wrenched Boots's face so that her nose was mere centimeters from Orna's. Her eyes bored into Boots's, her expression that of a child torturing an ant.

"You're just cattle now. I can butcher you whenever I want."

"I... know where the"—Boots gasped—"*Harrow* is."

"For your sake, I hope you do."

Ranger shoved once more and stepped back, leaving Boots to slide to the ground, hacking her lungs up. She had about a million things to say back to Orna, but none of them seemed wise.

The quartermaster loomed over Boots, her muscled arms tense

with fury. "This is the captain's ship, but it's my home. I ought to at least take a hand for what you did to us."

Boots rubbed her neck, then touched the delicate gash on her cheek. "You did shoot me with two knock rounds."

She smiled. "So I did."

A low rumble shook the walls, and Boots jolted as all the lights went red and klaxons wailed.

"Battle stations! I repeat, battle stations!" came Aisha's voice. "Combat gravity engaging in three..."

Orna slapped the armor's shoulder. "Ranger, get suited up!"

"Two..."

Ranger wrenched open the door to the cargo bay and loped away on all fours, his claws screeching against the deck.

"One. Combat gravity engaged."

A feeling of semi weightlessness washed over Boots, one she knew all too well from the bad old days. Combat gravity was one eighth what it was normally, to give the crew the chance to get around in large leaps. Falls were less deadly, and crew were less likely to show up to their stations winded.

Orna wrenched Boots by the collar and yanked her to her feet. "Get up."

"Where are we going?"

"Your cell is too far. You're going to wait this out on the bridge."

Boots and Orna burst onto the bridge, which had become a maelstrom of activity. Cordell stood at the captain's station, his chair folded into a hidden panel in the floor. Armin, the first mate, frantically punched at terminals, bringing the combat displays online. On the second tier, Didier traced a glyph and sunk his hands into a pair of mechanical sleeves. Servomotors lowered a helmet over his eyes, and a pale, lime-green light bled out around the seams.

On the lowest terrace, Aisha sat glued to her console, the antique flight stick in her nimble hands. Stars wheeled across the glass canopy, and Boots didn't see the enemy until two fighters came screaming past.

"What's she doing here?" Armin shouted the second he saw Boots.

"Easier than the brig," spat Orna. "Watch her, because I'm going out."

Through the open door to the bridge, Boots saw Ranger's chest and legs pop open, revealing a cushioned seat and a plethora of heads-up displays. Orna jumped inside, then the armor snapped shut and stormed away in the direction of the nearest airlock.

"So she's finally decided to use the battle armor as actual armor," said Boots.

Armin drew his slinger and gestured to a chair. "Strap in and shut up."

Cordell traced his shieldmaster's glyph, and a series of matte gray panels lowered around him, nearly hiding him from view. "All right, people, let's get this done!"

A three-dimensional projection of the *Capricious* and the surrounding hundred kilometers spun into being from the aether, filling up the vaulted space in the center of the bridge. A crystal ball emerged from the wall, and Armin slammed his hand against it, still keeping his weapon trained on Boots.

"Resonance reflections are negative," he called. "Life signs?"

"Scanning," replied Didier, his head locked in place. "Got 'em, man. Relaying to the aggregator."

Five pings flashed up on the display, circling the *Capricious* like a pack of wolves.

"Five bandits," called Armin. "Hotel eight-fiver-three, carom one-four-six, distance fifteen hundred!"

Going to be coming in from above us. Boots knew Cordell's strategy—the *Capricious* was a marauder class, used for dropping into combat zones with supplies and reinforcements. The toughest part of the ship was his belly, and unlike normal ships, sensitive gear was housed on his back. With a good shieldmaster like Cordell and a set of amps, they could protect the support gear and prolong the engagement until the police arrived.

Cordell splayed his fingers, and a set of two large, white discs appeared on the display, hovering above the *Capricious*. Those were his shields, amplified through high-powered defense systems to deflect even the best spells. He whipped his arm around to block a strafing run from the closest fighter.

"I've put in a call to the nearest patrol," said Didier. "They say ETA sixty seconds."

"Sokol, do you copy?" called the captain.

Her voice reverberated through the bridge. "I'm here. Heading out the airlock now."

"Do not engage," said the captain. "We just have to hold out until the gate cops catch up."

"How long?"

"Fifty-three seconds," said Armin, and a countdown appeared on the readout.

Boots let out a sigh. Five fighters against a marauder was bad, but if they had reinforcements inbound, they'd be all right.

Then she remembered what Nilah had told her back in the cell about the Fixers getting compromised. Nilah thought the cops had put a bounty on her for no reason, or to slow her down. Worse, Cyril's statements about a grand conspiracy still rattled around in Boots's head. Boots hated to sound like one of her delusional clients, but what if all of it was connected?

"You can't trust the authorities," said Boots.

"Shut up, or I'll shoot," said Armin. "They're targeting our comms first."

"On it," said Cordell, flicking his hand. Boots watched the display as a shield whipped across the surface of the *Capricious* to block a hail of spell bolts. Cordell winced. "They're using some pretty quality stuff. Going to be tough to keep this up long."

A tiny version of Ranger crawled across the holographic ship. "I'm on the outer hull," said Orna. "Permission to engage."

"Permission denied," said Cordell, wincing as another shot rocked the ship. "We don't want to get in the way of the cops. Time until the patrol arrives?"

"Thirty-two seconds!" called Armin.

Aisha spun the ship, and stars streaked across the dome as she maneuvered its belly toward the strafing fighters. Boots wished Aisha had been around at the Battle of Laconte.

One of the holographic ships landed a bolt near Ranger. "Permission to engage!" Orna insisted.

"Denied," said Cordell. For a man in his early fifties, he could move like a teenager. He made sweeping blocks across multiple lines of fire, drawing them all into his shield.

"Fifty-point-eight percent of their fire has been focused on our comms array!" shouted Armin. "It's not going to survive another hit."

"Noted," said Cordell, moving both his shields to overlap in front of the set of dishes and antennae that allowed the ship to call for help.

The three priorities of any ship combat action were: comms, gravity, and life support. Take out comms so they can't report their location, take out gravity so they get slung all over the cabins, and destroy life support so they slowly suffocate. Against five fighters, there was no way to protect all three systems for more than a few minutes.

"Eighteen seconds," said Armin, his eyes pulsing in time with the crystal ball. "The patrol is telling us to deactivate our counter-measures so we don't catch them in the cross fire."

To Cordell's credit, he said, "Can't get much more deactivated than this. We won't shoot the cops."

"Deactivate your countermeasures? Are you hearing yourself, Cordell?" Boots unbuckled her belts, gently rising from her chair. "They're either not coming, or they're coming to kill us!"

Armin let go of his crystal ball, locked back the hammer on his slinger, and marched straight to Boots. "Shut up! I've had enough of this!"

Ten seconds.

"Get back to your station!" shouted Cordell.

"As soon as I take care of this," hissed Armin. "I told you to keep your mouth shut."

"Put the gun down and do your job! That's an order!" bellowed the captain, drowning out all other sound in the cabin. The other voices died away, and Armin lowered his slinger, eyes wide. Boots had heard that voice before; it got the results that changed the course of campaigns.

Three seconds.

"Yes, sir," said Armin.

Two.

One.

The alarm chirped in the display, its four zeroes blinking with a painful, incessant noise.

No one came. Not one jump signal pinged their detection system. Boots looked from Armin to Cordell, both men stunned to see that a patrol had broken its promise.

"I told you," breathed Boots, trying to keep the quaver from her voice.

Armin bared his teeth like a wolf. "So you did."

A colossal blow rocked the ship, and it listed, each person

growing weightless in the wake of the explosion. The contents of Boots's stomach surged in the sudden loss of direction.

"They've taken out our artificial gravity!" yelled Aisha. "Can't maneuver!"

A standard maneuver cranks out twenty G's. No more hard pitching. No more spinning the belly to block shots. Straight, predictable lines only.

Cordell snapped out of his funk long enough to swear. "Okay then. They want to play like that, we're going to play like that. Orna, permission to engage granted. Light them up."

Ranger reared back, and the readout filled with thousands of orbs—a veritable star field of bullets. She filled slices of the grid with hazards, far too many to count, as each ship dove in to make a pass.

"Ammunition at ninety percent," said Orna. "Why did you stop your evasive maneuvers?"

"We lost gravity in here," responded Aisha. "Anything bigger than minor corrections might squish everyone."

"Understood." Ranger's long-barreled, back-mounted slingers pegged one of the inbound fighters, its fuselage smashing against the hull. The remains of the assault craft raked across the communications array, and a sickening static bled into the speakers.

Gravity down. Comms down. Life support is next.

Boots took a step forward. "I'm going out."

"The hell you are," said Armin. "We're about to lose imaging."

The projection in the center of the bridge distorted, then unraveled into tendrils of arcane energy.

"Cameras up," said Cordell, and an array of huge screens unfurled all around his feet. He guided the shields by their images, though he looked less steady than before. He hooked his feet into two special stirrups so his constant twisting wouldn't cause him to float away.

Boots peered over the console to see Orna wreaking havoc on the screens. As a tiny holographic projection, Ranger wasn't that impressive. Up close, Boots could see it loping along the hull like an ancient lion. It would burst onto frame, all six guns blazing, then dart away. She never saw it for more than a split second, and she could only describe it as majestic. Apart, Orna and Ranger were destructive. When she rode inside him, the effect was devastating.

Boots grit her teeth. "She needs support, Cordell!"

"Captain, this is another trick," said Armin.

Cordell licked his lips, sweeping away part of a volley. Spells pinged the ship's hull, eating through it like acid. He sighed. "Get out there, Boots. Armin, run alternates, and get our imaging back on line."

"Thank you," she huffed.

"Boots, remember: you're my only wing."

So you'd better stay on this bird. He'd said that to her a hundred times, before every escort. She'd chased the *Capricious* over a half dozen skies. She'd killed at least nineteen other pilots in its service. The phrase was like a needle in her heart, with its thread tied firmly to the ship. She cursed him under her breath.

Boots kicked off the console, gliding effortlessly toward the corridor. The door slid open before her, and she had to acclimate to the spinning sensation of no gravity. Low-grav maneuvering was a spacer's first skill, though, and she had her bearings back in no time, bouncing off the built-in kickplates and yanking along the handholds that ejected when artificial gravity failed.

She slung her weight around the stairwell door before diving down the central shaft, winding between railings. The ship rocked with the force of a hit, and the sudden tilt smashed her against a wall. All of her aches and bruises rang like alarm bells, but she righted herself and kept going. Any moment they were going to lose pressure, and she could only hope they had an emergency seal on the bridge.

Once in the cargo bay, she laid eyes on the Runner, about to slip its moorings. She launched from the floor toward the central part of the scaffolding, not wanting to overshoot and bounce off the ceiling. She hoisted herself the final few meters onto the loading ramp and found the cockpit open and waiting, its glimmering charge lamps beckoning her.

No time to suit up, and she didn't remember the preflight checks. She pushed off to the nearby intercom and hailed the bridge.

"Captain," she started, but spluttered as the long-forgotten word left her mouth. "Cordell. Your comms are out, so I can't hail you from my—your—fighter."

"Get him warmed up," said Cordell, his "serious captain voice" tainted by soft laughter at her mistake. "We're going to pop the cargo bay in thirty seconds. You're cleared hot the second you get out."

"Acknowledged," said Boots, kicking off the wall. She floated back to her craft and caught the corner of the open windscreen before throwing herself into the pilot's seat. She looked over the controls and—

"Oh no."

Each MRX-20 could be quickly activated by tracing the pilot's sigil on the glass pad that also served as the central console. Linked to a ship's internal database, it relayed information like the pilot's personal preferences, dashboard layout, seat firmness, weapon selection order, and other features.

Except Boots didn't have a sigil.

Even if she did, what version of the database was this? She'd been added to the ADF pilots' roster in 2871, so if it was a 2870 that had never seen action, it wouldn't be up to date. Boots sorely wished Orna had answered her question about the parts sourcing, because if she didn't get that cockpit sealed, this would be a very short engagement.

She flipped up the glass pad and found the mechanical keys, an accessibility feature for pilots whose magic was too exhausted to trace another sigil. She pressed the "mn code" button, then went to punch in her old code: 280419.

INCORRECT OR INVALID CODE. 2 TRIES REMAINING BEFORE LOCKDOWN.

Was she not in the database, or was the code wrong? Her pulse slammed in her neck as she tried to guess which possibility caused the fault. If the code was invalid, then it didn't matter, she'd never get the cockpit closed, and she'd die an agonizing, choking death. In light of that, she might as well keep trying.

The code had sounded right in her head, but felt wrong when she entered it. She hovered her fingers over the keys, trying to dredge up the muscle memory of her personal key. At the lightest touch of the eight, she realized she'd transposed the first two numbers.

82...04...1—

Another blast rattled the ship and her finger landed on the two.

1 TRY REMAINING BEFORE LOCKDOWN.

She snarled and carefully began punching in her code as the bay door lights began to flash. Not long now. The whole ship began to vibrate, and she knew one of the engines had been hit because of a subtle pull to the left. The keypad shook under her fingertip, already unsteady with adrenaline.

"Oh, for the love of—"

She slammed her finger down on the nine as hard as she could and had to draw back her hand as the glass panel folded down with its welcome message. The canopy closed over her, and she breathed a sigh of relief as she heard it pressurize.

All of her old settings cascaded through the cockpit, from her favorite seat height to the placement and style of her spatial reckoner. She wrapped her fingers around the flight stick at either side and tested the pedals.

WELCOME ELIZABETH "BOOTS" ELSWORTH.

"Hello to you, too, boy," she breathed, eyeing the scaffolding. This wasn't standard ADF, so there was no docking interface. How was she supposed to detach? On the deck below, Orna's unsecured tools slid toward the closed door, drawn outward by the ship's spin. When they opened the cargo bay, it was going to cost them more than a few argents. *That's why you always put your crap away, Miss Quartermaster.*

The Runner's engines ignited, their dull roar reverberating through her hull. Her console informed her that the oxygen content outside the ship had dropped rapidly, so they were depressurizing the bay. With a final klaxon, the cargo bay opened and the mag locks disengaged. Boots breathed a sigh of relief, since she hadn't wanted to tear out of the scaffolding.

Aisha had stabilized the *Capricious*'s spin, so only a few of Orna's precious toys drifted into the blackness of space. An incoming fighter went for a strafing run on the open cargo bay, and Boots flinched. She wasn't even going to get out of the ship before being blown apart.

Cordell's shield batted the spells out of the way, sizzling with each hit. The fighter veered off at the last second, but caught a tool chest across the canopy, flattening it and the pilot inside. Could she count that as her twentieth kill?

Easing the throttle forward, she pushed past the dock and out into space. Once she crossed the edge of the cargo bay, she gunned the engine. Cordell's shields were a blessing, but they could cut ships in half if they caught them just right.

She cursed as the throttle smashed her against the back of her seat. Young Boots had tuned the inertial dampers to sport mode so she could feel the maneuvers. Old Boots didn't appreciate that. She wasn't going to be able to finish this fight if she blacked out, so she quickly opened her control mapping.

Here was an honest-to-goodness space battle, and she was screwing with the settings panel. She finally found the secondary mapping and got the dampers fixed when her radio chirped: a call from Ranger.

"Watch out!" commanded Orna. "You just pulled one on your phase!"

Right. Phase. One hundred eighty degrees. Boots instinctively dove and dumped the throttle, forcing her ship to tumble. The enemy craft came into view, sleek and sinister, lightning pops from its high-cal slingers. Boots clicked the triggers, and her twin cannons blazed, pumping round after round at the weaving target. A single enemy round pinged her pristine hull, but no alarms sounded. It'd still leave a mark.

"Oh, no you don't!" shouted Boots, blasting after him as he broke from his path, whirling off to the side.

He made full-speed away from the combat zone, ducking and weaving, the flashes of fire receding behind the pair. Just a bit more, and she'd have him.

You're my only wing.

"Get back here," said Orna.

Boots swore and broke away to return to the battle. The little twit had tried to lead her away, and out of practice as she was, she'd almost fallen for it. She laid into the throttle and raced toward the *Capricious*, where two more fighters remained. That guy would be back soon enough, and she'd be ready for him.

The radio chirped. "You scratched my Runner's paint!"

"Deal with it. No seekers on this bird?" asked Boots, dodging stray fire from the fight.

"No," huffed Orna. "Couldn't afford them. Just dispersers and cannons."

Boots's breath hitched as she spun and dove after the nearest fighter. The maneuver nearly put her in red-out, and she felt an upward pull on her jowls that hadn't been there last time she flew. The enemy pilot dropped incinerator charges, little suns that would fry anything that got too close. Boots flipped the Runner so she passed over them with its belly, shielding her from the radiation. She hit two more with her dispersers and laid into the craft with her slingers.

She landed a solid shot in his power plant, and his eidolon core went up, spraying the entire craft across the stars in a sparkling crimson haze. She veered off; eidolon debris was nothing to play with.

"That makes twenty," said Boots. "You tell Cordell if I die today, I die an ace."

"You die today, there won't be anyone to tell. Make a low pass by the resonance tower. This bastard won't come in range."

"Why the tower?"

"Because I said so, old-timer."

"Salty little..." Boots circled the *Capricious*, staying just out of range of Cordell's shields before dipping under the half-mangled tower. Out of nowhere, Ranger bounded up and leapt onto Boots's maneuvering thrusters, riding her like a horse.

Boots winced as the armor's claws raked across the hull, digging in. "What was that about scratching the paint?"

"Shut up. It's my ship and this is awesome."

Together, they swept after the enemy fighter. Ranger's mass considerably altered the flight dynamics, but Boots could compensate if she concentrated. The sluggishness actually helped, since Boots still wasn't up to speed on the thrusters. The MRX-20 was so much more violent than she remembered.

When Ranger's guns thundered, the whole hull shook with their fury. Up close to their target, Orna switched to homing fire, her monstrous sigil canister rotating out with the spent one. The enemy fighter popped a disperser field, destroying the spells on contact, and Boots climbed to avoid the inert shells.

"Ammunition at five percent," said Orna.

"I've still got guns."

"Then show me what you can do."

Boots rolled the fighter so her canopy faced the bandit and yanked back on the flight stick, dipping toward him. Ranger lost its footing, but quickly scrabbled back into place and leveled its cannons. Both women opened up on the fighter, their craft rolling past disperser fields and incinerators. Boots neutralized all the countermeasures that she could, though Ranger had to swing down out of the way of an incinerator, pulling them off course. Boots quickly corrected, but not before Ranger had found its place atop her again.

Orna's homing fire rounds penetrated farther into the disperser clouds as the enemy ship began to lose power. Countermeasures exhausted, Boots tore the fighter to pieces with her guns.

Ranger banged its canisters with a metal fist. "I'm dry."

"That makes twenty-one kills."

"No dice," said Orna. "That was mine."

"Twenty-point-five?"

"Twenty and a quarter, and there's another one behind us."

The Runner lurched as Ranger leapt from her engines. Boots righted herself, gliding backward just in time to see Orna land atop the enemy fighter, punch through the canopy, and rip out the pilot. Boots winced as her comrade hurled the lifeless body out into the stars.

"That all of them?" asked Orna.

"I think so. They didn't show up on resonance, though, so they've got some kind of stealth."

"Can't hide life force. Let's get back to the ship, and I can ask Didier."

"How's your life support?" asked Boots.

"Holding steady. I've got five more hours out here."

They were a few klicks from the *Capricious*. Orna stood perched on the dead fighter; its engines automatically slowed and shut off without the presence of a pilot, leaving it to drift toward infinity. Boots took a look at her fuel reserves—more than enough to get back to Gantry Station.

"Well," said Boots, stretching her arms, "I hate to be the first to leave the party, but I think I have an engagement elsewhere."

"What?"

She spun her craft to put some distance between them. "I'm sure they'll come rescue you. Oh, and sorry about your tools, but that's what happens when you don't clean up your mess."

Boots was about to throttle up when her glass went black. A white, cartoonish version of Ranger's head hovered over the console, followed by the words: RANGER AUTOMATIC PILOT TECHNOLOGIES.

Boots flipped up the glass and punched in her override. "Oh no."

The craft spun to reveal Ranger atop the other fighter, its metal arms conducting Boots's ship like a symphony. "Oh yes."

"Look, kid, I was playing with you. It's a joke."

"The joke's on you."

Flight controls unresponsive. Weapons offline. "You said you didn't modify this thing!"

"I didn't. You've got an out-of-date defense system and I'm a mechanist. All I had to do was touch you and cast my spell."

"So that's why—"

"I rode your ship into battle? Yes." The Runner came alongside the downed craft, and Ranger climbed aboard. "Let's get back to the *Capricious*, shall we?"

Chapter Six

Pit Stop

N ilah's day hadn't gone as well as she'd hoped.

She should've been standing on a podium back on Gantry Station, waving before throngs of adoring fans. She imagined hoisting the Awala GP trophy aloft, the spray of alcoholic bubbles from sparkling wine scintillating in the artificial sun. Then she'd be back on Lang's private yacht, bound for a week of rest on Taitu. She could dream of lilac fields, then awaken to walk outside the Brio family estate, the soft petals of her custom-designed flowers sweet in her nose and creamy on her fingertips. There'd be a fireworks spectacular, a personal concert, and too many men and women to count in her bed.

Instead, she found herself terrified, plastered to one wall of a holding cell on a strange ship, its engines violently out of control. The lights browned out, leaving her in the purple glow of her dermaluxes.

She traced her glyph, placed her hand to the deck, and felt for a connection with the *Capricious*. Connecting to a small system like the Hyper 8 was one thing, but the size and scale of the

Capricious took a toll on her already worn muscles. She'd been careless before, trying to directly deactivate the force field, but perhaps she could get a status report. Anything was better than sitting in the shadows, waiting to die.

Main drive two-seventy damaged: no power. Communications error. Artificial gravity intermittent. She sensed the ship's damage like scabs, and she bit her lip. The *Capricious* had three engines: two on the sides and one on the back, and one of the side engines was out. If she could route power to it, she might be able to get it back online.

The link to primary engine control was tenuous, and scorched conduits pockmarked its path. She spotted an auxiliary routing, but she feared the ship's defense system. It was one thing to observe damage. Reaching out and touching it might cause another violent reaction like the one from the force field. Some defense programs could even fry mechanists by connecting them directly to the main power grid.

Nilah hesitated. She'd taken quite a beating. Every cool breath stung her nostrils, like the lining of her sinuses had been stripped away. Her eyes were a pair of boiled eggs, slow and swollen. Bruises pooled in her joints from neck to toes. If she got any worse, there wouldn't be enough recovery time before the next race.

If she didn't do anything, she might not survive to the next race.

Nilah pushed more of her magic into the ship, tensing up at the exertion required to penetrate its basic portals. The *Capricious's* network materialized in her mind like a fortress. Primary engine control would be heavily guarded, so she couldn't go after it right away. If she could take out the defense program, she'd gain access to the ship's core functions.

Find the point no one watches. Somewhere on the *Capricious*, a pantry lock began to slide open and closed. Nilah toggled it repeatedly, thrice per second for ten seconds. When she felt the hot surge of the ship's defense program, she jolted back out of sync. She dove back in and started slamming the closet door in the captain's quarters. When she finished that, she opened all the cabinets in med bay, then closed them in alternating intervals. She led the defense program on a wild goose chase, burning down its resources in the process.

Half of the defense program went to protecting all portals, so Nilah moved on to toilets. Then she flipped light switches. She adjusted the temperature by one degree on alternating decks. She turned on music in the crew bunks. She locked all the showers on cold.

Finally, she moved to fix the two-seventy engine. The defense program appeared before her, stretched thin with her probing—defenseless against her magic. She tore open its threads of code with a mighty pull of her spell, and it dissipated.

She bandaged the engine as best she could. The fix wouldn't bring the engine to full, but it beat nothing.

She then patched into the intraship comms system and listened to the chatter. They'd been attacked by five ships, and it sounded like Boots and someone named Orna fought them off. The pilot sounded excited to have her engine back, so Nilah set to work on the artificial gravity. The racer didn't much feel like helping her kidnappers, but she also didn't want to be blown to bits.

Nilah inspected the long-range communications array and saw only hopelessly destroyed wreckage; so much for calling for help. The next best thing: force them to put her somewhere less secure in the future. With the defense program out of commission, she cross-wired the force field generators on her cell, burning them out with a loud hiss and a chemical stench. They'd have to be completely gutted and replaced.

The spells had taken a lot out of her, but Nilah's days on the racetrack had done a lot to prepare her: two hours at a stretch of hard synchro with her car under intense conditions. Even in her beaten state, she could handle more punishment.

She crept out of her cell, where she found a hardwired console with field controls, lights, and all other types of access. With her hand directly on a conduit, she could do a lot more damage. She patched into the ship's speaker system as she sealed the bridge doors.

"Listen up. This is Nilah Brio, and your ship is mine."

Orna's remote landing protocol did a better job than Boots would have. The *Capricious*'s two-seventy had taken damage, and it spun lazily as it drifted through space. Boots was sorely out of practice, and docking with a cartwheeling ship wasn't a challenge she felt like facing. They passed through the open cargo bay and into the scaffolding, but before the mag locks could engage, the ship stopped spinning.

The screech of metal tore through Boots's eardrums as the Runner scraped along the ceiling and slammed into the wall, snapping off one of its maneuvering thrusters. The starfighter listed before Orna cut the power in half and sent them plummeting to the deck. Sirens and proximity alarms went wild with the teeth-rattling crash, and Boots opened her eyes to find she still lived. It had been a painful impact, but not nearly as bad as taking a direct hit to the power core. The ship would still fly again...one day.

Boots's arms settled over the control sticks, and she realized the artificial gravity had returned. The cargo bay slammed closed, and the swell of pressurization echoed through the chamber.

Ranger's heavy footfalls sounded from above on the rear engines, followed by the metallic thud of the suit landing hard on the cargo deck. He tromped out in view of the canopy, but Orna wasn't inside him. His chest plate hung open, exposing the cushions where a rider might sit, which meant Orna was still hanging around on the ship. It wasn't pointing its guns at Boots, probably because it was empty, but she hadn't forgotten it tearing a man from the cockpit.

Right on cue, a knocking came on top of the canopy, and Boots turned to see the quartermaster standing directly on top of her, brandishing her high-cal slinger.

"I'm going to open this ship, and you're not going to do anything stupid."

Boots shrugged and held up her hands. "What would be the point?"

Orna bared her teeth and locked back the hammer. "You wrecked my ship, so I'm including 'talking' in the list of stupid things you could do."

The quartermaster climbed to the wing while the canopy slid open, all the while keeping her weapon trained on Boots. Together, they climbed off the ship, and Boots got a good look at the outside.

The fighter had suffered cosmetic damage all over, and Boots saw the telltale signs of overthrust ringing the outer boosters. The spotless paint job appeared to have been attacked with a knife. Sections of the fuselage were warped from numerous impacts, the nozzles would have to be changed out before it would be airworthy again, and the landing struts had taken a shearing hit.

Angry lightning flashed in Orna's eyes as they crisscrossed the wreckage, cataloging each tiny nick and dent for Boots's indictment. Orna's breath heaved in her chest; her cheeks flushed with anger. Every muscle in her body was coiled taut, and Boots prepared herself for a beating.

Then the quartermaster's gaze left the ship long enough to recognize a new, critical fact: all of her tools and special projects were gone.

All of the color that filled her livid form drained away through her feet, and she whipped her head around in wide-eyed horror. Her gun left Boots, and Orna stomped from place to place, screaming at the voids where her precious instruments had once lived.

Boots could only look on in fear; to move or speak would be certain death. But then, failing to put some distance between them might also spell doom. Ranger stood impassively by, a nightmarish giant of clacking armor, its fingers twitching with each howl Orna made.

When Orna had finally confirmed the passing of her most favorite spanners, the quartermaster rolled over to Boots like a molten wave of star stuff, her gun snapping into place at Boots's forehead.

"You need to think about what you're doing," breathed Boots. "Think about what Cordell is going to say."

"How many people have I killed for less?" Orna's pupils shrunk to pinpricks, leaving only the blue of a gas flame.

"I know, but I . . . but I didn't leave the tools out . . ."

Orna's lip quivered. Whether she was about to cry or had merely lost control of her face, Boots would never know, because the next words she heard were:

"Listen up. This is Nilah Brio, and your ship is mine."

It'd come from the speaker system, and bounced off every wall to hit Orna again and again.

The quartermaster smiled—not a happy grin; more like a tiger being released on its captors to lay waste to their flesh.

"Pilot," said Nilah, "you're going to lay in a course for the jump gate and get us to Taitu, or I'm going to depressurize the bridge. Do you understand me?"

Orna's eyes sliced into Boots, but the frightful grin never left her face. For her part, Boots only raised her hands and shrugged. Any comment might be taken as an excuse for execution.

"I say again," came Nilah, "do you understand me?"

Orna laughed out loud: a hoarse bark, like she'd been punched in the gut. Then the laugh came again, longer and more sustained. It died to a chuckle, and she checked her weapon's clip, spun on a heel, and marched for the door. Boots started to follow, but the quartermaster's pistol barrel swung in her direction without even a broken stride.

Boots raised her hands, backing away slowly, as her captor disappeared into the bowels of the ship.

"That's just what we were doing, sweetheart," said a man's voice over the ship intercom. "Keep your pants on."

Nilah pressed her palms to the sides of the console, projecting her speech across all intraship comms. "Call me sweetheart again and you won't have air to do it a third time. Identify yourself."

"Cordell Lamarr, captain of the *Capricious*. And you're Nilah Brio."

"Why have you kidnapped me? Money? You're not getting anything."

"You seemed like you were in a spot of trouble, swee...Nilah. We couldn't just leave you unconscious on Gantry Station," said Cordell. He cleared his throat. "Also, uh, our quartermaster didn't know who you were."

Nilah snorted. "And that's a reason to kidnap someone?"

"She figured you had a beef with Boots, and that was a good reason to bring you along."

The racer started to respond, but her voice distorted and fell out of sync with the ship as she was cut off. A powerful presence cleanly sliced her connection to the *Capricious*...did the defense program reboot? It couldn't have; she'd ripped that thing in half. She slapped her hands back onto the console and linked into several low-level circuits. Once again, she saw the shape of the network in her mind, humming pathways and conduits pulsing with light.

In her mind's eye, a black shape, swift and vicious as a cat, swept down upon her, rending her from the ship with a howl. Her psychic connection fizzled out, leaving her back in the real world. Nilah screamed, pulling back her now-cooked palms and blowing on the hot skin. It had to be another mechanist intervening, but Nilah hadn't seen anything like that before. At the academy, she'd done a bit of countersynchronization, but hadn't been very good. She'd always been a tuner.

Still, she wasn't about to back down. People didn't die in PGRF racing, but it was still a dangerous sport, full of quick thinking and daring wagers. She was the best in the galaxy, and she'd be damned if she let some trash from a defunct warship take her out.

Gingerly she laid her burning hands across the console screen, tentatively feeling for a connection. As soon as she penetrated the ship, the black shape was upon her. Nilah weaved across pathways and pipelines, throwing interference and shields into her path as she fled. To her surprise, the other mechanist made no effort to avoid these traps, instead smashing through them with no regard for his or her own safety. Nilah wove a sever circuit into the infrastructure, and the other mechanist slammed into it, vanishing from the system with a woman's scream. Nilah grinned as control of the ship returned to her.

Whoever the other mechanist was, she had no tactics or talent. Her strategy was blind attack with as much strength as she could muster, and that was her undoing. With a little finesse, even the strongest opponents could be destroyed.

Except the jet-black presence began pouring in from a conduit in the midship, flooding across the systems and obscuring them from view. Nilah found herself retreating again, ceding more control than she'd intended. When she was ready to retaliate, the other mechanist disappeared. She was about to try to tap into the camera system to find her opponent when the inky shape reappeared, knocking out the lighting and camera systems outside the brig.

"Bloody—" Nilah began, but stopped short when a tall, raven-haired woman stomped into the room with her, slinger at the ready.

Oddly, the gun wasn't what transfixed Nilah as she surveyed the newcomer—it was the woman's taut, sweat-slicked arm muscles, covered in tiny scars like she'd gotten in a fight with a wildcat. The scars crisscrossed every inch of exposed skin, rising to her face. The largest cuts ran across her cheeks, just under her icy eyes. Her chest heaved with each quivering breath, but her gun remained steady and locked on Nilah's head. The racer knew beyond the shadow of a doubt: this was the enemy mechanist.

"Hi," Nilah said, never breaking contact with the ship's console.

The woman's eyes bored into her—a snake transfixing its prey. She snapped back the hammer on her slinger. "If I pull this trigger, you won't exist anymore. I won't even have to scatter the ashes."

"Do you know who I am?" asked Nilah.

"Yeah, I know your name. If you don't take your hands off my ship, I'll write it on your tombstone."

The woman looked down her nose and cocked an eyebrow, and a prickle of heat traveled over Nilah's skin. She told herself it was the cool malice of the statement, but there was something about this brute.

Nilah grimaced as she fiddled with the ship's controls, disabling a set of safety overrides. "I'd love to take my hands off, but...I've switched engine containment to manual, so if you don't back down, I'll blow us all to space dust. Are we crystal?"

The engine bucked like a wild animal as Nilah adjusted the shields inside a half dozen times per second. Before she'd taken the safeties off, she imagined it would be like tuning her car on the fly during a normal run on the track. Faced with the raging energies of a destabilizing core, she realized she'd underestimated the ship's scale. This wasn't a race car; if she made a mistake, or broke contact for even a second, the whole thing would go critical.

The woman's eyes went wide, and she pressed her palm to the ship. The mechanist's dark cloud circled the periphery of systems, but Nilah knew she wouldn't interfere. She only wanted to see for herself.

"You're crazy," whispered the woman.

"No," Nilah grunted. "I'm the best tuner in the galaxy...and right now...I need concentration." She spared a nod at the slinger. "What's your name?"

"Orna."

"Orna, disarm your slinger and toss it over here."

The woman did as she was told, and Nilah's eyes roamed over the rest of her body. Someone like her would have more than just one weapon.

Nilah sucked in a quick breath as the engine almost escaped her control. She couldn't keep this going forever, and this woman was too much of a threat. "Strip to your skivvies and kick your clothes over here."

"What?"

"You've got more weapons. I'm sure of it."

Orna shook her head. "You're not going to kill us all."

Nilah's heart thudded. "I am. I defy death every time I race."

The tall mechanist took a large step into the room, bringing her into arm's reach. "A pampered, pretty thing like you? I doubt it. You want to live just as much as everyone else."

Nilah's hands were glued to the console, and it took all her concentration to keep the system contained. She could do nothing as Orna reached up and wrapped her hands around the racer's throat, squeezing lightly.

"Put the containment fields back," Orna growled into her ear, "or I'll snap this skinny neck and end us all."

Nilah tried to reply, but Orna's vice-like grip pulsed, silencing her. The engine core thrashed wildly at its surroundings, scorching one of the control panels. If she didn't set it right soon, there wouldn't be enough left to save them.

Orna whispered into Nilah's ear, hot breath tickling her sensitive skin. "You wouldn't believe the things I've done to survive against far worse threats than you. I'm impressed that you carried it this far, but no more negotiations."

Klaxons blared once again, and the radio echoed through the ship. "This is the captain again. I hate to bother you down there, but we've got two jump ships rolling up on us, and they're not responding to hails."

Orna's grip tightened, and blood filled Nilah's cheeks. She took a last reedy breath before her airway closed altogether. Dizziness overtook her, and she started to lose control. Nilah didn't have a choice; she set the fields back the way they were, returning the systems to nominal operation.

Her assailant relaxed just enough to let her have a tiny sip of air. "Now let go of the console."

And for the second time that day, color drained away from the world around Nilah, and time sunk into syrupy slow motion. She recognized it instantly: Mother's spell.

Nilah's body lagged under the weight of magic, and her eyes strained to follow commands. The ship's systems, however, were millions of times faster than a human body, and with her hands still on the console, she connected to the external camera feeds.

It didn't take long to find the two bright yellow cruisers half a kilometer away. They must've jumped in next to the *Capricious* to get that close without a fight. And the *Capricious*, lacking its own jump engine, would never get away. Intricate designs crisscrossed the newcomers' hulls like silver vines, and she couldn't identify the make.

She did, however, recognize the missile launchers emerging from pod bays on both ships.

Patches of color ran across the *Capricious*'s plating where Mother's spell was either unstable or ineffective. Nilah thought back to Mother's murder of Cyril. He'd been in color as well, and able to move normally, which meant... Nilah swiveled the camera and cross-referenced the locations against the ship's critical systems. Flicking through the internal cams, Nilah saw a cone of color extending all the way down to life support.

The recent arrivals were planning to drive a spike through their hearts—no running, no evasion, no shields.

She flicked back to the exterior cameras. Flashes popped along the enemy hulls as a half dozen missiles launched toward them. She tried connecting to the amp to retarget the captain's shields, but they wouldn't move without him. Ship dispersers wouldn't target in time, since they still had to physically swivel.

She thought back to her car, the way it had teleported when she mixed energy from the Arclight Booster into Mother's spell. There had to be a dimensional element to Mother's power, the way space bent when it was broken, but the effect was unpredictable. If she could dump energy into the spell again, maybe she could bend space once more. But then, who knew where they'd end up?

Missiles closed on the *Capricious* like a school of hungry piranhas.

Nilah connected to the main drive to flush all its energy reserves in an uncontrolled burn. She hoped there was no one in the engine room, but there wasn't time to worry about that now.

The ship jolted under her feet, and for a moment, she thought they'd been hit. Light bent and diffracted, smearing around her as the spells mixed and the ship teleported without the aid of a jump gate or drive. Nilah didn't know where they were going or how far they'd get, but the spells interacting here were orders of magnitude larger than her little race car. She prayed it would carry them far away from Mother and her cruisers.

The deck pulled out from underneath her, and she flew backward, smashing into something soft. Alarms filled the air and automated systems chanted warnings about gravitational anomalies. Nilah heard a groan behind her and jumped as Orna slid to the floor, out cold.

"Oh god, I'm—" *Sorry?* Was she sorry? After all, this woman had been strangling her just a few moments prior, so maybe "sorry" wasn't the right word. Of course, Nilah had threatened to kill everyone on the ship, so maybe Orna had been a little justified.

The ship rumbled under her feet, and Nilah wondered if she'd done some damage to the core in the teleportation attempt. When she'd teleported her car, they hadn't even gone off Gantry Station. What if she'd moved the *Capricious* only a few hundred feet, or even a few kilometers? The ship would still be well within the sensor range of its hunters.

"What the hell was that?" shouted Cordell, his voice hollow in the speakers.

Nilah limped over to the console, her whole body beaten down by a difficult race, a horrid escape, and two strong zaps from some nasty spells. She renewed her glyph, and her palms stung as she placed them on the circuit and reconnected to the ship. She didn't see Mother's battlegroup on the external cameras, so she switched to the bridge intercom.

"We teleported," she croaked.

"What?" barked Cordell. "That's impossible! We don't have a—"

"Jump drive," said Nilah. "Yes, I know. It's complicated. Where are we?"

She could tell from his stammering that he wasn't often at a loss for words. "Uh, yeah. Okay. My navigator says we're about five days away from the nearest jump gate, which is the old Goodall Colony."

That was light-years away from Gantry Station. Nilah breathed a sigh of relief. "Okay then. I've...I've got someone wounded down here. Orna...I think her name is?"

"The doc is coming to you."

Chapter Seven

Strategies

Two days ago, Boots hadn't imagined herself dining at the captain's table on board the *Capricious*. In fact, she would've done everything she could to stay away from the place. Now she sat before an opulent spread of fresh vegetables, succulent meats, creamy cheeses, and tender pasta. If she'd been at home, she'd have been scarfing down a cup of Insto before tucking into a nightcap. She cursed her aching head and sore bones as the bottle of wine landed in front of her, courtesy of Didier. At least she had something to look at with her meal.

The hours prior had been her strangest ones on board the ship, including her time served in the Famine War. The bizarre teleportation event had rocked the ship and sent Boots flying across the cargo bay, along with Ranger. Apparently it'd knocked Orna unconscious, because the robot shut down, leaving Boots free to walk herself to the bridge. Boots was just glad it'd happened after the Midnight Runner was magnetically secured, because she'd have been squished otherwise.

Didier distracted her as he leaned over her shoulder to pour her a glass. He smelled of salt and grease, but also of something distinctly herbal. Boots discreetly took a deep breath of him.

"Malik told me you turned down your pills," said the cook.

"Wanted to drink," she replied. "Besides, I ain't hurt that badly."

"You need rest, man."

"I need food. Rest can come later."

"I'll pair you a wine for your pain, for now. Then it's sweet dreams for dessert. Malik might seem nice, but let's stay off his bad side."

Boots pointed at a steaming tray of tender shoots with her fork. "What is all of this?"

Didier explained his meal choices, but she hadn't heard of any of the dishes before. They definitely weren't homeworld favorites, but then, Clarkesfall wasn't known for having food at all. It all smelled and looked good, so she figured she ought to go ahead and dig in.

"How's your quartermaster?" asked Boots before taking her first bite of a savory beet pancake.

"No broken bones, so she's better off than she usually is."

The door to the captain's quarters slid open, and Cordell strode in, adjusting the cuffs of his shirt. It was a ratty throwback to his ADF days, but he wore it like it was brand-new. The sight of it awakened a few unpleasant memories, and Boots frowned, returning her attention to the meal.

"Thank you, Mister Thomasi," said Cordell, seating himself at the table. "I think I can serve our guest well enough from here."

"Just thought I'd walk her through the wine pairings, sir," said Didier.

Cordell grinned and poured himself a glass of rich red. "They're wasted on Miss Elsworth, Cookie. She may not look it, but she's a hard-bitten soldier."

Boots deliberately scraped her fork across the fine porcelain, provoking a wince from the gathered men, then resumed slicing into her entrée.

Didier stood up straight. "She looks like a lady to me, sir, and ladies deserve to be entertained."

As the chef made his way from the captain's quarters, Boots hazarded a glance at his backside. Not bad for a guy who had to be ten years older than her. Certainly not bad for the first guy to call her a lady in twenty years.

"Where'd you dig him up?" asked Boots, feigning away her blush.

"Thoen. He was a Kandamili chem smuggler."

She laughed bitterly. "Captain Arca let a Kandi on his ship? You're kidding."

"The war is over. We may have fought over the planet, but we're two sides of the same dead coin."

"You're the one with the Arcan icon hanging in the corner."

Cordell grimaced. "What am I going to do with you, Boots?"

"Let me leave."

"Not going to happen." He helped himself to a few ribs from the spread. "But I'm tempted. Those cruisers that came after us were big and expensive... so that means you've got big, expensive enemies. It might be fun to see how far you got before you disappeared. But here's the kicker: I bet we'd vanish right after, no matter what we did with you."

She rubbed the bridge of her nose, willing away the aches and pains of the day. "Buddy, disappearing is going to be step one of my plan when I get out of here."

"Looks like you tried to do that once already today."

"It's an officer's duty to escape at every opportunity, right?"

Cordell tore off a piece of meat with his teeth and put down the bone before wiping his fingers. "Yeah, but you aren't an officer. You're not even a soldier."

She narrowed her eyes. "That's real fine talk coming from a deserter."

"I was there when we lost. That's what matters. You should've stayed with your ship."

Boots looked around for effect. "And, uh, where are all the crew members who were on board when we deserted? I seem to remember you had a nice quorum. All in favor except me. They all stayed, right? Leon and Gary, Sera... Who else am I leaving out?"

She'd meant to stick the knife in with that one, but Cordell guffawed. "They're rich, Boots, and retired. Sure, we got into some scrapes when we started smuggling, but nothing we couldn't handle. Once they had their shares, they cashed out. I'm still going because it's more fun than drying up on a beach somewhere."

She took a sip of wine. "Oh. Sounds like they did a lot better than the crew at Laconte."

"You really are a coward, you know that? Trying to rattle me with crew losses like you're going to tell me something I've never thought before. You'll do anything to stop us from talking about you."

"I'm not like you, Cordell. I don't have to make everything about me."

"Fate gave you a second chance on that mountainside, and you wasted your life."

She rolled her eyes. "Yeah. I should've been a smuggler. Ma would've been proud."

The captain refilled his glass and held it to his nose, drawing in the scent. "Absolutely. You would've been dynamite. And it's not too late. You could still come work for me."

"I tried to steal your ship. That's not the best start to a job interview."

"I can make an exception, considering we go way back." His smile vanished. "I tell you what, though: if you betray us again, I'm going to let Armin and Orna do whatever they want with you.

Let me just say, a friend would shoot you sooner than hand you over to those two. We crystal on that?"

Boots looked into his eyes for a long time, searching for a bluff, but found none. "All right."

"Attagirl."

"What's the plan then, jump over to the *Harrow*'s last known?"

"That depends on how accurate your intel is. You're going to level with me now: how much of what you told me was a load of crap?" He held up his hand before she could speak. "And before you answer, I might take lies as a betrayal."

Boots swallowed. "It's all speculation. I don't have any hard evidence at all."

"So that lady didn't burn down your office?"

"No, she did. I've got it on Silas's authority. He's a lot of things, but he isn't a liar."

"And you still think it's the same woman trying to kill Nilah... and now us," said Cordell.

"Yeah, I do. So, I guess that's my evidence that the *Harrow* exists. You still got Kin plugged in?"

The assistant's voice chimed in, "Maybe I can help?"

"Kin," said Boots, "can you show me the image of the *Harrow* from Goulding Station?"

The holographic image of the *Harrow*, captured from the window of the space station, sprayed into the room. Its chitinous hull shone black in the lights of the station. Against the inky veil of stars, it was a mere suggestion of mass, save for the gargantuan brass rune disc underneath. A set of grapplers protruded, spider-like, from its belly, to secure the disc in place and serve as actuators. The pink light of eidolon crystals rippled over the surface of the runes, a dire warning to any who might try to attack the ship.

It wasn't difficult to imagine such a vessel destroying an entire country, but a spellship like that could be used for any number of purposes. It could've brought life to a dying Clarkesfall, and maybe averted the Famine War altogether.

Both diners rose to have a closer look at the glowing image.

"So this is my evidence," said Boots. "This is the whole thing: a twenty-two-year-old picture."

Cordell whistled. "This is a different picture than the one I've seen."

"Well, yeah. I'm here to sell treasure maps. If I handed out everyday images from the Link, no one would ever buy them. I've got a reputation to maintain, you know." She ran her hand through the hologram, disrupting the ship around her fingers. "I had to make an investment in my future, and that meant buying this bad boy."

"Kinnard, can you show us a picture of the *Harrow* off the Link?"

"May I?" asked the computer.

Boots agreed, and another picture of the ship appeared, this time from a different angle. The ship was much farther off, and the image had the sort of framing that suggested it was taken by a station docking camera.

"Yeah. This is the one everyone knows," said Boots.

"And where did you get your picture?" asked Cordell.

"The family of a miner. The guy died during an airlock transfer, and they hadn't even bothered opening his ruck since then. Some weird Carré custom. Got his name from the Goulding personnel records, cross-referenced against active miners who'd been on board the station that day. There weren't a ton of hits, so I blasted a message out to all the families, asking for any information they had on the *Harrow*."

Cordell peered from one to the other. "There's a difference here."

"Yeah, genius. They're two different pictures."

He snatched up a cigarette from his desk and lit it, returning to have a better look at the ships. "I meant in the content of the image. Do you remember the protocol regarding image capture of ADF starships in transit?"

Boots shrugged.

"It's strictly prohibited. Do you know why?"

Boots shrugged again.

"Did you pay any attention in flight school?"

"Listen, buddy, I'm a fighter pilot, not a photographer. And no, I didn't get your fancy officer training, so I don't know your answer. Just tell me what you know."

Cordell held up his hands. "Testy, testy. I think it's cute you're still calling yourself a fighter pilot."

"I literally just blew someone up in a space battle. I'm an ace now."

"Oh yeah. Congratulations."

"You going to tell me the difference or not?"

Cordell pointed to the energy signature across the rune disk. "This ship is about to make a jump. That's the pink light you see."

"Yeah. I see that every time I go through a jump gate. Big deal."

"Jump gates connect two known points. This ship was going somewhere using its onboard jump drive, so theoretically it couldn't be traced—but we can see the energy signature."

"Which means..."

He licked his lips and took a long drag. "It means we can trace where it went, provided we have a real-deal datamancer—and Armin is the best there ever was. The *Harrow* is a beautiful ship. We could go after him if..." His shoulders fell. "If we weren't all scraped up ourselves."

Boots rubbed her aching elbow unconsciously. "Yeah. They put a few dents in us. Any idea how bad?"

"Extremely. Long-range comms are toast, the two-seventy engine only has a few more weeks in her and the ninety isn't far behind. Our grav generator is currently held together by glue and happy thoughts. Orna's tools are hovering somewhere outside of Gantry Station."

The door chimed, and Cordell slouched to the table to sit down. "Come."

The portal slid open to reveal Nilah on the other side, looking considerably better than Boots remembered. The lack of purple vomit flecks somewhat improved her appearance. She wore a fitted white top and pilot's pants, which probably belonged to Aisha. She took a tentative step into the room.

"Nilah Brio," said the captain. "We haven't officially met, but my name is Cordell Lamarr. This is my ship."

Nilah surveyed the food and grimaced. "Hi."

"I talked to Doctor Jan," said Cordell, stubbing out his cigarette. "He says you're good to go, but you need to eat something."

"We don't eat animals on Taitu."

Boots smirked and sat back down before helping herself to a heaping plate of flesh. "When you're from Clarkesfall, you eat anything slow enough to catch."

"I'm sorry about that," said Cordell to Nilah. "I forgot. I'll have Cookie whip up something more to your liking. I think there are a few things here already..."

The racer's eyes wandered to the pictures of the *Harrow*. "What's that?"

He took a sip of wine and cleared his throat. "Based on what Boots has told me, that image is the reason Cyril Clowe was killed."

Nilah walked over to have a closer look. "How do you mean?"

"That's the *Harrow*, a legendary Taitutian warship," said Boots.

"I sold that image, along with a set of bogus coordinates, to an investment group, and from what I can gather, Cyril was the money man."

Nilah helped herself to a glass of wine and sat down, pushing back the tray of meat to keep the steam away. "I think you're a liar."

"I sold that picture, and a woman showed up, burned down my office, killed Cyril, tried to kill you, and chased us with a pair of warships. I think we can assume it's the real deal."

Cordell pursed his lips. "And we can guess she'll come for my crew next. Boots says they were powerful enough to buy off the Fixers?"

"Yes," said Nilah.

"What we need to do is—" Boots began.

Nilah cut her off. "Drop me off on Taitu and never talk to me again. I've got a race in five days; the team will already be there. I promise no harm or legal action will come to you if you do."

Boots shook her head. "Are you serious right now? We've got a bunch of murderers after us and—"

"Of course I'm bloody serious! I'm going to be champion! I didn't fight my whole life to get here, just so a couple of losers from the wrong side of space could ruin it all!" Nilah said, her voice a mix of anger and panic. "Do you know the sacrifices it takes to get this far?"

Boots narrowed her eyes. "You think...we're trying to ruin your championship?"

"No," said Nilah, "but you're not equipped to handle this. On Taitu, I've got a security team, a legal team, and my father!"

"Okay, okay," said Boots, trying not to openly laugh at her naïveté. "I think you can trust your dad—just not anyone who works for him, or the police, or the intelligence agencies, or anyone on your planet. Because you know what, kid? They bought off the Fixers and hit us *with two fricking battle cruisers.* And you seem to forget the bounty on your head."

Nilah's nostrils flared, but she didn't immediately retort.

Cordell shot Boots a glance. "Anyway, we're not going to get there in time."

The racer's lip stiffened. "I believe you misspoke. I'm going to get back to my team, and we'll work out the bounty thing with my lawyers and—"

The captain leaned back and folded his fingers behind his head. "No, I didn't. The ship is half wrecked. It's not going to make the jump to Taitu. I'm not sure it'll make the jump to the closest docks once we make the jump gate."

"And where are the closest docks?" she hissed.

"Harvest or maybe Yearling," said Cordell. "Nearest big world we could limp to is Carré."

"Carré!" Nilah repeated, furious. "That's in the middle of nowhere!"

Boots sucked her teeth. "I take it you've been before?"

"Of course I've been before! I took the podium twice there."

"You gave a speech there?" Boots said.

"I won two raccs, you blasted moron! Those people know me. They love me, and they're going to get me to Taitu in time for the Cormir GP."

"So, wait, you're happy to be going to Carré?" asked Boots.

"No!...Yes! I'm not sure, but I do know I'll be pleased to get off this rust bucket."

"If that's your wish," Cordell began.

"Of course it is. Don't be stupid," Nilah spat.

"You know you can't trust anyone else, right?" asked Cordell. "It's like Boots said, they can whack you anywhere in the galaxy."

She turned up her nose. "I thought I just asked you not to be stupid. Let me make myself clear: I was able to take over your ship once, and I can do it again. I've got an army of people looking for me and more money than god. So, if you'll please kindly let me off at Carré, I won't smite you in return."

Nilah held the steaming-hot cup of tea in her hands as she wandered the decks. There wasn't much else to do on the bloody ship, and she certainly wasn't going to help those scoundrels out with their daily chores. She was happy to be away from Mother, but she'd still been kidnapped and dragged to the middle of nowhere at the height of the season. Her comfortable lead over Kristof would rapidly dry up, and if she saw him wearing the Driver's Crown, she'd tear this place apart.

If she was lucky enough to see him wear the crown, that was. The crack of Cyril's skull still echoed in her ears. There were still police scouring the galaxy for her—some of them corrupt. And what was the excuse they were giving for the bounty? Fleeing the scene of a crime? For the first time, the thought that she might not survive this settled into her bones, and she chased it away with another swig of hot liquid.

Her remaining time in the sport was short. The oldest racer in the league was thirty-one, and there was already talk of him retiring. That gave her twelve chances to be the Driver's Champion, and she'd have to do it five times if she wanted to beat the greatest driver of all time. She was already on track to be the youngest champion in history. This was a once-in-several-lifetimes opportunity.

And the crew of the *Capricious* didn't get it.

The only tolerable member of the crew was the cook, who'd given her the tea leaves. He'd dug them out of his private stash and was extremely proud to share them with a Taitutian. The way his eyes glittered when he looked on his precious supply had been adorably disarming. She found the rustic blend quaint, though it scarcely compared to her usual fare in the Lang Autosport Hospitality Suites. Lang served real tea...but the cook had been so excited to see her reaction, she'd faked enjoyment.

If Nilah had Cordell and his crew arrested, she'd make sure the cook got a box of the good stuff in jail. She owed him that much.

She entered her new quarters—the converted brig—and brought the mug under her nose to calm her nerves. They may have given her a sleeping pad and access to toiletries, but it was far from comfortable. She didn't have a window, massage bed, entertainments and stimulations, control over the scents and temperature, or precise lighting. She'd asked the captain for access to Orna's supplies so that she might craft a few passable alternatives, but he'd refused. The force field that had formerly kept her confined to the cell was removed, but it left a large, open space where anyone could come and go as they pleased.

And it still smelled a little like her vomit.

At least they'd slid a dividing wall between her area and Boots's. All Boots did was glare at Nilah when she was around.

Was Boots in her quarters now? Nilah hadn't checked the other side of the brig to see. She started in that direction and paused. Why did she care if Boots was there? Then again, Boots was the only other kidnapping victim. Maybe they could talk. Nilah ached for some decent conversation, but she could settle for Boots.

She poked her head around the corner and spied her flatmate sitting on a cot, fingers tightly woven together, elbows on her knees. Was she angry or sad? Perhaps both, Nilah decided.

"What?" called Boots.

Nilah straightened and strode around the divider. "Nothing. Just seeing if you were here."

"Well, I am."

"Yes, I can see that."

"Glad to hear it."

Nilah grimaced. "All right, now. No need to get spiky about it."

Boots sat back. "I've got every reason to be annoyed. I should be back on Gantry Station."

"Tell me about it." Nilah took a sip of her tea, which had a subtle sweetness like honeysuckle with a strange, savory aftertaste. She still didn't love it, but it was growing on her.

The woman regarded her with trepidation, but softened. "Yeah. I guess we both got a raw deal, kid."

Nilah laughed. "This will wreak havoc on my contracts. I've probably lost a million argents on this."

Boots's face soured. "Maybe some of us got it worse than others."

"Thanks for understanding," said Nilah, before she realized Boots was being sarcastic.

Boots scowled. "It's not easy to be back here."

"Because you gave them a barmy salvage map?"

"No." Boots met her gaze. "Lot of bad memories locked up in this bucket."

"Oh. Sorry."

"Not your fault." Boots grabbed some kind of food bar from her nightstand drawer, unwrapped it, and took a bite. It looked like pressed protein garbage, but smelled heavenly.

"What on earth is that?" asked Nilah.

"Ration bar," Boots mumbled through the chewing. "Used to eat three of these a day when I was on a mission. High protein output, tastes pretty good, makes you poop on the regular."

"It looks awful. Why does it smell so good?"

Boots smirked and held it out for inspection. "Never seen one of these? The eggheads at High Command found a way to enchant them like the hoteliers do. It's specially engineered to stimulate your appetite, even if you're pinned in a firefight. Want to try a piece?"

"No, thank you. I can't spare the calories."

"For one bite of a ration bar?"

Nilah set down her mug. "I'm carefully regulated at fifteen hundred a day with an excruciating regimen. If I stray even a little bit, it changes the aerodynamics of the car. The engineers have to work so hard to shave each kilogram of equipment, so a little fat from me is unacceptable. If you're not a racer, it's hard to understand."

"Must be tough when you're away from your chef. How do you know what to eat?"

"On this ship, who knows? That cook doesn't know what ought to go into my meals. He may be able to prepare a few dishes from my homeworld, but the ingredients make all the difference. It's about quality."

"Yes, of course. Quality," said Boots.

Nilah deflated, catching the sarcasm. "All right. I see. You think I'm pampered, but I'm not."

Boots chuckled and leaned back against the wall, folding her hands behind her head. "No one called you pampered."

"But you think it."

"You're like some kind of exotic animal. Can you even eat food if it costs less than a thousand argents?"

Nilah rolled her eyes. "Healthy food doesn't have to be expensive, you know. You can eat well for five hundred argents a week."

"That's expensive, lady. My income is three hundred on a bad week, before you take out rent."

"If you owned your own house, you could install a few modcons to reduce the cost of cooking."

Boots squinted at her.

"Okay," said Nilah. "I take your point, but I'm really not pampered. I run twenty kilometers a day in addition to some severe aerobic workouts. I spend three hours a day in the simulators, which are grueling on the neck and back, then it's off to the press junkets."

Boots shrugged. "You work hard. I get it."

"You do?"

"Sure. If you want the best athletes, you've got to treat them like prized beasts. Spend a week in my shoes, and you'd be too fat and drunk to get around the block, much less the track. I don't work half as much as you, and that's the way I like it."

Nilah blinked, stunned.

"But you're pampered as hell," Boots said. "Let's be real, here."

"I suppose you're right." Nilah leaned against the divider. "You know, it's nice to talk to someone around here who isn't completely ridiculous."

"Oh?"

"Yes. God, yes. The captain, for example? He's so wrapped up in all this war stuff with the Arcan flags everywhere."

"Most can't let it go."

"I understand that, but we've got some real problems here, and he's awfully cavalier about them. He's not equipped to handle this, and we should be figuring out who to call for help, not . . . whatever the hell he's doing. He hasn't been a soldier for twenty years, but he acts like he's got it all under control."

Boots's face darkened. "Cordell has dealt with his share of 'real problems' in the past. If he says he's got it under control, he does."

"I'm sorry, mate, but some washed-up nobody from a forgotten world scarcely qualifies as an authority on—"

"None of us forgot about our home," Boots said, derailing Nilah's train of thought. The woman leaned forward, her voice firm. "You may bust your ass to get in shape, but it's just so you can drive in a circle for a couple of hours on end. Big deal."

"That's not what I meant. Athleticism is a worthy—"

"I flew sixty-three sorties with the captain, and I've killed more than my share of folks with skin in the game. Clarkesfall lost ninety percent of its population, including my family and all of my friends. The other ten percent were the lucky punks like me who made it offworld. You'll have to excuse us for failing to give a damn about racing."

Nilah swallowed, her tattoos flooding the room with green light. She took a step back. "Perhaps we got off on the wrong foot."

"Yes, you did."

"Okay. I can see that…and…I'm sorry."

Their eyes locked for a long series of breaths. Finally, Boots tore another hunk off her ration bar and chewed. "You don't seem like the apologizing type."

"Yes, well…" Nilah grimaced. "I…was out of line. This is my first kidnapping, and I don't know how to behave."

"And you only think about yourself. Don't bother blaming your circumstances."

"Boots—"

She held up her hands. "A little selfishness is probably good for a racer. Not saying it's always a bad thing. It just makes you completely intolerable."

Nilah looked at the ground. "Yes. I deserved that for my comments about—"

"About the death of my home planet?"

"Yes."

"Good talk, Brio. You can leave now," Boots said, wadding up the ration bar wrapper and tossing it at Nilah's feet.

"I really am sorry."

Boots's jaw tightened, and Nilah stood to leave, unfamiliar shame burning in her breast.

"Okay, kid, don't just…" came Boots's voice behind her. "Look, I know you're just scared. We all are. I'm betting that's why you want to get back to the race so bad, isn't it? You may think you can go back to your old life, bury yourself under a pile of wealth, and make all this disappear, but you can't."

Nilah turned back. "I've never cared about anything as much as standing on that podium and getting the crown. I test myself and push harder than anyone for weeks, so I can prove that I'm the fastest. Hitting the track with two dozen of the galaxy's best is the most addictive feeling there is. There's the strategy, the huge team...everyone has their hopes invested in you to bring home gold. Until you've matched wits at that speed it's hard to explain."

"I'm an ace, kid. I think I know what it's like to fight it out at high speed."

"Then you see why racing gets me out of bed before day cycle and keeps me up every night. I've spent every day since I was five years old working for this. So I'm not *merely* frightened. My dreams are at stake."

Boots chuckled. "Well I'm 'merely frightened,' and I don't mind saying it. If you have any sense in your head, you're going to learn to get along with the crew."

Nilah pulled up an empty transit case and sat down across from Boots, happy for the opportunity to talk with the only other captive. "Okay, then let's start with you. Tell me about yourself."

"What's to tell? You already know most of the important bits. Forties. Veteran. Had a show back in the day on the Link."

"Yes, I remember. *Looking for*—"

"*Finding Hana*," corrected Boots. "It was about the, uh, Chalice of Hana and, you know, finding it."

"I take it the Chalice wasn't an ordinary cup," Nilah said, trying to lead her in a talkative direction.

Boots sat up. "Yeah. It was an artifact from the Renwick Dynasty. You drink from it, and you get to cast the barrister's mark, but on a level few ever could. Most folks never heard of the spell."

Nilah narrowed her eyes. "We have barrister's marks in the PGRF. The magical compulsion keeps everyone from breaking their contracts."

"Yeah," said Boots. "So, like, I flew a lot of escorts during the last days of the Famine War. One of the final ones was guarding this culture ark into orbit. Basically, my people knew they might get bombed to glassy smithereens, so they smuggled out their most precious treasures." She motioned like she was picking up a box and dropping it onto a starship. "This particular ark, the *Saint of Flowers*, contained our most powerful artifact, the Chalice of Hana. This thing was used to sign interplanetary treaties for crying out loud. It was supposed to go to Taitu for safekeeping, back when we thought we could trust you people to have our backs."

Nilah nodded and ignored the insult. She vaguely remembered some of these details from the show.

"Except the *Saint of Flowers* never landed at the Taitutian banks. It diverted through a couple of jump gates and went AWOL. Anyone who wanted to find it was going to need to do a ton of sifting through historical data and information requests. I'd gotten good at looking for the fates of dead relatives after the war, filing with various refugee agencies and archives...so I thought I'd take a crack at the data trail. I followed the jump receipts and fuel purchases, and when I figured I'd hit a dead end, I found a docking receipt for slip time, but the time had never been cashed."

"So the *Saint of Flowers* paid for the dock, but never landed there?"

"Exactly. Given his cargo, he couldn't call for help, either, for fear of bringing bandits down on Clarkesfall's precious cultural heritage. But after the war, there was no planet, so there wasn't a heritage to preserve—just a ship full of dead soldiers floating somewhere around a half-dead star: CGS-280. I ran the numbers, and we had a few million years before that red giant ate everything in its system. I figured an enterprising sort could team up with the right salvager and make a fortune. I found a producer, Gemma Katz, willing to follow me around and pay for the story."

"So you found the Chalice?"

"Yeah," said Boots. "We did."

Nilah crossed her arms. "Then why aren't you rich?"

"Because my partner murdered Gemma when we finally got to it. Stetson Giles. What an asshole. He was soft on me, though, on account of us fighting together. He held me at the end of a slinger and made me sign a contract with him that I'd never do anything to harm him, even if it meant sending cops after him." Boots sighed heavily. "That artifact was going to be my ticket, even more than the show. I could've made a fortune negotiating treaties between planets and corporations. We were going to start a company, and I was finally going to get to cast magic."

"Do you know where Stetson is now?" asked Nilah.

Boots nodded.

"But you can't tell me?"

Boots nodded again. "Can't tell anyone."

"Is that why you wanted the Chalice? Because of your, um, arcana dystocia?"

Boots shook her head slowly. "I ain't got to talk to you about my physical burdens."

"No, sorry. You're right," said Nilah. "It's just, I don't know much about it. You're the first... one of you I've met."

"What's to tell? Everyone gets a cardioid, and I didn't."

"I thought you couldn't live without it."

"*You* can't. Magi die when it's damaged. Docs still don't have a clue how *I'm* alive."

"It starts that soon?"

"Yeah. Mom said the scanners went crazy when I was born. Said I was dying, but... I had a healthy set of lungs and I used them."

"So can they tell... you know, before a child is born?"

Boots looked at the ground. "No. If my parents had known when I was in the womb, well, I wouldn't be standing here, I think. I used to get sick a lot, and every time my crippled magic came into play, Mom would get inconsolable. Doctors have always been doom and gloom about my condition, but when I look at you magi…I don't see most folks doing anything so damned special. What else you want to know?"

Nilah smacked her lips. "So you don't have any family. Any friends?"

Boots chuckled. "Sure. Loads, all over the place. No drinking buddies, but as it turns out, I can drink alone. You?"

"Me what?"

"You got any pals?"

"I have a few. I don't do much recreational drinking, myself." She found her face growing hot. "I mostly hang around with celebrity types, you know; my publicist arranges for me to be seen with them."

"Sounds like she makes playdates for you."

Nilah folded her arms. "It's a lot like that, I'm afraid. I even have a drink that I'm obligated to order: Marshanda Fosser. Disgusting stuff."

"Never heard of it."

"It's a hibiscus rosemary liqueur. *Hibiscus rosemary*, Boots."

"Why are you obligated?"

Nilah rolled her eyes. "They pay for the ad space on my fire suit, as well as the rear wing of my car, so I choke one down when I can."

"Sounds like swill."

"It is," Nilah sighed. "High-calorie, expensive swill. And when I'm required to drink one, my nutritionist has to dock me a breakfast."

Boots reached up under her cot and pulled out a bottle; a clear liquid sloshed inside, clinging to the glass with rich legs.

"What's that?" Nilah eyed the bottle, suspecting she already knew the answer.

"Some kind of rum, maybe. There's a still in the kitchen. I mean... it smells like booze. Could be paint stripper."

"You nicked it?"

"Sure. Why not? I was thirsty."

Nilah took the bottle and unstoppered it before holding it to her nose: fuel and milled steel, notes of rubber. On the one hand, nothing consumable by humans should have such a smell. On the other, it was the scent of a racetrack.

She handed it back. "That's not safe to drink."

Boots shrugged. "Suit yourself, but it ain't Marshanda Fosser, and no publicist paid me to talk to you."

Of course she was right. Nilah had wanted to spend some time with anyone other than her kidnappers, and Boots was offering her a drink, waggling the bottle like a dog treat. Nilah took it up, examining the liquid again.

She shouldn't drink. After years of clean living, she had basically no tolerance. She needed every single brain cell for the race to come, as well as all the press junkets, the meetings with lawyers—and the mountain of other work that had to be done when she was reunited with her team and family.

But she was lonely.

Boots chortled as Nilah wiped the mouth of the bottle on her shirt and put it to her lips. The taste was like licking the fluid off a car's limited slip differential, and she couldn't decide if she found it pleasant or not. She didn't splutter or wheeze, and she swallowed without complaint, savoring the burn all the way down.

"Now then," said Boots. "I've provided the refreshments. You have to supply us the next topic of conversation."

Nilah smiled. "I've had rather bad luck talking about the war."

"And I couldn't care less about life in a race car. I doubt we have one thing in common."

Nilah searched her memory to find some intersection. "Have you heard of Sam Mitcham?"

Boots's eyebrows knit. "Why do I know that name?"

"He was a racer," said Nilah, taking another swig. "He went insane a decade ago and disappeared into the Erantis System. Sam was a friend of my father's."

"Rich, crazy people go missing all the time. Still doesn't explain why I know the name."

"Because his ship was a Class A Star Yacht, and because he was carrying a supply of weapons-grade eidolon crystals when he vanished. He was worth close to a billion argents, and most of his assets were with him."

"Okay. This is ringing a bell," said Boots.

"But in order to know where he went, you have to know why he lost his mind. And in order to know that..." Nilah pointed the bottle at her. "You have to understand life on the track."

Boots snatched back the liquor and took a long pull. "So it's racing and legendary treasures?"

"That's right."

"You are full of surprises, aren't you?"

Chapter Eight

Shifting Gears

Nilah concentrated, sending power down her forearms, across her fingertips, and back into her elbows. She took slow breaths and focused, creating shimmering waves across her dermaluxes. With the mechanist's art, she could sense the nanomachines implanted in her flesh like some people sensed the breeze tickling their hairs. She used that awareness to keep her fighting tight and locked into lightning-quick movements. In the vast space of the cargo bay, she could run through her combat forms uninterrupted, free to run, jump, and flip as she pleased.

And to think, Kristof trained by jogging. What a fool.

They had no mat for her, but she didn't mind keeping her bare feet against the diamond deck as she moved. The damaged Midnight Runner dangling overhead was a little distracting, but it made for an interesting chandelier.

She chanted the martial arts forms to herself, just as she did her racing lines: *Accretion's pull to nebula's birth, then rising rocket. Disrupted orbit, cold star. Singularity to finish.* She modeled the target's responses in her mind: the way he ducked to avoid her kick, only to fall to the elbow. She remembered the snap of the bounty hunter's jaw on Gantry Station and stumbled.

A door slid open behind her.

"Your captain promised no one would disturb me," she huffed, sweat streaming down her neck, still going through the forms.

"This is my bay. The captain won't stop me," said Orna, her boots thumping the deck as she emerged from the shadows. The quartermaster's head was partially wrapped in biobandages, dimly lit by cool, blue magics. She walked with a bit of a limp, and didn't wear the circlet from before, so her battle armor wasn't likely to be around.

"I'll be done in short order. You can come back then."

"Is that Flicker?" Orna asked, cracking her neck and looking over Nilah's body.

The waves on her forearm blushed pink before she forced them back to white. "It is. You've heard of it?"

"Oh, sure. 'The unbeatable art.' Banned in the match leagues for brutality and all that."

"I'm Nilah, by the way. I don't think we were properly introduced when I held your ship hostage and whatnot."

"Orna. Quartermaster...and I don't buy the unbeatable stuff."

"If someone loses with Flicker, they didn't train hard enough."

Orna snorted. "Wouldn't that be true with any fighting style?"

"No. Flicker is a cut above."

The quartermaster crossed her arms, her muscles hardening with the gesture. "I want to see it firsthand."

Nilah took a few steps back and flashed through a powerful combo that should've ended with a broken kneecap for her opponent. She executed each move flawlessly before coming to a standstill in front of Orna, who cocked an eyebrow.

"That's it? That's the big, bad Flicker? I guess it was pretty."

"It's not a matter of what you saw," said Nilah. "It's what you didn't see. Misdirection is key; if I can achieve that, I can strike you twice as hard as a guarded adversary."

"So it lets you punch chumps?"

Nilah rested her hands on her hips. "People are far more susceptible than you think."

"You'd never take me out with that, and it's no good against a slinger, so who cares?"

"I've defeated dozens of opponents in training, most of them bigger than you."

Orna slid her bandages off her head; her oily hair was matted in places. Nilah doubted Orna had cleaned herself in a few days, but there was still something oddly compelling about the scarred woman. Nilah blinked to stop herself from staring.

" 'In training,' " chuckled Orna. "School is out. What do you say we play?"

Nilah had to struggle to hide her exhilaration. "You want to fight? I doubt it'd be entertaining enough."

"Let's make a bet then."

"Excuse me?"

Orna slid a large chronograph from her wrist, walked to the wall, and set it down next to the door. "Deadly serious here. I want to fight you, and Flicker looks like a joke to me."

"A wager!" Nilah's laugh went all the way to her belly. "Oh, but you can't possibly bet against me. The casinos where I play don't take the paltry change people like you earn. I'd have to bet half the value of this ship just to feel it."

Orna shrugged. "I don't care. Ask me for anything, and I'll put it on the action."

This upstart had just become ten times as entertaining as before. Nilah bit her lip. "I'm not joking around here. Are you sure you want to play in my league?"

"Ask me for anything."

"If I win," Nilah began, her breast swelling with pride, "you sign a contract to be my personal security escort for two years, following any order I give you to the letter. Your duties will be unlimited, and you will live at my beck and call. We'll seal it with the barrister's mark when we get back to my home planet."

"Great. If I win, you replace all of my tools and repair the ship and the Runner. That'll be a few hundred thousand argents, but I'm sure you're good for it."

"Hardly seems a fair bet."

"Half a million in exchange for two years of service? Sounds like a raise."

Nilah sneered. "You have no idea how much I'm going to humiliate you. My only concern is that you understand that Flicker can destroy you. I won't be holding back."

The quartermaster pointed to one of her many scars. "I think I'll live." She held out a fist for Nilah to bump.

The moment their skin made contact, Nilah danced away, her upper body in a tight fighting pose. Her dermaluxes shimmered with delight as she evaluated Orna's stance. How much damage could she do and still keep her new assistant valuable?

The quartermaster barely raised her arms, apparently content to watch Nilah bob and weave across the deck. Orna had a long reach, and getting inside her circle would prove tough for any normal fighter. If Nilah had arms like Orna's, she would've kept them close, not hanging down like some half-dazed rookie. When Nilah circled to her back, Orna turned to face her, so she wasn't a total fool, but she still failed to show any concern. If the quartermaster wasn't going to take the match seriously, it wouldn't be fun.

Nilah flashed her tattoos to the rhythm of her bouncing, establishing a beat to her stance. She rushed into Orna's range, peppering her with a series of attacks in time with the flashes. Each movement was carefully telegraphed, and Orna blocked them with ease before unleashing a powerful backhand—but Orna had fallen in time with the beat.

Nilah ducked the strike and broke her sync, slamming her knee as hard as she could into the quartermaster's gut. The blow sunk in better than she could've hoped, and Nilah watched her opponent go stumbling backward, gasping for air. It would've been unsporting to chase her down and finish the fight right then, so she gave the other woman time to regain her breath.

"What do you think?" asked Nilah. "You can still quit before I beat the devil out of you."

"I won't," she wheezed, "back out of a bet."

Nilah laughed. "I wasn't offering that. You'll still be my servant."

"Hah. Well, then . . ."

Orna straightened up, wincing. A normal fighter should've tensed up to reduce the impact of Nilah's knee, but the quartermaster had been caught flat-footed. From the look on Orna's face, she had begun to understand the power of dermaluxes.

"I forgot to ask," said Orna, "are we going until pin or knockout? It changes how I make you scream."

"Let's go for a knockout, then. The next time you wake up, you'll have a new job."

"One more thing—"

Whatever Orna was planning, it was a stall tactic, and it wouldn't work. Nilah's arms went violet as she dashed low and inside. Human eyes couldn't perceive the color very well, a fact often exploited by the polychromatic Flicker wielder. To Orna, Nilah's arms would appear blurry and borderless. She wove her attacks in between Orna's guard, snapping off repeated jabs into the woman's face and stepping deep into her enemy's stance. Nilah finished her combo with an uppercut and a foot sweep, and Orna hit the deck hard.

She stood over her huffing opponent, a cool wetness on her knuckles. She'd drawn blood; a bit of crimson spilled from Orna's brow into her right eye. If Orna rose again, she'd be fighting blind.

"You're beaten," said Nilah, holding out a hand, but ready to coldcock her opponent. "Now concede, so I don't mess up your pretty face any more."

"I'm not sure anyone has ever accused me of being pretty," chuckled Orna, her shoulders falling. "Now as I was saying, before you interrupted me, I have a question about how I'll be serving you."

"Hm?"

Orna's eyes locked onto hers. "Will it be clothed or nude?"

Nilah's tattoos went bright pink, and the quartermaster seized her hand, tracing her own glyph. In a split second, Orna's mechanist magic connected with the dermaluxes' nanomachines and shut them off. She yanked Nilah down into her fist, plowing across her cheek. Stunned, Nilah tried to jump backward, but caught a glancing blow against her temple. The quartermaster never let go, a crazed smile on her face as she delivered a sharp hook into her ribs, then another into Nilah's jaw.

Stars flooded Nilah's vision, and she tasted blood as Orna threw her to the deck and wrenched her head back by her hair.

"Nighty night," whispered the quartermaster, right before she slammed Nilah's face into the hard steel.

By the time the world reassembled itself out of blackness, Nilah lay face down in a pool of her own blood, sick with the realization of what had occurred. Orna knelt before her, her own face streaming with crimson.

"Well now," she began, grinning. "I guess we see how good Flicker is, don't we?"

Nilah shakily rose to her hands and knees, each joint quivering with adrenaline and concussion.

Orna rose; only her boots remained in Nilah's ground-level view. "Med bay is on the lower deck. Thanks for paying for my ships, chump."

Then the quartermaster clomped away, chuckling as she went.

Boots blinked, and shards of broken glass danced through the cockpit, glittering before her dazed eyes. She reached out with a gloved hand and clumsily batted at one, trying to clear it from her view.

"I'm sorr—" His voice crackled across her earpiece, followed by a static screech.

She blinked, trying to refocus on the planetary landscape below. A shake of her throbbing head fixed little. On the distant surface, orange orbs of flame, miles wide, bloomed one after another in a steady march across an ocean.

She managed to catch the canopy in sharp relief, and her eyes adjusted. Her protective screen was shot to pieces, open to the great void of space. Flashes of blue traced the lines of shattered glass, reflections of her fractured engine core and the exposed eidolon crystals. A torn section of her fighter's hull tumbled in her view, far away from where it was supposed to be. Among the tide of wreckage, she knew that piece was hers, because it had ELSWORTH written on the side above her call sign, BOOTS.

Less than a hundred feet away, an enemy pilot clawed at his visor, floating panicked in space. He must've had a crack. His fingertips flared with light as he tried to draw a spell, which sputtered out like a dying flame. He thrashed, then fell still.

"—on't know if you can hear me, Lizzie, but you were right." It was a transmission from ground control.

Her face tingled and her teeth ached. She licked her lips, tasting blood. "I'm always right, Kin," she groaned.

"Are you up there?"

"Yeah." Her suit had begun to hiss. She was going to die in orbit, but at least she could say goodbye.

Soft static filled a long pause. "Elizabeth?"

"Yeah, Kin."

"Elizabeth?"

"Oh. You can't hear me." She straightened, and her torso lit up with pain. Her harness had gotten damaged and felt as though it would cut her in half. She unbuckled it, and it snapped away, letting her drift freely in the remains of her cockpit in renewed agony.

The explosions planetside had almost reached the coast of Arca. In a moment, she'd see the shield kick on, and the collision of powerful spells would give her something beautiful to watch while she suffocated.

She swallowed. "You're not supposed to be calling me, Kin. Supposed to leave this line open for ops."

"You were right wh—you said—s . . . wouldn't work—Grid didn't hold." The first massive wave of ordnance struck the coast. "If—still alive, I want you to take—ship and go."

What was he talking about? What happened to the defense grid? "Say again? I need you to repeat that last communication."

"Lots of things . . . never got to say to you. I'm g . . . you can g . . . t me."

Then a plume of raw power engulfed the capital city of Elizabeth Elsworth's beloved home. The Command Center was down there. Kinnard was down there.

"Kin?"

The crackle went dead.

"Kin, come in." She tapped the side of her helmet. "Kin, answer me."

The flash dissipated, replaced by a shock wave that pushed aside the clouds like the gentle hand of a giant.

"Answer me," she commanded. She drove a palm into her helmet, and her radio squawked in protest. "You say something to me, you pile of garbage."

Nothing came. No one spoke, save for the whispering hiss of death. The wreckage of a former destroyer floated gracefully past, a bucket of corpses. With a surge of adrenaline, she bashed her head into the side of her cockpit, then again as violently as she could. Hot tears bounced around the inside of her visor as she slammed her radio package into the wall over and over again.

"Answer me! You aren't dead, so talk!" Her broken chest heaved with sorrow as she came to rest. "Damn you."

Her earpiece chirped, and her heart thudded so hard she thought it would burst.

"Hello? Yes? Hello! Kin, are you there?" she stammered.

"This is the ADF *Capricious* transmitting on all emergency frequencies. Anyone alive up here needs to start talking, because we've got to split."

She hugged herself, almost like she thought it would stop her lips from quivering. "Captain Lamarr..."

"Boots? That you, girl?"

"Kin's dead. They're all dead down there."

"But you're not. We're coming to pick you up."

She thought about it, then shook her head no, as if anyone could see her.

"Where are you at?" Cordell sounded rock-solid for a guy flying through a field of debris.

"It doesn't matter." She reached down and yanked a lever marked with snaking yellow and black caution tape. Her ejector seat shot forward, shoving her out of the cockpit along with her survival package. Untethered as she was, the seat took off in one direction and her body went in another. A flashing beacon on her back pinged with a constant radio pulse.

"I see you, but so does the enemy, Bootsie. You need to shut that off."

She didn't care. She'd done her duty, and there was no home left to save. Part of her hoped the enemy would blast her tiny body out of the sky and end it all.

In ten seconds, she'd fall into the deep trance of a hibernation spell. "I guess it's a race, then."

After a pause, he replied, "You're going to learn not to bet against the *Capricious* one of these days. Tag up is in thirty seconds."

Boots blinked, the brig coming into focus. Her whole body ached from the battles of the past few days, and sleep had only made it worse, like she'd been beaten from head to toe. She'd fallen asleep with her arm above her head, and now her shoulder throbbed like it might snap off any second. On the other side of the divider, Nilah snored away like a saw blade. The racer had come in injured and drugged, and Boots hadn't asked questions.

"Kin," she whispered, hoarse.

"Yes, Lizzie?"

Cordell had been kind enough to leave him connected to the ship's network, though Kinnard was segmented so he couldn't access the *Capricious*'s files.

"I had a dream about you."

"I need you to disambiguate. Me, the computer? Or me, the human model for this computer?"

"The real Kinnard."

"Neither of us is fictitious, though I think I take your meaning. It's been almost six months since you reported one of those. Would you like a whiskey?"

"Why would I want a..."

"You've reported eight dreams about Kinnard in the last four years. In each instance, you drank a whiskey before returning to bed."

Boots sat up and massaged her shaky shoulder. "Yeah. That's not a bad idea."

"Actually, it is a bad idea. Any blood alcohol content during sleep disrupts—"

She stood and began pulling on her clothes in the darkness. "Thanks. Don't care, Kin."

"All right, Lizzie." A short chime indicated Kinnard didn't intend to say anything else.

Did computers get frustrated with people? She considered asking him, but the last thing she needed was an artificial guilt trip in Kinnard's voice. Barefoot, she padded out into the hall, headed for the mess.

Cordell had promised her she could wander around at her leisure, though Boots had yet to test her privileges. The last thing she wanted was to run into Orna again, though she wouldn't mind meeting Didier in the dim night cycle. There were worse things to look at. Maybe it was just the way he treated her, but no one had called her a lady in a long time. He was unconditionally friendly, which was a damned sight better than Cordell, whose friendliness was extremely conditional. Unlike the captain, Didier didn't ask her for anything or try to order her around, or beg her to jump on the ship she'd never wanted to see again for the rest of her life.

Creeping downstairs, she spied a light inside the mess and smiled. Maybe she'd get her wish.

The warmth in her belly disappeared when she came upon Armin, clad in red velvet pajamas, seated at one of the tables. He froze, a spoonful of cold cereal midway between his bowl and his lips.

"Good evening," said Boots, at a loss for what else to do.

He returned the spoon without finishing his bite and smacked his lips. "Well, it *was*."

She rolled her eyes. "I guess I'd better be getting back to bed."

He smiled like someone had pulled on the corners of his mouth. "Oh, please. Come eat some of our hard-earned food. Can I recommend some of Cookie's Jordacan truffles? They cost a fortune."

"There's no call to be nasty."

He pinched the air. "Miss Elsworth, I was this close to getting the captain into a real shipping contract before you showed up."

Screw it. She walked across to the kitchen and began to dig around in the liquor cabinet. "That tells me you don't know Cordell as well as you thought you did."

"The Flemmlian ten-year whiskey is on the bottom shelf, near the back," he called to her.

Her favorite whiskey. Boots straightened up and peered back at him.

He smirked. "You served on this ship for two years, ten months, and eleven days. That's a total of thirty-one shore leaves. Each time you came back on, you declared a bottle of that swill. I've had access to all of the ship's logs for a long time."

"Right," she said, "datamancy. Well, smart guy, say what you will, but you don't know Cordell. You couldn't make him go straight if you gave him two points with nothing in between."

Armin tapped his bony chin. "Actually, I know Cordell very well...though I think he doesn't know you."

Boots narrowed her eyes, unsure of where he was going with this.

"He's told me you're a soldier, and that you'll come around. I'd wager you don't have one shred of integrity left in you, and according to the financial records I obtained off Kinnard, I'd be right."

"You hacked him?" Anger burned in Boots's cheeks. "You've got some nerve!"

"Relax. How do you think we found out about your farm on

Hopper's Hope? And don't look at me like that. You sent our ship all over the galaxy searching for garbage. Now, I want you to pour yourself a drink and have a seat."

Boots did as he bade her, and the sweet spice of whiskey wafted into her nose as it burbled into her tumbler.

"Between Orna and I," he began, "we can break any data source. Even Kin. I was surprised at some of the military capabilities he had…"

"Cordell acted like he hadn't tried to crack Kin, and all this time…"

Armin shook his head. "I didn't ask him for permission. It was so easy that it was a matter of procedure. Now, I don't think you want to be complaining about our honesty when you fleeced us out of thousands of argents, do you? Our hacking Kinnard scarcely makes us even after what you've done."

Her anger faltered. "A ripe mark is a ripe mark. A starship captain can't afford to be gullible."

"And a charlatan can't get sloppy. You were so easy to track down. Your patterns on Gantry Station might not be apparent to everyone else, but they were a snap for me." He folded his fingers. "However, I'd like to call a truce."

Boots nearly snorted out her whiskey, but managed to stop herself. "Between me and you? But you enjoyed threatening to kill me so much."

"Promises and plans, Ms. Elsworth, but never threats." He smoothed back his hair. "No, I think the time for our spats is over. You see, you've brought two things of value. The first is the image of the *Harrow*. Thanks to you, I'll learn where it completed its last verified jump."

She gulped her drink. The idea of flying toward that dark ship, treasure or no, wasn't a comfort. It'd certainly bring them back into contact with Mother. "Okay, well, uh…you're welcome. What's the second thing?"

"Your randomness."

"What?"

"When you tried to steal that Midnight Runner, it fell outside of my predictions. If I'd even remotely predicted that, I would've shot you on the bridge. It was as though we were playing a game, and you moved your piece outside of the board. The substantial data I had on you suggested you'd never do such a thing."

"Steal a ship to save my own skin?"

Armin smiled, his teeth flashing in the bright lamplight of the galley greenhouse. "Not twenty years ago, you dressed the captain down for doing the exact same thing. You turned yourself in and faced disgrace. It's hard to believe a core tenet could change that much."

"You learn a lot in twenty years…a lot more when no one will give you a job because of a dishonorable discharge on your record and a lack of magic. I guess stealing a ship is the right thing to do from time to time."

"So if you could go back and change your mind—stay with the captain—would you do it?"

Boots considered it. She thought back to walking down the ramp of the *Capricious* that awful day, her derelict order papers clutched in her hand and Cordell shouting at her back. There'd been a deep and abiding numbness in her bones that year—the year her planet fell apart. "Nah."

Armin folded his fingers together and rested his chin atop them. "Fascinating. You know, I have to wonder if your arcana dystocia has something to do with your slight unpredictability."

"Excuse me?"

"Magi work by magical assumption and occasional fiat. You

don't have those luxuries, and so the world that swirls around you becomes cloudier, difficult to aggregate. Your condition merits further study, to be certain."

Boots pushed back from the table. "All right, buddy. If you're going to start in with the 'dull-fingered' crap—"

"I would never call you such a thing."

She paused.

Armin showed his palms. "I'm not asking you to join up with us out of the goodness of my heart, which is undoubtedly in short supply. You should stay because you can give me knowledge, and we can give you peace."

"Peace? Is this some kind of religious thing?" That tickled her. "I don't think god cares much for folk like me."

"Not like that. Do you like wagers?"

"Too broke to gamble."

He sat back. "No cash required. I wager that I know why you're wandering around the decks in the middle of night cycle."

"I'll bite. Why?"

"You had another dream about Kinnard."

Boots felt a fire well inside of her.

"I'm right, aren't I? You've been logging them, and it never fails: within the week of making contact with Captain Lamarr, you report one to your computer. Then your system logs activity at all sorts of odd hours."

"Listen, I don't know what your game is, but—"

"My game is safety, Miss Elsworth. The captain wants us to chase down a ghost ship and insists you be around. I want you to be part of the crew, and not planning your next big ship-jacking. I want you to help with security, and in order to have that, I need you to be a team player." He straightened his glasses. "Captain Lamarr is a good man, and that might be why he has trouble getting through to you. Allow me to speak your language: join us,

and we'll cut you in for an even share of the *Harrow*'s salvage…
and, just maybe, you can find out why you keep having these
dreams."

"The captain put you up to this?"

"We've spoken on it, yes."

Before she could decide, he added, "And also, this Mother character is going to kill us all before long. For a group with their resources,
finding the crew manifest of the *Capricious* should be a snap. If we
separate, our odds of survival go down, and make no mistake, I
know odds better than anyone you'll ever meet."

She tongued the inside of her cheek as she thought it over.
"Interesting… I figured you'd be happier with me dead."

"Oh, I might. But I should also point out that your presence
reduces the chance I'll be shot first. So do we have a deal?"

He snatched up her whiskey bottle and tipped the neck slightly
toward her. She clinked her tumbler against it.

"All right. Until we salvage the *Harrow*, consider me part of the
crew."

Chapter Nine

Planetfall

And so, contract signed, Boots found herself in an old, sweaty spacesuit, buffing out slinger scorch marks on the outer hull. It was backbreaking labor, the process of Armin "breaking her in" after years of slovenly civvy life.

She could handle it. She'd certainly seen worse. For her first posting, she'd been stationed on the plains in the civil air patrol, a place she'd lovingly dubbed "spider country." Passing a few days buffing and grinding burrs off the ship wasn't so bad.

On the third day, she was standing among the stars, working on a particularly arduous patch of twisted hull, when the ship made a gentle bank for approach. The gray sphere of Carré rose into her view.

This was the site of her country's surrender negotiations, where Arca ceased to be.

"Hey, Boots," came Cordell's voice on her radio.

"Yeah?"

"Yeah, what?"

"Yes, Captain?"

Calling Cordell "Captain" was the only part of ship life that alarmed her. On the one hand, his rank on her tongue was an old, familiar dish, cooked at home by those she loved. On the other hand, most of those people were dead.

"*Capricious* docks within the hour. Button him up and come to the ready room."

"Yes, sir."

Boots did what she could to get temporary covers over the burned-out spell punctures, but Cordell would project a shield across the belly during reentry. His amplified magic could stop military-grade slingers, so a little atmosphere wouldn't matter much. Once preparations were complete, she closed the airlock and stripped out of her spacesuit.

When she got to the ready room (which was what they called the mess when they wanted to do mission briefings), she found the entire crew assembled and waiting. Cordell leaned against a wall, while Orna, Malik, Aisha, Didier, and Nilah remained seated around the tables. Armin cocked an eyebrow.

"Could you be any slower?"

Boots choked on an unsaid retort, clearing her throat. "Had to change, sir."

The first mate sneered. "Did you need a shower, too? I believe the captain gave you an order to get in here. Leave the suit on next time and get in here when we tell you."

Boots knew the first mate routine all too well: Armin needed to be the bad guy so Cordell wasn't hated. It was a classic out of the military playbook, so Boots played along... though she considered asking if she should still take time to close the airlock or just leave it open.

"Absolutely, sir," she replied, and took her seat.

"Ladies and gentlemen," Cordell began, pushing off the wall. "As you know, we're about to dock at Carré for repairs. However, I have some news: for reasons known only to her, Miss Nilah Brio has graciously offered to pay for our substantial fees. She has not asked for recompense, and none of your shares will suffer from our sudden expenses."

A hushed gasp went through the room as all eyes fell on Nilah, who gave an embarrassed little sigh. Didier whooped.

Cordell continued, "That being said, she's going to need to get access to her funds, and she can't do it from the ship. The bounty on her still calls for her safe return, but I'm concerned that hunters will ignore that. They're not known for being…subtle."

He crossed his arms. "To that end, I'm assembling an away team to escort her to her bank, where she'll transfer the money to us. Then, Nilah's time with us is at an end. She'll be disembarking at the palace of Duke Thiollier, who will conduct her to Taitu and the waiting arms of Lang Autosport so she can finish her season."

Boots glanced over at Nilah, wondering what that look was on her face. It could've been shame, or some regret of some kind.

"Miss Brio sought out Boots for answers, and we may happen across some of those in our future travels. We will continue to share information with Miss Brio via the Link after she's safe with the duke," said Cordell, "and indirectly coordinate with the authorities if need be. It falls on all of you to protect her until then. If something happens to her, our shares all get a lot smaller."

"The duke is an old friend of mine," said Nilah. "Perhaps I could arrange for your crew to be guests?"

Another gasp went up, and all eyes fell on Cordell, who shook his head in disappointment. "Y'all are some sorry folks. Are you telling me there's somewhere in the galaxy more comfortable than your sweet bunks?"

Boots refrained from commenting alongside the rest of the clucking crew. Being planetside near the high-profile bounty was an unpleasant thought at best.

"All right, then," said Cordell. "I guess it's shore leave. Crew, prepare for landing. We dock at Saison Shipyards. And Nilah, I hope you won't try to escape on the surface."

Nilah narrowed her eyes and affixed him with a stare.

Cordell showed her his palms, as though surrendering. "I'm saying that we're trying to deliver you in the safest possible way. Any escape attempt on your part could create dangers to your health. Stick with the people who know escort duty."

"I still don't understand why you won't dock at the palace," said Nilah. "The mechanics there are top-notch."

"I got my own guys, and not everything on this ship is strictly legal," said Cordell. "Let's just leave it at that."

Before Boots could leave, the captain stopped her with a hand on her shoulder. "Miss Elsworth, I've got a question needs answering."

"Yes, Captain?"

"The miner's family that sold you the picture, the one that started all this trouble... They're from here, aren't they?"

"Yes, sir—way up north, near the poles."

"Have they got any more of his effects?"

"I don't know, sir."

"When we land, I want you to take Didier and find out. He's got a chit with ten thousand argents on it. I want you to buy anything else from that estate you can find."

Boots thought about the long ride she'd have to share with Didier and inhaled sharply. She'd played it pretty cool with him, kept it professional, and she worried about that mask slipping.

"Yes, sir."

"Oh, and Boots?"

She paused.

"Can you at least pretend to be unhappy? It's killing me to be this right."

"About what?"

149

He shook a cigarette out of his case and lit it. "About you belonging on this ship. You snapped in here like a puzzle piece, and you know it. You're a spacer, and you always will be."

"Speaking of which," she began, snatching the cigarette from his mouth and crushing it underfoot. "No smoking in the mess, Captain. ADF regs."

Surprise, then a hint of anger, cooling to a grin. "This ain't an Arcan ship anymore."

She leaned in close enough to smell his sweet cologne and old smoke. "Then maybe you ought to take down their banners in your quarters, sir. Those had me confused, you see."

She spun on her heel and made all speed for the door, not waiting to see if she'd gotten a rise out of him.

"God, I am bloody ecstatic to be getting off this bucket," said Nilah, her feet clanging across the cargo bay.

Orna followed with Ranger in tow, the mechanical beast's footfalls banging along. The three of them marched a quick waltz beat as they crossed to where Malik stood waiting. The ship's doctor reminded Nilah of her personal trainer back at Lang—always smiling with his perfectly bright eyes. There was little more obnoxious than a chipper face in the morning.

"I would urge caution," said Malik. "There's the matter of the bounty on your head, and Carré isn't the safest of worlds."

"Nonsense," said Nilah. Cordell's words echoed in her mind, but she brushed them off. "I've been here loads of times. It's no Taitu, but it's a beautiful place. These are my second people."

"Orna, I think it would be safer if you let her ride inside of Ranger," said Malik. "No one would be any wiser for—"

"No," said Orna, and her armor stomped behind her. Orna reached back, stroking the sides of his cameras, and the armor rumbled in response, purring as his exhaust ports warmed with orange light. "She can wear a rebreather. That'll stop the curious and the bank cameras. No one touches Ranger."

Nilah swallowed. She hadn't considered what it'd be like inside that armor. It probably smelled like Orna—a scent that carried both the acute memory of being knocked unconscious and inexplicable exhilaration. She couldn't help but feel a tinge of disappointment that she wouldn't have the experience of being surrounded by Ranger's powerful bulk.

"Won't I look a bit odd being the only one in the rebreather?" she asked.

"Not at all," said Orna, taking a rubbery full-face mask out of her pack and passing it to Nilah. "There are plenty of people who can't live on sea level without hacking up bits of lung from the allergens. We can just pretend you're a local."

Nilah turned the rebreather over in her hands, inspecting the seals. They were worn, and in sore need of replacement, but they'd probably hold. The system was an older model, with a utilitarian, robotic face. "The locals don't wear these... I've been here before, Orna."

"Don't wear it then. Open him up, Ranger," said Orna. She snapped on a thin particulate filter as the cargo bay doors swung open.

Tendrils of rotten mist crept into the ship's open cavity, instantly offending Nilah's sensitive nose. She couldn't quite place the stench—like a cross between flowers and rotting meat. She snapped the rebreather onto her face without another word. It carried its own signature scent—old sweat—but it was far better than the mystery mist swirling into the bay.

"The Gray, a byproduct of eidolon processing on this world," Malik said, placing a calming hand on her shoulder. "Mostly harmless, but point one percent of the population develops an allergy over time. Many, but not all, locals wear masks."

Nilah's eyes darted to the outside, where she saw the bloom of city lights haloed in the murk. "You parked in the Gray? Why?"

"Because we can trust the shipyards here," said Malik.

Orna took a deep breath, exhaling with telegraphed satisfaction. "More accurately, we know they'll stick a knife in our front... not our backs, like the places upworld."

"But no one lives down here. How are we going to find my bank?"

"Not so," said Malik, gesturing to the opening. "Almost everyone lives down here. Shall we proceed?"

As they set out into the mist, past the spaceport gates, Nilah found a bustling metropolis. As above, numerous dwellings were carved into the bedrock of mountains, but the buildings were far shabbier, and the air thundered with the movement of vehicles on the skylanes above. Colorful holograms danced through the emptiness above shops, but when she peered into the cracked, barred windows, she found only junk. In each instance, Nilah wondered how these people could make a living. She recognized a few of the symbols of the Galactic Common Semiotic Set: food, fuel, hotel, drugs. The pictograms were accompanied by the Carrétan alphabet, which Nilah couldn't read.

"I'm surprised you've never heard of this place," said Malik. "It's Carré's legendary Forgiven Zone."

Nilah jumped as another pedestrian muscled past her: an old man with anemic flesh and a patchy beard.

"Why would I have heard of it?"

"Been in the news a lot, lately," said Orna. "Remember the Blixen Bomber? Killed on Taitu by the Police Special Branch. After they gunned him down, they traced him back to here."

"I don't watch the news if it's not racing," she said. "Why is it called the Forgiven Zone?"

"Everything here is governed under civil law," said Malik,

cutting in. "Everything except heresy, which remains a capital offense, punishable by death."

"So it's all contracts and lawsuits down here?" asked Nilah. "What about murder?"

"Everything," replied Malik.

Nilah shuddered. "The civil stuff mostly sounds good, but I don't believe in the death penalty. We shouldn't kill sentient creatures."

Malik nodded, but when she looked to Orna, the quartermaster merely laughed.

"How many people do you think I've killed?" she said.

Nilah chose not to answer, and they continued on the labyrinthine streets for the better part of an hour. Malik was chatty and pleasant, and enjoyed waxing poetic about the plight of the average Carrétan, while Orna's eyes darted nervously from corner to corner each time they reached a crossroads. She would only join the conversation to scoff at Nilah's ignorance or say something generally demoralizing about their surroundings. Ranger brought up the rear, constantly sampling the air and sneezing out minor particulate and carcinogen warnings.

The longer they were down there, the more foolish Nilah felt. She'd never seen this side of Carré, and had long considered the planet a second home. It had been hidden from her, an embarrassment to the regals high above. Easy to do, as the schedule of a racer at a grand prix was carefully controlled. From the moment she landed to the moment she left, there were simulations to run, princes to meet, press to charm. Her handlers had done a lot to steer her to the best parts of every planet, and anywhere she went, the cameras followed.

This Carré, the Forgiven Zone, seemed dirty and difficult, impossibly complicated for a foreigner. She didn't know much about how the galactic press selected their news items, but half of a planet's population living under a cancerous haze seemed at least a little important.

"Straighten up," said Orna. "You look like your dog died."

"This place is depressing."

"Yeah, well. You weren't on Clarkesfall in the last days."

Nilah looked her over. Sure, she was scarred up, but she didn't look a day over twenty-five. "I wasn't born yet when Clarkesfall dried up. You would've only been a child when the last people were evacuated."

Orna shot her a cutting glance. "I was a child. Everyone lost their damned minds back then."

Nilah swallowed and shoved her hands into her pockets, getting a few paces' distance between her and the quartermaster. In a desperate attempt to change the subject, she nudged Malik. "What makes you think we're going to find a bank down here?"

He smiled and gestured to a marble edifice emerging from the fog. "Because when the law is for sale, everyone is in debt. We're here."

They passed under a gargantuan archway and through a series of blowers that cleared away the Gray.

A grand gallery appeared before her, one that would rival the main hall of a palace. Warm light painted chandeliers in glittering flecks of gold, and kiosk after inviting kiosk offered smiling, fresh-faced attendants. Though the bank employees dressed in sharp suits, their faces shimmered with the telltale signs of advanced force field rebreathers, unlike Nilah's leather and rubber mask. Whoever these people were, they didn't live down in the Forgiven Zone with everyone else.

Nilah knew her clothes were inadequate, but a quick survey of the room revealed that the other customers weren't doing much better. Only a few patrons possessed clothing equal to the bankers', but there was something off about their fashion choices; they were more likely criminals than commoners, with their aggressively flashy suits and overabundant jewelry.

"Which bank is this?" she whispered to Malik.

"Banc Royale, so named for the family that runs it," he replied.

Her thoughts of the royals had grown less than charitable in recent minutes. "Maybe they ought to spend as much on the streets outside as they do on this building."

He cocked an eyebrow. "That could be construed as heresy, Nilah. Be a little more careful."

The image of the Lang Hyper 8 race car caught her attention from the corner of her eye. The Carrétan News Service flickered above the automated kiosks, showing her car entering the tunnel at the Awala GP alongside Cyril Clowe. It then cut to Gantry Station's chief inspector, a grizzled woman with skin like dark leather. The broadcast was subtitled in Carrétan, but the interview audio was conducted in her native Standard.

"At this point," the inspector began, "the people of Gantry Station hereby charge Nilah Brio with the murder of Cyril Clowe."

Nilah's rebreather couldn't keep up with her gasp, and she nearly ripped it off her face. A cold sweat beaded up on her cheeks, pooling around the seals as her eyes burned.

Murder. Why would she ever kill Cyril? She barely deigned to speak to the loser before that fateful day. Her breaths came faster and faster, and she dug her fingernails into her palms. She had to calm herself, or the other patrons were going to start asking questions.

A news anchor appeared onscreen. "Taitutian Prime Minister Mandell issued a statement that Brio is still a Taitutian citizen, and that the Gantry racetrack module belongs to his planet's government."

"While we respect the sovereignty of Gantry Station," the prime minister began, his dark, chubby face filling the screen, "we require the extradition of Miss Brio to her homeworld, where she can face justice from her peers. She is a respected citizen and will be accorded those rights." The sight of him triggered a pang of longing. She knew him well, and they would've been dining together that night, celebrating her future podium on her homeworld grand prix.

The feed cut to the racetrack on Taitu, inside the Lang paddock. Nilah should've been there, answering questions about her upcoming drive, not wanted for... the thought of it nauseated her. She glanced around to see if anyone was looking at her, and thankfully, she only had Orna and Malik's attention. The other customers found Ranger far more interesting than the three people accompanying the suit.

Claire appeared in the projections, her golden hair frizzed. Nilah had never seen her boss so disheveled, not even after the crash with Kristof.

"Obviously," said Claire, "I want her to turn herself in so we can move forward. If she could—"

A man's voice joined Claire's, talking over the team boss. Nilah recognized him: Harmon Kelley, a small-time journalist who'd made the mistake of hitting on her a few times at the track. "Do you believe she's guilty? The police claim they have compelling evidence."

"I've seen the videos, but I'm not a forensic arcanist. I... I don't want to believe she's capable of doing something like that... but I don't know how to disagree with what I've seen."

Nilah recognized the look on Claire's face. The team boss was as transparent as glass, always wearing her emotions on her sleeve, and Nilah knew: her boss believed she had killed Cyril.

The interview kept going, but Nilah could scarcely hear it over the pounding in her ears. Her vision grew watery, and she blinked out a hot tear. How could Claire believe something like that?

Another cut brought Kristof onto the screen, and Nilah braced herself for an even worse savaging.

"With the charges levied against Brio, your chances of winning the Driver's Championship have gone up considerably. A lot of people are saying you've got it locked," the reporter said.

Kristof looked down his nose, squinting at the interviewer. "What do you think you're doing?"

"This is a major story. I'm reporting it."

"No. You're being vulgar. One man is dead, and the points leader is missing. This has nothing to do with my championship hopes."

"Obviously, if she doesn't race tomorrow, it does."

Kristof sneered. "I'm going to make two things clear. First, I was always going to beat Nilah Brio, but I can't do it if she's not on the track. I want her back here where she belongs."

"I, uh, see..." Harmon stammered. "And the other thing?"

Kristof leaned closer. "I've been with Nilah since the karting days. There is no chance Nilah murdered another racer, period. I know her, and I stand by her. Now get that lens out of my face before I break it."

First she was accused of murder, now Kristof was defending her. If her world turned upside down twice, was something righted? Claire's interview had been enough to send her to pieces, but Kristof's kept her on her feet, if only just. Everyone in the entire galaxy hated her, except her bitter rival, and there was a tiny spark of comfort in that.

Nilah jumped as a hand fell on her shoulder, and she turned away from the broadcast to meet Malik's concerned eyes.

"Maybe we should step outside so you can have a moment," he said.

"No," she said, her voice quivering without her permission. "A promise is a promise. I said I'd fix the ship, and I will."

Orna crossed her arms. "I don't think anyone was offering to let you out of that, but it might be better if you don't blow our cover by weeping all over the teller."

Nilah took a deep breath and squared her shoulders. "I'm fine. I'll make sure your money goes through. Wait here, though. Ranger is going to make people nervous."

"Yeah, we'll be outside," said Orna. "Come on, Doc."

Nilah approached the teller, who greeted her in Carrétan before switching to heavily accented Standard. Her heart pounded as she gave the man her IGF unsigned account number. When she got her first drive in the big leagues with Oxcom, Nilah's father had insisted that she set aside 10 percent of her contract value in an unsigned emergency fund, if only because she'd become a ransom risk.

And now, here she was, actually kidnapped and about to hand over her ransom money to her kidnappers. Her father would be furious when he found out, and her chest ached a little when she thought of seeing his livid face again. She imagined him heartbroken in a hotel on Gantry Station, patiently awaiting the police capture of his little girl. She wanted to call him, to make contact somehow, but then remembered the dead Fixer and thought better of it. Contacting her father would only put him at risk.

Once the teller validated the account number, he handed Nilah a pad to punch in her secret code. The IGF Banking network didn't require unsigned accounts to have names or information of any kind, but anyone with the code could get the money—as long as they could enter it in person at an IGF participating branch. Nilah couldn't begin to guess at how much laundering that system facilitated.

If she was wanted for murder, Nilah's plan to stay with the duke was doomed. Carré was a fringe world, but it still had an extradition treaty. Staying with a noble would almost certainly result in her being turned over to the authorities, and she couldn't have that. That meant she would be stuck on the *Capricious* for an indeterminate amount of time: until she could clear her name. She transferred a million argents—more than triple the requested amount—into the *Capricious*'s corporate holdings and punched her code again to confirm the request.

She'd have to ask Cordell if she could stay a bit longer, and a million argents seemed like the right number to sweeten the deal. After all, she was relying on him to provide her protection.

She returned the code pad to the teller, who smiled as though he saw cash numbers like that every day. Given the criminals doing business in the sector, perhaps he did. Summoning every ounce of calm she could, Nilah casually strode to the front entryway and back out into the fog, where she found Malik, Orna, and Ranger waiting for her.

"Did you transfer the funds?" asked Orna, and Nilah nodded.

"Fantastic," said Ranger in Cordell's voice. Its lenses flashed a bright green in time with the captain's words. "It's there, and then some."

"I might need to stay with you longer. Is there a problem?" asked Nilah.

"No, but let's have a sit-down when you get back," said Cordell. "Orna, the shipwright is here, and we've got a lot to discuss. Did you need anything else?"

"No, Captain. See you in an hour or two. Sokol out," said Orna, and the green light faded from Ranger's lenses.

Wanted for murder. Nilah's chest tightened. She'd been fine inside the bank, but as the stress of the money transfer faded, the weight of the news report toppled onto her like a rockslide. The rebreather filled with hot air, and her lungs heaved. She needed to get it off right that second, or she'd surely suffocate. She struggled to push it off her face, gasping.

Malik wrapped an arm around her and reseated the mask where she'd gotten it free, gently lowering her hands. "You have to stop. Remember where you are."

"I can't breathe," she said, though she knew it was only panic. "They really think I killed Cyril. Claire thinks I did it. Do my parents?"

Malik stroked her back, his gentle warmth a minor comfort. "We have to get off the street, Orna."

"I could have Ranger just pick her up and run back to the ship," said Orna, her eyes searching for any parties too curious about Nilah.

"Too conspicuous," said Malik. "Nilah, I want you to hold tight to me. You're going to be okay."

"Yeah," she said, the strong facade she'd given the teller now completely gone. "Just... let me take this off."

"Don't do that here," said Malik. "Facial geometry will pick you up from the bank's cameras. You can be brave. You can do this. Just hold it together for a few more minutes."

Malik quietly led them along the misty paths until he found a restaurant he trusted. The tables were battered slabs of metal, and the building looked as though it might come down on them at any second, but the plates and cutlery arrayed before empty seats seemed clean enough. Soothing scents of frying dough and seared vegetables wafted through the filters of her rebreather. Malik asked, in perfect Carrétan, to have the trio seated in the back, where there was a small, private dining area.

As soon as the curtain closed, Malik cast a glyph and pressed his palm between Nilah's shoulder blades. Her heart slowed and the room grew brighter as her irises slightly dilated. Hunger rumbled in the pit of her stomach—a healthy appetite she'd not expected. She could breathe again, though her mask's stench still offended her nose.

Nilah yanked her rebreather off with a sucking gasp. "I'm sorry. I'm so sorry. I didn't expect... that. This place. Any of it."

Orna smirked. "What happened to 'This is my planet'?"

Nilah pulled up her shirt collar to wipe her face, but the stink of the Gray had soaked into the fabric. "It's been a long day." She picked up her menu, but found only an unfamiliar language and a few Standard numbers. "I can't read these bloody menus. Are we really going to eat when we're on high alert?"

"I can read them," said Malik. "And yes. We need to stay off the streets for a bit after your small panic attack at the bank."

"Would you..." Nilah began, but paused. She hated asking her former kidnappers for help. "Would you mind helping me order?"

"Of course not," replied the doctor, his expression unsullied by the clear enjoyment Orna had taken with their situation. "What do you like?"

"Anything, doctor, provided it's not an animal," said Nilah, pushing her menu away. "Please select something at your discretion."

"Milks and creams are okay?" asked Malik.

"Yes," said Nilah, wiping her nose on a napkin. "And... and I apologize for being so curt with you back on the ship."

The quartermaster leaned in close and narrowed her eyes. "Did that news break you?"

"I'm accused of murder. Of course I'm bloody upset," she whispered.

"As she has every right to be, Orna. Leave her alone," said Malik. "You're safe for the moment, Nilah, and we can make a plan when we get back to the ship. Just focus on getting a meal into yourself."

"So, be honest here: did you kill that guy?" asked Orna, and Malik snapped at her. "What? I'm just asking. It's not like we're going to turn her in."

"No," said Nilah. "I've already told you how he died. Mother killed him."

Orna propped an elbow on her chair and leaned back. "You know, if that battlegroup hadn't come after us, I wouldn't believe a word of your story."

Nilah grit her teeth together. "I take it you're happy to see me accused."

The quartermaster chuckled. "I am. You're kind of an ass."

"And you're a stone-cold criminal, so I suppose we deserve each other."

"Ladies, please," said Malik. "Can't we just eat?"

Once the order was placed, the four of them sat in silence, with only the bustle of the kitchen and clicks of Ranger's servos to punctuate the span. The doctor seemed perfectly comfortable in his own skin, but Orna's predatory stare never strayed from Nilah. The chef set plates down in front of the three of them, a panoply of delicious fried cakes, tubers, and cream-covered dishes. They were full of fat, sugar, and salt: three things Nilah almost never ate. But after the stresses of kidnapping and framing, she didn't bother to stop herself. Who knew when she'd get back in a race car?

Orna took a bite from Ranger's fork. The battle armor sliced apart her meals, queuing up bites in order of the quartermaster's preferences. It was an off-putting effect, seeing the armor go from pet to caretaker. "I mean, I *do* believe you. Anyone who'd get broken up over something so small isn't a murderer."

Nilah's heart thumped, and she pushed food around her plate in an effort not to look into Orna's eyes. "Thanks."

"You are so cute like that," said the quartermaster. "A little bruised, a little flushed. This is a big meal, but I bet I could just eat you up after."

Nilah choked on her drink as her dermaluxes flashed pink. She'd had her fair share of admirers, but no one like Orna—fit and fierce at the same time. As she coughed, Malik's warm hand patted on her back.

"You're okay," he said.

Orna rolled her eyes. "Or Malik can ruin the moment by acting like everyone's dad."

"You're out of line, Miss Sokol," said Malik, his voice so sharp and final that the two women were stunned into silence. "A quartermaster is an officer, and your conduct around Miss Brio is shameful."

Ranger put down his fork and Orna cocked an eyebrow. "I'll do what I want, Doc."

Malik nodded. "I know you're unaccustomed to guests on the ship, but if you continue to dishonor the *Capricious* by hurting Miss Brio's feelings, I'll find some consequences for you. Are we clear?"

"We're basically pirates. What are you going to do, tell the captain?" asked Orna.

He swallowed a bite, his slender neck bobbing with effort. "Would you like me to? I could recommend he discharge you from service."

"I was playing, Doc."

"I'm not."

Rage seeped into Orna's face, prompting Nilah to her feet.

"I'm full," said Nilah, brushing a few stray crumbs off her pant legs. "How about we get on with things?"

"Yeah, let's," said Orna, pushing back from the table.

As they paid, Nilah remembered her rebreather and yanked it back over her head, its ancient seals slurping onto her moist skin. She peered out into the fog through the open front door, but didn't see anyone lurking in the streets. Once the check had been settled, they stepped out into the thrumming air of the Forgiven Zone.

The whine of ships had grown louder, even as the streets and pathways emptied of people. One man, clad in formfitting leathers and a black rebreather, came wandering out of the mist. He raised a hand to them in greeting, and Ranger receded from their group. Nilah exchanged wary glances with Orna; she'd probably sent Ranger into the mists to get a flanking position on the newcomer.

When the man was mere feet way, Nilah saw silver accents glinting on his mask, red bars upon his epaulets, and a badge in one hand—the police.

"Pardon me," he said, his accented voice a growl. "You're Nilah Brio."

It hadn't been a question.

"I'm chief inspector Emile Le—" he began, but was cut off as Orna's fist crashed against his nose, snapping his head back.

"Run!" shouted the quartermaster.

Nilah turned to go, but the air around her electrified with pulses of yellow and cyan...the colors of the Carré police lights. Everywhere she turned, she saw flashing lights descending from the skies, blocking her exits. She heard Orna cry out in the fog, but she didn't dare look back. Hard-nosed attack fighters slammed into the ground, vomiting forth an army of police goons, armed to the teeth. She heard the telltale whiz of knock rounds and Malik's strangled scream.

And so, she did the only thing she could: she raised her hands and waited for them to take her.

Chapter Ten

Condemned

B oots grimaced at the buildings outside as they blew past her transport. The miner's house wasn't on the other side of the planet, but it certainly wasn't in the same duchy.

Carré depressed her. It always had since she'd landed there for the Clarkesfall Armistice. She'd screamed for Cordell to let her off the ship after Arca fell to Kandamil, to let her turn herself in like a good soldier, and he'd complied, releasing her on this god-awful rock. And when she went through processing, through all of the hassle and toil of surrender, the enemy had saddled her with a dishonorable discharge and a lifetime of struggles. The Carrétan government had helped them screw her over.

Another tattered green Kandamili flag shot through the Gray underneath the transport, and Boots scoffed. Both countries had died on Clarkesfall, but Kandamil had a lot more survivors alive and well on Carré.

"You got a hair ball, man?" asked Didier.

She glanced at him across the ratty cabin, and even though she knew the answer, she asked, "Where are you from?"

He leaned back into a torn leather seat, folding his hands over his ample belly. It was the only part of his physique out of place, like a skinny man who'd eaten a balloon. She was more than willing to forgive it for his muscular, hairy arms. "All over. You?"

"Arca."

"Oh. If I had to pick somewhere I was from, I guess I'd say Kandamil."

Her nostrils flared.

"Sure. I mean, I wasn't born there, but I kind of adopted it."

She folded her arms and leaned against the window. "Then congratulations. You fooled me. I thought you were a decent fellow."

"Thanks, but you're the first."

She scratched her nose. "To be fooled?"

"No. You're the first to think I'm decent."

Boots rolled her eyes.

"No, no, I get it. Kandamili guy in Carré is an easy sell. That's where most of our refugees went. No one looks crossways at me. I'm pretty sure I've got a bunch of family here somewhere."

Boots frowned. "My family is dead."

He smirked. "Oh, come on. A person has got a lot of family out there, man. You can't tell me some of them didn't make it offworld."

"If they fled, they're no family of mine. Real Arcans fought to the last."

"Then how are we talking? Shouldn't you be some skeleton on the subcontinent? You seem pretty spry for a corpse."

She chuckled, against her better nature. "Shut up. You're the enemy."

"If I'm your enemy, you don't have any problems at all."

The transport hit a patch of rough air before righting itself. The violent rocking shoved Didier against her, and she scooted back on reflex, if not on principle.

"I think you're forgetting that the Kandamili bombed my

capital into a thicket of glass and wild magic. Your people make pretty good enemies."

"Not me, though," he said, bringing his hands up like a dog's paws. "I'll roll over for anyone. Allegiance for any person who wants to give me belly rubs."

She smiled. "Shut your fool mouth."

"Undying loyalty for anyone who rubs something farther south," he said.

Boots pinched the bridge of her nose, glad that there was no human pilot on the death trap of a taxi. "Oh lord."

"You don't strike me as the religious sort."

"Just believe it enough to blaspheme."

Didier smoothed out his bushy mustache, twirling the ends until they curled. "That's too bad. The churchy ones are always good in the sack."

No one had spoken to her that way in years. The more she thought about it, no one had spoken to her that way ever. Kin had always been too keen on chivalry, and before that, there had been an endless litany of schoolboys ready to do anything for the lithe, skinny girls. Not her; never her—especially since she could wrestle them to the ground or break their noses. It electrified her to think Didier looked at her the same way she'd looked at him.

"You're out of line," she said, more quietly than she wanted, her cheeks growing hot.

He nodded. "Then it stops. My apologies."

"I mean, you're cute," said Boots, her words coming slow like syrup. She'd spent too long without the touch of another, not so much as a handshake, and the thought of blowing off some steam with Didier was overwhelming. "But I think we could focus more on the task at hand, you know?"

"Did you mean that?"

"Yeah. I don't think you should hit on me for now."

He shook his head, incredulous. "No. You think I'm cute?"

"What are we, children? Yes."

He raised his eyebrows. "And what did you mean by that?"

She sighed. "It means I'd take you in a hotel room and break your hips if we had time, okay? But we don't, so chill."

"I don't know how to follow that."

"Then you shouldn't. Just take the compliment and don't press your luck."

She regretted saying it, because two painful hours passed before they finally reached their destination—a tiny village on the outskirts of the Forgiven Zone, far beyond where the sane folks lived. Bitter wind blasted her as she clambered out of the taxi, her face blistering in the cold. For a woman who'd spent the last decade on Gantry Station in the perfectly calibrated room temperature of an orbital colony, Carré's far north was like stepping out into the frigid vacuum of space—painful, inevitable, and terminal.

"Whoa! It's cold, man!" shouted the king of the obvious. "This sucks!"

Boots agreed, stepping down into the dirty snow. This place wasn't like most colonies: hospitable and engineered for comfort. No life existed out here—or very little. This hellhole was frozen solid. She may have been dull-fingered, but she recognized the look on Didier's face. Magic came from the presence of life, and all magi got paranoid when they realized there wasn't much life energy to draw from. On starships, they solved this problem with biobatteries, food stores, and other crew. Aside from a few microbes, this icy waste was dead.

"I've got to admit," he said, crunching into the snow, "I'm freaked out being out of comms range with the ship."

"Please. We left comms range four hours ago."

"We should've taken the *Midnight Runner* up here."

"I assure you, it's better this way. You ever done an eight-hour mission in one of those?"

"No," he admitted, rubbing his arms to stay warm.

"It ain't a picnic, I can tell you that. Give me a nice automated transport any day."

Didier authorized the transport to wait for them. It'd cost argents for every minute they remained, but it was better than getting stuck out in the snow with no way home. Boots looked over the small village: a couple of domes poking out of the snowstorm, their antennae thrust high in an attempt to capture any signal they could, no matter how thin.

Boots gestured to the series. "I've never been to the miner's house in person. Conducted the last transaction over the Link, but I never met the family face-to-face."

"I'll be damned if I know which house is his. Want to just knock on some doors and see what happens?"

"Beats freezing my ass off," she said, taking exaggerated steps through the accumulated frost. "These coordinates were the ones listed on the initial contact."

"How did you know to buy this one picture, anyway?"

She grinned back at him. "Spammed a bunch of dead miners' families who'd been at Goulding Station when the *Harrow* was imaged. Just my luck this one widow had an unopened rucksack and a couple of data cubes she thought had pics. I picked up a picture of the *Harrow* for a few hundred argents."

"Who took it?"

"The late husband, I'm guessing. Some guy named Jean Prejean."

"Nice name," huffed Didier.

"I'm guessing his parents weren't all that creative. According to records, he's survived by his wife, but they never had any children."

"Can't imagine you'd want to have any, not in a place like this."

Boots scoured the snow-caked village for any signs of life. "This is a widow's town. When a Carrétan man dies, his holdings become his brother's by custom, and personal effects go to the wife. It's the brother's job to buy the widow a place to live."

"Seems like he could've done a lot better than some shack in the middle of the tundra."

"People only treat each other as well as they have to. That's what makes the king and his planet such garbage."

"That's heresy," said Didier with a wink.

"Wish I could tell his majesty what I thought of that. What a joke."

"I may not know much about Carré, but I know insulting the royals is a capital crime."

"At least if they killed me, I wouldn't have to suffer through their crap planet anymore. Can you scan for signs of life? I want to know which one of these rust heaps is inhabited."

"No amp, not much juice, but sure, I can try." He traced out a glyph, ragged and smoky along the edges, like the green light was bleeding out of it. The magic flickered, weakened by the surroundings. Didier's birth defect of a malformed mark didn't help.

It was funny to her: even if she couldn't cast a spell, she knew an unhealthy one when she saw it.

Didier finished his glyph, which wrapped around his fingers like glowing spiderwebs, and he stretched out his hands toward the houses. He lowered his hands and sighed.

"You're not going to like this," he said, his mustache twitching. "What?"

"Just vermin living in those domes. There's no one home."

His words tangled around her like a trip wire. They'd been stuck in that transport for eight hours, and no one was home? She'd just purchased the image stack a few weeks prior. There was no way the village had been abandoned in that short time. With sickening certainty, she knew exactly what she'd find in those houses.

She drew her slinger and checked her ammo: discus rounds.

Didier frowned. "Who are you going to shoot? There's no one home, man!"

"No one alive, you mean," Boots growled, edging toward the nearest dome.

Didier put a heavy hand on her shoulder. "Yeah. So my question stands. There's no one to shoot. Even if it's wall-to-wall dead bodies, you don't need to blow them away. Dig?"

"What about bots?"

"Oh yeah," he sighed, drawing his own slinger.

Boots spied the telltale purple glow of overloader spells in the chamber of Didier's gun and shook her head. "Those don't work on bots. Can't stun something without a brain."

"It's all I've got."

"You're kidding."

He grimaced, his mustache going lopsided with the motion. "I've never killed anyone. Wasn't about to start."

"We're an away team, Didier! Away teams shoot stuff!"

"And when they're done, I can cook them a nice meal."

"You didn't think to bring some utility rounds like knocks or rebounds or ... something?"

He shrugged. "Then I might accidentally shoot someone."

Boots's eyes stung in the chill air from going so wide. "Exactly why are you on my mission?"

"I'm not. You're on *my* mission. The captain didn't trust you to carry the money, so you're just here to guard me while we buy what's left of this guy's stuff."

Boots rested her hands on her knees, the frigid metal of her slinger's grip digging into her leg. She couldn't go charging in there with some rank amateur hoping to shoot up any bots she found. He was just as likely to shoot her as an enemy.

"Okay," she sighed. "Wait here."

"And do what?"

"Look pretty," she called as she tromped off toward the houses. When she glanced back at him, he'd posed stick-straight, one hand smoothing out the sides of his mustache like he was some great thinker. She wanted to call back for him to stand guard, but thought better of it. The last thing she needed was for him to fire off rounds at some gust of wind.

Boots circled around the tiny installation—a series of six domes with doors all facing a central courtyard. A pillar of tanks, tubes, and antennae stretched skyward from the center of this formation, a shared system for filtration, power, comms, and climate adjustment.

She headed through the snow to the nearest door and checked the console. Power still flowed through the installation, and it wasn't locked. Since there probably wasn't another human for a hundred kilometers, she figured the inhabitants didn't need to lock up.

Bracing her back against the wall for cover, she tapped the open button and waited for a trap to go off, or maybe a bot to come storming out. She didn't know if she hoped to find Jean Prejean's survivors or an empty house. If they weren't present, it'd be nigh impossible to track them down. If they were... Didier hadn't detected any life force.

The scent of blood told her all she needed to know. She ducked out of cover and peered inside, slinger at the ready. As her eyes adjusted from the blinding snow to utter darkness, dread metastasized in the pit of her stomach.

Twenty-two years ago, at the Battle of Laconte, the *Capricious* had gone down hard with no internal gravity to save him. Cordell was a master wizard with shields, so he survived without a

172

problem, but three crew members had been in the cargo bay when the ship rolled. When Boots landed her Midnight Runner and rushed inside, she found her shipmates had been smeared all over the walls by debris and cargo. They were nothing but scattered blood and bone, tumbled away like imperfections on a river stone. Boots tried to shake the image, but it coated her mind.

Whoever had lived in this room, their blood was now all over it.

The far wall was splashed with crimson, which slid down in a wide trail before hitting the floor and dripping down some stairs. Boots edged into the room just a hair, checking the corners and keeping her guard high. The room contained a bed, sink, and a toilet—no food preparation of any kind. A faint light reflected up from the bottom of the stairwell, glinting in the syrupy blood.

She stomped back out of the house and through the waist-high drifts to Didier. "Hey. So about that house…"

"Yeah?"

"Why don't you come in there with me after all?"

He waggled his eyebrows. "Did you find a bed?"

Boots started to explain the sight he was about to witness, but her mouth went dry. She smacked her lips together and smiled wanly at him.

"That bad, huh?" he said, his grin fading. "Why don't I go in first, so I can—?"

"No. I've got more training. I'll take point."

Together, they stepped into the house. A pile of snow toppled in behind them, wicking up blood as ice became water. Didier swore under his breath before retracing his glyph. Green light glowed over the bloody room.

"What are you doing?" she whispered.

"I was far away before. I just wanted to make sure I didn't miss anyone."

"And did you?"

He swept his palms to and fro, scanning the area. "No. And given our current surroundings, that's a good thing, man."

She found the lighting panel and tapped it on, but it only confirmed the grisly details. Boots focused more on the contents of the room, ignoring whatever had happened here.

It was scarcely a home in the traditional sense. Yes, it was a well-insulated shelter, and it had a place to rest and clean, but there were no images on the wall, no holoprojection lenses, and no personal effects. Even the bed was perfectly made, as though no one had been horribly murdered nearby. If this was where Jean Prejean's widow lived, there had to be some strange reasons for it.

"Stairs?" she asked.

Didier nodded. "Stairs."

As they crossed the threshold toward the darkness below, Boots inspected the entrance. She noticed a lip around the stairwell, along with a hidden switch behind the nightstand. "Looks like these stairs weren't meant to be left open like this," she said.

"How so?"

"Hidden switch."

"Neat," said the cook, focusing his attention on descent.

There were only about twenty steps through a switchback before they hit the bottom. On the lower landing, they found a blast door, cut from its hinges in large, drippy welds. Acrid dust had settled into the scene, tinging the air with chemical scents. Boots closely examined the welds and found unblemished silver surrounded by carbon scoring.

She ran her hands over the shiny surface: surprisingly rough. "Fire magic cut this open, or something like it."

"How do you know it wasn't just explosives?"

"Micro-abrading. When the cutting area gets too hot, the subsurface can't keep up and causes these little cracks. Chemical explosives don't get hot enough to do that."

Didier smirked. "Where did you learn that?"

"On the *Capricious*'s fifth run, a Kandamili fire mage landed on our hull and sliced a hole into it. He depressurized a third of the ship before we knocked him off. Killed two decent folks."

His smile melted.

"It's fine," she said. "When we came in for repairs, those entire panels had to be recut, because the welders couldn't patch it."

"I'm sorry for bringing it up."

She shrugged. "It also gave me pretty good fodder for a salvage legend a few years later. Treasure hunters love little details like that. Ready?" Boots peered in through the door, but only darkness greeted her.

Didier reached into his pack and drew out a small lumon flare orb. He touched a glowing finger to its surface, and it responded with brilliant, green light. He then gently tossed it into the empty space beyond. The lumon bounced over a few feet of anti-slip treads before rolling underneath a railing and disappearing. Didier's finger glowed brighter, and the device popped, leaving thousands of glowing motes suspended throughout the room.

The landing door led to the second-floor balcony of a cavernous archive. Shelf after shelf of inactive data crystals, each the size of Kin, lined the walls. Boots forced herself to blink. The room below had to be as long as a small starship, and if those crystals were full of information, they'd hit some kind of preservation project or military archives.

The familiar stir of the hunt blossomed in her gut, and her breath quickened. She remembered the exact moment, long ago, she'd seen that derelict starship containing the Chalice of Hana. She remembered Gemma and Stetson, and their forced calm as they docked, camera crews in tow.

Another one of her legends was true. They really were on the path of the *Harrow*. What did the stars hold for her this time?

She stepped through the gaping doorway into the green shadows of the lumon, creeping to the edge of the balcony. Three bodies lay sprawled across the floor of the massive data gallery, each riddled with slinger wounds. Given the extent of slicing damage and the destroyed concrete floor behind them, they'd been shot with discus rounds.

An array of hallways branched off the mezzanine balconies, each one with a vault door scorched to pieces. She pointed them out to Didier.

"Ten to one those go up to the other houses in the area."

"What do you think we'd find there?" he asked.

"More bodies."

From her new vantage point she could see the central control array, or what was left of it. It had been washed in a sea of fire, mostly melted away into slag. Data crystals littered the floor, having been blown from their sockets by concussion spells or conventional arms.

"Whatever went down here, it happened fast," Boots breathed.

Didier joined her at the railing. "Oh yeah?"

She pointed to the corpses. "All outside of cover. They're unarmed."

"They could've surrendered and been executed."

From the way the floor had been destroyed behind them, Boots knew the shooter had been standing exactly where she was. "Doubtful. The killer or killers came in through the house above. Tore that person up, then came down here and started blasting. That's why they needed a fire mage—so they could slice through the blast door in under a second."

"What do you make of the melted console?"

"They came to bury the information contained here. Which means it's going to be tough to get at whatever is left. This sucks."

Didier scratched his nose. "Yeah. Those people were murdered, man. Poor bastards."

She'd actually been talking about the fact that most of the info here was likely destroyed, but she kept her mouth shut. She'd been leading people to garbage and lies for so long, and now that she was standing at the precipice of a real-life legend, someone had melted most of it.

"You want to cast your spell again?" she asked as they searched for some stairs to the lower level.

"Nah. Getting tired. Besides, I did find life in here, it just wasn't human."

"What?"

He shook his head. "Don't freak out. I just found some microbes, bacteria, that kind of stuff. Just because those folks are dead, that doesn't mean everything is. I was really hoping there was some spoiled food down here and not a pile of corpses."

She sighed. "See, I was hoping for a warm welcome from an old woman, milk and cookies, and a bit of intel."

"I could've brought us food from the ship."

"Do you take everything literally?"

They descended to the lower level, where the stench of death mingled with burned electronics. She tried to keep her mind on the buttery flavor of warm cookie dough and the cool cream of milk. "Besides, everyone knows cookies are better when an octogenarian makes them."

Didier glanced back the way they came, ignoring her comment. "If they meant to destroy this place, why not blow it up?"

"Maybe the plume would draw too much attention, even out here. Or maybe..." They reached a bottleneck in the path, and she placed a hand to Didier's chest, stopping him in his tracks. "They wanted to leave enough data cubes intact to distract anyone who came after."

She pointed to the corner, where a lens glinted, mostly obscured by rubble. The pile of broken stone didn't look quite right, as though someone had heaped it over the lens after breaking the rocks apart. There was another, much larger pile behind it, and Boots knew exactly what she'd find under those stones.

"Springfly," she whispered.

"Here?"

In Clarkesfall ground operations, a springfly was the worst thing that could happen to a squad. Both sides loved them. The trigger lens could detect life, friend or foe, at range, and it could be hidden almost anywhere. When an enemy crossed its sight, a winged bot with scything arms and blinding speed would burst forth from a concealed case and perforate anything it could find. The flies could stay dormant for months or even years, and once operational, would continue to hunt their prey for weeks, provided they hadn't butchered everyone in under a second. They were deadlier than land mines and smarter than most marines, and the ruins of Arca were littered with them.

Boots followed the gaze of the lens; it was focused on the half-melted console in the center of the room. Whoever had planned the ambush was smart: lure everyone down to a choke point, then release a hunter in case someone escaped. It wouldn't matter if Boots had brought a squad of twenty meatheads strapped for action; that bot would finish them all in under ten seconds.

"Crap. There are a ton of intact cubes here. I bet we can actually get something out of the remains of that console if we can hook up Kin."

"Okay, so we shoot the lens, right?" asked Didier, gripping his slinger tightly.

"One: no we do not... not yet. And two: take your finger off the trigger. You're going to accidentally discharge. Any weapons fire will launch that springfly, and that's not how I want to die."

He did as she asked, donning a noble accent. "I assure you, madam, all my discharges are purposeful."

Boots scrutinized the second pile: one hid the lens trigger, the other hid the launcher box. "Here's the plan: on the count of three, you're going to shoot the lens with one of those overloader rounds, and I'll blast the bot after it launches. If it shoots straight up, I'll get a clean shot on it. The discus should tear it clean in half."

"What if it doesn't?"

"I'll have less than a quarter of a second to try again."

"Can we just sneak around the lens and get at the console?"

Boots shook her head. "That lens has a wide field of view. We're lucky it didn't catch us already. So you think you can do this?"

Didier scratched an eyebrow. "Or we could leave. We might not get anything out of that terminal, and nothing chops our heads off if we split."

"You make it a point to lie to your captain?"

"Only if he asks me to do something dumb."

Well, he couldn't be perfect, now could he? Boots grabbed him by the chin and planted a hard kiss on his lips, pulling away before he could slip her the tongue. "Brave boys are the only ones worth knowing. Should I give a damn about you?"

Didier smacked his lips. "I've got to admit, I expected that to play out a little differently. Like, not in a room full of mangled corpses."

Boots locked back the hammer of her slinger, and it gave off a light hum as it charged. "A kiss could play out in a hotel room if you just take the shot. You need to learn the art of not giving a damn."

Didier shrugged. "All right."

Without warning, he raised his pistol and thumped the trigger camera with a stunner round, sending dust and shrapnel spiraling into the air. Boots heard the telltale clacking of the springfly box, her eyes desperately sifting the haze for its package. A shower of flashing, blinding sparks burst from the trap in a phosphorescent storm, and she realized to her horror that she couldn't see the bot through the flares. She blinked back tears and the terrible feeling that the spell had seared her retinas, and put three discuses directly into the center of the cloud. They whined through the air before crashing against the far wall, but she had no way of knowing if they'd struck home. Her useless eyes would never give her a second chance.

Boots held her breath for a full five seconds, waiting to feel the slice of a springfly's blade across her neck. A mechanical clinking filled the gallery. Her trachea remained remarkably intact, and her head was still on her shoulders, so she straightened up. She pawed at her burned skin to see if she'd been hit anywhere.

"You nailed it, man! Sliced it right in half!"

She took a wild swing at the air where Didier had been standing. Her heart hammered as she tried once more to sock the bastard, to no avail. She couldn't see much more than blurs, but she heard his snickering as he ducked away.

She swung again. "What the hell was that?"

"You said I shouldn't give a damn!"

"There's a difference between dashing and dumbass!" She finally got a hold of his collar and dragged him in front of her burning eyes. "What were you thinking?"

"You convinced me to have fun and die young, man."

"Have fun, yes. But dying, not so much," she said, closing her eyes. The pain of it bored into her brain, stealing her breath. "Look, I think I got really hurt back there. Just...let me sit down."

Firm, calloused hands wrapped around hers and guided her to the floor. Chopped rocks underneath her butt didn't exactly make it comfortable, but it was better than staggering through the compound.

"Can you open your eyes?" asked Didier, his warm breath on her face. "I need to take a look."

"How come you can see?"

"I shut my eyes tight after I took the shot. Didn't want to see the end coming, man."

She laughed in spite of her pain and pried her eyes open to see his blurry visage. "You are seriously a wimp, and an idiot."

"Yeah, but that's why you think I'm so sexy. It, uh, doesn't look like you've got any damage."

"You can't know that for sure. These people lived out here alone, with little help from the rest of civilization. A place this big has to have a compounder, maybe even a regen system. See if you can find it."

"Roger that."

He rooted around for a while, moving debris this way and that. She winced every time she heard the faint tinkle of a data cube being kicked out of the way. Who knew what those crystals contained?

"I'm going to have to head upstairs into one of the other houses," he said. "No first aid down here."

"Okay," said Boots. "Just, like...be more careful, okay? There could be more traps."

"I'll be sure to scream if something kills me."

Then he raced away and left Boots alone with the corpses. Her eyes pulsed in time with the blood in her heart, and she bit her lip to distract herself from the pain. It was a relief when she heard Didier coming down the stairs, shaking a bottle.

"It's not as good as what Malik would cook up," said Didier, "but the compounder recommended this spray. Said it should get your sight back in eight to twelve hours. It also gave me these bandages to put over your eyes."

"Great."

"It also said you should take these pills."

"For what? Pain?"

"Yeah. You're not going to like this."

She scoffed. "I'm not getting doped up in an underground death trap. I can take the pills after we're out of this. Maybe I should just do the spray later, for that matter."

"No dice, Boots. Compudoc says you've got to do it now."

She forced her eyes open with a grimace. "Fine. Show me what you've got, then."

When he sprayed the solution into her burning eyes, it was like boiling, salty acid. Her pain went from barely manageable to swooning with nausea in a heartbeat, though Boots kept it together. After a few seconds, the compounder's anesthetic kicked in, deadening her searing eyeballs until she couldn't feel anything but cold pressure.

"See?" She wheezed, scrunching her eyes tight. "Not so bad..."

"Totally. I, uh, was wondering if I'd sprayed any in there at all. You were so...stoic."

"Good. Bandage me up and let's get what we came for."

Didier sucked his teeth. "Compounder says I need to do another pass."

"It's fine," she grunted. "My eyes are already colder than an open airlock. I'm not going to feel it."

She was wrong. Somehow, the second time was far worse, but she didn't remember the specifics, because she found herself hyperventilating on the ground. Didier kept any jokes or comments to himself as he propped her up, gingerly leaned her head forward, and wrapped bandages across the bridge of her nose.

"I'm sorry," he whispered in her ear as he tied the gauze behind her head.

"Don't worry about it. Can you hook up Kin without me?" She handed over her satchel.

"I can find some wiring harnesses for him, but I doubt we'll get anything."

Boots's burning eyes had evolved into a runny nose, and she

wiped it unceremoniously on her sleeve. "Do it for me? Kin isn't an ordinary cube."

"How so?"

"His cube came from my old Midnight Runner. He's ex-military. I kind of...stole him when I surrendered."

"And here Cordell told me you were an honorable soldier," said Didier. He might've been smirking.

"When I turned myself in, I was homeless, jobless, and penniless. Without that AI's help, I never would've made it. Kin can hack most systems if he has enough time, and you don't mind getting caught."

"Sounds like a useful guy to have around."

"He ain't a bad conversationalist, either."

"All right," said Didier. "You take it easy. I'll get on console."

A few minutes passed, timed only by the clink of wiring harnesses against her computer. Whatever Didier was doing, he was terrible at it. Eventually the rustling turned to swearing, then relieved laughter.

"Powering him up now," said the cook.

"Hello, Lizzie," came Kin's voice. "Now, this is an interesting place you've brought me."

"Can you access their network?" she called. "I want to know what they were trying to hide."

"Absolutely. This could take a few minutes."

Didier crunched back through the debris and sat down next to her. "You doing okay?"

"I'm better now," she sighed. "Just happy to have Kin up and running."

Didier's hand fell on her back, massaging her neck. "If we find anything out here, it'll be big."

"I've found something," said Kin, "and you're right. It's big."

"Play it," said Boots.

*   *   *

I wonder if that's you, Elizabeth, listening to my ghost.

I wish I could hear your voice, see your face.

My name is Marie.

Have you ever seen a god? I killed one tonight…Jean Prejean. I sank a pen into his eye and twisted until he stopped shaking. Like the other women here, I'm happily widowed to the corpse at my feet.

Ten years ago, I'd never have imagined this day. Jean was too dangerous, had me believing he was all-powerful. I'd tried before, and he shrugged me off like rainwater off his back—not that any of us had seen rainwater in a decade.

When we served together aboard the Harrow, *I fell in love with him. He warned me about the mutiny mere minutes before it happened. I never should have put on that rebreather. I wish I'd died with the rest of them, coughing out our lungs onto the floor in so many raw hunks.*

What we did with that ship; oh god, I can't even say it aloud after all this time. Jean used it, used us, and then kept us young for so many years.

Jean transformed. He could see his enemies days or even weeks in advance of their next move. He had time to prepare, then he could show up and butcher them at his leisure.

It seemed he had no weakness, but I knew better.

He suffered from a profound nearsightedness: when one faction hatched a plot against him, he couldn't see the others who longed for his downfall. And no one longed for his downfall more than me.

He had a prophecy about you, Elizabeth—that you would bring the Harrow *to light and ruin his greatest plans. He started talking about you day and night, and I took notice. He called you "Boots" in conversation, like you were friends. Though he wouldn't share his plans with me, he said you would unravel everything.*

Thanks to you, I could murder him. I drove that pen so far into his eye socket that the nib broke against the inside of his skull.

There are other pictures inside these cubes, other angles of the ship about to jump. I didn't want to send you everything, didn't want to share it all; if you knew I was telling the truth, you might have been scared away. No sane person would ever get involved.

Jean said you would delve the umbra and destroy everything. Do it.

He had a dead man's switch. Henrick and the others know what I've done. They're coming for my sisters and me. There's no point in running. I want to spend my last days with my family.

Time to sign off.

I'm so sorry.

"Cut it off, Kin," said Boots, and a chime signaled, followed by a wake of silence.

"I don't mean to talk out of turn here," Didier began, "but that's some serious heat right there. Did she say what I think she said?"

"Can't be. There hasn't been an oracle since the days of Origin. And honestly, I doubt those stories are true. No one has enough magic talent to see the future. It's just not possible."

"That you know of. What else could this be?"

If she hadn't had bandages over her eyes, she'd have glared at him. There were a hundred other things this could be, chief among them: a setup. There were hundreds of thousands of people in the galaxy who might know what to do with a photo of the *Harrow* mid-jump. With a little coaching, even the most boring citizen could be convinced to go on some wild chase after the most legendary ship of modern times.

The power of Jean Prejean, the Great Oracle, hadn't put that photo in her hands. It had been a conspiracy at best, and the sooner she could figure out who'd benefit, the sooner she could find her angle on the situation.

"Kin," she said. "Where was that recording buried?"

"That recording existed behind sixteen layers of encryption," said Kinnard. "In addition, I had to piece it together out of four discrete fragmented crystals. I have also located thirty-two other pictures of the *Harrow* in mid-jump from other station cameras. I'm storing them to my data banks."

"Wow. Nice AI," said Didier.

Boots pushed herself to her feet, her back against the wall. "Like I said: Kin isn't a normal computer. He can do a lot of things others can't."

"See, the oracle knew that," said Didier. "He knew you'd have something like Kin to help you find the *Harrow*. That's why he was afraid of you."

"This is so obviously a setup. There are no oracles, no matter how hard you try to make the pieces fit."

"Or you simply don't want to believe what's in front of your eyes."

"I can't see anything right now."

"Your metaphorical eyes."

She shook her head. "Why are the cute ones always so dumb?"

Chapter Eleven

Hairpin

When the police transport settled onto the mossy gardens of Duke Thiollier's palace, Nilah could do little else except blink.

The past few hours had been tumultuous, if not horrifying. She'd been shuffled from cell to cell, separated from Orna and Malik, never told where she was going or allowed contact with the outside world. The prisons of Carré were essentially caves and contained no windows of any kind. She'd been detained for hours with little contact, and every time the door opened, Nilah felt sure she'd find Mother on the other side, waiting to cave in her skull.

She'd seen glimpses of the darkest sides of Carré in that prison complex: starving people, beaten people, broken people. In the few short hours trapped there, she stopped fearing extradition to Gantry Station and started fearing they'd leave her there. Nilah tried to push away the fresh memory of a Carrétan prison, but it caught in her mind like a splinter.

The transport's doors opened, and rich, botanical scents filled Nilah's nose: bloody orchids, regal ganpho, and the wet, honey scent of the treasured nduwayo. Squinting, she crawled out of the back to be helped down by a pair of guards. They removed her handcuffs, gave a curt bow, and filed back into the boxy black cruiser. Nilah shielded her eyes from the thruster wash as the craft blasted off and disappeared behind a rocky peak.

She adjusted to the sunlight, and the garden's commanding view startled her. Stark granite peaks rose from the mist as far as the eye could see, each one dotted with the lights of distant palatial shields: blue spheres that collected near their apexes like dew on blades of grass. She'd been to the duke's palace last year, but that time she'd disembarked from the Lang Autosport luxury team yacht. It'd been nonstop galas and enchantments before and after her arrival, so the duke's gardens had scarcely held her interest. Now, after the *Capricious*, the Forgiven Zone, and a Carrétan prison, they seemed impossibly beautiful.

"Nilah Brio!" called a voice behind her. She spun to find Duke Thiollier striding across the wide, open lawn from his palace—a set of azure spires rising into the gray sky. "You don't look too much the worse for wear."

"I'm sorry?"

He reached her and brought her in for a kiss on either cheek. Nilah did her best not to recoil from her host's embrace—she knew she smelled foul and looked worse. In such a state, she'd be too embarrassed to be in the same room as a noble, much less be touched by one. Remembering her manners, she returned the kiss and summoned up her most polite smile.

"Duke Thiollier," she said.

"Please, Nilah. You know to call me Vayle."

"Vayle. I take it I have you to thank for my freedom?"

The nobleman gave her a flirtatious smirk. He had a body sleeker than any starship and a reputation for being twice as fast.

Nilah couldn't help but catch her breath at the sight of him—the product of the best surgeries and spells money could buy.

"Who says you're free? Maybe I just wanted to see you myself before they cart you off to Gantry Station."

Her heart thudded. She hoped he was joking. "One last autograph session on Carré, then?"

He regarded her with eyes like clear skies. "I'm sorry. That was in poor taste. I know you didn't murder Clowe."

Perhaps it was the sudden turn in the conversation, or perhaps it was the horrific day she'd had; maybe she just wanted someone to tell her she was innocent, but it took everything Nilah had to stifle tears. "And why's that?" she asked, holding her voice steady.

"Because you're the best driver alive today, and you wouldn't stoop so low." He crooked his elbow, offering her an escort. "So says Kristof Kater, and I couldn't agree more. I was surprised when he vouched for you."

"Me too."

"I'll always believe a compliment from a bitter rival."

Nilah smiled. "We weren't always so venomous, you know."

Vayle smirked. "Of course I know. I'm your biggest fan."

"So, um...Orna Sokol and Malik Jan...are they all right?"

The duke pointed to the tallest of his towers. "Malik has already arrived. He's inside, in the bathhouse, where you'll join us soon enough."

She narrowed her eyes. "And Orna?"

"The tall woman? I'm still trying to extricate her from the prison. She's apparently broken a lot of bones—not her own, of course. Two guards and three inmates, at last report. I'll pay off her reparations, and hopefully we'll see her before nightfall."

"Can I ask what you'll be doing with me then? If you think I'm innocent."

Vayle scratched his chin. "I think I'll hire the best legal team in the galaxy; we can challenge this murder nonsense from here. You can stay with me while we sort things out."

But why? What was he getting out of it? Was he just a superfan with too much money? He might enjoy keeping Nilah around for bragging rights, stranded in his castle during a court case. Maybe he was making an industry play. Vayle held shares in two teams that weren't Lang; he might want Nilah to consider switching teams next season. Whatever caused his generosity, she hoped it had nothing to do with the *Harrow* conspiracy.

"What about my other friends—the ones back on the ship?"

"I extended an invitation to them, but alas, Captain Lamarr and his first mate declined. Something about wanting to stay with the ship. Despite that, I'd prefer to know they're safe, so I put the port on lockdown and rented out the other docks. They're under my protection, but it would've been easier if they'd landed here at the palace."

"Yes, well," said Nilah, "you can understand why men like Captain Lamarr operate in the Forgiven Zone."

The ease with which Vayle spoke of her predicament unnerved Nilah. She couldn't clean the image of the dead Fixers from her mind. Maybe Vayle was playing her; maybe they'd already gotten to him like they'd gotten to the Fixers, and she was walking into a trap. She glanced back at the cliffside waterfall, tumbling into the endless abyss of the Gray. The police transport had already taken off, and they wouldn't help her anyway. The only road to freedom wound through the palace, so she had little choice but to play along with whatever the duke had planned. Besides, if he wanted her dead, she'd have had an accident in the prison and been wiped off the face of the universe.

Nilah smiled warmly and took hold of Vayle's elbow. "I'm in

sore need of a bath. If I can't be on the grid at Taitu, I'd at least like to watch the race in style."

Vayle ran his fingers over her knuckles and shook his head. "I can't believe what you've been through, but that's over now."

"Though," Nilah began, remembering where she was. Vayle would have access to technologies no one else did. "Could I use one of the palace's encrypted comms?"

Nilah's heart pounded in her throat as she waited in the darkness. Claire materialized in front of her, sitting on a translucent green chair behind the glowing projection of a desk. She was writing something, though Nilah couldn't see what.

"This needs to be good," grumbled Claire, not looking up. "We're on the grid in an hour—"

"I promise," said Nilah, "it's good."

Claire shot upright, her long blond hair falling across her face. "Oh my god, Nilah!"

Though Nilah would never openly admit it, she loved Claire like a mother. The sight of her mentor brought a warmth and weakness like she'd never felt—and an agony in its wake. Claire thought she'd killed Cyril.

The team boss rushed around her desk, as though she could run to Nilah and embrace her, and stopped before the camera.

"How are we, love?" Claire's voice came soft and low. "Holding up all right?"

"Great," said Nilah, smiling as she dabbed her eyes with a finger. She wasn't about to start crying here. "Couldn't be better, really. Just thought I'd call my boss and let her know I won't be at work today."

Claire laughed, her nose turning red. She always did that when she was about to lose her composure: when her husband passed away, when they took the Constructor's Crown last year, when Nilah lost the Driver's Crown shortly after to Jin Sung. "I'm sorry... for what I said at the presser. I...they showed me some videos and it looked...exceedingly bad. I didn't have any time to process."

Excuses for Claire's behavior jumped into Nilah's mind at Claire's statement. *It's okay. She never thought you could be a murderer. She was just confused and frightened.*

Nilah stiffened, fighting the urge to exonerate the team boss just yet. "I didn't do it."

Claire blinked, then a warm smile came over her. "I'm glad to hear you say that. It means a lot to hear it straight from you."

"And I want you to be clear with the press that you stand with me."

"Of course I do. Cyril was a crap driver. I'm sure his accident was a misund—"

"No, it wasn't a misunderstanding," said Nilah, raising her eyebrows. "Cyril was murdered. Just not by me. I know this sounds daft, but there's an assassin out there. What's the official story from the police?"

"They told us you built some kind of tiny jump drive. That you killed Cyril and then botched your getaway."

"What kind of idiocy is that? If I could build a tiny jump drive, I'd be bloody rich!"

Claire closed her eyes and sighed. "Nilah, you know the drivers are exempt from scans by the dispersers. No one from the outside would've stood a chance of casting a spell onto the track."

Nilah laughed bitterly. "But they think I could miniaturize a jump drive?"

"They're casting you as some kind of mad genius. They keep playing that clip of your radio over and over."

"Which clip?"

Claire cleared her throat. "'If he gets in my way, I'll leave him pasted to the tarmac.'"

"I was speaking metaphorically!" Nilah nearly lost control of her volume, but reined it in. "I was just trying to rile him!"

"So you've seen the assassin?" asked Claire.

"Yes," said Nilah. "It's an old hag in a black cloak. She has a helmet that enables her to see in all directions. Why didn't the dispersers fire? I couldn't have shut them down!"

"The police think you did—before the race. They're framing this as premeditated."

"Why? What could I possibly have to gain from killing Cyril?"

Claire held herself, unable to meet Nilah's gaze. "Did you have a relationship with Cyril? Outside of the track?"

Nilah recoiled. "Are you bleeding serious? Cyril? These days, I've lost patience with boys entirely."

"They...have you on access logs to his hotel rooms for the past six races."

"That's ridiculous! If I was going to kill my boyfriend, I could do better than Cyril. And of course they have me on the logs; *I'm being framed.*"

But she could see the doubt in Claire's eyes. Nilah's team boss wouldn't question her honesty, but her sanity would be fair game. Nilah had a reputation for childish tantrums, unreasonable demands, and bullying. It was a reputation she'd enjoyed, until Mother murdered Cyril and framed her for it. She could see how it would be easy to pin the guilt on her with a few well-placed pieces of evidence.

"I'll...I'll look into it, okay?" said Claire. "But you need to turn yourself in if it's this crazy. Just let the professionals handle this. We're out of our depth."

"No."

"You're the most politically protected woman in all of space! I urge you to reconsider."

"I'm sorry, Claire, I—" It gutted her to turn down the invitation. "I have to take care of myself."

"Are you okay? Can we send you any help? Supplies?"

Nilah thought about it, but decided against sharing her location. Claire was trustworthy, but if she knew where Nilah was, she'd be at risk, too.

"I'll be fine," said Nilah. "I just need you to make sure they don't disqualify me."

"Nilah, you have bigger problems!"

"I'm taking care of them. I want you to keep the PGRF in line."

"That's beyond my control," Claire said, mustering her sympathetic schoolteacher face. She always did that when she had to say no to Nilah.

"No, it's not!" said the racer, taking a step closer. "Lang is a shoo-in for the Constructor's Crown and the most powerful player in all of racing. You've got the seat at the head of the Strategy Group, for god's sake! If anyone can keep me in the championship, it's you."

Claire massaged the bridge of her nose. "Look, I'll talk to them. That's all I can promise you."

"I can come back from this, Claire. I will be back on the track."

Silence fell across them as the two women regarded each other for a long moment.

"Okay," said Claire. "I'll make the case. In the meantime, you're to stay safe."

"That was the plan."

"Good. Don't do anything stupid." Claire stepped up like she wanted to hug the driver, but she was only a projection. "The PM has been asking me about you."

Of course the prime minister had been bothering her. Nilah's father had likely sicced him on the poor team boss.

"I know. I'm sorry. Can you just tell my father that I miss him? That I'm okay?"

Claire nodded. "Absolutely, love. This isn't over, all right?"
"No, it's not," agreed Nilah before severing the connection.

It had been easy to forget just what real wealth was. Nilah had a home on Morrison Station: nearly two thousand square meters of nonstop luxury and security hovering high above Taitu, the richest planet in the universe. Her front door was nothing more than a magic portal, teleporting those who wished to enter into whatever room she chose. Her kitchen contained a thousand enchantments to craft any food she could possibly want. She had a spell for everything and worlds of possibilities to indulge her creativity.

That was not real wealth.

Duke Vayle Thiollier was attended by hundreds, if not thousands of staff. They catered to his every whim, from sensory preferences to corporate interests. There were no spells in Vayle's kitchens—there were humans, tirelessly laboring to provide delectable new experiences in far-reaching cuisine. The breadth of knowledge at his culinary staff's command stretched light-years with a depth of eons. Nilah's spells could bring her any food she wanted, but the ideas still had to flow from her. Duke Thiollier was so wealthy that he could add the greatness of the best culinary minds to his own.

Nilah didn't have even a single person under her employ at home. Her house, replete with the latest magics, cleaned itself when she found the time to inhabit it. Here at the palace, staffers scurried to and fro, organizing and dusting, maintaining no illusions about their visibility. They were there to serve and be seen, but never heard.

"This may be in poor taste to ask, but is it expensive to maintain a human labor force like this?" Nilah inquired.

"I suppose the food and lodging is a bit much," he replied, "but the service they provide is invaluable."

"I would think that salary—" she began, but he cut her off with a sharp laugh.

"You misunderstand their positions. These people owe me money—lots of it—and they can't pay. So, I give them a home and a place to work off their debts."

Nilah watched the flurry of ongoing work with some consternation. "You've made this many loans to people who can't pay? That sounds foolish."

"Not at all. It's an investment in both my future and theirs. They take care of a few obligations, then they come to work for me. And some of them didn't borrow money; they're heretics who besmirched my family name."

"I thought that was a capital crime."

"Yes, but everything is for sale in the Forgiven Zone. If I am owed a life, can't I use it to barter?" He gave her a guileless, good-hearted look, as though he had this sort of conversation every day, and perhaps he did.

"Can someone ever repay that type of debt?"

"My word, no. Oh, don't look so horrified, Nilah," he said, waving away her confusion. "My staff are well cared for, receive ample food and medical care, and when they grow old, we give them palliative care at a hospice facility. Many of them live much better lives than their counterparts in the Gray, and I enjoy the company of commoners. I'm the best thing to ever happen to many of these people. I know that my palace may not be extravagant to a racer like you—"

"Oh, it's plenty impressive."

"But it's our home, and my privilege to share it with these fine people."

"You do seem a bit . . . overstaffed."

"A debt isn't a debt unless it's collected."

Nilah knew Vayle had other interests, including Carrétan mines, but refrained from asking him who staffed those.

Vayle thrust his hands into his pockets, an oddly relaxed stance for a noble. "I'm surprised to hear these kinds of questions from a highly respected driver. You sound like one of those offworld journalists."

"Yes, well..." she stammered. "This is my first experience with, um..."

"Indentured servitude built the Circuit Perrin Espy, so racing owes it a greater debt than you think."

She tried not to think about her drive on Carré the year before or the backbreaking work that must have gone into creating the state-of-the-art track. They approached a cadre of tan-suited soldiers whose violent, snapping steps came to rest before the duke. Their hands all shot to dutiful salute, frozen in place above stern brows.

Nilah was surprised to find that their uniforms were the only consistent thing about the squadron. They had all colors of skin, various body modifications, and were diverse in age. Even their weapons varied from soldier to soldier: slingers and swords of all shapes and classes.

"How are things, Captain?" asked Vayle, inspecting the troops.

"Excellent, sir. We've doubled the perimeter guard, as you asked, and the automated systems are in perfect order," said the most decorated woman in their ranks.

"Very good," said Vayle, and the elite squadron marched on, disappearing around the corner at the end of a long corridor.

Nilah watched them go with some interest.

"Those are my Flamekeepers," said Vayle, noting her gaze. "Each and every one of them is a fire scribe, in the ancient traditions of Origin. They're cross-trained in arcane combat tactics, intelligence gathering, psychological operations, and counterinsurgency."

She grimaced. "I've yet to meet a fire scribe who could impress me. Most scribblers barely surpass a cheap lighter in terms of power."

"Then I should introduce you. These men and women are athletes, magi of the highest order, and hold unparalleled destruction in their palms. Hooked up to the right amp, these people could easily level a city block. I recruit them from all over the galaxy and pay them a small fortune to stay here with me."

"Why arsonists, though? Wouldn't you rather diversify your, uh, portfolio? There are so many other destructive marks: conductors, zephyrs, corruptors..."

Vayle traced out a glyph and flicked a match flame from his index finger. He waved it around for a moment, then snuffed it with a breath. "My dear, the mark I carry inspired me to start a new dynasty. Instead of simple family ties, I share something deeper with my Flamekeepers—a common spell."

Nilah chortled. "And you could destroy a city block with an amp?"

He averted his sparkling eyes in mock embarrassment. "Oh, no. I'm one of the match-flame scribes you were talking about before, I'm afraid. I've almost no skill in the arts." He straightened up, summoning his noble stature into his shoulders. "I'm glad you got to see them, though. I want you to know just how safe you are while you're here with me."

"I *should* be safe on Taitu, prepping for the race."

"Yes, you should. It's a damnable shame that you're forced to sit this one out."

Palace halls gave way to rock walls as they descended through cavernous passages. Gone was the Origin colonialist-era architecture of the palaces above, replaced by a more modern set of lighting and design patterns. Huge perimah birds, their clawed wings outstretched in battle, had been carved into the rough-hewn walls. Nilah recognized them as the same ones from the Thiollier family crest.

When they reached the baths, they found Malik luxuriating in the water. Glowing, aquamarine pools glimmered in the granite cavern underneath a twisting field of magically projected stars. Strains of a distant crystalphone warbled in through the cave, lending a ghostly air to the scene. Warm steam seeped into Nilah's lungs, a welcome balm after breathing in bits of the Gray.

Malik lay against one of the rocks with his hands clasped over his chest, his eyes shut and slow breath disturbing the steam around him. He'd fallen asleep, which seemed to Nilah to be his default state.

"He seems comfortable," said Vayle, attendants approaching him from seemingly nowhere.

"He's a hibernator. He says sleeping so much makes you healthy."

Malik popped open an eye. "Not quite." His gentle voice echoed through the cavern. "I said this much peace makes you healthy."

The duke stripped out of his clothes, handing them off to his attendant before slipping into the water. Nilah enjoyed the sight of his sculpted body, even though she hadn't appreciated his conversation much. The Vayle she'd met last season had been less eager to talk about trapping people in lifelong, exploitative contracts. She considered some of the comments she'd made about her own contract with Oxcom in previous seasons and felt a little stupid.

Another attendant approached her from behind and cleared his throat. Nodding, Nilah peeled out of her clothes, ripe with the scent of the Gray, the prison, and a tense day, and handed them over. Malik's eyes returned to a closed position, but Vayle made no secret of watching her as she'd watched him. Too bad he'd spoken too much earlier, or she might've had some fun with him.

She stepped to the water's edge and allowed the moist, temperate air to soothe her skin, then sunk a foot into the pool.

She nearly tripped as her tensed, knotted muscles fell slack in the hot water. Vayle laughed as she sat down, gasping and cheeks flushed.

"Do you like it?" jibed the duke. "It's water from the Prokarthic Ruins. The whole spring is essentially enchanted, so take your time climbing in."

"Are you serious?" she shouted, then wrestled her voice under control. "All of it?"

Vayle winked. "My grandfather's grandfather shipped in every last drop, save for the few liters he sold to the academics. My family was one of the two claimants on the Prokarthic site."

"The other claimant's family was exterminated to the last scion," added the doctor, not budging.

"Malik!" Nilah wasn't sure about the customs of Carré, but she knew it was rude to imply the murder of a noble family.

"It's fine," said Vayle. "Serenity brings honesty. And I can handle it, because he's right."

And because you're stewing in several million argents' worth of magic water. "I see," she said.

"My family has made some difficult decisions, decisions I had no part in. And they've done some harsh things, but their choices bought me this life," said Vayle, spreading his arms wide as if to embrace the entire cavern. "And I love the way I live. I'm grateful for it. Now come inside. Surely you're cold out there."

"I'm not sure I need this much honesty in my day."

"Honesty is good for you," slurred Malik, barely conscious through the pure bliss. "Live longer."

Nilah took a deep breath and slid into the hot pool, her derma-luxes flaring gold with the sudden sense of all-encompassing well-being. "Oh god," slipped from her lips before she could stop it, and every stress melted from her frame. She'd never felt anything comparable—like she'd been frozen solid before being dropped into a warm bath. She uncoiled—her mind, her muscles.

Hard truths burbled to the surface of her psyche. Even after her call to Claire, she was still smarting about the things her boss had said during the presser. In spite of all the horrible things Vayle had said and done, his nude form was perfection, and still worth bedding. She was obsessed with Orna, and desperately hoped the quartermaster would show up before it was time to get out of the baths.

And she wanted Boots to be her friend.

The last truth struck Nilah as strange, since she couldn't imagine the reason for feeling that way. The short, odd woman wasn't like the svelte racers and the hangers-on inside the PGRF. No one at any of the glamorous parties even remotely resembled Boots, and they would be summarily dismissed if they did.

Nilah admired the woman's survivalist nature, her relentlessness and occasional ferocity. She saw in Boots a toughness she wanted for herself.

Vayle's honey-smooth laugh interrupted her thoughts. "Are you all right?"

Nilah blinked. "Of course I am."

"We were just wondering, because you've been staring straight ahead for the last ten minutes."

She glanced at Malik, who mustered enough togetherness to smirk at her. The water wasn't like any drug she'd tried—if she relaxed, it would envelop her mind, freeing her to think without restrictions or ego. When she snapped out of it, the water only left behind vague pleasantness, its intoxicating power gone in a flash.

She blushed, trying to keep her focus.

"Would you care to watch the race, Nilah?" Vayle suggested.

"You have a stream?"

Vayle winked. "I've got better than that."

Motes of light swirled across the ceiling of the cavern, speeding over the rocks to swallow them in multicolored flashes. The sparks twisted and contorted into the shapes of grandstands, purple fields of lavender, the red and white stripes of rumble strips along the side of fresh black tarmac. The roar of a hundred thousand people filled the cavern like a waterfall, and only open road stretched before her. A ruddy sunset filled her eyes, and she recognized the skies of her beloved homeworld.

She was in the cockpit of the Lang Hyper 8, or rather, the entire bath had become a larger-than-life representation of the bleeding-edge race car. The steering wheel didn't quite look like hers, and the gloves were the wrong color; this was Kristof's car, and he was sitting in pole position. She felt a stab of nostalgia—even through the numbing effects of the baths. If she hadn't been inside the calming influence of the ancient waters, she'd have thrown things. The angrier she got, the more the felt her surroundings leeching her emotion away.

It should've been Nilah in that cockpit, but there could be no changing it now.

"Welcome to Wilson Fields," boomed the race announcer, "and thanks for logging in for this—the seventy-third Taitu Grand Prix!"

Nilah watched through Kristof's eyes as he scanned the crowd, lingering on the vast patches of purple in the sea of team colors. The commentators called out the hue: it was the purple of Taitutian lilacs, to symbolize Nilah's innocence.

Kristof reached down and took hold of something, bringing it in view of the camera—a violet silk scarf, clutched in a quivering fist. He held it high, like a conqueror's flag.

The crowd went insane.

Kristof could've tried to make a pariah of her, rallying everyone to his cause with ease. He could've wooed her personal sponsors, adding a big bump to his earnings. Maybe she would've beat the charges and triumphantly returned to racing, but no one would've faulted him for accusing her of murder.

The gesture complete, one of the paddock crew approached to take the scarf, but Kristof waved him away, tying it around his left wrist. Once again, he thrust his fist skyward.

The pride she felt looking upon that scarf melted into the waters, as did her shame; she still hoped he failed to finish the race, keeping her shot at the title completely secure.

"Right, let's start him up," came the voice of Gertrude Schack, Kristof's race engineer.

He traced his glyph and gripped the steering wheel, and the car sang a metal opera in Kristof's capable hands. All those systems falling into sync at the same time still thrilled Nilah's tuner heart, even though she was only watching. She could almost feel the pulsing veins of the engine, its power flowing through the chassis and into her back. They took a formation lap, then reassembled at the pole.

The lights cut out and Kristof launched from the line toward a desperate skirmish in the first turn complex.

"What do you think?" asked Vayle, and Nilah tore her eyes away from the glorious image overhead. "This is the way to watch a race, no? Every detail comes to us in perfect scale, magnified a hundred times. It's larger than life."

"It's bloody brilliant."

"Better than being there?"

She shook her head. "There's nothing better than being there."

"Why don't you have a look at this, then?"

Vayle called out the drivers' names in turn, and the image snapped to each of their cockpits. He raised his hand, and a luminescent pane of glass materialized in his palm. It held the figures for car telemetry, charge levels, lateral forces, tire temperatures, and brake biases—most of the critical stats watched by the pit crews. The stats weren't dumbed down for public consumption, either. These were raw engineering figures.

Nilah stared at them in disbelief. These were basic data feeds from the track, the same things her bosses would pore over for weeks after a race. "I knew you liked racing, but you actually understand those? The majority of analysts have advanced engineering degrees."

"Most of it. That's the reason I fell in love with your driving. The public thinks you're boring, but I know better. I see all the little ways you adjust your drive to become one with the car. You don't take chances, but you play that car like a maestro with a prized instrument. Once you fall into the beat of the track, you're inexorable—a rising tide to swallow the competition."

Vayle looked down his nose, not gloating, but beaming with pride. "I have unedited feeds from every driver in every race for the past five years. Track owners get that."

Nilah stood straight out of the water. "You what?"

The ripples of her sudden ascent reached Malik, who grumbled and turned away like a sleepy child not wanting to leave bed.

The cool air felt like sandpaper on her skin after soaking in the Prokarthic baths. "You've got my drive from last week? You've got Clowe's?"

Vayle put up a hand. "It cuts out when you reach the tunnel. The authorities claim your spells interfered with it."

That's probably because the authorities, the Fixers, and the PGRF have all probably decided that I need to go. "Oh," she said, sinking back down.

She cycled through the drivers until she arrived at Cyril Clowe's teammate, Uziah Lesinski. Both Hambleys were jokes of cars:

poorly tuned, driven by second-rate racers who'd been good in the lower leagues but couldn't hack it in the big time. Journalists never interviewed them, sponsors regularly dropped them, and they were essentially speed bumps for the better drivers. Nilah wondered just how bad Uziah's line would be—probably a waffling fool with an oversteering problem.

Instead, she found a controlled, almost robotic driver. He took it easy on the revs, and she couldn't imagine his gearbox, discs, or tires were ever in any danger. If he'd push his car twice as hard, he'd be competitive. The Hambley might've been a garbage ride, but Uziah clearly had the skill he needed to get more out of it.

Aside from his slow speed, his only flaw was that he fired his Arclight Booster at seemingly random times. Nilah had lapped the Hambleys on track after track, and she remembered clear annoyance every time one appeared in her view. Riding along in his cockpit, she watched Uziah execute a full burn on the booster around a hairpin without ever using the engine to supplement his acceleration.

He'd boost, but keep the same speed, almost like he enjoyed spraying magic all over the track. Again, his fingers flickered over the controls of his steering wheel, mechanical and knowing.

Every lap, Uziah did the same thing: charge up his Arclight and either give it a ten-second burn or two five-second burns. He always let off the throttle to keep his speed consistent, even if he'd gain an advantage by accelerating, as on the straights. He boosted through curves and occasionally took escape lanes, even when he wasn't about to overshoot a turn. Every time she felt as though she grasped his purpose, it slipped away.

"What are you doing?" she thought out loud.

"Sleeping," muttered Malik. "I love this bath."

"Not you. Uziah Lesinski, one of the drivers."

Malik creaked open his eyes and sat up. "What do you mean?"

She explained what she was looking at, but he didn't seem to follow. Nilah couldn't fault him for that. The data points were a bit much for non-racers to understand, especially those who'd never seen raw telemetry.

"I've got no answers," he said, "but if you're looking for patterns, one option is to flatten out."

She gave him a quizzical look. "Flatten out?"

"Yes. Change your waking brain waves to look more like your sleeping brain waves. A weak hibernation spell can do that."

"Won't that just make me go to sleep?"

"Almost. That's what makes the spell much better. I can calibrate what stage of sleep you're in. Most people think that sleep is only three stages, but it's actually fourteen, including several that take place while you're still awake. With arcane stimulation of neural—"

"Do it."

Malik stretched and wiped the water from his face, standing up out of the pool with glistening skin. She found it hard to believe he was Captain Lamarr's age. If beauty sleep kept him looking that young, Nilah needed to consider hiring a hibernation specialist for herself.

Malik traced a purple glyph and placed his palms against her temples. Aside from the focus skewing in her eyes, she felt no different. He spun her to face the hovering telemetry display, her vision smearing into streaks of light as she turned.

Her mind held no questions, only queer clarity.

"Relax," he whispered into her ear, his low voice like the drawing of a cello string—smooth and harmonic.

With that word, her legs gave way and she melted into the water. Malik caught her, and she was vaguely aware of his naked body pressed against her back, but she couldn't tear her eyes from the glowing telemetry readouts.

She focused on the outputs from Uziah Lesinski's Arclight Booster, placing each firing on the track map. Over fifteen laps, a pattern emerged: clouds of magic from the Arclight laid one over another. They became distinct curving strokes, slicing around the back double apex, the three-four-five complex, and the long sweeper at turn eleven.

The strokes meant nothing to her, and normally, her lack of information would've been frustrating. However, in the thrall of the spell and the water, Nilah felt nothing—less than nothing—like an observer on the outside of the universe. Her mind dilated, and she leaned back against Malik, taking in everything in the room: the scents of steam and the men who accompanied her, wet drops on the rocky shore refracting the chaos of racing above, Kristof's long, polychromatic burn of his Arclight up the central straight.

Uziah was spraying magic through the turns where no one else would. The other racers laid down clouds of it on the obvious straights. Between the two groups, a shape began to form in her mind—

A glyph.

Chapter Twelve

Foxhole

C arré's southern snowstorms were legendary. Boots and Didier watched pale blue light filter in through the blinds of their hotel room, reflections of a sign outside which beckoned travelers out of the storm.

Boots rolled over onto her stomach, away from Didier's hot, sticky skin. They'd had sex three times that night, and her joints were sore from the effort. She'd always thought of herself as tough and salty, but she wasn't as young as she used to be. As she popped her hip joint, she decided that she regretted nothing.

She couldn't remember the last time she'd climaxed so hard. The chef's hands, calloused though they were, had been the perfect mix of gentle and unyielding, like they were carved from wood. For the first two times, her medical compress still obscured her vision, and he'd taken advantage of that with expert ministrations to her blindfolded body. When it had come time to take off the bandages, the sight of her lover sent her into a frenzy, and they coupled once more. Now they lay spent, sweat-slicked, and happy.

He caressed her lower back, fingers tickling the base of her spine, but she was too tired to laugh or even shiver.

"I'm so glad this was an overnight trip," he sighed.

"Me too," she grunted. "Me too."

"So are we going to talk about that recording? I'm concerned, man."

She thought about it. The prophecy that directly mentioned her as the downfall of Jean Prejean was nothing more than a frightful mystery at this point: all questions, no answers. She tried to place it on a timeline between the ravaging of Prejean's lair and the burning of her office, but all analysis came up short. Antiquity was full of myths about people who'd been singled out by prophecy; too many of those stories were tragedies.

It couldn't be real; there had to be a trick. Scientists had long made it clear that the amount of magic required to produce a prophet was inconceivable, even with modern technology. It couldn't be done, and so prophetic visions were relegated to the realms of myth and wacky conspiracy theories.

There was no comfort to be had in the discussion—not now.

"Not really," she said. "I'd rather use the bed we paid for."

"The bed *I* paid for."

"That's the one," she said, closing her eyes.

"All right, then. I'm hungry, though."

"What?"

"It's almost breakfast time," he said.

"I'm not getting up with you."

"I didn't ask you to. I figured I could go get us some food from the place across the street. I'll bring it back here and we can catch a few winks before heading back."

"Well, now," she said, "you're speaking my language."

Didier's clothes lay in a convenient pile, but hers had been removed haphazardly, strewn about the room. After he'd found his way into his clothes, he winked at her and left.

Boots hated the little flutter her heart did as he exited the hotel

209

room. She wasn't the type to have a crush, and she didn't plan to start now. The men in her life hadn't been anything to rely on. Cordell had gone AWOL and Kin had up and died. She wrestled the sheets over her body, but they stuck to her at odd angles.

Boots finally kicked them off and fetched Kin's cube from her traveling bag, running a thumb over the shiny data contacts. She socketed him into the room.

"Good morning, Lizzie. My, there's a lot of interesting network traffic in this hotel. I'm a little concerned about viruses."

"Don't be ridiculous, Kin. You're military-grade. Do you think you can safely use Carré networks to relay our findings to the *Capricious*?"

"Not really, no. If anyone is looking for you, a meta-analysis of the data could provide strong indications of your location."

"I just wish we could send our location to Cordell."

"Understandable, but you'll recall he gave you two days to complete your mission, so constant updates will not be necessary unless you're in danger."

"I know," she sighed.

"I'm sure you do. That's why I have to wonder what else I can do for you."

"What do you mean?"

"You're a fighter pilot. More than anyone else, you under-stand emergency protocols in the event of a separation. I may be endowed with your memories of Kinnard, but I also possess your memories of you. There's a reason you plugged me in, and I doubt it has anything to do with calling the *Capricious*."

She felt a redness welling in her cheeks. "What do you know?"

"I know you're worried about something, and that you often plug me in when you just want to talk. Data aggregation of voice patterns and breathing over the last two minutes yields—"

"Okay, fine. I'm upset."

"About what?"

She slicked back her hair and sat on the edge of the bed, her skin folding in places she'd rather it didn't. "I think I'm being stupid."

"Help me understand how."

"I don't think I ought to be sleeping with people. I'm not sure that I deserve it. I mean, I'm no good for anyone. You know that."

"You'll recall that you had sex with my human inspiration before your final mission."

"Yeah, and I disappointed you immediately after." Boots shook her head and leaned forward onto her knees. "Kin, I need you to do something..." Her face prickled with heat. Was she embarrassed? Angry? "When you talk about Kinnard, the dead one, I want you to talk as if it's you."

"That would be exceedingly unhealthy. Perhaps when operational security calms down, I can contact a therapy center on your behalf."

"That's an order, Kin."

She could almost hear his processor cycles trying to sort out the conflicting priorities. "Okay."

"Now say what you were going to say."

"You'll recall that we made love before your deployment."

She swallowed. "Yeah."

"So how was that different from now? You're saying you can't sleep with someone if you're going to disappoint them, but you left me."

"Yeah. I guess that makes me a hypocrite."

She regretted plugging him in. Her computer, just like the real Kin, was always right; it hadn't been what she wanted to hear.

"I think you're talking to me because you want absolution," he said.

"Shut up." She clenched her teeth. "I...I don't need to be touched...I mean, I do. I just don't deserve it."

Tears remained hidden inside her. She sat in silence, fuming at the carpet, not daring to look up for fear of finding Didier standing over her.

"Kin?"

"You told me not to speak."

"I think maybe I did love you a little. Maybe that's why I never really bothered with any other guys."

The whirr of high-speed data processing filled Kinnard's crystalline structure. "When you first created me, the death of Clarkesfall and the destruction of Arca were fresh on your mind. The mnemonimancer imprinted your memories of that day upon my schema, a filter through which all memories of my human form could flow. I have often revisited your memories of my last transmission."

She could hear his fragmented words in her flight helmet at the mention of it.

Kinnard continued. "I believe I've pieced together the things I said that day. I would like to play them for you."

"Why haven't you played them before?"

"Because you haven't told me to treat myself as Kin before. If I were still alive, I'd want you to hear this."

"Play it."

The sound of her breath in a spacesuit transported her back to that day, twenty years ago, when she lost him.

His voice became hoarse, tinged with fear. "You were right when you said the warships wouldn't work. The grid didn't hold. If you're still alive, I want you to take your ship and go."

She could clearly see the battle, the shattered pieces of canopy, floating corpses, and the blossoms of fire as they obliterated her home country.

"There were lots of things I never got to say to you. I'm glad you can go on without me."

She should've been there for him in the days before they bombed him. She should've made him happy.

And there he was, telling her to go AWOL, just like Cordell. His dying wish had been for her to find a way out of Clarkesfall, out of the ADF and the whole Famine War. He'd only wanted her to move onward. When the Defense Force collapsed, her instincts were to stay and give up. Were there any willing surrenders, or had she been the only one to offer herself up to the consequences of war?

Move on.

"Thanks, Kin."

Boots rearranged her clothes into a neat pile, placing her slinger holster on the nightstand. It wouldn't do to step on it in the middle of the night and blow off a leg. She pulled on her skivvies and crawled up onto the bed. The sheets had dried out a little, so she could tolerate slipping into them.

"Lights?" she called, and the hotel's ambient lighting dimmed to a cool blue. Glass polarized and blocked out Carré's rising sun. "Kin, play me something sweet from home."

A quiet tune, swishing reeds and hums, came wafting in from the room's speakers. Wooden flutes and dulcimers joined it. She recognized it as one of the Legends of the Landers, the first people to settle her planet.

She'd been about to close her eyes when the door slid open and Didier entered, brushing the snow from his shoulders, a pair of bags in each hand.

He cocked his head. "Not going to sleep without me, are you?"

"Took too long to get back," she said, pretending to snore.

"Oh, man. That's too bad, because I found a little Carrétan

bakery with the best chocolate bread you can imagine. I also managed to find some fresh fruits and a little wine."

She turned to face him, sizing up the bags with renewed interest.

He opened his mouth to speak. A strange flash bloomed from him, momentarily wilting the colors to gray. Boots squinted, trying to understand exactly what was happening, and he disappeared.

It was like his very presence had been torn from the hotel room.

The bags he was carrying shot to the ground, not thrown, but vanished and reappeared, inert. They looked as though they'd been there for minutes, instead of freshly falling from his hands. Thick blood coated the bags, and Boots sat up to see it running along the carpet. A hot mist settled over her face, and she blinked dumbly.

Her eyes ran along the trail, yet they did not want to see what lay at its end. Gore dripped from the furniture and bedclothes, leading to what remained of Didier.

Terrible, weeping slashes covered his windbreaker, and his arms hung limply at his sides. He was like a wounded animal, his fur coat torn open to the meat underneath, bone and cartilage. Boots couldn't understand how he was even standing. At last she was able to wrap her mind around the woman in the exosuit poised behind him, a long blade passing all the way through his skull to pin him in place like an insect. Boots had seen enough deaths to know his fate was sealed, and yet she screamed, fury and agony crushing together in her throat.

The woman's appearance was exactly what Nilah had described: a tattered black cloak, brassy exosuit, high-powered actuators peppered with magic sigils and an ovoid mask covered in lenses, each pointing in a different direction. This woman had to be Mother.

The crone shot her palm out, and Boots flinched as fingers formed a glyph, lightning fast. This was it—whatever she'd done to Didier, she'd do to Boots, and that would be the end. The world began to distort, gray seeping into the corners of her vision like the frost outside. Boots made to grab her slinger from the nightstand, but it was like trying to snatch away part of a stone statue. The weapon was locked in place by the spell, cold and immobile.

Mother dumped Didier's corpse off to one side with a sickening slosh, both she and Didier still possessed of brilliant color, still able to move and be moved. She calmly flicked her sword free of blood. It flashed in a wide arc, the sort of speed that could've cut someone in half. She took a step toward Boots, who backed away against the headboard.

Everything in Boots's sight had become completely inert, and there would be no escape. Mother had locked the three of them outside of time, and she could easily dice Boots with that sword at her leisure. She took another step closer, and Boots yanked desperately at the slinger, knowing it would be to no avail.

Mother paused. There was something wrong with the spell; Boots could sense it, too.

Air wrapped in distorted strands around Boots's arms, like clear plastic, before snapping violently. All colors returned. Her slinger came loose from the nightstand without any resistance, and she brought it to bear on Mother.

The crone frowned. Boots loosed a discus round into her would-be assassin's torso.

The glowing, spinning halo erupted into hot shrapnel as it crashed against Mother. Unstable sparks of the spell bounced around the room, slicing into the furniture as well as Boots's own exposed arms and legs. Mother was thrown clear over Didier's body and into the window. The tough glass spiderwebbed under her heavy suit; a regular body would've just bounced off.

But the discus had been broken. The spell round designed to shred armor off vehicles, slice through doors, and tear soldiers

215

asunder had shattered like cheap dishware. A shot like that should've cut Mother in half, but the assassin straightened up as though it had never happened.

The crone slashed out her glyph again, and Boots leapt from the bed as its magic entangled her. This time the spell snapped free even faster, and Mother snarled, charging in with her wicked blade.

Boots fired again and Mother crossed her arms over her exposed chin, withered lips sneering all the while. The spell exploded against her, and hot shrapnel tore through the wall and ignited the curtains. It speckled the window, presenting a host of new holes. Boots fired twice more, and on the last shot, the window shattered, and Mother tumbled backward into the snowstorm.

Boots rushed forward to catch sight of the assassin's fate, and found Mother flat on her back. To Boots's horror, the crone slowly clambered to her feet to stare back, a snarl on her thin lips.

Smoke curled upward from the freshly lit curtains, and the hotel fire alarm pierced the night. The snowstorm took on a queer glow as the village's first response unit mobilized in the distance.

Mother looked between the oncoming lights and the hotel. With a scowl, she sheathed her sword and took off into the night.

She'd fallen six stories without so much as a sprained ankle. The coward wouldn't be back that day. Not while she'd lost the advantage of surprise. Boots wondered if she'd ever see Mother's face again, or if death would come swooping from the shadows with no warning.

She turned back to where Didier lay in a pool of crimson. She didn't know how to drag him out of there, he was so mangled. She looked into his unfocused eyes—eyes that had been locked onto hers during the passionate embrace only hours before. She needed to get him to the transport before the authorities arrived.

The police would be there to help at first, but they'd be bought off in time.

In a daze, she made her way to the bathroom, washed her face, and pulled on her clothes, which had been spared the splashing of his blood. She couldn't leave him here. As she crept out into the hall, and then the lobby, she learned that her task would be considerably easier than expected—everyone in the hotel was dead.

Boots wrapped Didier's body in layers of sheets and hoisted him over her shoulder, just as she had with so many others during the war. The pair of decades had taken their toll on her muscles, but her memories of the bad times were as youthful as ever. Her back ached and her knees creaked, but she still had the strength to haul him back to the transport. Boots had to get back to the *Capricious*, to safety.

She had to warn Cordell that Mother had made planetfall.

Duke Thiollier had been less than convinced when Nilah told him what she saw. He'd given her the sort of understanding nod one gives out of concern for the speaker, as if to say, "Tell me more, so I know what to say to the doctors." And why wouldn't he? She was accusing the most powerful body in motorsport of a vast, methodical conspiracy that would have taken years of planning and billions of argents to pull off. Of course it was laughable.

When she pointed out the "roughly glyph-shaped" nature of the track, he rightly countered that there were thousands of glyphs in existence, and almost everything complex enough could be described as "roughly glyph-shaped." Furthermore, it was a known fact that humans liked to build glyph-like objects; it was ingrained in the nature of their psyches like a perfect ratio.

At the heart of their disconnect, however, was the fact that he was a scribe and she was a mechanist. He could trace a single, solitary glyph, and she could build intricate machines to replicate and supplement all kinds of spells. There was always tension between scribes, who saw spellcraft as a natural art, and mechanists, who saw magic's boundless potential.

After her outburst post-bathhouse, he'd partitioned himself from her, suddenly indisposed for all manner of reasons. Nilah had two theories about what that meant. One annoyed her, and the other terrified her. Maybe he'd imagined himself the white knight, rescuing her so he could court her favor. If that was the case, he was distancing himself because he now understood how much trouble she'd be. Sleeping with a racer would be a good story, but a crazy racer would be too much trouble to pursue.

The more frightening theory was simple. Maybe he was part of the conspiracy. Maybe behind every gilded column, every immaculate statue, there was a knife, waiting to strike. But if that was true, it would have made more sense to leave her in the prison, where criminals and police could both do unto her as they would. From what she'd seen of the massive borehole prisons of Carré, no one would ever find her again.

When Orna arrived—unharmed but pissed off—Nilah knew Duke Thiollier wasn't part of the conspiracy. The quartermaster had been given all her weapons, and Ranger strode patiently behind her with enough firepower to level half the building. If Vayle had been planning to murder Nilah or hand her over to the masterminds behind Clowe's death, Orna needed to be out of the picture.

Nilah met Orna in the gardens, the twin lights of Carré's two moons splitting the shadows between a tidal green and rusty orange. Ranger's head spun in place as he tromped along, snapping in the direction of any movement. From what Nilah could tell, he was tracking the guards, the attendants, and maybe a few distant targets invisible to her.

"Heavens, am I happy to see you," said Nilah, taking long strides before embracing her companion. Orna smelled horrid and tensed up under her grip, but eventually relented and returned the embrace.

The quartermaster pulled away. "Tell me where I can bathe."

"I have exactly the place."

But she didn't. Nilah and Orna were refused entry to the Prokarthic baths on the grounds that the waters needed to recharge after having so many bathers. When Nilah argued, Orna told all assembled that she didn't need any of that garbage, and regular water would be more than enough.

And that was how they found themselves in a spacious, well-furnished bath attached to one of the palace rooms, Nilah sitting in the anteroom as Orna cleansed herself. Ranger stayed with Nilah, simultaneously keeping watch while relaying the conversation between the two women. Nilah had found a nice chair and nicer liquor, and despite any impending doom, she'd managed to relax. Someone accustomed to the stress of races always had to know where to find bliss the night before.

"You really should try the oils," Nilah urged, for what had to be the hundredth time.

"I just want soap. Where is the regular damned soap?" said Ranger in Orna's voice.

"A good routine doesn't use anything as harsh as soap. First, you want a sugar scrub to stop your calluses from getting worse."

"I like my calluses. They keep my fingers from getting cut while I work. And you're not going to get grease off with a damned sugar scrub."

"Well, sure, but you could be more careful while you work. I saw the way you'd been storing your tools. You could benefit from some cleanliness."

Ranger shrugged, which was odd for a death machine. "Why?

If I lose them, I can just beat the snot out of you and get some more."

Nilah sloshed her glass around and watched the rich red legs of the liquor drip down the sides. She'd grown used to Orna's constant jabs, and the more of them she suffered, the less painful they got. "That was a pretty good trick, shutting off my dermaluxes like that."

Ranger cocked his head, his lenses traveling up and down Nilah's arms. "Yeah, well... it was the only way to win, and I don't think I could do it again. Beat you, I mean... I don't think I could beat you again." Ranger looked away, perhaps ashamed. "You must be pretty happy with yourself right now."

"About getting a compliment?"

"About getting off our ship. It's all you've been able to talk about since you came on board." Orna's mocking impression of a Taitutian accent whistled through Ranger's speakers. "'I can't live in these conditions. It's disgusting. Where are the servants?'"

"You really have no idea how tough I am."

"Tough enough for ship life?"

Nilah considered the question for the first time. In the whole of the galaxy, there were precious few people she trusted to have her back. Her father and the prime minister were sure to protect her where they could, but those two were far away at the moment. Kristof showed unwavering support for her, even when Claire buckled. And lastly, the crew of the *Capricious* had treated her as well as one of their own. Better, even, since she wasn't required to do any chores.

She'd only been able to focus on escape, yet now that she had, Vayle's palace felt wrong in so many ways. Perhaps it was a disappointment. Perhaps it was a danger. But when she thought of being back on the ship, her heart calmed.

"Actually, yeah. I kind of wish I could stay."

Ranger's lenses locked onto her eyes. "I wouldn't kick you off if you wanted to come with us. Beats hanging around in a place like this."

Nilah blushed, and her dermaluxes gave off a bright shade of pink.

Orna groaned. "I don't know how you can stand to wear your emotions on your sleeve like that."

"I can suppress them."

"Except when you forget to, which is basically all the time. I always know what's happening in that tiny head of yours."

Nilah frowned. "Which is?"

"Oh, you're hot under the collar for me, little miss racer. The way you fawn is so pathetic with those puppy dog eyes."

Nilah took a long swig of her liquor. After the first bottle, she was starting to feel its effects, and her tongue had loosened. "Please. It's not like you're any better! You act so tough, like you're some kind of loner, but I've seen the way you look at me, too. Even without dermaluxes telling me your every bloody thought, your eyes linger just a bit overlong, don't you think?"

No response came, and Nilah squinted into her glass. Had she offended? Was Orna thinking it over? A little drunken flame inside her egged her onward.

"You know, if you were really tough, you'd do something about it, instead of hiding behind some little act. You'd come in here and—"

Orna's bare feet squelched against the tile as she appeared in the doorway, steam rising off her wet body. Her balled fists shook, and it seemed like the quartermaster had nerves. Then Nilah looked past her scarred belly and breasts to Orna's quivering white lips and clenching jaw. Her eyes were narrowed, her nose wrinkled with rage.

Nilah's breath caught. She'd made a critical mistake.

Then Orna said, "Ranger received a message from the ship. Boots just got back—flew an all-nighter to get there..."

"O-okay..."

"Didier is dead. The *Capricious* is coming to get us."

Chapter Thirteen

Double Apex

O nce dressed, Orna made her way through the palace like a cyclone, blowing past statues and colonnades, through galleries and salons. Ranger strode a few paces ahead of her, shoving attendants, staffers, and guests away, clearing the way for his master. Nilah followed in their wake, silently towed along behind the pair as though she were riding in their slipstream.

Orna's eyes remained red, but the quartermaster wouldn't cry. Quite the opposite: she possessed a violence in her countenance that Nilah hadn't seen before. She feared what her companion might do once they arrived at Vayle's chambers. And all the while, the words kept cycling through her mind: *Didier is dead.*

When they got closer to the duke's offices, things got a little more dicey. Two armed guards stepped between them and progress, blocking Ranger's path. Both men kept their hands on their rifles, but didn't level them. Ranger clacked his metal claws, and his servos let out a low, electronic growl.

Nilah swallowed. "We, uh, have some news for Vayle."

"We need to see Duke Thiollier, immediately," said Orna, her voice a flat contrast to her simmering expression.

"I'm afraid he's indisposed," said one of the guardsmen.

"It's important." A hot edge entered Orna's voice.

The guardsman cocked his head, then whispered something to the other man beside him, who jogged away. "If he's willing to see you, I'll need to see that you're disarmed."

Orna sneered. "Yeah. *If* he's willing to see us. I'll just hang on to my crap until then."

"As you wish."

They waited a few minutes, and when the other guard returned, he did so with a small cadre. Ranger went and stood against a wall, and Orna shoved her guns into the battle armor's hands. The guards searched Nilah with scanners, and Orna was subjected to a more thorough pat down. Satisfied that the pair posed no threat, the guards allowed the women to pass.

They found the duke in his office, a sprawling room of white marble and gold adorned with his pervasive family tapestries. Gargantuan statues flanked the room: the Thiollier matriarch and patriarch atop solid bronze bases that rose almost as high as Nilah. Vayle sat behind a desk formed of glass blocks, inlaid with refractive pathways to channel magical systems to its surface. He wore his royal uniform, medals adorning the breast of his doublet. When he stood, Nilah spotted his family saber at his side, the one he always wore to the races.

"We're leaving," said Nilah.

Vayle sighed. "And why are you—"

"One of our friends is dead," said Orna. "So our ship is coming to get us. We don't want to have a problem with the palace anti-air defenses."

"I see. I'm sorry. I'll let the guard towers know," said Vayle.

Nilah couldn't help but eye his outfit. Why was he wearing ceremonial garb? "You're dressed up."

He raised an eyebrow. "Yes, well, I've been on a call with His

Majesty's legal counsel. I've been strongly advised to extradite you to the Gantry Station authorities."

"I'll end up dead if you do that."

He crossed his arms. "I'm starting to come around to your way of thinking on that. I've been inundated with calls since I informed the planetary security forces of your arrival."

"You *what*?"

He shook his head. "Don't look at me like that. I kept it classified at the highest levels, so that only the heads of the great families know you're here."

Several soldiers in tan uniforms bustled into the room behind Nilah and Orna, their faces drawn and urgent. Nilah recognized them as Flamekeepers she'd seen on the way to the baths. The duke scowled at the interruption, and she could see that he'd become exasperated with all of the goings-on. The lead Flamekeeper, a bald fellow with striking brown eyes, stiffened under Vayle's gaze and saluted.

"Sir, we're here to arrest these two," he barked, pointing at Nilah and Orna. "Please stand clear."

"Hold on," said Vayle. "On what grounds?"

"Espionage and heresy," said the Flamekeeper. "They were spotted infiltrating your vaults and stealing from the royal family."

Vayle gave Nilah an ashen look of betrayal, and outrage bubbled over in her.

"Oh really?" shouted Nilah. "Do you have any bloody cameras on these vaults of yours? You're a liar!"

"You will be quiet," said the Flamekeeper, stepping closer, hand on the pommel of his sword. "The duke will not suffer a heretic to speak!"

"You think we'd steal from you when we're staying with you?" asked Orna.

"Heresy and theft..." said the duke. "From you of all people, Nilah?"

"Vayle, please!" said Nilah, looking to him with pleading eyes. "I know these are your men, but something is wrong! Don't send me away without checking the cameras. You owe it to yourself."

"Do not make demands of the duke," said the Flamekeeper. "Sir, I must advise against reviewing the evidence in the presence of the accused. Her lawyers—"

"She's right," said Vayle, sitting down at his desk and folding his hands. "I want to see for myself."

Maybe it was because Nilah didn't trust anyone. Maybe it was because she felt the presence of a spell building. Or maybe it was because she saw the man's face harden in the split second before he cast. Either way, Nilah understood the onrushing betrayal, and her racer's instincts kicked in.

The Flamekeeper cast his glyph, lightning-fast, and seized hold of it like a ball before flinging it at Nilah. She jumped and shoved Orna out of its path, slamming both of them onto the hard marble. The ball struck Vayle's desk, and she heard the duke screaming amid licking flames. Nilah rolled and saw the pack of Flamekeepers, each tracing glyphs while looking at her with murder in their eyes.

"Go! Go! Go!" she cried, yanking a dazed Orna to her feet.

They dashed in the direction of the matriarch statue as the sizzle of completed spells filled the air. Both women barely managed to skid behind the bronze base before the whole world seemed to catch fire around them. Years of racing safety had taught Nilah something important for this day: if she was ever trapped in flames, she had to hold her breath. Her hand shot to Orna's nose and mouth, and they backed up against the burning-hot pedestal to shield themselves from the crashing waves of fire.

When her bare skin touched the bronze, it burned, but Nilah felt the presence of an arcane machine within. Her mechanist's senses described the system's purpose to her in fuzzy details, and she forced herself to stay in contact with the hot metal. The statues were dispersers—and someone had switched them off.

Nilah traced a glyph and slapped her free palm against the pedestal, fighting through the pain to link with the machine and search for its activation. Security was light, probably because no one expected a physical hacker in the duke's inner sanctum. With all of her concentration, she was able to switch on the dispersers.

The bass thud of arcane waveforms filled her ears, and things got a lot colder as the raging inferno popped out of existence. Nilah thanked her maker that these dispersers worked better than the ones at the track, overloading any exposed glyphs they could find. She hazarded a glance at Vayle's desk, but given the blackened scorch marks all over it, he was certainly dead, his beautiful body burned to a crisp.

At least they couldn't cast anymore, and the dispersers would knock down any slinger bolts, too. It'd be hand to hand from here on out, and Nilah had full confidence that she and Orna could punch their way out of the room.

Drawing swords sliced the silence that followed, and Nilah swallowed hard. *Oh right. They have swords.*

The rumble of high-caliber slingers echoed from the open doorway to the office.

"Ranger is trying to get to us, but he's taking fire," Orna whispered. "I'm going to remote pilot him. You keep them busy while I concentrate."

"I thought you could operate him and fight at the same time!"

"You might be surprised to find out the palace guard is pretty good. They've got him pinned, and we need him to escape. Now get out there."

"Do you see a sword in my hand?"

Orna winked. "You said Flicker was unbeatable. I had no idea you were such a chicken."

Nilah clambered to her feet, where she could peek around the column and see six Flamekeepers leering at her. "This conversation isn't over."

"Make sure you survive to finish it, then," Orna chuckled.

Nilah shook her head. Why did she always like the crazy ones?

She kept her hands visible as she crossed into the room, all swords pointed at her. There were two women and four men, each one equipped with particularly nasty-looking Carrétan heavy sabers. Vayle's body had begun to stink up the room, and she tried not to focus on the smell. "All right, boys and girls, here's what's going to happen: I'm going to hurt you—a lot—unless you turn around and walk every one of those hideous uniforms of yours out of here."

The leader glanced at his companions, and they began to laugh.

She rolled back her sleeves, exposing her dermaluxes, which began to flash in time with her bouncing stance. She pointed to the man at the front of the vanguard. "You. Come here and get broken."

The leader charged her, unmasked murder in his eyes as he swiped his sword at her. She ducked under the deadly crescent, and in a single swift movement, she took him by the throat and slammed him neck-first into the marble. His sword went skidding across the stone, and for good measure, she straddled him and gave him three swift blows across the nose, snapping it.

When she stood, his blood dripping from her knuckles, and smiled at the others, the mirth melted from their expressions. It would be all business from here on out. They dashed in after her, and it took all of her speed and reflexes to keep them corralled to one side. Provided that they only attacked from one direction, she could dodge and weave, and their strikes would get tangled.

If they managed to flank her at any point, though, it would all be over.

Her Flicker master had tested her against multiple opponents in the studio, but never anything like this. The Flamekeepers were swift, driven, and vicious, and she only gave ground. With the momentum against her in the face of myriad flashing swords, she couldn't find the room or time to strike back, and they would have her cornered in no time. A forceful lunge brought one Flamekeeper too close, and Nilah snapped a jab into the woman's chin. The punch was weak, off-balance, and utterly ineffective. Nilah took another step back, and her heel touched a column. The Flamekeepers quickly responded by closing ranks around her and leveling swords to skewer her.

Nilah rushed toward them, ramping her dermaluxes to blinding intensity and juking past the tips of blades. She latched onto the pommel of the nearest man's sword, twisting it in his grasp while fanning her arm to distract the others. When he didn't want to let go, she struck his eyes with stiffened fingers and drove her knee into his groin.

Taking his sword, she swiped wildly to open up some space, but the others easily riposted the attacks. She wasn't trained in the art of the blade, and they obviously were. She danced around the other columns, leading her attackers and trying to keep them to one side as best she could.

A stroke of luck took a blond man off balance, and Nilah knocked aside his blade before palm-striking him in the dead center of his throat. He reeled back, sputtering, and she saw an opportunity to drive the blade into his heart.

She'd never killed anyone, though.

In the moment's hesitation, another woman planted her boot into Nilah's back and sent her sprawling to the floor. She went down hard, her saber spiraling away across the marble. The Flame-keepers lunged for her, inexorable death closing in.

In a whirl of screeching teeth and claws, Ranger blasted through a wall and into the melee. Nilah took the opportunity to get clear, glancing back as the chaos unfolded. Ranger sliced into two of the tan uniforms with his talons, then snatched another one by the head, smashing it into the nearby column. Their blades clanked harmlessly off his armor, and Ranger seized their swords, shattering them with his fist. He cut throats. He snapped necks. And as the last Flamekeeper tried to crawl away, Ranger leapt onto her and tore her to ribbons.

When the dust settled, not a single tan uniform remained unsullied by crimson. The beast stood in the center of the carnage he'd wrought, servos hissing and fingers flexing.

Nilah blinked and checked herself for wounds; no punctures, no blood on her, nothing except a mild burn. Orna emerged from her hiding place, checking her circlet to make sure it was still tight around her head.

"Oh, my god..." Nilah breathed.

Orna dusted her hands, and Ranger followed suit, flicking away the blood of his prey.

"The next time you get a chance to kill a killer," said Orna, gently taking Nilah by the shoulders, "you drive that blade in deep, understand? End them."

Nilah nodded, shaken. "Okay."

Orna clapped her on the shoulder. "You're okay. Dust yourself off and let's call the *Capricious* and let them know there's a problem. They might not get a warm welcome from the palace guard after what's happened."

"It's worse than that. Those dispersers...someone had deactivated them. Someone in the palace guard might be in on this."

As if on cue, a series of klaxons sounded, followed by a general announcement: "Thiollier Palace is under attack. Repeat. Thiollier Palace is under attack. Apprehend Nilah Brio, Orna Sokol, and Malik Jan. Use of deadly force is authorized." Flashing lights dropped from the ceiling, painting the ornate palace a shade of vermilion.

"We've got to warn the ship," said Orna, sprinting over to guard the door alongside Ranger.

Nilah made her way to Vayle's smoldering chair and gently pushed his corpse away with her foot. She wiped the crystalline surface free of soot and tapped in the *Capricious*'s comm code.

Cordell's harried voice came over the other side of the line. "Duke, I don't know if you're in on this, but so help me—"

"This is Nilah. Duke Thiollier is dead," she cut in. "And we're under attack. You need to get us out of here."

An explosion crackled across Cordell's transmission. "Interesting. And tricky," he grunted. "You're going to have to hold that thought a moment." He barked some orders to Armin and Aisha before returning. "We're kind of under attack now ourselves. The airspace over Thiollier Palace is a death trap. If we try to go in there, only bits of us are coming to your rescue. We can't extract you from your location."

Nilah's heart jumped into her throat. "You can't rescue us?"

"I'm sorry. Not unless you can get some distance." Another explosion. "Damn it, I just fixed this thing!"

Nilah pressed a button on the desk, and a glass rod the length of her palm emerged from a recess. She held it to her ear. "Captain, track on this comm unit. I think we can get clear within fifteen minutes."

"All right. We're loitering. Get my crew out of there, and I'll take you anywhere you want to go."

Nilah pocketed the comm crystal. She wasn't a professional spy, but even she knew that the *Capricious* wouldn't be the only one tracking her with it. The duke's murderers would be on them every step of the way. But she'd have to deal with that later. She jogged to Orna.

"The captain can't pick us up from here," Nilah said. "We're going to have to get clear of the palace."

"Steal a flyer? That could be fun." A spell ricocheted off the wall next to Orna's head, and Ranger loped down the hall in its direction.

"Cordell said the airspace was locked down."

Screams rang out from Ranger's direction. Orna cocked her head. "What do you want to do then? Surrender? Doesn't seem wise."

Nilah smiled. "Vayle was a rich race fan. And what do rich race fans have?"

Orna nodded, catching her idea. "Fast cars. Let's get Malik and get the hell out of here."

When Nilah and Orna reached Malik's hallway, they found no blood or gore, but a pile of clean bodies outside his door. The men and women there had dropped like sacks of bricks, weapons strewn across the floor, and there wasn't a single spell's scorch mark to be found. Whatever had killed these soldiers had been swift and surgical.

Then Nilah heard one of them snore.

Upon closer inspection, each and every soldier was merely unconscious, their chests rising and falling with slow, peaceful breaths. Nilah, Orna, and Ranger stepped over the slumbering killers, gingerly approaching Malik's open doorway.

"Malik," hissed Nilah when they got close enough. "Don't shoot us."

The doctor came striding out of his room, dressed and clean, as though he'd just been preparing to depart for an evening on the town. He adjusted his cuffs and inspected the trio, his eyes lingering overlong on Ranger's bloody carapace.

"Good," he said, his face impassive, "you've arrived."

"What did you do to them?" asked Nilah, her voice a whisper.

"What's it look like?" said Orna. "He's a sleep mage."

"It's true," he said. "Undisturbed, they won't wake for a few hours. The alarms provide a constant noise pattern, so they'll sleep through them."

Nilah watched in astonishment as one of the soldiers snuggled up to another, nuzzling into the crook of his neck.

Malik shrugged. "I thought it was best not to kill anyone, given the political ramifications. I see you've taken a different approach."

Ranger unholstered his large-caliber slinger and took aim at a sleeper's head.

The fury in Orna's eyes could've melted steel. "Didier is dead. These men tried to slaughter us. Maybe a little killing makes a lot of sense."

"I know. The captain called me before he called you," said Malik. "Save your ammunition. There'll be plenty of people to shoot between us and our escape."

"A nap is getting off too lightly," she growled.

"I agree, but we're better than them. Let's get to the gardens and call for pickup."

Orna nodded at Ranger, who put the slinger back. "We can't. Palace airspace is too hot, but Nilah has a plan that takes us to the garage."

"Interesting. Lead on," he replied.

The grand galleries and sprawling corridors of Duke Thiollier's palace offered dozens of hiding places for aggressors, and swift death awaited the band of fugitives around every corner. With Malik's help, however, they were able to remain largely undetected. If a guard stood in their way, Malik would draw his murmuring purple glyph and hurl the spell into the sentry, who would collapse under the weight of his own exhaustion.

Outside the garage, however, they encountered a patrol of six men, all armed and alert. Nilah recognized the pink glow emanating from the tips of their rifle barrels: expensive homing fléchettes. It took her a moment to realize that those darts would be coated in a deadly neurotoxin.

Nilah's two companions exchanged a series of complex hand signals, and Nilah stopped them. "I don't know your bloody gestures," she whispered. "What's my part in this?"

"Nothing," said Orna. "Hang back, and we'll handle it."

Malik nodded his assent.

"Hold on, hold on," said Nilah, glancing around. "I am not going to simply sit here while you two trot off to play hero. I'm not useless."

"We don't think that," said Malik, "but we've got to protect you because you're the most important person here."

Ranger's armor quietly popped and hissed, opening to reveal the operator's seat. Nilah's eyes darted to the armor's soft, rubberized chinks—the joints, the neck, anywhere a flechette might worm into his interior.

"The most important?" Nilah began.

Orna smirked as she stepped backward into Ranger. "You're the driver, dumbass. Malik, you ready?"

"Try to keep them grouped up," he replied.

Ranger sealed Orna inside and sunk into a low, catlike crouch before bolting into the open garage antechamber. The guards' cries of alarm were stifled by dozens of automatic pops from their slingers. Nilah had been right: they were hybrid slingers, firing projectiles coated in spells to home in on Orna's suit. Pink streaks filled the cavernous space like swarming bumblebees, clanking off Orna's suit as she bounded from floor, to wall, to ceiling, then dropped down, leaving jagged claw marks in her wake.

Orna didn't shoot at them, she only defended herself as best she could, though Nilah could spot several glistening fléchettes embedded in Ranger's soft parts. A single prick from any one of them on Orna's exposed arms could mean her demise. Nilah racked her brain for any way to help, but given the swarm of dancing pink death, she couldn't charge into the room. A large spell hissed beside her, and Nilah turned to find Malik mid-cast, his purple glyph at least a meter wide.

Nilah could finally see Malik's age with his face distorted in exertion. The glyph clearly taxed his stamina, but he carried on with the inscription, bringing the last ligature to a close. The spell snapped to life, then collapsed into a strobing ball of energy. He shooed her out of the way, pushing the flashing magic into the group of guards before ducking back behind the corner.

But it was too late. One of the soldiers had caught sight of him and fired off a volley of screaming metal in their direction. It whizzed down the corridor toward them, rounding the corner. Nilah's reflexes kicked in, and she rolled away, hearing the fléchettes embed in the wall beside her.

A low boom sounded inside the anteroom, followed by shuffling, a clank, and finally, silence.

Malik brushed himself off and smiled. "See? Easily done."

Nilah's eyes locked onto a golden glint just above his foot. Her mind wanted to make it a piece of rubble, part of Malik's outfit, anything but a fléchette. But there it lay, buried in his calf muscle: a trio of guidance fins, a smooth barrel, and a deadly payload delivery system. A spasm tugged at the corner of Malik's mouth, and his fingers flexed.

"Malik?" Nilah's voice was weak. "You...There's a..."

Malik's legs bulged as though electricity coursed through his body. His eyes darted to his hand, and he raised it to carve a shaky spell. "It's o-okay. I just need to h-hibernate until you c-can get me to m-m-med—"

He tried to write a glyph, but his convulsing fingers wouldn't listen to him, the soft luminescence of purple smoke dissipating before he could make any progress. Malik shook his fingers out like he was freezing cold and tried again before grinding to a halt. His hand locked in place, and he cried out in pain.

"I've got this," he whispered, his tongue sticking on the "s" sound. "I can—"

Nilah rushed to him and yanked the dart from his calf, a wicked barb taking with it a squirt of blood. "Malik, stay calm! The poison will go slower, if—"

The bands of muscle through his legs creaked like an old rope being pulled taut. His lips pulled back in a rictus, and for the first time, Nilah saw panic in his eyes. His neck bulged as the poison worked its way toward his brain.

"Come on," said Nilah, tears forming in her eyes. "Concentrate."

His fingers flared purple, guttering like a match flame, and held. He scowled at his hand, as though chastising it. Haltingly, he began tracing a glyph.

"Put me in c-coma. Get...m-m-me to sh-ship. F-fast."

Hot streaks of water ran from Nilah's eyes. Malik had been such a paragon of calm and rationality, and seeing him afraid shook her deeply. She kept him as steady as she could, for fear of interrupting his casting. He wouldn't get a second chance.

"S'okay." He sucked a shallow breath and tried to speak, his voice barely audible. He pushed himself to the last stroke of the spell. "Tell...Aish—s'okay."

His spell snapped to life, a whistling ball of violet energy. Malik fell forward into Nilah's arms, and it was like being struck with a statue, his body was so rigid. Nilah had to tear herself free as he began to curl around her like a dying insect, each muscle going taut.

Nilah eased him onto his side and placed a hand on his shoulder, finding only strips of hardened muscle. "Oh, god, Malik. Okay. You're going to be okay. We'll get you to the ship," she whispered, stroking his back.

His eyes remained fixed on hers until his spell wrapped around him, sucking into his flesh like water into a sponge. Its work done, the poison began to thaw from his body, muscles slowly going limp, and he let forth a gurgling sigh.

Nilah placed a hand in front of his mouth and nose—and felt nothing. Sobbing, she wiped a tear away and reached out again with the wet side of her hand.

A coolness—breath out. She waited, teeth clenched, lips quivering, for him to inhale.

He breathed—slow, weak, but breathing all the same.

She stood and wiped her nose. *No time to go to pieces.* Her eyes darted to what remained of the antechamber: a pile of bodies, and at the center of them, deathly still, Ranger, its joints peppered with the poisonous little darts. Pinpricks of gold riddled it from groin to neck, and it lay like a slain lion.

"No!" Nilah dashed toward it, not bothering to look for threats anymore.

She couldn't lose Orna, too. Not now. Not after all this. She traced her glyph as she reached Ranger, knelt down, and thumped her bare palm against his chestplate. The system rose against her, and she wrestled its AI out of the way of the armor locks. The computer's defenses evolved quickly, but Nilah was faster, and she disengaged Ranger's bolts. With their brief contact, however, it had become a much more formidable opponent; Nilah prayed she wouldn't have to fight it again anytime soon. The armor popped open, revealing the still body of the quartermaster inside. Nilah couldn't see where any of the darts had pierced the protection, but even a little puncture would've done the trick.

With trembling fingers, Nilah reached down to Orna's neck to check for a pulse. "No, I'm begging you, no. Please get up. Please."

Orna's breath caressed the underside of Nilah's arm as she reached across. Nilah dared to hope.

"Orna?"

The quartermaster yawned and blinked the sleep from her eyes with a lazy grin. She sat up, brushing Nilah's hand away. "I take it we got them all?" She glanced about for danger, then soured as she noticed Nilah's tears.

"Where's Malik?"

Nilah's breath caught. With all her might, she managed to force the words, "They...they got him. He forced himself—into a coma. We have to get him back to the ship right now or—"

She barely managed to snap her hand back in time as Ranger's chestplate slammed shut. The mechanical beast rose underneath her, sending her tumbling off, and its knife-claws clacked in its hands. The armor hissed and whirred, and when it turned to face Nilah, it didn't offer her help rising to her feet.

It merely said, "Get to the garage."

"Not without—"

"Find us a getaway car."

Nilah backed away through the garage doors, leaving the enraged quartermaster standing amid the pile of sleeping bodies, blades sharp and willing.

The garage stretched before her like a cove teeming with exotic fish. Sports cars and flyers of every color of the rainbow filled the bay, just as breathtaking as the first time she'd seen them. Duke Vayle Thiollier's collection of fine vehicles rivaled any in the galaxy, valued in the billions of argents. The first time she'd visited the duke's palace, she'd wandered this hall for hours, marveling at the sights within: the archrome finishes, the hypertuned engines, the brilliant and bizarre automotive histories contained therein. The duke's garage had been a temple as holy as any race paddock.

And now she had to steal one of these cars or die.

A scream rang out behind her—one of the guards in the antechamber—and she tried her best to ignore it as she sprinted down the row. She couldn't take a flyer; the airspace was too well defended. The wheeled vehicles would be tricky too; the roads around the duke's palace were fraught with blind corners and bluff faces, scarcely protected by ancient guardrails. She ran down the specs in her head as she jogged down the row:

Robison R70—too slow through the corners, notorious understeer.

Start XR—good brake horsepower, low top speed.

Langheim GP Papania—a classic, but not exactly quick on a modern scale.

On and on she went, imagining the scenario to come. The palace guard was clearly a part of the conspiracy, or they'd been tricked into thinking she and Orna were the murderers. They would come after her with everything they had, and that meant fast flyers, homing missiles, and worse. If the pair really wanted to try an overland getaway through the mountains, their drive had to be the total package: speed, acceleration, cornering, and braking.

That was when she saw the Carriger Hyper 1, the groundbreaking vision upon which her own car had been based. Before Lang Autosport bought the team, Michael Carriger had pushed his people to sixteen galactic championship victories.

She looked at the fragile bodywork and wondered if it would hold Ranger. When the far doors slid open and a pack of slinger-toting palace guards slipped into the garage, she decided there wouldn't be time to test; she'd just go for it.

Nilah popped off the steering wheel, hopped into the cockpit, and slid low. She wished she could get low enough to hide in the footwell, but the car wasn't exactly spacious. The seat had been uncomfortably molded to someone else's posterior, but this was only supposed to be a getaway, not a two-hour race, and a little survival was worth a lot of discomfort. She slid the steering wheel home and locked it, running her fingers over the controls. What was the startup sequence for the Hyper 1? Did Vayle keep his cars fueled?

She wrote out her spell, and her mechanist's art linked her to the computer.

It responded that it did not, in fact, have any fuel.

Oh, good. I've climbed into my own coffin.

The computer chirped; there were two eidolon crystals in the engine with some juice. The feature predated the Arclight Booster, and was for boosting and overtaking strictly within designated zones. To use them to operate the car on all parts of the track would've been against the rules...and it would burn out the engine.

She could probably keep the car together for ten minutes once she routed power from the crystals to the main engine.

Guards fanned out through the rows of cars, their slingers popping off shots at her exposed head. A bolt landed on the intake next to her head, sending tiny shards of stinging fibron into her exposed neck.

Nilah yelped and traced her glyph. The connection made, the Hyper 1's engine screamed to life, causing the guards to jump.

Nilah wasted no time getting underway, slipping it into drive and lurching forward. The cold wheels refused to grip, so she slammed down the throttle, spinning out clouds of choking polymer dust. The guards staggered backward, covering their faces and firing wildly into the smoke. Nilah winced as another shot almost took her nose off.

The second her wheels were the right temperature, she rocketed forward. She struck a guard in mid-spell, and the man bounced off, encased in a shimmering bubble of magic. Nilah hurtled down the row of sports cars toward the open door—but she didn't have Orna. She veered hard right, and the Hyper 1 understeered, nearly sending her into one of the duke's all-terrain vehicles. Her own Hyper 8 was so vastly different, so much subtler in its handling, that she needed a moment to readjust. She glided past an array of stunt fliers and watched in horror as the oncoming palace guards fired at her from behind cars. Nilah whipped left and right in a serpentine pattern, as though she was warming her tires on a formation lap. A hail of spells slammed into the cars around her, and Nilah recognized the white oval of a discus round. One shot from that, and her car would be cut in half. One of the guards twirled out a glyph and lassoed the race car with a green arc of power.

Nilah felt the magic trying to wind its way inside to gum up her gearbox, and so she connected it directly to the eidolon output. The shock of power traveled back up the line and popped in the guard's face, throwing him onto the hood of the car behind him.

As she completed the loop of the garage, she slid directly in front of the door to the antechamber, her front wing lined up exactly on the garage doors. She couldn't stick around here. They'd button the place up and she'd never get out.

Come on, Orna.

The only thing louder than the roar of the Hyper 1's engine was the sickening crash of Ranger landing on top of the chassis, its clawed feet digging into the body panels. The car would've been priceless to collectors, but now, with a rapidly melting engine and punctured aero work, it was junk.

Really fast junk.

"Drive," commanded Orna, booming through Ranger.

Nilah dropped the hammer, only to be rewarded with wheel spin. She'd been afraid this would happen. Ranger was heavy—far too heavy to start the car from a dead stop. The grip would be all wrong, the aerodynamics would be broken. A discus round whizzed over Nilah's head, and the robot dodged, returning fire and shredding several priceless cars. Orna fired two bright orange spells from her slinger and millions of argents' worth of automotives burst into flames.

"Damn it!" shouted Nilah, unable to help herself. "That was a Devlin ST!"

"And now it's not," said Orna. "Let's go."

No more spellfire echoed in the wake of the explosion; the guards were dead or hiding. Nilah glanced into her rearview mirror and saw Malik hanging limply underneath Ranger's arm, his hands drooping to the ground.

"I need you to push!" Nilah called back.

Ranger locked its claws around the rear wing with a clank and ran forward, shoving the car. Nilah let off the brakes and dropped into first, slowly taking over for the robot. Once they were coasting, the metal beast leapt onto the body, its talons barely missing Nilah's head as it straddled the intake port behind her. The harsh scratching of regraded steel on fibron filled her ears, and she wished with all her might for a helmet. One slipup from Ranger, and it would have jammed its foot into her head.

"Hang on!" Nilah shouted, dodging flaming wreckage. The

handling was sluggish, but with her psychic link to the Hyper 1, she could soften the suspension on the outside and compensate a little. Nilah downshifted and laid into the accelerator, zipping toward the garage door and the open night air around Thiollier Palace. The lights outdoors flared, and she recognized searchlights. They'd be waiting for her in fliers, perhaps with more of those fléchettes. They'd certainly launch a volley of rockets.

Human reaction times were terrible. If she could get up enough speed, maybe she could get clear before a wave of magical death crushed their escape. She downshifted again; too much acceleration, and it'd be wheelspin, not enough, and they'd emerge too slow. She watched her revs: *a little more.* Nilah white-knuckled the wheel as they shot through the opening in the palace wall.

They burst forth into the courtyard, a line of fire from Carrétan scout fliers decimating the palace wall behind them. Though Nilah felt heat surge around her, they'd gotten clear. Orna straightened and returned a few rounds, but Ranger's grip was too tenuous to hang on to the car, Malik, and the slinger. With a final shot into the front gate, Orna gave up on trying to fight back and stowed her slinger.

They raced through the remains of the gate and down into the serpentine paths of the mountainside. In years past, Vayle would take these roads while redlining the revs of his favorite sports cars, almost like a racetrack. Nilah had joined him once, and had dreamed of doing it again one day, but not like this. The roads would be easy to close, and the authorities would be all over them. She took a sluggish corner in her overweight race car, and several flaming rounds from the fliers melted the front wing. It wasn't a problem to lose it—her current configuration had plenty of downforce.

"I'm switching to knock rounds," said Orna. "If they set up a blockade, just keep driving. I'm going to hammer it off the road."

"A knock round won't lift a car!"

"The ones I make do."

Only a flimsy guardrail on the left side of the car protected them from a sheer drop down the cliff face and into the Gray below. Nilah rounded a downward-sweeping hairpin and spotted flashing lights. Ranger's slinger snapped into its hand, and two blue bolts went flying from the muzzle, striking the center of the blockade. Thudding bursts of energy swept the cars over the face of the bluff and sent policemen flying like rag dolls—some of them into the Gray with their vehicles. As she weaved between the prone bodies, Nilah forced herself not to look to see whether or not they lived.

"You can't just shoot policemen!"

"This planet runs on corruption," grunted Orna. "It's kill or die."

Nilah had to veer across the lanes to avoid a strafing run from one of the fliers. The pavement exploded into lava before her, and she had to take care that she didn't roll over it and blow a tire. Meanwhile, the other flier blasted the corner ahead with frosty rounds of ice spells, freezing the sharp turn solid. They'd never take it at speed, if they could take it at all.

"Orna!"

"I see it," she said, and fired a knock at it. The blue bolt burst in the air, its shock wave instantly powdering the ice. A second airburst round blasted the ice free.

They shot around the turn, barely maintaining traction, and the lights of a mountainside village loomed large in the distance.

"We've got to get rid of these fliers," said Orna. "When we hit that town, get ready to head around the block a few times."

Nilah shot down the road toward the blaring lights of the town. A glance into her rearview showed a smoking spire above the mountaintop, the Flamekeepers' treacherous blaze roaring out of control on the top levels—the end of a short, sad relationship with Duke Vayle Thiollier.

"Look out!" boomed Orna, and Nilah barely weaved between a pair of parked delivery trucks. "Keep your eyes on the road and double back. I've got to get rid of a few pests."

The suspension strained in agony as Ranger leapt free of the Hyper 1 and began to climb the nearest townhouse, its claws shredding concrete to dust as it scrabbled up the side.

Free of her burden, Nilah felt the grip of her tires catch in that familiar way. She wouldn't be able to establish the flow of a PGRF track, sinking into a perfect rhythm from turn to turn, but she could certainly react, and she was one of the PGRF's finest. The Hyper 1 screamed under her fingertips, and she forced her spirit deeper inside, her magic intertwining with the car's subsystems. The few blocks that comprised the little palace town may have been littered with civilian vehicles, bystanders, and less-than-perfect road paving, but they still formed a circle...

And this was racing.

Chapter Fourteen

Extradition

Boots keyed on the Midnight Runner, the glow of its heads-up display filling her eyes with prismatic light. The *Capricious* bucked with an explosive hit, and she grit her teeth. Even though the belly of the ship was its most reinforced part, she couldn't be sure it would survive a direct hit from an advanced anti-aircraft battery. She'd felt the crunch of heavy magic a thousand times, and yet she tensed with every glancing blow. Surely military spells hadn't come so far since the Famine War that they rendered Cordell's shields useless. Their captain could deflect almost anything, right?

Her mind flashed to the flaming wreckage of the *Capricious* in the Battle of Laconte. For a marauder-class crew, it was always do or die.

Sometimes, it was both.

"*Capricious*, this is Boots, check in."

"Boss here. Copy that. Sixty seconds to release," radioed Cordell, his voice tense with concentration. She knew he'd be on the bridge, focusing his magic through the amps. Hopefully their recent repairs would hold.

"Yes, Captain. Sitrep?"

Armin's sour voice filled her comms. "Prince here. Nilah's locator is making circles in the town of Arbrevert, attracting the attention of every provincial guard throughout the region. Given the speed of the movement, she's still alive."

"And the extraction point? How is it?" asked Boots, but she already knew the answer; it would be bad. She squeezed her eyes tight and tried to get back into the zone. Fighting Mother's battle-group had been a pain, but that was open, airless space. Here, she'd face the effects of gravity and atmosphere. It'd be a live drop zone, like the bad old days.

"You've got sixteen bandits: five provincial fighters and a motorcade," said Armin. "I hope you're good."

"Just remember," said Cordell, "our ship is solid. This is what he was designed for, so let's go get some. Aerial supremacy is ground supremacy."

It'd been almost twenty years since she'd dropped in gravity, and it was quite a trick back in the day. If the *Capricious* maneuvered too hard during Boots's egress, she could be bounced around inside the hull, only to emerge a pile of debris. The idea was to minimize risk by firing her front impulse thrusters as hard as she could, slowing her to a dead stop while her hosts sped away from her. Then she could fall for a short span to rile everyone's targeting before boosting away. Her nav glass showed their altitude at just under four hundred meters—not much room to move.

Cordell added, "Boots, we don't have to win this one. We just have to fight through. You're my only wing."

"Copy, Boss," she said, and the cargo bay door wailed behind her, the rushing wind full of deadly spells and magic shrapnel. Any enemy craft present would recognize a launch, so it was time to drop before they could fill the *Capricious* with a firestorm of spells. "Mag locks disengaging in three...two...one..."

Her dampers blunted the edge of the thrust, but Boots's head still slammed forward with their force. Like a damned rookie, she'd left her fighter's internal gravity calibrated for space actions, and as she began to fall, she cursed her weightlessness. She may have been a hardened spacer, but falling still felt all wrong. Open, starry sky filled her view, along with the ruby gleam of more than a dozen threat warnings.

Her ship's dispersers immediately kicked on, knocking out two of the larger attack spells headed her way. Fragments of glyphs twisted across her hull, and she boosted through them like gossamer webs. The thrusters glued her back into her seat as she accelerated past the swollen armored belly of the *Capricious*, and her canopy shields glowed with the friction of atmosphere. Boots tapped on the console glass, increasing the power of her dampers as she rolled out of the way of another huge fire spell. It sizzled past her, its connective strands hot enough to slice through the toughest materials in the galaxy.

Boots wheeled her Midnight Runner in a wide arc, soaring around mountain peaks until she came full circle to her home ship. Streamers of energy from the city below split the night sky in two as round after round pelted the *Capricious*'s shields. The city's antispacecraft measures would tear apart a normal ship in seconds. A marauder-class vessel could withstand more punishment, but not much.

"Get to work, Boots," said Cordell, the strain of his shield spell thinning his voice. "First target is Ratchet eight-one-four, two kilometers, five hundred ASL."

Boots zipped toward the scrambled palace fighters, her slinger cannons armed and ready for business. As she coasted over Arbrevert, she slipped a few exploding rounds into a surface-to-air gun, transforming its tower into a pillar of flame and debris. She glanced over her shoulder as she sailed clear of the city limits and spotted the other anti-air tower. Sensing her desires, the Runner's glass highlighted the remaining objectives on the heads-up display. She yanked back on the stick and sank back into her seat as she rolled the craft, executing a spinning turn.

Ahead of her, fighters attacked the *Capricious* from above while Cordell kept the shields directed at the antispacecraft slingers below. As long as the surface-to-air guns were operational, he wouldn't be able to protect the ship from the smaller threats above.

And there was the vehicle convoy, taking potshots at Boots. She peeled off and sunk below the city's elevation, roaring along the mountainside as she circled. Thankfully, the Carrétan starfighters didn't give chase. If she was lucky, that mistake would cost her enemy the battle. She surged above Arbreverr's skyline and planted a series of shots into another gun tower, striking all along its length. She lined up for a strafing run at the remaining cannon, but stopped short of firing when she couldn't get a clean shot. A skirmish in space was one thing, but a missed target in a city meant she might hit a house, a school, a hospital. Someone outside of the battle would die.

She hadn't always been so soft. During the last days of Clarkesfall, there was no such thing as a civvy. Famine had destroyed everything, and each person was part of the mad dash for scraps. But this wasn't war. At least, not that she knew of.

The surface of Cordell's spell arced and spit where slingers hammered it.

"Boots, I'm losing my shields here!" Cordell had genuine panic in his voice.

"You can hold it, Boss!"

"Prince here. He can't. Take out the remaining gun or we're dead in five seconds," added Armin.

There wasn't time to circle back for another strafing run, and in the planet's gravity, she couldn't execute a backward spin. She had to keep moving forward or she'd drop out of the sky like a rock.

"Four..."

She'd have to make it a wide loop if she didn't want to fly directly into the path of the antispacecraft spells, so she opened up her thrusters and pulled back on the flight stick.

"Three..."

The *Capricious* and the city buildings appeared before her as she hit the zenith of her loop, followed by the hot, steady stream of arcane energy lancing across her vision. Upside down, she could almost line it up.

"Two..."

"Shut the hell up!" She loosed a pair of bolts into the cannon structure and watched a satisfying fireball envelop the whole thing. She threw the ship into a hard bank and nearly blacked out as her blood pooled in her legs. Even with the dampers active, a fight inside a gravity well was no joke.

"Good kill," said Armin.

"Now we're talking!" shouted Cordell, and the ship's shields swung from his belly to the upper decks, taking out one of the fighters that had strayed too close like a giant hand swatting a fly from the heavens. The other fighters scattered away, frightened, but they'd be back. If Boots could get in there and mix it up with them—

"Orna here. We could use a little help!"

Boots searched her keel slinger cameras to find the quartermaster almost directly below her. Ranger jumped across the road, its slinger roaring with sparkling magic. The robot seemed clunkier than she remembered...encumbered. Was it carrying Nilah over its shoulder? As if reading Boots's mind, a race car screamed up the main drag, a couple of pursuers shooting over the lane after her. It wasn't Nilah in Ranger's arms, so it was...Malik?

"Copy, Ranger. Help is on the way," said Armin. "Boots, light up that convoy."

Boots whipped her craft around, slammed home the throttle, and braced herself to line up for a strafing run on the goons dogging Orna's path. She'd have to place her shots carefully, or she might plant a round in someone's living room. The motorcade was easy to spot, their slingers carelessly frying everything in sight as they burned across the streets of Arbrevert after their prey.

"Are you going to shoot them or what, Boots?" Orna hissed, scrabbling across an exploding rooftop.

"Maybe I might." Boots lined up parallel to the street and squeezed the trigger, blistering the tarmac with molten magic. Two of the lead cars hit the patch and went skating into a spin as their tires melted.

The force of her shots shattered windows, and Boots winced. "We shouldn't be fighting here!"

"Tell that to them!" Orna grunted.

The Midnight Runner thumped as her dispersers auto-fired. Someone down below had smacked her hull with a rust-inducing sabotage spell. She only hoped her countermeasures had caught it in time.

"Help! Help over here!" cried Nilah over the comms, and the Runner's heads-up display highlighted her location.

"Headed to you." Boots fired impulse thrusters and pulled the craft up into the wind, groaning as inertia yanked her stomach into her rump. Above her, the *Capricious* destroyed another fighter with a perfectly placed shot from its single cannon. Aisha must've been using her marksman's mark.

Boots spotted Nilah's race car wailing down the main drag

with a couple of Carrétan police cruisers flying after her. "Captain, I've got eyes on Nilah. I'll clear you a landing zone."

"Zap it with a beacon," said Aisha. "I'll drop this big boy on your mark."

Boots scanned the street ahead of Nilah for an open space and caught a lucky break: a large, decorative fountain, all lit up for the evening. She pinged the site with her designator.

"Acknowledged," said Aisha, and the *Capricious* banked toward Boots's side of town.

"This is Prince. Eliminate her attackers," barked Armin. "We're not equipped to repel boarders if they get inside with Nilah."

"Roger that," said Boots, air-braking her craft as best she could. She was too low and couldn't line up a shot on the police vehicles without possibly hitting Nilah.

So Boots got right in front of the cruisers and throttled up to full, blowing them away with engine wash. The blast caught Nilah as Boots rocketed upward, sending the race car flying forward like a kite in an updraft.

"What the hell, Boots?" screeched Nilah.

Boots watched through her keel cameras as the car almost flipped, then came down on all four wheels. It was going too fast, though. It'd get to the fountain before the *Capricious*.

As if sensing Boots's fears, Aisha gently said, "Stand by to board, Nilah. Captain, I need shields on the belly."

Then the pilot of the *Capricious* dropped the ship out of the sky. like a boulder, devastating the fountain, the park, and surrounding buildings with the impact.

As it turned out, Nilah's white-hot eidolon crystal was the least of her problems. First came the scorching wash of Boots's engines, which nearly sent the Hyper 1 end over end. Nilah's front right suspension locked up, folding in on itself like a piece of paper.

She could feel it as acutely as a sprain in her ankle. She couldn't turn, and she couldn't stop. Then came the *Capricious*'s thunderous landing, and with it, a suicidal drive into a shock wave.

Nothing Nilah could do would let her avoid the cloud of rocky shrapnel, so she triggered the Hyper 1's emergency crash systems and hoped they still worked. She threw her hands in front of her face as phantoplasm exploded from jets, slathering her body. Rocks shot through the gelatin, harmlessly thumping against her skin, and Nilah's stomach flipped. The crash systems must have been expired, in need of replacement. The debris shouldn't have been able to pass through the gelatin, much less touch her.

That meant she could still be crushed if the car flipped over and struck something.

All these thoughts rushed through her head in the time it took the car to ramp off the remains of the road and flip over onto its open top.

The roll bar screeched and sparked as the chassis struck metal, tumbling over and over again. The world went light, then dark, then light, before finally settling down. She'd stopped, but where? Her blurry vision was full of phantoplasm and caked debris, and she wouldn't know her situation until the goo melted away.

A familiar sickness settled over her as the gelatinous compound dissolved into indolence gasses, rendering all magic inert and severing her magical connection to her vehicle. Her heart hammered and a cold sweat covered her skin. She brushed the rocks and dirt from her eyes to find the interior of the *Capricious*'s cargo bay.

They'd dropped the ship in front of her and she'd ramped into it.

"I'm on board!" she coughed, but no one could hear her. The relays to the ship's nerve center were arcane, and also subject to the effects of the gas. She shook her hands, expecting her connection to magic to return any moment, but it didn't. The hull began to vibrate as the ship lifted from the ground. The old fear gnawed at her, the one that haunted her every single crash: what if she never felt the arcane ever again?

She unlatched and staggered to the cargo bay doors, trying to pull in as much fresh air as possible. She took the crystal comm she'd stolen from Vayle's office and polished it on her clothing. It squawked with the fragment of a transmission. The suppression effects of the gas were wearing off.

"I'm in the ship! I'm on board!" said Nilah. She began to sense the machines around her, and traced her glyph just to be sure.

"Just you?" came Armin's reply.

Nilah leaned against one of the large actuators that moved the doors. The streets of Arbrevert fell away beneath her as the ship rose higher. "Yeah. None of the palace guard made it in with me."

"Where's my husband?" asked Aisha, and Nilah swallowed hard.

This wasn't the right time. Nilah wasn't part of the *Capricious*'s family, and even if she were, Aisha was in the middle of a combat. She ducked away from the bay opening as a fighter whizzed past, slingers blazing. "He's . . . He's with Orna." Not a lie. Not the truth.

Orna's voice sizzled across the relay, cut through with the automatic whir of slinger fire. "I'm sorry, Aisha. They poisoned him. He's in a coma."

Aisha's wail was so raw, so painful, Nilah felt sure the bridge canopy had taken a direct hit. She'd never heard a scream of its particular quality: mournful, twisted around primal.

The *Capricious* arose in steady flight. The ship's cannon blasted shot after shot, and from the proximity of the explosions, Nilah knew fighters were getting skewered. She watched out of the open bay as one of the missed spells crashed against a clock tower, toppling it into a nearby building.

"If you've got Nilah, I need immediate evac over here," said Orna. "It's time to go."

Boots responded first. "I'm coming for you. Can you do your ship-riding trick in the atmosphere?"

"I'll try. If I can't, I won't live long enough to regret it," she said. "Make a slow pass down the western boulevard. I've got to time this just right or I'll wreck us both."

Nilah searched for Orna's location, and had little trouble spotting the streams of spells arcing from the battle. Light diffracted into rainbows and flashed gray. A familiar chill ran up Nilah's spine; she knew that gray spell—Mother's magic.

She jerked the crystal comm to her mouth. "Mother incoming!"

"What? Where?" Was that panic in Boots's voice?

Nilah saw the gray flash again, its epicenter on the western side of the city. "Look west!"

The Midnight Runner broke off its run to Orna, strafing toward the west.

Nilah scarcely recognized Boots's voice through her growl over the crystal comm. "Nowhere to hide, you withered scribbler."

With her mechanist's art, Nilah sensed Boots crank the active scanners on the Midnight Runner up to full blast. Every satellite orbiting Carré would detect Boots's fighter: an enemy craft in their airspace. There was another gray flash, and the Midnight Runner banked toward its source.

Armin's warning echoed Nilah's fears. "Planetary defenses coming online!"

"Shut that off, Boots, or we'll shoot you down ourselves." Cordell's voice was like a brick wall; there was no room for arguing with his tone. "Two seconds to comply."

Nilah felt the sensors switch off, and the tightness in her chest eased off—until the next gray flash, almost directly beneath the Midnight Runner.

"Boots—" Nilah began.

Cordell cut in. "Boots—get Orna. Now."

"Acknowledged," was her simple reply.

The Runner pulled off into a hard bank low enough to skim the buildings with its keel. It shattered windows and collapsed roofs as it shot across the town. An iridescent explosion rocked the area where Orna had been, and in its light, Ranger's silhouette climbed up a long steeple.

"Tell me you see me!" hissed Orna.

"Get ready to jump," said Boots. "One klick to you."

Ranger hunkered down, then jumped through a hail of sparking spells. Nilah held her breath, unable to see if the suit had struck home. For a moment, the battlefield seemed impossibly silent. Boots's ship wobbled as it banked toward the *Capricious*'s cargo bay, impulse thrusters popping across its hull.

"Captain, I'm on board the Runner," said Orna.

"Then let's get the hell out of here," said Cordell, and the ship began to rise a little faster.

When the Runner came closer, Nilah could clearly make out Ranger's form and the battle damage across his surface. His shiny regraded steel plates had been scored by dozens of slinger shots, and one of his cameras hung freely from its socket. Nilah's heart skipped with the fear that Orna had been shot. Malik lay unconscious in her arms—she must've taken a few hits to protect him.

Nilah started forward and almost missed Mother, her brass arms clinging to the Runner's landing skids like vise grips. The old woman heaved ragged breaths through clenched teeth, her tattered cloak whipping about her like a murder of crows. Mother traced a sigil, and in the gray flash that followed, she appeared behind Orna. Nilah pointed and screamed, and Ranger turned its half-blinded head to see the new threat, but it was too late.

Mother shoved a brass claw through Ranger's abdomen like punching through water. Blood caked Mother's hand, and her lips twisted in a delighted sneer. Malik slipped from Ranger's grip and banged to the deck, rolling toward the night sky.

He was going to go over the edge. Nilah dashed forward and slid across the deck, catching Malik's collar. Her other hand locked around one of the cargo bay's tethering rings, and she strained to keep him on the ship. Overhead, the Runner's engines filled the air with a choking heat.

"Damn it!" Orna gurgled, her armor sparking as Mother struck her again and again, yanking at the plates like picking meat from bones.

Ranger lashed out at the assassin, slamming Mother squarely across the chest. The woman went flying backward off the craft and tumbling toward the city below. Before she passed behind the open cargo door, Nilah spotted something in Mother's hand—a detonator.

The explosion nearly ripped Nilah from her handhold, and her ears filled with a singing silence. She felt a tear in Malik's collar and redoubled her grip. She'd be damned if she let him go.

The Midnight Runner spun with the blast, choking smoke billowing from its keel. The fighter barely missed Nilah, its impulse thrusters popping every which way as it made a mad spin toward the far wall—behind which lay the critical systems and the bridge. At the last second, the ship righted itself, skidding across the deck with relative gentleness. The Runner's nose would be ground to pieces, the canopy would shatter, the thruster ports would all require extensive bodywork, and he wouldn't be airworthy any time soon, but it was better than a huge ball of fire in the cargo hold.

A second explosion came, this one smaller than the first, but because it was enclosed within the bay, it struck Nilah like an avalanche. Stars flashed in her eyes and her equilibrium vanished. The *Capricious* pitched to one side, and the Hyper 1 came grinding toward her like a giant hand, about to scrape her out of the cargo bay and into the city beyond. Dizzy, Nilah mustered every ounce of strength to hoist Malik from the wailing opening. She dragged him clear just as the Hyper 1 banged through the entrance and tipped over the ledge into nothingness.

"We're in the ship," Boots grunted, "and we've got wounded!"

The cargo bay slammed shut with startling speed, and the ground seemed to swell beneath Nilah through the sudden kick of artificial gravity. Ranger sagged across the roof of the fighter, but remained firmly attached. Nilah leapt to her feet, still woozy from the blast, and made a mad dash for the Midnight Runner. The ruined canopy slid open and Boots emerged, ripping her helmet from her head as she climbed around the side.

"Get over here and get Orna!" Boots commanded in a voice Nilah hadn't heard before—calm, yet powerful. She had the sure stride of a woman who'd already seen a million worst-case scenarios.

Nilah hoisted herself up to where Ranger was, her eyes darting to the open wound, terrified that she'd see intestines hanging out. Instead, she found a thin mesh of duraplex weaving over the gaping hole. Nilah's fire suit was supposed to have a similar apparatus, but she'd never had occasion to use it. Nilah ran her fingers over the sealing wound, tracing her glyph to test the health of the system.

Ranger's code erupted against Nilah, slashing her with the ferocity of a cornered animal. She broke the psychic connection before the armor could short-circuit its batteries into her brain. It wouldn't let her hack it again. The armor was incredibly hostile, and Nilah had little doubt that the suit would physically attack her if it could. Before the system cut her off, she had been able to make out a flurry of warnings, cautions, and advisories beneath the surface. Two of them stood out above all the others:

BLOOD O2 43 PULSE 0

PILOT CRITICAL STABILIZATION FAIL PROTECT 3506AC$

"She's dying!" Nilah cried, hammering the armor closure with a fist. "Oh god, get her out of there!"

Ranger backhanded her, and Nilah almost lost her footing as metal claws tore across her cheek. Hot blood spilled across her neck, splattering crimson against the hull of the Runner.

Fury wrapped around her, and Nilah's reflexes kicked in like they never had on the track. She traced a glyph, took hold of Ranger's arm, and lanced at the core of his code with a pinpoint mechanist's attack: for blood, for victory, for Orna. Her power shot right through his personality, his critical functions, everything. With a tug at this thread of arcane energy, she unraveled Ranger like a tattered tapestry.

The mechanical beast's arms went completely limp, and he hissed open with a metallic chime to reveal the devastated body inside. Orna's cool, glassy eyes gazed into nothing; her scarred flesh was pale with the loss of so much blood. The duraplex graft remained stuck to her abdomen, holding Orna's guts in place.

Boots called to her from the deck, two gurneys hovering obediently before her: one with Malik, one empty. "Med bay! Let's go!"

"She—I don't think she—" Nilah sobbed.

"I said let's go!"

Nilah jumped down, and together they loaded Orna onto the empty gurney. Boots and Nilah raced through the corridors of the ship. With every step came the sudden nauseating shift of the artificial gravity; the *Capricious* was doing heavy maneuvers as they ascended. The ship rattled and groaned under the weight of a barrage of explosions, but Boots looked unfazed as they pulled into the deserted med bay.

"You get Malik into the sleep pod," said Boots, gesturing to the convalescence bed in the corner of the med bay. "And hook up the oxygen. We'll hook up the feeding stuff in a bit."

"You should do that. I can help Orna—"

Boots wheeled on her, face like stone. "I have more training with battle injuries. Do as I say, *right now*, and maybe we can save both of them."

Nilah grimaced. Boots was right. Her legs unsteady, Nilah pushed Malik's gurney to the convalescence bed. When she couldn't figure out the levers to unload him, she traced her glyph and compelled the bed to do it for her. She used her mechanist's art to decipher how to start up the oxygen, and fitted Malik with a mask and pulse monitors. Out of the corner of her eye, Nilah glimpsed Boots unceremoniously slice off Orna's tattered clothes, avoiding the place where the quartermaster had been impaled.

As soon as the convalescence bed registered steady—but weak—vital signs, Nilah rushed back to Orna's side.

Boots wheeled the old nurse cart to the side of the bed and began plugging up wires and sticking down sensors. The medical bot ran diagnostics and responded to what it found. It attacked Orna's exposed flesh with a variety of syringes and tubes, sinking needle after needle into her body.

"That thing is ancient. Are you sure it's safe?" Nilah asked.

Boots picked up the pace as she laid out tools for the bot to grab. "We can't do any worse by Orna. Connect up to the sensors and make sure it's reading right."

Nilah wove her magic into the robot, and aside from a little wear and tear, found it to be in pristine condition. Malik had taken excellent care of it. Synchronized with the ship's sensor array, the bot could locate all of Orna's life-threatening injuries, and Nilah saw them too—hot red on a sea of cooling blue.

The nurse bot extruded mechanical tentacles and plunged into the quartermaster's abdomen. Orna's skin writhed with their movement, and Nilah felt them spinning duraplex grafts across Orna's injured organs. It pumped her heart for her. It sank a tube into her neck and pushed an oxygenated blood substitute through her jugular. Syringes emptied, and Nilah called out their contents as Boots rushed back and forth, always making sure the nurse was supplied. The scanners reported the state of Orna's brain: all waves flat, but not dead.

Orna could die or live. Maybe she would be whole, maybe she'd never be the woman she was in the prime of her life.

The nurse noted old scars, broken bones, torn grafts from a dozen years or more of violent struggle. Not a single one of Orna's ribs had made it to adulthood without being crushed or broken at some point. The nurse's cycles idly suggested possible causes for the internal scar tissue: contusions and shearing, lacerations and debridement. It was like the quartermaster had been dropped in a meat grinder and reconstituted over and over again.

Given her medical history, the nurse estimated her odds of survival: 28 percent.

Gradually, the thud of detonations gave way to smooth space and smoother gravity. Nilah realized they must be free of Carré's planetary defenses, or they'd be dead by now. Somehow, they'd shaken away the fighters and found freedom without Boots and Nilah ever leaving Orna's side. Maybe the *Capricious* had already slipped through the gate, and they were on their way to god-knew-where.

The bot chirped, "Stand by for cardioid resuscitation."

The nurse began to shave Orna's oily black hair, and Nilah

swallowed hard. She'd seen plenty of dramas where a shaved head was the last gift a person received before the universe decided they were a lost cause.

The bot cast a net of shining, barbed probes across Orna's naked scalp. They fell in even spacing, drops of artificially circulated blood falling where they'd landed.

"Stand clear," said the bot. "Charging crystals."

Nilah winced as the nursing bot pushed a long orichalcum wire through the edge of Orna's eye socket, just to the left of her nose. The penetration looked too forceful to Nilah, but it was their only option. The mechanical nurse gripped Orna's neck and forehead with specialized forceps, pinning the quartermaster's skull to the gurney.

Monitors flickered on all around the med bay, Orna's darkening life essence mapped to her dying brain. The predicted path of the arcane spark overlaid the image, a warm red energy signature traced out for the benefit of surgeon magi. The nurse started its calculations to find the exact order to ignite the probes. When it reached 100 percent, it'd fire.

"Gonna be okay, kid," murmured Boots. "Orna has some strong magic keeping her here."

Nilah looked to Boots and knew the older woman was thinking of her arcana dystocia; if it was Boots on the gurney, she'd be dead. They had no way to bring her back from the most catastrophic injuries. Nilah's heart felt as though it was tearing in half, and she took Boots's hand, gripping it tightly.

Boots returned a smile. "Don't worry about me. This ain't my first rodeo."

To shock someone's cardioid was devastating to their system; more than a few attempts would kill Orna outright.

"Calculations complete," buzzed the nurse. "Contact."

On the monitors, a cascade of magic sloshed through Orna's

brain, racing along her skull and down her spine. The afterimage of the roughly heart-shaped cardioid faded from her head like a lightning strike, leaving only darkening neurons. The screen readout showed the new odds: 13 percent. *One in eight or so.*

"Recalculating spark path..."

Nilah squeezed Boots's fingers as tightly as she could. The nurse would hit Orna again, this time harder, and it would keep doing so until there were no odds of survival.

"Contact..."

Nilah focused on Orna's eyes, willing them to blink around the orichalcum probe.

"Negative."

Six point three percent. *Was that one in fifteen?*

What would Malik have done if he were there? What drugs would he administer? What machinery would he have hooked up? A trained doctor was so far beyond a mere triage robot. Nilah glanced around the bay, looking for anything she could add to the equation, but was interrupted.

"Contact..."

Blink, Orna. Close your eyes and open them.

"Negative."

One point eight nine percent. *Almost one in fifty.*

"Recalculating... contact." Its voice was like a harsh antiseptic, and Nilah's breath caught at the sound.

"Orna!" screamed Nilah, and the monitors froze in place. She traced her glyph and slapped her palms against the med bot.

"Nilah, stop! You don't know what you're—"

Boots tried to pull her back, but Nilah knocked her away with an elbow to the gut. Every fiber of Nilah's knowledge channeled into making this bot work in the most optimal way. She fused with it, overcharging its eidolon crystals, retuning its probes to fire the perfect shot.

The monitors flashed with the discharge, the whole med bay growing bright with their radiance.

At first, Nilah thought she'd shorted the monitors out. They were stuck on the image of the cardioid, magic flowing from it the same way the probes had predicted. Then she spotted tiny waves in the blue flow of energy; it was a live image of a living brain.

"Complete. Subject sustained."

Orna gasped and screamed, swinging her fist at the nurse bot, but it easily held her in place as it filled her blood with sweet anesthesia and euphoric medicines.

Nilah turned back to Boots to find her companion on the ground, clutching her stomach, mouth hanging open in shock.

"You..." Boots started, blinking. "You actually did it."

Nilah gave her a shaking nod, frowning hard so she wouldn't start crying. "I bloody well did, didn't I? I told you PGRF tuners were good."

She helped Boots up and threw her arms around the woman, clutching her so tight that Boots grunted.

"Thank you. Sorry I hit you. Thank you," Nilah whispered into Boots's ear. "When I thought we couldn't save her, I...You kept me together."

"You did good," said Boots, smacking her back. "You did really good."

Boots pulled back, and they looked over to where Malik lay locked in his hibernation spell, his heart beating in slow motion. He was stable, but the system had little it could do for him. They needed to get him to a major hospital where the best surgeons could work on him.

But dropping him off now would be like signing his death warrant. Mother would find him in no time.

"I meant to say, back in the cargo bay..." said Boots, pulling Nilah back into the moment.

"Hm?"

The fighter pilot grinned warmly, nodding her approval. "Malik: nice catch."

"Thanks."

Boots shooed her off. "And now, I want you to say good evening to these two. The bot has a lot of work to do setting up Malik's food. I'll take first watch, okay?"

Nilah hugged herself, surveying Orna's scarred face, her blood-stained skin. "You'll call me if..."

Boots nodded. "The doc bot will be by to check your face in a bit. You need to get some rest. Take one of the beds in the corner. I expect a relief watch in four hours."

The adrenaline began to fade from Nilah's system, exhaustion flooding her in its place. She agreed and went to a nearby cot, settling down onto it. The cool pillow soothed her bare neck, and she closed her eyes, taking a deep breath. Boots switched the lights to the sleep cycle, and Nilah opened her eyes to the dim sunset glow.

"Hey, Boots?"

"Hm?"

"I don't know what happened, but I'm sorry about Didier."

Boots turned away, returning her attention to the monitors, checking the status of the nursing bot. "Yeah...me too. Get some sleep."

Chapter Fifteen

After Action

Boots squeezed a lever, lifting the Midnight Runner's banged-up husk into the cargo bay mag clamps. The damage wasn't extensive, but its maneuvering thrusters wouldn't get the ship into place anymore. Until Orna could be up and about servicing the fighter, it wasn't going anywhere.

Her hands stung from a morning of heavy lifting and cutting. The new tools Nilah had ordered on Carré were scattered and tipped by the explosion, and needed straightening up. She'd had to cut the Runner's panel free from where it had sliced a nasty groove into the deck plating. Carbon scoring dotted the deck from where Mother had blown apart the Runner's skids. Boots wiped her sweaty cheeks with a gloved hand, not caring if she got a few metal shavings on her skin. Things were too bad to worry about a couple of cuts.

The far bulkhead swung open, revealing Cordell, his captain's jacket scuffed and disarrayed. His hair was matted in odd spots, no doubt from a night of restless sleep. He pulled out a cigarette case, tapped one to pack it, and lit up.

Boots didn't salute, because they weren't in the military

anymore. Instead, she called to him, "You can't smoke in here, Captain."

He gave her a mirthless smirk and a smoky sigh. "The hell I can't. This is my ship."

"I understand if you prefer to make special rules for yourself, sir."

"Why did I take you on again?"

Boots shrugged. "You kidnapped me. I guess you wanted to go legit."

"Very funny."

She grimaced at his constant puffing. "You're going to make the whole place stink of smoke."

The captain swept his open palm over the scene—the burnt pylons, the carbon scoring—and scowled. "This whole place was nearly burnt to a crisp. A little cigarette smoke ain't going to hurt anything, girlie."

"Remember the first time you called me that? Right after I came on board the ship."

He leaned back against the wall like some kind of juvenile delinquent. "Yeah, I do. You filed a complaint with Command, and we were attacked during the disciplinary hearing."

She kicked a piece of scrap out of the way. "It was a hell of a way to get out of a harassment charge."

He grunted an assent as he took a drag. "What do you make of that story Nilah told us, about the racetrack being a glyph?"

Boots mopped her forehead with the back of a glove. "Damned if I know how any of this fits together. But I'm sure she was telling the truth. What glyph?"

"Armin can't figure it out. Says he thinks it's only partial." His eyes cut to the wrecked Midnight Runner hanging from the mag clamps. "You ever going to name that thing?"

From where Boots stood, she could see the shredded keel and twisted landing gear. "Probably going to name him *Salvage*."

"And why is that?"

"It'd take one hell of a mechanic to get this thing back in the air. Probably two of them, if we're being honest."

Cordell pushed off the wall with his shoulders and sauntered over to her. "Then I've got good news: Orna and Nilah are two of the best mechanics I've ever seen."

"You're assuming Orna survives all of this."

He licked the inside of his mouth, as though tasting his response. "She'll make it. After the famine took most of Clarkesfall, she fought in the cages for food."

"Are you serious?" Boots asked. "Did you rescue her or something?"

"Not exactly. Armin and I responded to a distress beacon from the surface. When we got there, she'd killed most of the slavers and assembled a pretty decent antenna. Fight gone wrong or something. Anyway, she took my ship by force and offered to spare us if we brought her along."

"Wow. Then this must've been when she was...what... seventeen?"

"She was twelve."

Boots tried to visualize a small child holding the *Capricious* hostage, but nothing came to her. "You're really not joking."

Cordell shook his head. "She's good with a bomb."

"Damn. I guess she'll make it after all."

"The famine made for some pretty hard kids. So what are you doing in here?"

Boots pointed to the damaged Runner. "Cleaning up this guy's mess. What else would I be doing?"

A long wisp of smoke curled across Cordell's upper lip before he exhaled, blowing it away. "You were reckless out there with your sensors. Carré's planetary defense grid almost got us."

Didier's blood on her hands, as well as the heft of his corpse, flashed through her mind. "Yeah, well. I had reasons."

"I do, too. Mine are named Armin, Aisha, Malik, Orna, Nilah, and even Boots. Revenge is never a good reason to do anything."

"It wasn't just about revenge."

"The hell it wasn't. You took all that risk, and for what?"

"The flight data recorder."

Cordell took a step closer. "Excuse me?"

Boots looked him dead in the eye. "I recorded Mother's spell, from beginning to end, within one of the active sensor sweeps."

He blinked, clearly not sure whether or not to be angry. "Which means—"

"Which means we have comprehensive data on two things: what her magic is and how it works. You combine that with datamancy and a pair of genius mechanists, you might just get a viable countermeasure." She folded her arms. "I'm tired of getting ambushed. I'm tired of her gutting anyone and everyone who gets too close to us. I don't know if we can find the *Harrow* with the crew we have left, but I'm sure we can put a spell through Mother's head."

Cordell's cigarette slipped from his fingers, and he stooped down to pick it up. "Is that why you did it? Almost got us all killed for some data?"

"Not really. I was hoping to fry the old witch."

Boots watched his face for any willingness to concede the point. He wanted Mother dead as much as anyone, but he gave no sign of relenting. He'd always been a hard-ass.

"I could've blasted her if you hadn't stopped me. I was about two seconds away from target acquisition."

"Too risky. Not worth it, Boots."

"You're the captain."

Boots brushed past him and disappeared into the holds of the ship, in search of her bunk and a fitful night of sleep.

Mother's claws, dripping red. The witch's thin, hateful lips.

Nilah stirred to the sounds of clanking metal and turned over in her bed. The sheets carried a queer, inhuman smell, like no one had ever slept in them. Her face throbbed, and she briefly recalled the reason for her presence there: Ranger's claws had taken thin ribbons of flesh out of her cheek. Her eyes drooped as painkillers returned a measure of intoxication to her.

The metallic noise came again, weak and insistent: a light scratching, followed by a few taps. A tray perhaps? She pressed her cheek into the pillow, trying to will the noise away, but was rewarded with searing pain across the bandages on her face.

The scratching stopped, replaced by a low moan, and Nilah bolted upright. The med bay was dark, but faint light lined the floors. Sensing that occupants were conscious, the ship brought a few of the accent lights online, providing a bit of definition. Once her eyes adjusted, Nilah found Orna lying on the bed across the bay, her fingers curled like talons. The metal tray table contained Orna's circlet, which Nilah assumed was the source of the noise.

Nilah's entire body complained as she slipped from her bed and rushed to Orna's side.

"Okay, okay," Nilah cooed, surprised at how much she sounded like her own mother. "No need to move. Let's just lie back."

The quartermaster stared at her, wide eyes full of violence like a wild animal. Nilah gently pushed Orna's arms to her sides and ran her fingers across her sweat-soaked forehead. Orna's black, stubbly hair glimmered in the low light, and Nilah grabbed a nearby towel to gingerly pat her head dry. Thin, even trails of blood from Orna's scalp came away on the cloth.

"You've still got a lot of healing to do. You won't be up for another day or two," said Nilah. "If you don't relax, it'll only take longer."

"What..." Orna's eyes traveled about the med bay, and Nilah understood the question.

"Mother put her hand through you. No better way to say it."

The quartermaster's eyes traveled to her circlet, and she weakly pointed to the tray. "Pu...p...Give t—me."

Nilah picked up the silver band, and her ambient magical senses wound over its circuits. It was a primitive design, but effective, and it felt like looking at some of Orna's earliest work. Just how old was it?

Orna interrupted her train of thought by running a finger across Nilah's bare forearm and closing her eyes. She wanted Nilah to slip the circlet over her head.

Nilah started to comply, but then froze. If Orna wore the silver band, she'd know Ranger was dead. She wasn't ready for that sort of news.

"I don't think this is a good idea right now," said Nilah. "You need to be resting."

"Want...to walk...around," Orna said, wincing on that last word. "Ranger can..." She tilted her head toward the door.

"Let's not worry about that right now."

Orna weakly reached for the circlet, and Nilah pulled it from her grasp with little difficulty. She found it sickening to see the quartermaster with the strength of a child—a majestic beast laid low. Nilah thought of those scarred fists and powerful hands that had beaten her thoroughly, and she took a step back.

A scream ripped from Orna's lungs as she attempted to sit up. Klaxons and alarms echoed her cry, and Nilah rushed to restrain her.

"Where's Ranger?" Orna shouted, her eyes watering.

"You have to stop!"

"Where is … he?" she gasped, half fury, half terror. "Where— is Ranger?"

"Lay down!" Nilah slammed the emergency button, but the nurse bot had already arrived. "Please! I'm sorry!"

The quartermaster froze, and locked her gaze onto Nilah's. Tears streamed from her eyes. "You're s-sorry?"

She knew. In that split second, everything collapsed around Nilah. The nurse bot's purple sigil thrummed with power as it bellowed arcane smoke. Alarm cries drew out to long howls. Info panels hovered still in the air with seized vitals. And Orna's eyes registered a betrayal unlike any Nilah had ever seen.

The nurse bot's preloaded sleep spell cracked against Orna's skin, and she fell limply against the bed, purple tendrils of vapor curling from her mouth.

In a fluid movement, the boxy bot shoved Nilah back toward the door, stopping just short of taking her feet out from under her. "Leave now."

"But—"

"Outcome negatively influenced. Leave now. You are well enough for quarters."

Nilah's eyes darted to the unconscious woman on the bed; she'd subsided, but the medical alarms hadn't. Nilah took a wobbly step back, then another, feeling behind her for the bulkhead. The stalwart nurse made no move to advance, but its shock prong remained deployed nearby in case Nilah decided to do anything stupid.

But she hadn't the energy for stupidity after all that. Her fingers brushed the metal frame of the bulkhead, and she backed into the hall. The med bay door slammed in her face, leaving her stunned in the corridor, the low rumble of the ship's engines the only sound in her ears.

Her back against the wall, Nilah slid to the floor, and a hard sob burst from her lips. She wasn't the crying type, not like those prissy racers when they lost the precious podium. She was the work harder, get even, do better type. But here she sat, racked with guilt for perhaps the first time in her life. Nothing she could do could make it better; she didn't know Ranger enough to rebuild him, and the robot's personality would never be the same. Maybe she was crying because there was nothing to be done. No training. No fixing.

Boots gingerly stepped into Armin's quarters, a vast network of plugs and wires hampering her progress. She couldn't quite see past the jungle of screens, each flickering with seemingly random information. For a blink, she might make out the unforgettable picture of the *Harrow* about to jump, only to have it replaced with star charts and data sheets: the texture of information.

She shouldn't have come, but she had scarcely seen Armin in the days since they left Carré. She'd already given him the dozens of pictures of the *Harrow* to speed his calculations. She wanted to personally give him the crystal containing her scans of Mother's magic, to explain to him why she'd endangered everyone. She knew it would curry some badly needed favor with him; datamancers were suckers for raw input in much the same way mechanists loved their machines.

"Armin?"

Farther into the maze she went. Had his quarters always been this big? Coolant lines and chunky data ports now slithered across the floor, dynamically configuring and reconfiguring in the snow of a thousand floating readout screens. She smelled dried sweat behind the chemical stench of cleaners, and it reminded her of the training hall at Fort Halloran. When she pushed through the last curtain of cables, she found Armin perched over the ship's computer sphere, hands stretched over its surface.

He didn't look like the first mate who'd threatened her after her Gantry Station kidnapping. He was a shell: hollow cheeks that quivered with each painful swallow, sunken eyes darting about with insectoid precision, pallid skin aglow with the light of information.

"Armin..."

"I am the first mate," he wheezed without looking up, his lips cracked. "It's 'sir,' or have you forgotten how starships work?"

"Sir..."

"Don't speak to me right now. Dismissed."

"Okay, but I have—"

The screens vanished and the sphere turned a dismal blue as Armin's head snapped up to look at her. She spied madness in his pale eyes.

"You dare speak again?" he hissed.

"It's about Mother—"

He pounded the globe and snarled. "I'm searching for the damned *Harrow*! Do you hear me?" He had a powerful roar for a man so weak. "That is the only priority. Take your grudge and get the hell out of my sight."

During the Famine War, the thought of a first mate shouting her down like that would've frozen her heart. In Clarkesfall's most dire days, the cost of insubordination might be summary execution. Now, there were no bases with more soldiers; no replacements. He needed her help, and for that she pitied him. Her gaze fell to his feet.

His joints were swollen—she could see it through his pants legs. How many days had it been since he'd eaten? Since he'd drunk a cup of water or slept? His knees knocked together like an old man's, though Armin couldn't yet be in his fifties. Had he been locked in this room since they left Carré?

She opened her mouth to answer him, or perhaps ask after his health, but thought better of it.

"*Dismissed,*" he repeated, and she didn't dawdle.

She nearly bowled Nilah over as she backed out of Armin's quarters. The door slid shut, leaving them both in the corridor, and the racer looked her over with some trepidation. Nilah's eyes were red.

"That good, huh?" asked Boots.

Nilah blinked. "What?"

"Things are going that good, huh?"

"Yeah," she replied, and turned to go.

"Nilah."

The racer stopped. "Yeah?"

Boots jammed her hands into her pockets. "You've got a lot to be proud of. Can't be beating yourself up about what happened on Carré."

"Ask Malik and Orna how they feel about that."

"I'll be able to because you saved them."

"Malik might not make it, though."

"Look, I'm going to tell you something, and I want you to really listen to me. I know I ain't got any business giving you life advice. You're rich and—"

Nilah's fists balled up at her sides. "Just say it."

"In a battle, whatever happens, happens. You're going to have to be okay with doing the best you could."

She nodded and turned to face Boots, a wry smile on her face. "Learned that from experience, did you?"

"Yeah. I lost my whole crew on an escort mission."

Nilah's stunned pause gave Boots plenty of room to finish her thought.

"I'd been serving with those folks for months when we were

shot down during a drop. I say 'we,' but it was really the *Capricious*. He went down hard after they took apart his artificial gravity and smeared my friends all over the inside of the hull. We had to replace everyone after the salvagers brought him back online."

"Where were you during all of this?"

"I was flying a Midnight Runner, just like the one you see out in the cargo hold." Boots crossed her arms. "It was my job to keep everyone in the air... but sometimes, your orders ask too much of you. Sometimes, they ask for everything."

"How did Cordell survive?"

"He's a good shieldmaster. Those guys can live through any crash, jump from any height, you name it."

Boots had played through the incident a thousand times in her head, turning over and over what it must've been like on the bridge in those final moments. With the impulse thrusters gone and no artificial gravity, they'd known they were going down and that nothing would save them. All radio transmissions from the bridge had been absolute bedlam.

Cordell's orders had them drop at Laconte, one of the strongest points of enemy control. He would've had thirty or forty seconds to watch his friends realize there would be no tomorrow for them. He, like everyone else on the ship, knew his magic would save him, and he had to live with the fact that he'd sent them to their deaths.

Nilah mulled over Boots's words, clearly stunned out of her typical derisive comebacks. "I'm sorry. I know...I know I did everything people expected of me...It's just that I make my living on perfection."

Boots shrugged. "Don't be sorry. You can be as perfect as you want, and you still wouldn't have gotten Malik out of there in one piece. A little bad luck in a fight turns into a whole lot of misfortune."

"That's cold comfort."

"It's reality. We've got a long way to go before you and I are safe. If you can't figure out how to live with this and move on..."

"I'll try."

Boots tried on a warm smile. It fit a little tightly, but she managed. "You don't strike me as the 'trying' type, champ."

She returned a weak grin. "Yeah. Maybe not. I just wish I knew what to do now."

Boots felt in her pocket for the memory crystal from the Midnight Runner—the one that contained scans of Mother's spells. She held it out for Nilah to see. "I think I know exactly what you can do to help."

"What's on the crystal?"

"Mother's magic, recorded from start to finish. Between you and Armin, I bet you can figure out how her spells work...maybe even come up with a countermeasure."

Nilah's eyes widened as she took the crystal. "Why haven't you given this to him yourself?"

"He hates me. That's just how it is. Can't say I blame him."

"Really? He's always nice to me. You should get the credit for this."

"I don't want the credit, sugar. I want the job done," Boots said.

Nilah gave the crystal a quick squeeze and opened her palm, inspecting it. "When you were on the Link...going on that big adventure to find the Chalice of Hana, I bet you hated every minute."

Boots smirked. "The adventure? Never."

"No. The fame. It obviously doesn't suit you. I'd never turn down the credit for something."

Nilah sighed, pocketed the cube, and took a few steps in the direction of Armin's door before pausing. "Do you know the worst part about being stuck on this ship?"

Boots grimaced.

"Being so wrong about you. It's embarrassing. I'll make sure Armin knows where I got this."

Nilah gave Armin the memory crystal, and he jumped at the chance to analyze it. When she'd told him the scans came from Boots, he'd scoffed, "She can't be worthless all the time," but he softened a bit.

Nilah spent the next few days keeping the half-crazed datamancer alive. He'd had little sleep, no baths, and paltry amounts of food and water. Despite Orna's presence on the ship, no one had built anything ergonomic for the first mate, and he didn't know what a skilled mechanist could do for him in that department.

In between races, Nilah liked to work hand in hand with Lang's Safety and Human Factors Group, and as such, knew how to carve her own seats for rapid prototyping, weave moisturizing gel mesh fire suits, redirect ambient energies into nourishing spell shapers, and on and on.

With these skills, she constructed a throne for Armin to make any datamancer jealous. While seated in it, he would never have to drink or eat, and his body temperature would be perfectly regulated. The throne stimulated his muscles and massaged his skin, eliminating the bedsores and joint pain that plagued many datamancers. She used arcane circuits to model copies of Malik's sleep spells, helping Armin to flatten out.

She built it using Orna's hardware while the quartermaster remained under sedation. Nilah felt like a thief every time she stole down to the cargo bay to fetch tools that didn't belong to her, but she got the job done.

While Armin crunched the numbers on Mother's scans, Nilah had taken to wandering the decks, looking for things to fix. The *Capricious* was covered in tiny problems: broken lights, clogged ventilation ducts, and stressed wiring, among others. Small repairs were the sort of thing in which Nilah could lose herself, and she took some joy in traipsing from glitch to glitch, smoothing them out. For the first time since she'd boarded the ship, she felt a creeping, natural contentment.

And so, when she'd gone to repair the comm terminal in the crew mess, she didn't notice Aisha in the room with her. The pilot set down a tray on the table with such a clatter that Nilah snapped from her reverie. Nilah glanced back at her, pulse pounding, but Aisha simply stared at her food.

"Sorry," said Nilah, pushing the maintenance access closed. "I didn't know you were, uh, eating."

Aisha's eyes were deep set, and the whites of her eyes had been rubbed a raw pink. Her hair had come undone, frayed in places. Nilah's chest ached to look at her.

"The captain," Aisha began, "told me what happened to my husband. Did you know the duke's palace would be dangerous before you went in there?"

"I...I didn't. I thought it would be safe for me to hide there after Cordell dropped me off. I honestly felt like it was the only place in the galaxy where these... these people couldn't reach me."

"'Safe for me,'" Aisha echoed bitterly.

"I'm sorry." Nilah had said those words far too rarely in her lifetime.

Aisha's reddened eyes bored into her. Crow's-feet cropped up along the pilot's formerly perfect skin. "For what?"

"Malik was only there because of me."

"No." Aisha smiled, a storm brewing behind her eyes. Nilah could scarcely tell if the pilot was spiteful or caring, accepting or furious. "Malik was there because of Cordell. They were old friends, you know, and Cordell begged him to join the crew. If it wasn't for their time together, Malik would be by my side right now."

"He was there because of Orna. He didn't want her going with you alone because she's so hot-tempered. He knew she'd get in trouble with the local authorities." She wiped her cheek, but a steady stream of tears replaced the missing drop.

"And worst of all, he was there because of me. Because I liked being on a ship with my husband. If he'd taken that position at the sleep clinic on Taitu, I never would've seen him. Here, I—I could have him to myself almost every day."

Nilah crept closer, but didn't venture a comforting hand. "You're trying too hard to make this your fault."

Aisha gripped her fork. "I know you're right. And I want you to feel the same way. If I didn't put him in that coma, neither did you."

"Do you really think that?"

The pilot smiled at Nilah, but the expression didn't extend to her eyes. "For everyone's sake, I'm trying to. And Boots told me how you caught him when he almost fell."

"Orna carried him to you. She took a lot of hits to keep him safe."

Aisha's eyes bored into Nilah. "I will never have words to express the depth of gratitude I feel for you two. And I saw the contraption you made for Armin. I recognized my husband's magic in the sleep circuit you built. He must've cast a spell on you on Carré, and it inspired you. He has that effect on people."

She set her fork down and stood up, her chair squawking against the deck in protest. Nilah took a step back as the pilot hefted her tray.

Aisha continued, "I like knowing that, even if he doesn't make it, he's still helping people. You made those sleep circuits because of him, and...and that means there's a little bit of him in you, too. I can't...hate you for that reason alone."

Then the pilot strode to the cycler and tipped the contents of her untouched tray into it. She didn't turn back to face Nilah. "But maybe that's why I can't stand to see you right now. You were... You were the last person he saw. It should've been me."

Nilah wanted to excuse herself, but Aisha stood between her and the door. She'd never known how to comfort others, having grown up racing. Racers were all so selfish, so childish.

Aisha's shoulders fell. "When I walked past Armin's quarters, your chair... I thought I sensed Malik again, that old, familiar spell of his. When it was you, my heart just... I didn't think I could take it." She stiffened and turned to Nilah. "My husband is comatose, and I have to share the bits that remain with everyone."

Nilah jumped as the tray slipped from Aisha's fingers and banged to the floor.

"I'm sorry," Nilah repeated, feeling stupid.

Aisha's haunted eyes raked her over. "No one can be sorry enough. Thank you for making the chair for Armin."

Then the pilot turned and wandered away, her soft footfalls scarcely there, like a ghost.

Chapter Sixteen

The Back Straight

Nilah hadn't expected to hear shouting from Armin's quarters as she made her way through the ship. His hoarse voice rang out, startling her, and she tried the door—locked. She banged on it, and his shouts grew louder. Panic set in. What if Mother and her hunters had slipped onto the *Capricious*?

Nilah traced her glyph and connected to his lock, disabling it and sweeping aside the door so she could rush inside, dermaluxes strobing. She almost tripped on the cables, and had no idea how she'd fight in there, but she had to try.

She found him sitting on his throne, a crooked smile on his face.

"I did it," he sighed, shaking his head.

Nilah shut off her tattoos and followed his gaze to one of the ethereal monitors. The screen depicted a nebula with a small cluster of planets just outside the cloud, and Nilah drew closer to find that the tiniest planet had a geomarker dropped on it.

The Harrow's *jump coordinates.*

"You did it," she said.

Armin's uncharacteristic laugh unnerved Nilah. "I did it!"

She smiled and nodded, thrilled to have the coordinates and deeply concerned for Armin's mental health. He'd been sequestered away for a week, and there was only so much Nilah could do for him with the chair. "Yes! Uh, congratulations!"

"I need actual sleep!" he shouted, blinking his red eyes. "Am I being loud?"

She nodded again.

"Okay! Please tell the captain so I can go to bed."

Nilah had scarcely made it down the hall when Orna's rough hand spun her around and shoved her against a wall.

"Whoa, whoa, whoa!"

"Just listen to me," said the quartermaster. "I'm sorry in advance."

Nilah recoiled as though struck. She'd seen a lot of strange things since coming on board the ship, but a woman like Orna apologizing never entered into her imagination.

"Orna, I—"

"I said listen." She locked her ice-blue eyes onto Nilah's. "Ranger meant everything to me. He was my friend when I was alone, and he protected me when I was scared. When some bastard or another hauled me in from the dust so I could fight for food, he was there for me. I made him, and I owed him my life a thousand times over...and you killed him."

Orna slapped her palms against the wall on either side of Nilah's head, trapping her between scarred, bare arms. "I need you to understand something. I need to have said it in the plainest damned words I can so I can be sure you heard me." Her eyes sparkled and her nose reddened, and Nilah thought back to the raging, half-dead woman in the med bay.

"O-okay..."

"Ranger wasn't attacking you, okay? He wasn't. There was nothing wrong with him, he…he was just trying to protect me." She sniffed hard and ran her fingers over the bandages on Nilah's face, fingers warm on the painful cuts. "I need you to get this. Ranger was a good boy, and I loved him."

Boots emerged from the mess and spun to see the two of them standing there, concern immediately washing over her face. Nilah gave Boots a reassuring glance and waved her away with a flick of her fingers. The older woman nodded and crept back into the mess without a word.

Orna's lips quivered and her head sagged, but she wouldn't cry. She wouldn't let it out, even though it must've been killing her.

"He was a good boy…He was just scared for me. And for the first time, I feel so alone. When I wake up at night, he's not there for me. I can feel everything in this ship—the engines, the computers—but he's not there. He was the home I made, and he's gone."

Nilah's stomach flipped. What was she supposed to say? "I'm sorry. I had to…had to kill him or I'd lose you."

"I know that!" Orna's head shot up, and her hot breath came like a dragon's. "Don't you think I know that? I just want to hear you tell me—tell me he didn't do anything wrong!"

Nilah stared down the quartermaster. Orna's eyes were an ocean of rage, fear, and grief—an expression all too common around the *Capricious* those days.

And she craved the kind of absolution that she could only get from another mechanist.

"Ranger was perfect, to the very end," said Nilah. "He was a masterpiece."

Orna's breath hitched, and she blinked out a tear. She wiped it on the back of her hand, then inspected it as though she'd found an oil leak. She wiped her cheek twice more and stood up straight, releasing Nilah from her prison.

Nilah started to relax, but Orna wrapped her fingers around the back of Nilah's neck and pulled her in for a hard kiss. The quartermaster's other arm snaked around her waist, reeling her in like a steel cable, and Nilah arched her back, leaning into the warmth of Orna's breast. The quartermaster's breath mingled with hers, and Nilah closed her eyes as Orna's tears dripped onto her cheeks.

As quickly as it had started, Orna shoved her against the wall and pushed off, turning her back to Nilah.

"Thanks for saving my life," Orna mumbled before storming around the corner and disappearing.

Nilah remained in the hallway, her lips still tingling.

"So this," said Armin, pointing to a small planet in the ethereal projection, "is Wartenberg. That's where the *Harrow* jumped after Goulding Station."

Boots leaned across the table in the darkened mess hall to get a closer look at it. It wasn't much of a world, barely large enough to warrant classification as a planet—more like a moon.

Cordell had gathered her and Armin for a consultation; Armin had the strategic authority, and Boots had the knowledge of obscure planets and ancient treasures.

"That's Wartenberg?" asked Boots. "I always thought it'd be bigger."

At the end of the table, Cordell crossed his arms. "You've heard of it?"

"Sure, Captain," said Boots. "There are all kinds of doomed mining missions throughout the galaxy. They make for great salvage legends, you know. 'Go here, there's a bunch of abandoned equipment and the like.' Rubes love it."

"I appreciate your candor, Boots," said Armin, shaking his head. "I'd almost forgotten that we were some of your rubes."

She gave him a tight smile. "Sorry, sir. I just meant that I've come across Wartenberg before."

Cordell grinned. "I knew you had to have some real truth in all the lies you peddled. Fill us in."

"Here's what I know: this big company had a mining outpost there before the Famine War. They'd supposedly found a huge strike of eidolon crystals, so they set up a ton of infrastructure. Only, the veins were dry—barely anything to mine. They sold the real estate after the mine went bankrupt."

"That's more than I got," said Armin.

"I bought a logbook of mining inspections a couple of years ago," said Boots. "It's in my apartment on Gantry Station if we ever make it back there."

Armin nodded. "I couldn't find much on the Link. Just a deed registered to a private holding company, the Hatch Fund, based in Taitu. Strict no-trespassing policy. No listed permanent residents. The company claims demi-sovereignty with Taitu."

"So if we land there, and they shoot us…" Cordell began.

"They'll claim self-defense under Taitutian law," said Armin.

"With all due respect, sir," said Boots, "*someone* is going to shoot us no matter where we land. Does it really matter if it's our enemies or the local authorities?"

Cordell nodded. "That's fair. Armin, could you at least find some survey data?"

"I did, sir." Armin tapped the planet, and it expanded to fill the entire mess. A satellite pinged above Wartenberg, sending glowing echoes through the room. "This is recent—just a few hours since the last sweep of the system. They have a registered orbital defense system, though it's not much. Just enough to keep out any curious ships."

The captain rubbed his chin. "One slinger sat could knock down a yacht, but they're nothing a marauder-class ship couldn't handle. Any downsides to blowing apart their defenses?"

Boots smirked. "It opens them up to piracy?"

"Nearest jump gate?" asked Cordell.

The projection rotated and zoomed out to show a course between a jump gate and Wartenberg. "Torm: one day away."

"So we jump in next to the planet and swat down the defenses," said Cordell, "but if we have to hot-foot it out of there, it takes a day."

Cordell folded his hands in front of him, resting his elbows on the table. The projector illuminated his face from below, giving him an eerie appearance. "I don't like this at all; my Midnight Runner is barely operational, I'm down two crew members, and we've got no way of knowing what we'll find. We still don't have analysis of Mother's spell or a countermeasure. If we see her, we have to run. More to the point, Mother knows we have the jump images. She's *going* to follow us there."

"Correct, Captain," said Armin.

Cordell frowned. "What the hell was the *Harrow* doing at Wartenberg?"

"Only one way to find out, sir," said Boots.

The captain stood, prompting Boots and Armin to their feet. He called for the lights, and the projection disappeared. Sunny illumination flooded the mess, bringing all of Didier's plants back into focus. They were overgrown, poking out of the tops of their enclosures; the crew had been eating out of the ration stock without their cook.

"Okay," said Cordell. "The sooner we get this done, the sooner we get Malik to a real hospital. Inform the crew that we're jumping at the next gate."

Nilah stood on the bridge, watching the stars streak past. Familiar pre-race nerves hit her, like having rocks in her guts. Red light suffused the space, summoning all crew to battle stations.

The Midnight Runner still wasn't spaceworthy after the damage to its skids and thrusters. They didn't have the materials to repair it, and Cordell deemed it too risky to land on any civilized worlds. Nilah could've fixed it with Orna if she could just buy the parts—

—and if she'd spoken to the quartermaster since the kiss.

So, no parts, no Runner, no wing to protect the *Capricious* on approach. At least Nilah had been able to get Orna's tools organized in the cargo bay.

"Dropping into normal space in three…" said Aisha, and Nilah glanced to the captain. He looked as collected as ever, and she wondered if anything ever fazed him.

"Two…"

Nilah's eyes traveled over the others. Orna stood by her, face unreadable. Armin waited patiently by the captain's side, hands folded behind his back. Aisha tensely gripped the controls in the pilot's chair.

"One," said Aisha, tracing her glyph with one hand and pulling a throttle with the other. "Normal space."

The craggy little gray sphere that greeted them was pockmarked with craters and ice rifts. Nilah saw no atmosphere, no lights along its surface, no evidence of any human life whatsoever.

"That's it, huh? Weapons free," said Cordell. "Take out that defense satellite. I want us on the surface in under an hour. No point giving them time to prepare."

"I got a fix on the sat, Captain," called Boots, pecking at the radar station where Didier once sat. She clearly wasn't accustomed to working a bridge station, given the way she tapped at her console. "Relaying to the aggregator."

The projection hovering in the center of the bridge lit up with a single red point—the hostile satellite.

"It's requesting access codes," said Armin.

Cordell smiled. "Missus Jan, why don't you knock on their door for me?"

Aisha rolled the *Capricious* so its keel gun could acquire the target and planted a shot directly into the center of it. The red dot exploded into mist on the projection.

"Good kill, Missus Jan," said the captain. "Scan for the mining settlement and—"

"Uh," Boots interrupted. "I'm still reading hostiles, I think..."

Nilah stepped down the terrace to look closer at the cloud of scanner contacts. Debris should've flown off in all directions at random. This set of pings seemed more organized somehow. They drifted into a configuration Nilah vaguely recognized as a colossal grenadier's mark.

She spun to face Cordell. "Look out!"

The captain was on his feet with his shield spell cast in the blink of an eye. The satellite collective lobbed a ball of energy in their direction, and the ship's dispersers failed to collapse the spell in time. The liquid fire sphere crashed against the *Capricious*'s canopy like an egg. White-hot plasma congealed against Cordell's blue shields, arcing and flashing.

And to Nilah's shock, his shield broke into fizzling shards.

"Evasive maneuvers," Cordell grunted through clenched teeth. He clutched his forearm as though physically struck. "That's some next-level tech right there."

"Looks like we're in the right place," said Armin as stars whirled through the canopy overhead. "Going to see if I can ID the system and find a weakness."

"Combat gravity engaged," said Aisha, and Nilah's weight dropped considerably.

Aisha traced her glyph and fired again. On the projection, the red dots split apart, allowing the spell to pass harmlessly through their center. Lightning-fast, they reorganized and cast again, throwing out two grenadier's marks, then another four, then eight. A net of deadly plasma swelled to encompass the projection.

"Odds of survival are low on a retreat, sir," called Armin. "We can't get to the jump gate, and the sat looks a lot faster than us in open space."

"Get us to the planet's surface," said Cordell. "We can find cover in those canyons."

"We'll have to go through the field," Aisha called back.

"Ahead full. Ram it," ordered Cordell. "I've still got one shield left."

Nilah's stomach flipped as internal gravity tried to compensate for Aisha's corkscrew dive. The satellite collective came into full view—a slithering silver mass of machines, dynamically reconfiguring and pumping out a minefield of star-hot plasma.

She braced as they slammed into the grenadier's marks, the blobs of light sliding across Cordell's shield like lethal raindrops. The ship rocked with the impact, and Nilah nearly lost her footing.

They dove full-speed, wheeling as the satellite collective pushed shot after shot at them. It gave chase, and Nilah watched the scanner projections in wide-eyed horror as it matched pace. Aisha couldn't let go of the sticks to cast her marksman's mark, and even if she could, the *Capricious*'s keel slinger was designed to hit single targets, not swarms.

"We can't identify the make, sir," called Armin.

"Got to improvise, then," said Cordell. He cried out as his other shield cracked, then he cast his spell again.

"Your shields are too weak to hold off another direct hit, Captain," said Armin.

"From the sats maybe, but not the ice canyon walls," Cordell shot back. "If anyone knows how to return fire, I'm all ears!"

"Orna and I can do it," Nilah said before she could stop herself.

"Spacesuits, mag boots, and tethers—you open the cargo ramp. There's no atmosphere to blow us away."

"Do you concur, Miss Sokol?" asked Armin, and Orna nodded.

"We've got Ranger's old slinger," added the quartermaster, looking to Nilah. "Zero out the gravity and we can lift it."

"Go!" ordered the captain, stepping into his stirrups. "We can't take another hit and this is the best plan we've got. Zero the gravity, Missus Jan."

Nilah kicked off a nearby railing and sailed for the door, Orna hot on her tail. The quartermaster took the lead in the corridor, and together they flew down the center of the stairwell to the cargo bay. Upon landing, they launched into the bay toward their suit storage lockers.

Nilah had never donned an EVA suit so fast in her life, but Orna was even quicker—obviously more accustomed to emergency combat action. When Nilah locked her helmet into place, the comms chimed.

"Prince here," said Armin. "What's your ETA?"

"This is Nilah. I'm suited up."

"Orna here. Same."

"Tether up," said Armin. "The *Capricious*'s inertial dampers lose effectiveness the closer you get to the cargo bay ramp. We can't have you swept off the ship."

Nilah found a cargo winch on the wall and clipped it to her belt. Orna had already attached, and was busy pushing Ranger's massive slinger out of storage. Nilah switched on her mag boots and tromped over to help. Even with the gravity zeroed out, the sheer mass of the weapon surprised Nilah. It was tough to get it moving, and once they had it going, it was hard to stop.

"Stand by to pop the bay ramp," said Armin.

Atmospheric alarms sounded through the bay, growing dimmer by the second as the *Capricious* vented their air.

"Hey." Orna nodded to the tools, which had been meticulously mounted on the walls. "Thanks for, you know, organizing my stuff."

Nilah smirked. "Thank me after we stay alive, darling."

Orna fetched another winch and looped it through a tie-down, clipping it to the titanium ring on the butt of the huge slinger. "For recoil," she said. "We're ready, Prince."

"Opening the bay now," said Armin. "Good hunting."

The ramp descended in front of the pair of women, revealing canyon walls shooting past at terrifying speeds. Sunset light from the nearby star filtered through the ice crystals like glassy waves, flashing with each crease and crag. Iron deposits tinged the ice crimson in places, giving the canyon an unsettlingly blood-spattered appearance.

On the bridge, Nilah had failed to grasp the scale of the satellite collective. A dozen machines, each the size of her race car, comprised the body, and lines of arcane energy shot across their ethereal conduits like lightning. A grenadier's mark formed in the space between them, creating a ball of sunlight.

Its radiance baked Nilah's suit, and sweat erupted from every pore. It was like driving on the burning sands of Wylde—the galaxy's hardest endurance race.

Except in this case, the sun was coming straight at her.

The *Capricious* rocketed around a corner, and the spell crashed against the canyon wall, erupting into billows of roiling fire and steam. Jagged chunks of ice filled the canyon behind them, and the satellite collective just barely dodged through the shrapnel of its own spell.

Orna grasped the butt of the rifle and Nilah held the barrel, assisting with aim.

"Ready?" asked the quartermaster.

Nilah nodded, her eyes never leaving the charging satellite nodes before her. "Fire!"

The slinger thundered in Nilah's hands, recoil slamming the muzzle upward. She almost lost control. The last thing they needed was a stray friendly shot hitting the inside of the cargo bay. Nilah's aim was wide, and the bolts of fire harmlessly exploded against the canyon walls in the far distance.

A lucky shot went straight for one of the satellite nodes, but it dodged out of the way with little difficulty. Its displacement, however, misshaped its next grenadier's mark, and the satellite's spell failed.

"We just have to keep disrupting it when it casts!" said Nilah.

"Negative," Armin buzzed over her comm. "We're going to get cornered sooner or later. You must destroy it. Look for a controller unit."

Nilah and Orna shared a glance. "They're self-organizing, sir," the mechanists said in unison.

The pair opened up with another volley of shots at the satellite, this time scoring a clean hit on one of the nodes. It burst into glittering shards, but the other nodes immediately filled in the gaps to cast the mark.

"Damn it!" said Orna, firing again to disrupt the spell, and though it worked, she hit nothing. Worse, Nilah felt the empty click of a used spell canister. "Got to reload!"

"Prepare for incoming!" shouted Nilah. There was nothing to stop the satellite from casting.

Again came the heat, the blinding light, and the orb of plasma coming straight at them. The ship dipped into the shadowed depths of the ice rift as the ball passed overhead.

"Brace for impact!" shouted Cordell.

Then Nilah felt the silent, bone-rattling crunch through her mag boots as the *Capricious* plowed through a hail of icebergs, snow and shards filling the view from the cargo bay. The satellite collective scattered and wormed its way through the gaps in the avalanche, but two nodes slammed into the falling ice at full speed.

The remaining nine nodes reorganized for another attack. How many more would it need to lose before it lacked the resolution to create a glyph?

Orna slapped another clip into the base of Ranger's slinger and wrapped her finger around the trigger. "Ready?"

"Wait!" called Nilah. "Blast the canyon walls!"

They were too deep inside the cargo bay for a decent shot. Nilah gestured to the line in the deck where the ramp was attached. "We have to get closer!"

Orna pulled a remote from her suit's belt and gave them a good amount of slack on the winches. "Hurry up. The drones are regrouping for another shot."

The pair unclipped Ranger's slinger and rushed to the tie-down on the ramp, where they tried to pass the carabiner through with bulky gloves.

"No time!" said Orna. "Look!"

The satellite collective swarmed closer than ever, its nodes charged and ready to fire another miniature sun into the *Capricious*'s cargo bay. Nilah went down on one knee, bracing the massive slinger in her armpit like a tripod. Orna squeezed the trigger, and they sprayed the canyon walls in front of the nodes. Orna aimed a little high, so the collective couldn't simply ascend out of the canyon.

"We've got another tight fit!" called Cordell. "Brace!"

But Nilah and Orna were at the edge of the inertial dampening field, and when the ship entered a nauseating corkscrew, the tether snapped from Ranger's slinger, and Nilah was slung outward. She bounced off one of the hydraulic ramp struts and screamed in agony. Her cable snapped taut ten meters outside of the ship, and she twisted at the end of the cable like a worm on a hook. She clutched Ranger's slinger as tightly as she could and shouted aimlessly into her helmet.

Looking past her feet, she saw elemental explosions as the nodes crashed against jagged chunks of ice, obliterated in the moment of impact. Only one node made its way through the avalanche, and it bore down on her at high speed.

Its directive was clear: if it couldn't cast the grenadier's mark, it was to use itself like a cannonball. Nilah was the closest target.

It blasted out of the ice storm, a glittering trail in its wake like a comet. Nilah wrapped her legs around the barrel of Ranger's slinger and braced the butt with her belly before jerking the trigger. A wild spray of spells ripped from the muzzle, and she closed her eyes against the recoil hammering her body.

One of the shots struck home, and the node collapsed into jagged metal shards.

"Negative scanner contacts," said Armin. "Good kill."

"Reel me in! Oh god, reel me in!" Nilah gasped as they took another turn that brought her a little too close to the wall.

The *Capricious* slowly rose up out of the trench so as not to slam Nilah into any large hunks of ice. She clutched the slinger with one hand and the cable in the other, the sound of her fast breathing filling her helmet. Her harness finally scraped against the bay ramp and she scrambled inside. Getting to her feet, she swung her arms around Orna and squeezed as tightly as she could.

"Okay," said Orna. "I've got you. You did it. You're okay."

Nilah pushed back and looked at her companion with wide eyes, their scratched visors reflecting stray sunbeams. As the fear drained from her body, Nilah cracked a smile.

"Tell me you saw that bloody shot," said Nilah.

Orna returned her grin. "It was pretty badass. Quick thinking, keeping hold of Ranger's slinger."

Nilah hefted the metal weapon, struggling against its inertia. Even weightless, it was hard to manipulate. She presented it to the quartermaster.

"I cost you so much of him," Nilah said. "I didn't want to lose the last piece."

Orna's smile faded to quiet reflection, and she took the slinger from Nilah's hands.

"Okay, Prince," Orna said into the comm, turning away, "button him up and give us some atmos."

As the cargo bay ramp closed, Nilah added, "And may I please have some gravity? I miss it."

Chapter Seventeen

Waystation

Boots peered into the various scopes and scanner readouts on the bridge as she relayed the best approach vector for the Wartenberg Mining Colony. She hadn't been a scanner tech since her days in the Arcan Civil Air Patrol, and she sucked at it. Her readings on arrival at Wartenberg had been slow, and she was ashamed of her performance.

If Mother hadn't blown the skids on her Midnight Runner, Boots could've been flying wing out there with a set of scanners she knew far better. It was probably too much to hope that they'd be able to repair her fighter before they located the *Harrow.*

They came into visual range of the colony, and the *Capricious*'s high-powered scopes locked onto it. Boots squinted at her screens, then routed them to Armin. "I'm seeing something weird here, sir."

"Good," said Cordell, before Armin could reply. "I'd hate it if we shot down someone's satellite for no reason."

Armin looked over Boots's readouts and mixed them with countless other data tables, collating the results and teasing meaning out of them. "This is a good find, Boots. Captain, those red deposits you saw are iron. They've been magnetically aligned to confuse sub-surface scanning. This entire moon was realigned by a large spell."

"Okay," said Cordell. "So that means..."

"It means," said Armin, "we don't know how far down the Wartenberg Mining Colony goes, nor do we know its layout. It could be a few feet, or it could be miles. The *Harrow* might be here and we'll never know without feet on the ground. That'd be a real shame, though."

"And why is that, Mister Vandevere?" asked the captain.

"Wartenberg claims demi-sovereignty," said Armin. "We'd lose any salvage rights."

Cordell shook with a short, bitter laugh. "These people killed one of my crew and put another in a coma. Forget the law. I just want to find out their secrets so we can take what we can from them. I'd like to ruin everything they care about, if it's possible."

"How do you think they did it—magnetically aligned all of those deposits?" asked Aisha.

"With a ship like the *Harrow*," said Cordell, "I bet you could do anything."

The *Capricious* drew closer to the colony, and Boots got a good look at the docking clamp. "Look at this ring, Captain. It's the old style, older than our bucket."

"We're not going in the front door," said Cordell. "We're going to cut our way into one of the isolated rooms and go from there. Ten to one the docking tubes are wired to blow the second they engage."

Boots shrugged. It was a fair assessment. A large, rectangular imaging artifact flickered on her screen some two kilometers from the colony, then disappeared. It was like catching a brief reflection through several panes of glass—hard to pin down exactly what she saw and where. She dropped the playback into the aggregator.

"Sir, we may not have to cut anything," Boots called out. "One of our scanner reflections caught a subterranean structure the size of a docking bay."

Armin took the playback and cross-referenced it against dozens of resources like ice brittleness indexes, meteor strike patterns, and the *Capricious*'s active scans of the surface, narrowing down the possible origins of the reflection. "This trench here," he said, "is big enough to dock a ship like the *Harrow*, located within a klick of the colony, and appears to be highly stable. Captain, I'd recommend taking us there."

"Very good, Mister Vandevere," said Cordell.

They proceeded to the designated point in near silence, save for Armin's occasional approach orders to Aisha. They descended into the wide canyon, where Boots's scanners went dark, except for the immediate pings from the canyon walls. They descended past the level of sunlight penetration, into shadow. Aisha cranked up the ship's searchlights, but there was little need for them in the massive trench.

"Should be something at eleven o'clock," said Armin, and the ship slowed to a stop. Aisha swept her searchlights across the canyon wall face, but found nothing.

"False positive maybe?" asked Cordell, and Boots flushed with embarrassment. Of course she'd read it wrong—this wasn't her usual setup.

It had made so much sense, though: the large trench, the secluded docking point, Armin's calculations and the reflections. Boots racked her brain for a solution, only seeing a blank ice wall before her.

"We could drill it with a few shots from the keel gun," said Cordell. "Maybe it's back there somewhere."

Armin shook his head. "Or we could bring the trench down on top of us."

"It's the old waterfall trick," said Boots, more to herself than anyone else.

Cordell leaned forward in his chair. "Explain."

"There are loads of stories about caverns hidden behind waterfalls where treasure is buried, sir," said Boots. "Every planet has a couple—even Clarkesfall. Take the Legends of the Landers, for example: when they stole Robert's saber, where did they hide it?"

Cordell nodded. "In the mouth of the cave behind Ranier Falls."

Boots cocked an eyebrow. "Exactly. I bet if you target that wall with dispersers, you'll unravel an illusion."

"Missus Jan, charge the dispersers and fire on the northern wall, full blast," said Cordell.

"Yes, Captain."

When Aisha fired, a huge swath of the trench wall shuddered and convulsed, and for a moment, Boots feared they'd destabilized it somehow. Aisha fired again, and the pockmarked ice writhed and twisted before disappearing entirely.

In its place lay a large blast door, the kind often used to cover atmospheric bubble shields. The *Harrow* wouldn't have fit in it, but this site certainly could've served as a shipyard.

"Come in, Miss Sokol," said Cordell, "this is Boss."

Orna's voice echoed across the bridge. "Sokol here."

"I think we need to give you some code names, like real operators," he mused. "You think you and Nilah could hack that bay door open?"

There was a long pause.

"You mean you want me and Nilah to jump across and try to physically access security?"

Kin chimed in, his voice clear and cheerful, "I can help. It'll go faster with an AI on your side. Would that be acceptable, Lizzie?"

"Yeah," said Boots. "Probably smart to breach as quickly as possible."

Boots heard Nilah groan in the background. She couldn't blame the racer for her recalcitrance after Nilah had been slung around an icy trench on a tow line.

"It'd be our pleasure," said Orna. "Stand by."

"Prince here. I'm going to suit up and join you," said Armin. "I can help you sift through the security access databases."

"Copy that," said Orna. "Sokol out."

"Do you think Mother is here, sir?" asked Boots, and she noticed Aisha wince out of the corner of her eye.

Cordell leaned onto his armrest, stroking his chin. "Let's crack this baby open and find out."

A dull three hours passed waiting for Nilah, Orna, and Armin to hack into the door on the canyon wall. Ready protocols required all battle staff to remain on the bridge, with a special exception for Armin. In truth, if they were attacked, there would be almost no way to fight someone off. The battle with the satellite had exhausted Cordell, and Aisha didn't look much better off.

Boots was the only one fully operational aboard the bridge, and she was bored to tears. She dropped another cube of coffee into her mug and leaned against the terminal, trying not to slow blink.

In the distance, three tiny lights bobbed by the once-hidden door: the spacesuits of the *Capricious* hackers taking apart an access panel. They were so small against the massive cliff face, and Boots kept her scanners trained on their position in case anything tried to sneak up on them.

"Doesn't seem like anybody is home, does it, Bootsie?" said Cordell, yawning. "You'd think they would've come out to meet us in force."

"Could always be a trap, sir," said Boots, as her cube melted and splashed into hot, caffeinated goodness. "At least we know we're in the right place."

Aisha lazily spun her chair to face them. She'd been watching the slow-motion breaching like a hawk, but it appeared even she couldn't stand it anymore. "This place makes no sense at all."

"Legendary warship, secret underground base," said Boots. "Perfectly reasonable, if you ask me."

Aisha shook her head. "No. The *Harrow* should've been all about fanfare and presence. By all accounts, it was the largest ship Taitu ever constructed. Why dock it in the darkness of a frontier world like a bunch of thieves?"

"It was highly classified," said Boots.

"*Every* warship is highly classified," replied Aisha. "Even a tiny marauder like the *Capricious* had classified systems. But states don't hide warships from the rest of the galaxy. A navy only exists to inspire fear in an enemy. So why keep it a secret?"

Cordell grimaced and rubbed his forehead, about to fall asleep in his chair. "I feel like that's what we're here to find out."

"What if it's not a warship, or a weapon at all?" asked Boots. "Then hiding it becomes a little more reasonable."

She'd only said it as idle nonsense to pass the time, but Cordell and Aisha both stared at her as though she'd laid an egg.

Armin's voice buzzed over the bridge comms with a loud laugh. "We got it! Well done, ladies, well done. That was some incredible hacking."

"I've never had crypto-analytics on a hack before," came Nilah's radio, followed by an obnoxious amount of back-patting and self-congratulation.

"At least the nerds were having fun," Boots chuckled, turning back to her station. "Active scanners coming up to full."

Boots held focus on the dock door as it slowly ground open, shaking loose years of ice dust into long swirls. Lights flickered on inside the empty bay, illuminating maintenance gear and several dozen workstations. They'd once been able to scramble fighters from here, but those ships were long gone, even if the tools weren't.

"Jackpot," radioed Orna, her tiny, distant body peering around the side of the door. "Let's steal all of their crap."

"You think you can repair the Midnight Runner with that?" Boots asked, technically breaking radio priority by transmitting to an away team when it wasn't important.

Cordell gave her a nasty look, and she shrugged.

"Just want to get back to what I'm best at, Captain," Boots said with a toothy smile, hoping to avoid a reprimand. "Also, scanner contacts negative, sir. Nothing inside the bay."

"Okay," said Cordell, shaking his head. "How about you take us in, Missus Jan?"

"Yes, Captain."

The *Capricious* passed from the shadow of the canyon into the harsh lights of the docking bay, easily able to fit where the *Harrow* couldn't. They drifted through the blue bubble of the atmos shield, and Aisha made course corrections, accounting for the addition of breathable air. The ship settled onto a set of docking pylons, and Orna, Nilah, and Armin came following inside with their maneuvering thrusters.

"Air samples look breathable, Captain," came Armin's voice over the comm. "No NRBC hazards detected."

"Does that mean I can get out of this suit, please?" asked Nilah. "I've been in here for hours, and it smells like an armpit."

"Not until we're sure we have control of the atmos shield," said Cordell, standing. "It wouldn't do to take off your suit and have someone vent the docking bay into space. No one takes off their suit unless we know the status of power and security."

"You heard the man," radioed Orna. "If you want to get out of the suit, we've got more hacking to do."

Cordell fished out his cigarette case and lit up. His inscrutable eyes surveyed the bay through the canopy. He took a long drag and sighed. "Missus Jan, I'm going to need you to keep the ship hot and his main gun trained on any entrances. We may need to beat a hasty retreat."

"Captain, I'm the best shot with a slinger," said Aisha. "I should be part of an away team."

"That's true, but you and Malik are the closest thing we have to an insurance policy. If something happens, I need you to take the ship and go public with everything we know."

Aisha gave him a grim nod.

Cordell turned to Boots and smiled. "Miss Elsworth, time to go earn our shares."

The bay was the typical setup to support a wing of starfighters, very similar to many that Boots had seen during her days as a pilot. The fighters were long gone, and a layer of dust covered all of the tool chests and equipment cages. Whoever had left here never closed it out, never liquidated their gear, as though they planned to return.

Boots walked from station to station, inspecting the belongings and looking through drawers, keying on consoles and testing commands. It all powered up and attempted to connect to the missing fighters. She supposed that they must be with the *Harrow*, wherever it was. She might've already shot them down with Mother's battlegroup.

With direct physical access to shield security and power generators, Orna, Nilah, and Armin were able to quickly take control of the bay systems and lock them down, guaranteeing emergency power and shield coverage. Everyone happily removed their spacesuits, and Nilah looked as though she might faint.

"Not used to long EVAs?" asked Boots, slapping her on the back.

"After all this is over," she coughed, "I'm buying you people some new suits."

"If we can salvage the *Harrow*," said Boots, "we can afford our own."

"Here's the plan," called Cordell, and everyone snapped to attention. "There is no element of surprise. If there was someone home, that satellite already warned them when we didn't take it out on the first shot. For all we know, a distress call has already gone out and there's a ship in jump headed straight for us. That's why we need to be in and out. We can't hang around for Mother to get here."

Boots looked behind her at the open door and the icy trench, imagining the *Harrow* descending over them, cornering them inside the base.

Cordell gestured at the *Capricious*'s open cargo bay, where the Runner hung from its scaffold. "To that end, we need two teams. Miss Sokol, I want you to use anything you can to get the Midnight Runner working. I know you won't find factory originals here, but I think it's time we gave up on an authentic MRX-20. Miss Brio, if you're willing to help, that would be appreciated."

"Absolutely," said Nilah.

"Mister Vandevere and Miss Elsworth, you'll take Kin and join me on a sweep of the rest of the base. We need to get whatever information this place has and get the hell out of here."

Nilah and Orna immediately set to work, inventorying the docking bay for assets to repair the Runner. Boots, Cordell, and Armin gathered at the interior door at the far end of the docking bay. They drew their slinger pistols and stepped behind Cordell, who cast his shield. It was a healthy cast; he'd had some time to recover since battling the satellite. They keyed the panel, and the door slid aside as lights came to life beyond.

A thin blanket of dust covered the gleaming white marble slab floors beyond. The corridor yawned before them, dotted with fluted columns on either side. Every five meters, a crystal chandelier descended, each fixture a masterwork of curving glass tendrils and faceted drops. Intricate copper latticework crisscrossed the path before them, the work of skilled artisans.

"Uh..." said Boots.

"My thoughts exactly," added Armin.

"I mean," Boots began, "I always joked that the Taitutians had nice stuff, but this might be overkill."

"Keep your eyes open for valuables," said Cordell. "I think it's only fair that we take what we can find, don't you?"

"We're going to need a bigger ship to loot this place," said Boots.

They crossed the threshold, and Boots marveled at the walls: flat, clear glass molded to the mottled shape of the ice beyond. Spark-lamps danced through the ice like will-o'-the-wisps in the darkness. The team came to the first offshoot from the main hall—a pair of black oak doors set into the wall. Cordell brought up his shield to guard his chest and tapped the door handle.

The door motors swung them open to reveal a room full of data cubes. They'd been arranged on intricately carved wooden shelves, each cube resting atop a red velvet cushion. A high-backed leather chair sat before a terminal of milled gold. The same patina of dust from the hallway had crept into here.

"What the..." the captain's voice drifted off.

"It's like we got stuck in the dream of some Origin-obsessed whack job," said Boots.

Armin strode past them, slinger lowered in awe. "Look at all of this data...what do you think is on all of it?"

"If we don't find the location of the *Harrow*, Mister Vandevere, you'll be sifting through these," said Cordell. "Now come on. We can't get stuck in here gawking. Need to keep moving."

"Captain, why don't we connect up Kin," said Boots. "He can try some analytics while we search?"

"Good call," said Cordell.

Boots stepped to the terminal and seated Kin's crystalline cube down into the mount. He lit with an eerie green glow before a chime echoed across unseen speakers.

"What a lovely repository this is," said Kin, his voice more faithfully reproduced than Boots had heard it in a long time. The audio setup made it sound as though the human Kinnard was in the room with them.

"What are we looking at?" asked Boots.

"Too early to tell, just based upon indexing 8 percent of one of these crystals," said Kin, "but I should have an answer soon."

"Can you access the systems outside of this room?" asked Boots. "Central control and all that?"

A brief pause. "No. This room is a completely air-gapped network with no external data connections."

Boots, Armin, and Cordell exchanged glances.

"What have you seen so far?" asked Boots.

"Paintings," answered Kin. "This first cube is a database of tens of thousands of perfect analog scans of paintings. Most of the classics from Taitu are in here."

"Not what I was expecting to hear," said Boots, turning to her companions.

"This whole place ain't what I expected," said Cordell. "Why don't we let old Kin cook on this for a bit while we check the rest of the base out?"

They followed Cordell back into the corridor, where he led them to the next door. They swung it wide to reveal a long, grand hall, arched buttresses meeting in the center like an ancient cathedral. Rings of golden light rotated slowly overhead, creating mesmerizing orbital patterns. In the center of the room, a long onyx slab floated motionless, ringed on all sides by high-backed, gilded chairs—four seats on each side, one larger one at the head of the table.

"Okay," sighed Cordell, shaking his head, "secret base or no, *none* of that is military-issue. I don't give a damn how rich your planet is—"

A telltale hum was the only warning they received before an autoturret popped out of the ceiling, pounding Cordell's shield with corrosion spells. Any one of those rounds could've melted the flesh from his bones. He hunkered down behind his shield, providing cover for Boots and Armin, who ducked out to return fire.

On the fifth shot, Boots finally nailed the turret, leaving a smoking hole in the ceiling.

"Traps," sighed Boots, checking her mag. "Always with the traps."

They fanned out into the room, ears pricked for the sounds of machines, but heard nothing. Boots reached the head of the table first, and a luminous inscription flickered to life above the mirrored black surface.

"Witts," she read aloud. "This must be the admiral that Marie Prejean was talking about. So these other chairs are...other ship commanders maybe?"

"Fulsom," answered Cordell, approaching the table at the third seat down.

"Jean Prejean sat here," said Armin. That seat was almost at the end of the table. Boots was no expert on weird, secret paramilitary base decorum, but Prejean didn't seem all that important by the measure of his placement.

They read all of the names: Witts, Gweder, Hopkins, Vraba, Novak, Owusu, Slatkin, Jeon.

"Do you know who any of these people are?" asked Cordell. "Like, are any of these names associated with a secret banking cult that runs the galaxy, or…"

"Not a clue, sir," said Boots. "I've never heard the names before. It'd be nice to have some pictures or something."

"Henrick Witts was supposed to be an admiral in the Taitutian command, right? We could index these people against the records on the Link when we get back to the *Capricious*. It'd be a good place to start."

Boots made her way to the back of the hall, where she found another set of doors. "There are more rooms this way, sir." She listened against them for any movement, but heard nothing on the other side. Again her team re-formed in a vanguard behind Cordell, and they pushed open the doors.

Beyond was an advanced comms center and listening post. Boots recognized the layout from dozens of joint missions.

"Finally," said Cordell, cautiously stepping into the room. "Something reasonable around here. They had to be using this area to route communications between all of those bigwigs who sat at the table."

"If we assume this is the *Harrow*'s home base," said Armin, walking over to tap one of the dead screens, "this would be the operations center where they'd get their intelligence from Taitu. They could probably coordinate a lot of ships out of here."

"Look at this," said Cordell, powering on one of the stations. "No signal. It's expecting to link up to fifty satellites. Did you folks see fifty sats out there?"

"No, sir," said Boots. "I doubt we could've survived fifty of what we faced."

Cordell smiled. "Aw, Bootsie, don't sell us short. Anyway, my point is that those sats are either gone or downed. This place is off the grid."

"Sir," said Armin, "this is a substantial installation. I can think of dozens of states and private interests who'd have a use for this. Why just shut it down and forget it?"

"Maybe it already served its purpose," said Boots.

Cordell nodded. "I don't know why yet, but I hope you're wrong. This place is giving me the creeps."

"If they'd followed any kind of comsec standard operating procedures," said Armin, "none of this stuff should've booted. I'm guessing a lot of the data here is intact."

"Why would they leave it like that, sir?" asked Boots.

"Look at the chairs," said Armin, "arranged precisely at each station. The holomarks are all where they should be. The screens aren't scrambled all to hell." He shook his head. "This preservation is deliberate."

They filed out into the central hall, where they made their way in silence.

"Let's see how deep this goes and double back," said Cordell. "Boots, watch our phase."

They crept, shield forward and Boots facing behind, until they were out of the corridor. At the end of the long hallway, they found a secured hatch with a heavy blast door. Unlike the other walls, it was solid regraded steel, and even a skilled fire mage with a focused spell would've had trouble cutting through. To the right of it was a guard station where a few soldiers could've sat ready—if anyone had been home.

Cordell took point, leading the trio into the enclosed space of the guards' office. Lights powered on at his approach, and Armin keyed on a few of the projectors. As three-dimensional images of the corridors spun into life all around them, Boots noted a small, red warning.

She motioned Armin to it. "'Sat cluster down,' it says."

"Let's hope this system is the only one that got the memo," he muttered in reply. Then the image of the corridors outside snapped into focus. "Okay, now this is interesting."

To say there were no eidolon crystals on Wartenberg would've been an understatement. There was no mining equipment, construction gear, processing facility, or crew quarters, either. The entire Wartenberg Mining Colony was essentially a deadly decoy. Tiny green dots appeared all over the upper levels of the mining colony: explosive traps, tripwires, springflies, hidden glyph launchers, and another copy of the satellite drone swarm from before. All of the traps reported in, online and ready to kill.

"They really, really didn't want someone investigating the lower levels of the mines," said Boots, thankful they hadn't tried coming in the front door.

Cordell laughed and pointed to the colony's upper-level docking clamp. "What'd I tell you?" he said. "Boom."

Boots took a closer look and saw that the docking tube was one giant lancer round. If they'd have clamped on, the spell would've impaled their ship. She swept her hand over the projection sparkling with deadly green traps. She grimaced. "It's a good thing you wanted to cut your way in somewhere else, Captain. I think there's a safe spot in the little maintenance closet on subfloor B."

The air approach was essentially doomed, with every single docking point rigged to blow. The land approach involved a decent number of landmines and offensive spells, hidden just below the crust of ice. Near as Boots could tell, they could cut their way inside with a good enough fire mage, but that would leave them in a labyrinth of doom.

There was a tunnel between their location and the mining colony, but it was a nightmare: sieve grids, autoturrets, and more springflies. Even if they'd fought their way through the traps on the upper level, they wouldn't have made one step of progress down the hallway on the other side of the guard station.

"They never mined a single crystal here, did they?" asked Armin.

"It's pretty clearly a front, sir," said Boots. "But Aisha said something that stuck with me: why hide a warship like the *Harrow*? From what I can see, this is a mission planning center, which could've easily been housed on Taitu, where it would be better defended and managed."

"So what you're saying is..." Cordell began.

"What if it actually had some clandestine purpose? We all assumed, based on the massive glyph disc, that it was a weapon... but maybe it's something worse than sheer might."

"Like what?" asked Armin.

Boots shook her head. "I haven't gotten that far yet. There were a few more doors to check back there."

They made their way back to the closest door, and Boots listened against it. The wood was cool to the touch, and she wasn't sure what to make of that. Then she noticed an inscription above the door, cut into a gold plaque: IN GRATITUDE.

Cordell and Armin joined her and readied in formation. Cordell reached out and tapped the door plate, and it swung inward. Blinding blue light poured from inside, along with gusts of freezing air.

When their eyes adjusted, they found a graveyard.

Crystal clear ice filled this area, just as it consumed Wartenberg's surface. The freezing process left it cloudless, and some magic, maybe the grenadier's mark, had carved a perfectly round borehole through it like a tunnel. This place had once been a barracks, built from the same marble as the hallway outside, majestic and stepped like an amphitheater, lined with rooms.

Human bodies clouded the ice, their faces frozen in shock, their forms twisted as though a tidal wave had just thrown them from their feet. They'd been swept together like leaves on a breeze, and Boots could intuit which direction the floodwaters had come from. Bubbles gathered at their shocked faces. Whatever had filled their barracks with ice had done it quickly.

Ever mindful of traps, Boots followed her comrades inside. The deceased all wore matching uniforms—Taitutian military in appearance, but slightly different from the standard-issue. These were sleeker somehow, made from finer materials. The medals and insignia were strange variants on the known Taitutian patches, accented with heavier design elements. Their military seals were more akin to ancient escutcheons than modern ship equivalents.

Boots counted the ones nearest her, then estimated the distance: had to be over a hundred corpses in there.

"Marie Prejean had said something about a mutiny," said Boots. "You think this is what she was talking about, Captain?"

Cordell put his hands on his hips and peered up into the icy dead. "I listened to that recording a few times after you brought it back. The *Harrow* mutineers used gas, remember?"

"Oh," said Boots. "So these were some other people who got betrayed over the *Harrow*."

"I think these are the people who helped the mutineers carry off their plans," said Armin. "Their uniforms are different, and think about that turret in the planning and comms area; there are traps all over the colony, but only one inside the base. I'd wager that even these people weren't allowed inside the room with the chairs."

Cordell mulled it over. "So some of the *Harrow* crew mutinies. They get the ship. Then they come back here and kill everyone who helped them?"

"That ship is priceless," said Armin, "and it'd be smart to silence anyone who could lead someone to it. It might be worth cutting one of these people out of the ice to find any identifying marks."

"You ever seen anything like this, Mister Vandevere?" asked Cordell.

"Magic this large, this tightly controlled?" said Armin, reaching out to touch one of the walls. "Never."

Boots continued down the corridor, inspecting each of the bodies. The clear ice gave the chilling impression of being under the water with them, and when she'd made it about halfway, she could see that the passageway widened into a stone grotto. Marble pillars rose from the floor, past the lip of the tunnel, and she crept closer to get a better look.

Only they weren't pillars; they were nine tall, robed statues—a central figure flanked by four on both sides. Their surfaces weren't smoothly sculpted, like the fluted columns outside, but rough-hewn, as though they'd risen from the floor like stalagmites. Hoods hid their faces. Stony renderings of jeweled chains hung from their necks. Each one was indistinguishable from the next, save for the size of the central figure.

Boots poked her head into the larger room to see just how high the roof went, and found an impromptu chapel. The ceiling rose at least twenty meters, with lights drifting behind prismatic panes of glass or ice—she couldn't tell from the ground.

"Cap," she called back down the hallway, interrupting his conversation with Armin. "You've got to see this."

Her companions joined her, eyes wide. Cordell moved to touch one of the statues, and Armin stopped him.

"Haven't been scanned yet, sir," said Armin. "Better safe than sorry."

Boots spied a plaque inset into the ground, its letters obscured by a shadow. She pulled out her flashlight and knelt over it to read.

HERE, LAID BARE, ARE MY REMEMBRANCES,
A LIVING RECORD OF MY GREAT UNDERTAKING.
THIS WAS MY FIRST TRUE STEP.
THIS WAS MY ALPHA.
FROM HERE, I WROUGHT MY APOTHEOSIS.

I WILL RETURN WHEN THE STARS HAVE BOILED AWAY,
AND WE ARE POSSESSED OF AN INFINITE NIGHT.
I WILL LIGHT THE LAST LAMP HERE:
THE FINAL ACT OF THE CREATOR.
AND THEN TIME WILL PASS BEYOND ALL MEANING.

EVEN IN DIVINITY, I MUST NEVER FORGET,
THE STRIDES I TOOK, THE SACRIFICES MADE,
THOSE WHO CREWED MY SHIPS,
THOSE WHO DIED HERE,
THOSE ON CLARKESFALL.

Boots's blood ran as cold as the corpses in the antechamber, and her eyes rose to the robed man looming over her. In her mind's eye, blooming fireballs marched toward the coast of Arca, and Kinnard spoke his last words once more.

What, exactly, had the *Harrow* done on Clarkesfall? What clandestine part had it played in the Famine War? It certainly hadn't fought on the side of Arca. Had the *Harrow* taken down their defense grid in the last moment? Was that the warship's secret purpose?

She felt a hand on her back, and she flinched out of her thoughts. She turned to find Cordell reading the plaque over her shoulder, his face darkening with frosty anger.

"I was never sure," he began, keeping his voice steady, "that we were going to find the *Harrow*."

"And now?" she asked.

"I'll never have another happy day until I see its hull in the flesh. Whoever this Admiral Witts is, we're going to get our answers."

Chapter Eighteen

Overtake

N ilah had all the tools and the best design partner she could've
asked for in Orna. The parts in the equipment cages were
meticulously organized and brand-new. Fabrication inside
the docking bay would've been a dream come true for Nilah—if
she hadn't seen what lay farther inside Alpha.

That's what they'd come to call the Wartenberg base, and it'd
given her a new set of nightmares to join her dreams of Mother.
The "cemetery," as the floating bodies had come to be known, terrified her to her core.

The crew had gone silent and ashen in the pursuit of their
duties. The frightening mention of Clarkesfall had them all on
edge, and Nilah could easily imagine what they'd been like in the
closing days of the war: sullen, hungry, desperate. Orna was like
a different person, and though she was a good mechanic, she'd
become a terrible conversationalist.

Boots pushed a crate of data cubes past Nilah, toward the *Capricious*'s cargo ramp. Nilah recognized the dusty cubes from the
"library"; Kin said they were collections of art from across the galaxy,
but mostly Taitu. According to Boots, the reproductions weren't just

archival quality; they were like the culture arks Arca had launched in its final days. It was like someone expected Taitu to be wiped off the map, and wanted to keep what they could.

Boots gave the racer an idle wave as she passed, but kept her head down. Even Boots was too preoccupied for her usual saltiness.

"Miss Brio," called Cordell, striding up to the platform where they were welding a new armor panel onto the Runner.

"It's okay to call me Nilah," she replied, hoping to get a smile out of him. "We're friends now, you know."

He did smile, though she sensed it to be a front he put on for her. "Apologies, Nilah. You never stop being an officer. Anything interesting?"

"Boots ought to be pleased to know that we found a small cache of missiles with seeker heads."

"Enemy materiel, huh? What kind of ordnance are we talking?" asked Cordell. He gestured to the missiles, which Nilah and Orna had mounted to the stub-wing weapons hardpoints.

Nilah shrugged. "Not sure. We had to hack the hell out of security to get them. Some kind of high-explosive, nonfragmentation. Orna couldn't understand them much better than I could, but they appear quite well made—bespoke, perhaps. There's a binary mixing chamber, but we can't be sure of what chemicals are inside without cracking the—"

"And you want to bring these things onto my ship?" asked Cordell.

Nilah swallowed. "The, uh, quartermaster said they were safe. I thought that's what quartermasters did."

The captain put his hands on his hips. "Uh-huh."

She gave him a nervous smile. "We also found a whole lot of unused ordnance. She, um...she wants to take all of that, too."

"Of course she does," said Cordell, snorting. "I'm going to need you for something that'll take you off the Midnight Runner for the remainder of our time here."

"And how long is that?" she asked.

Cordell scratched his chin. He'd developed a bit of scruff since he'd been so busy all the time. "My first mate tells me he and Kinnard are on the verge of a breakthrough."

"That's good. You shouldn't shave the beard, by the way. It looks good on you."

His grin grew a little more genuine. "Nah. A clean ship and a clean face for me."

She shrugged. "Suit yourself. If we live through this, I know a few designers who might enjoy working with you."

He chuckled. "I guess we'll just have to stay alive so I can find out what you mean." He nodded to the fighter. "How close are we on the Runner?"

"Got some new skids on him. Redrilled the thruster ports and swapped out some busted armor plating. Orna is recalibrating the guns now. That thing is tough, not like a monocoque race car. If you get so much as a dent in one of those—"

Cordell raised his eyebrows. "You know I'm too stupid for the technical details, right? Just an old starship captain."

"Sorry," she said. "I tend to get a little carried away. So what did you need from me?"

He gestured toward the creepy hallway with its marble columns. She didn't want to go back after seeing the graveyard. Its architecture reminded Nilah of the design of Claire's office on the Lang yacht: overwrought wood and ancient expressions of wealth. She'd never be able to meet in Claire's office again without thinking of bodies trapped in ice.

"The traps upstairs report to the guard shack down here," he said. "Is that a two-way thing? Can we send them messages?"

"I'd imagine so," she said. "What's your thinking?"

He led her farther out of earshot from Orna, who watched them with idle curiosity as she worked. "When you first came aboard my ship, you tore up my defensive software. Then you hacked Ranger apart."

Nilah winced as he said that. She didn't like to think of it as an achievement.

"Sorry. I'm not trying to get you down," he said. "I think you've got a real knack for ripping up software, and I want your help with the techie stuff upstairs in the mining colony."

"Captain Lamarr, for me to take out all of those traps would be impossible."

He raised his hands in mock surrender. "Oh, I agree with you there. See, I just want *one* of the traps."

Cordell's wrist comm pinged, and he tapped it. "Go ahead."

"Captain," came Armin's tinny voice, "we've cracked their satellite surveillance footage from the last time the *Harrow* jumped out of here. I've got the next set of coordinates."

"Get back to the *Capricious* and get him prepped," said Cordell. "Miss Brio and I have some business to attend to before we can leave."

"Miss Brio," said Cordell, "everything green?"

Nilah sat on the darkened bridge of the *Capricious* for the twelfth consecutive hour, her clothes rumpled and itchy. Boots had once told her about the "hurry up and wait" mentality of ship life, and Nilah finally understood what she meant.

"All good here," she sighed, stifling a yawn. Her breath fogged in the frosty air, and she wiped her nose.

Once Armin had secured the *Harrow*'s coordinates, the crew lit out of Alpha and up to the top of the trench, where they'd prepped the surface of the glaciers with the few supplies they could find. The *Capricious* then flew a good distance and settled down into a flat spot in the base of another trench.

Cordell ordered every system in the ship to be placed in its most passive mode; electrical, climate control, and gravity were on minimal power so they'd be nigh undetectable. Their long-range scanners had been shut off: no pinging, only listening. They'd be able to detect a jump entry, but little else.

Nilah had been excited to take a turn at Orna's station, but now that she understood the reality of watching a dozen cameras for a day, the glamour had worn off.

"You want me to wake Miss Sokol so you can swap out early?" he asked, and she shook her head no. "Okay. Just another hour and they'll take a turn."

Nilah looked over to the other bridge crew, sacked out on the ground by their stations in hibernation bags. They didn't look comfortable, but she would've happily traded with one of them for a chance to shut her eyes.

Two more shift rotations. If Mother hadn't chased them to Wartenberg by then, they'd make for the jump gate.

One eyelid went down, and the bridge blurred. Her eyes fluttered with coming unconsciousness. The light strobed with the twitch of sleep.

Except it was a warning light blinking.

Boots perked up in her chair, startling Nilah awake. "Captain! Jump detected! One bandit, Sparrow five-four-five, sixty thousand ASL and dropping fast."

Cordell leaned forward in his captain's chair, a sudden ball of energy. "Yes, ma'am! That's what I'm talking about! Rise and shine, everyone!" He clapped his hands, and the others roused instantly. "Battle stations, people! We're live! Let's go!"

Armin returned to his place at the aggregator, tracing his glyph and resting his palms atop the crystal sphere. Aisha carved her spell and took hold of the flight stick in one hand and the keel slinger in the other. Orna took a seat beside Nilah, and together they drew their mechanist's marks, psychically connecting to the console—and the set of hidden cameras resting on a pile of ice outside Alpha's doors.

"Miss Sokol, relay the feed to the aggregator," said Cordell.

"Yes, sir," Orna replied, and Nilah felt her sculpt a connection between the cameras and Armin's data sifter.

"It's coming down fast, sir," called Boots. "No atmosphere to slow him."

"You're going to need to tune this thing for maximum speed, Miss Brio," said Cordell.

"Of course," she started, and feeling out of place, added, "Captain."

"Odds of scanner detection," said Armin, "fifteen percent."

Nilah couldn't help but hold her breath. The *Capricious* lay dormant in a trench fifty kilometers from Alpha, but if they were detected, they'd probably be blown out of the sky. Two things gave her solace: much of the planet was opaque to conventional scanning, and if Mother caught them in her spell, Nilah could overload it again and cause an accidental teleport.

However, they might teleport straight into Wartenberg's core, so the comfort was cold at best.

The shadow of Mother's ship rolled over Nilah's hidden cameras, and she shivered. She had to hope that the ice dust across her lenses would make them harder for metal scanners to detect.

Mother's battle cruiser slowed and turned, aligned to Alpha's hidden door, and began to descend into the trench. Nilah could feel its scanners turned to full power like a hot spotlight. She couldn't shake the thought from her head: *They're going to see us.*

"Distance to Alpha, nine hundred meters," said Armin. "By now, they know we took down their illusion spell, sir."

"Zoom in on the hull," said Cordell, and Nilah complied, focusing her many lenses on its massive hull. "Oh, that's the big boy right there. He's got four engines."

Nilah bit her lip. There were no contingencies if this failed. "He still hasn't seen us, Captain."

"Seven hundred meters to Alpha," called Armin.

"Not yet," Cordell soothed. "Let the bastards get a little closer."

"Five hundred meters," called Armin as the ship sunk lower, closer to Nilah's cameras.

"Closer..."

The hot spotlight of Mother's battle cruiser fell on Nilah's lens. "It sees me, Captain!"

Cordell stood from his chair. "Now!"

At Orna's command, the charges detonated at the top of the trench, sending glacial chunks of ice drifting overhead. They tumbled slowly, until a set of secondary charges splintered them down toward Mother's battle cruiser in a scattershot pattern.

"Hold, Brio!" called Cordell.

For this plan to work, they needed Mother to cast her spell, to be unprepared for the coming assault. Nilah swallowed, hoping the ice was good enough bait. The blues and blood reds of the canyon smeared away in a gray flash, and a volley of slinger fire appeared, shattering the dozen glaciers into a blast of snow.

Mother had done exactly what Cordell said she would: she pulled her battle cruiser out of time to set up a counterattack.

"Go!" ordered the captain, and Nilah's drone collective sprang into life. The dozen satellite orbs erupted from the scanner-jamming ice crystals, casting the grenadier's mark as fast as they could. Nilah built the ball of plasma in the drones' care like she was rolling it around in her palm before chucking it straight into the engine of Mother's battle cruiser.

It was a good hit, melting the central mounting of one of the engines. The blue jet of flame sputtered and died as Mother's ship listed to one side. Another gray flash filled the cameras, and the ship reappeared elsewhere inside the ice storm. Nilah's reflexes kicked in, and she re-targeted the engines without a second's pause. "No you don't!" she cried, sending another ball of luminous energy straight into the nozzle of another engine.

The scanners snapped to Nilah's drone collective, and she winced. She had more damage to do.

"They're targeting us," said Orna. "Prepare to evade!"

Mother's spell pulled her ship out of time once more and the colors melted away. When they returned, sizzling slinger bolts came flying straight at each one of Nilah's drones, taking out two of them. The ship had moved once again, but it couldn't flee through the ice overhead. Nilah would get another shot.

"Take her out!" shouted Cordell. "Let's end this!"

This time, Nilah felt no hesitation, no fear at the thought of ending another person's life. She fired another grenadier's mark and slammed the battle cruiser's third engine, shattering its housing into thousands of pieces. Mother's ship belched smoke into the crowded canyon, the airlessness drawing it away like syrup down into the trench. She wanted revenge for Didier, for Malik. She lined up a shot, charging closer. She would put a ball of plasma straight through the bridge.

Another gray flash, and Nilah completely lost contact with her drones. She knew what had happened. They'd been shot to pieces because of her charge.

"I lost contact, Captain Lamarr," said Nilah. "Sorry."

"It doesn't matter, Miss Brio. They're going to limp to the docks with hits like those," he replied. "Missus Jan, take us out of here. We've got a jump gate to catch."

*   *   *

Boots wrung her fingers behind her back, not wanting her nerves to show. Combat strategy briefings never sat well with her— ground truth always ruined plans.

There'd been a day of planning en route to the jump gate, and Armin had spent it sequestered away in his quarters, crunching data. Once they'd jumped, Cordell called a meeting. The crew stood assembled in the mess—not on alternating shifts, not away at work stations. With all of them together, the holes where Didier and Malik once stood filled with a tangible nothingness. No one mentioned the gaps.

Cordell rubbed his palms together, as though about to pick up a heavy load. "Mister Vandevere, why don't we start with the bad news?"

Armin placed his palm onto the ship's data terminal, and the projectors wove together images of Mother's smoking battle cruiser. "I've been analyzing the combat footage of our previous encounter with Mother, and I believe we were less effective than we thought."

Boots knew what he was going to say before he said it. The countermeasures on advanced warships were so much stronger than most conventional weapons. They'd been lucky to score hits at all, and it'd always been a gamble.

"You can see their dispersers firing effectively here and here," said Armin, and the projections highlighted his designations. "Some of the damage is more superficial than it looks. Based upon their crew complement, ship class, available resources, and a few other vari- ables, I estimate their repairs to have taken under forty-eight hours. They're already chasing us, and I can guarantee they're going to catch up."

Boots glanced at Nilah, who turned ashen.

"Miss Brio," said Cordell, "you did a fine job hammering those engines. This is just the hand we were dealt, and we've got to play it."

Armin cleared his throat. "For obvious reasons, I've been spending the bulk of my bandwidth finding the *Harrow*'s last known coordinates. Now that we have those, I was able to turn my attention to Mother's spell. She's the vanguard of the enemy, and it's time we created a countermeasure."

A projection of a golden glyph filled the mess. The lights dimmed, leaving the crew in the dark with the sigil, glowing like the sun. Its form was intricate, yet severe, the mingling of genius and fury. Even Boots could tell this was no ordinary glyph.

"This," said Armin, "is Mother's spell. It was scanned from beginning to end by Miss Elsworth, one of several perfect captures she made."

Murmurs rolled through the mess, and the glyph's script took on a more twisted character in Boots's mind. It was the mark of a hateful witch.

"Through continuous analysis, and with Miss Sokol's support, we've been able to determine how it works," said Armin. "And it's not pretty. We should start with the fact that—no matter how horrid—this woman is a virtuoso. The amount of arcane throughput she'd have to muster to cast this spell is enormous, and the complexity of the glyph is far too much for most of us scribblers. I doubt many people in the entire galaxy have faced something like her. I hate her as much as the rest of you, but we must respect her perfection if we're going to deal with the threat."

The glyph moved aside to make room for a series of charts and graphs depicting arcane energy force curves plotted over nanoseconds. "Mother is capable of drawing targets of various sizes into temporary dimensions for short periods. Within those pocket dimensions, time passes at extreme rates, while on the home plane, no time appears to pass at all. That's why it so often seems like she teleports—she's just moving through the pocket dimension at ultrahigh speed. Nilah, you reported the colors leached from your surroundings, and I believe this is the clearest way to understand the phenomenon. All the things in color cohabitate the dimension that Mother creates with her spell. All the things in gray have been left back on your home plane, where time is slower. A colorless closed door cannot be opened, a gray gun cannot be lifted."

"So how does that help Mother?" asked Orna.

"I believe she behaves like any predator," said Armin. "She isolates you from the herd. If she can catch you without your slinger, you're dead."

"But I had my slinger, and it didn't ice her. Also, Mother's scribbling didn't work on me," said Boots.

"I believe that has something to do with your arcana dystocia," Armin replied. "Unfortunately, the medical establishment doesn't understand much about your condition. If we did, we could find a way to use it to protect ourselves."

Boots had never considered herself useful in that way, and it made her uncomfortable. She crossed her arms and adjusted her stance, trying not to think about it too much.

"We know we can defeat Mother's spell from the inside if we flood it with a substantial amount of power, like the Arclight Booster or the ship's core, causing a random teleportation. But if you're not on the ship, that doesn't help you. Dispersers won't cut it if Mother doesn't bring them into the pocket dimension."

Nilah spoke up. "Because things are happening too fast inside Mother's spell?"

"Precisely," said Armin. "And dispersers take up a lot of energy, or we'd give them to all of you. Miss Sokol is working on a system, but we're not confident that—"

"Indolence gas," Nilah interrupted. "We use it in racing."

Armin blinked. "I'm sorry?"

"Did any of you catch last year's Awala GP? The one where Vangen crashed out and fractured his arcane batteries."

Boots and the others stared blankly at her.

"None of you watch racing?"

A chorus of murmurs and "not really my thing" came in reply.

Nilah rubbed her brow. "Okay, well... whenever we crash, there's a chance that the mechanist components in the car will explode in unpredictable ways. You get gusts of wind, balls of flame, and so on. Indolence gas renders those high-speed spells inert, but it also disconnects you from magic for a short period of time."

Orna nodded. "They should use that in jails, instead of the dispersers."

Nilah shook her head. "Prolonged, constant exposure can cause permanent dull... arcana dystocia. It'd be like cutting off your legs to keep you from running away. It's too cruel... and, uh, sorry for the slipup, Boots."

Boots shrugged, stifling her reflexive annoyance. "It's fine. I know you're trying."

The crew shifted uncomfortably, and Nilah cleared her throat. "With Orna's help, we could manufacture indolence gas and eat up Mother's spell from inside the pocket dimension, instead of pumping the spell full of power. We could rig a device to release the gas when we're targeted by that specific glyph."

"If it does what you say, I'm not wearing that," said Aisha.

"No magic is better than dead," Boots replied. "I get along just fine, you know."

"It's perfectly safe in small doses," Nilah replied. "And if you can catch Mother in the cloud, you might short out some of that armor she's wearing as well."

"And it won't be a choice, Missus Jan," said Cordell, who then cocked an eyebrow at Boots. "What if Mother gets the whole ship again? I'm sure you all remember that one."

"That's easy," said Orna. "We program the ship to dump energy when it detects Mother's spell. We'll teleport from the disruption, but there are worse things."

The captain crossed his arms. "Can these countermeasures be ready in time to contact the *Harrow*?"

"That depends, sir," said Orna. "You haven't told us when we're arriving there."

Armin sucked in a breath. "Two days."

The crackle of anxiety that descended over the room was palpable.

"What?" Orna's eyes widened. "Why can't we have more time to prepare? A week, at least!"

Cordell straightened. "I'm sorry, Miss Sokol, but that's not possible. Whoever is after us bought off the Fixers and Duke Thiollier's royal guard, two of the most trusted organizations in the galaxy. We have to assume that they have infinite resources at their disposal, and that they'll catch up to us sooner or later... probably sooner."

"You're asking for a miracle, Captain!" said Orna.

"That's enough." Cordell's voice flattened the room like a hammer. "We've got a man dead. We've got another in a coma, and he is depending on us to be the miracle workers we've always been. Now there is only one correct answer here. They don't want us finding the *Harrow*, so we've got to get there as soon as possible. If they're trying this hard to kill us, that means they're afraid of us, and by god, I will make sure they should be. Now, I don't know what's on that ship, but I know we want it. Miss Sokol, will you or won't you be ready with the countermeasures in two days?"

"Yes, sir."

"Good," said Cordell. "Is there anything else we need to cover?"

"Missus Jan will take the floor." Armin nodded to Aisha. "You found something on the star charts, didn't you?"

"Yes."

The pilot waved her hand over the console, and a star map filled the mess. She pointed to one of the galaxies, and it unfolded before them. A yellow, blinking cloud ensconced a large portion of it, a red exclamation mark spinning in the center of the mass.

"This is why they haven't moved the *Harrow* in all these years: they found the perfect hiding place." Aisha gestured to a warning box that popped up next to the cloud. "There's a system-wide advisory that covers two hundred planetary bodies, including our destination. It's category five, which makes it a no-fly zone."

"What's the enforcing authority?" asked Boots. "Local navy?"

Aisha shook her head. "There isn't one. Category five means that if you enter, you die. Supposedly, the military won't guard it because it's self-policing. I checked all the records I could find. They said, 'intense arcane storms and disruption.'"

"That could mean anything," Cordell added. "Do we have any imaging of the area?"

Aisha gestured, and the cloud zoomed in on a blurry group of worlds. "Taitutian wide-band scrying and far field spellscopes took images thirty years ago. There are two worlds of reasonable size in all this mess. The *Harrow* supposedly jumped in next to this one: Chaparral Two."

One of the planets burned a bright green as Aisha reached out and touched it.

"We're not one hundred percent that the *Harrow* is still there. There's a chance it could've jumped away on its own," said Armin, "and the nearest jump gate is six days away at a full burn. If we go in, we're there for at least a week."

"It'll be there, sir. I can guarantee it," said Boots. "Think about it—they tried to burn down my office, they tried to whack Nilah with a battlegroup of starfighters, and later, they burned down the duke's palace. If they could move the ship, they would've, because it's a hell of a lot cheaper than killing Duke Thiollier."

Armin nodded. "I'm inclined to agree with your logic."

Cordell smiled. "So what do you think, Boots? What are we going to find when we jump in there?"

Boots scratched the back of her head. "The past two sites we've found have been full of deadly traps, so...yeah...that. We don't know the whereabouts of the other battle cruiser, either, so I'm pretty certain it'll be waiting for us. I'm assuming we have a plan to engage them?"

The captain let out a long sigh, breaking the regal composure he'd had only moments prior. "We'll need to use the one advantage a marauder-class ship has—the belly. If we can get in close with them and mix it up, we might be able to get a lucky shot on their bridge. I'm thinking we rush them with full shields, some improvised mines, and the keel gun while you keep their fighters off our backs. Bombs overload the dispersers while Missus Jan lines up the perfect shot."

An eerie silence fell over the mess, only punctuated by the occasional beep of a computer. Boots's hairs stood on end—he wanted to try the same strategy he'd used at Laconte.

Cordell affixed Boots with his clear brown eyes. They were the only two people in the room who really understood what he was suggesting. He jammed his hands into his pockets. "You saw their missile complement, Bootsie. If we keep our distance, we're dead. If you try to engage them one at a time, you're dead, *then* we're dead. Our only hope is to drop in fast and take them out before they know what hit them."

Boots lowered her gaze to stop herself from looking at her crewmates. Otherwise, she'd imagine them in the same states as those from Laconte: torn to pieces. That battle was Cordell's greatest career failure. He wouldn't suggest it unless he was sure.

"So we drop out of the Flow, I launch, we charge, and hope for the best?" asked Boots.

"Correct," said Cordell.

She might be able to talk him out of this. She could see in his eyes that he wasn't completely sure of the strategy, either. And yet, as she racked her brain, she didn't have any better ideas.

"Has a marauder... ever in history..." said Boots, pinching the bridge of her nose, "taken out a battle cruiser."

Cordell smirked. "You're the historian. You tell me."

Boots closed her eyes and nodded. "What the hell, I suppose. Maybe we can take a few of them with us."

"You know we will," said the captain. "Missus Jan, keep us up to date regarding our exit from the Flow. Nonessentials are dismissed."

Boots awoke to the lights in her room flashing red.

"All crew, ready stations in ten minutes. All crew, stand by ready stations," came Aisha's voice.

Swinging her legs over the edge of the bed, Boots gave herself a good stretch. They were coming out of the Flow right on schedule, and she'd been expecting the call any second, though she'd hoped they would be an hour late. The crew had been on standby for the past three days, which meant no showers and no disrobing, save for the few seconds it took to change clothes every day. The one exception to the rule was Nilah, who was classified as nonessential personnel. By the third day, being around the racer was like being in the presence of a divine creature—beautiful, polished, and pleasant—unlike the rest of the musky crew.

Boots stank, and her hair felt greasy. She flexed her toes in her sweaty shoes. "Kin, how long was I out?"

"Twenty-three minutes, Lizzie."

"Dang." She lumbered out of bed and pulled her covers back into place before heading out to the cargo bay.

Lights flickered on with her arrival, and Boots glanced up at the Midnight Runner, orange floodlights splashing across its hull.

"Go time," she whispered. *They're going to be okay. This will be different than Laconte. It's open space.*

They'd salvaged a couple of seekers for the Runner back at Alpha, and she wasn't sure of the exact make, but the missiles made for an impressive complement. Boots just hoped the nonstandard warheads were as mean as they looked.

For the past few days, Nilah had sequestered herself in her quarters with about half of Orna's tools and some dangerous-looking chemicals. She was creating a countermeasure for Mother's power, but Boots hadn't seen it yet. She only knew that the rest of the crew wanted nothing to do with the racer while she worked; something about the indolence gas kept them pretty spooked. For the first time, Boots was thankful for her natural immunity.

A pair of mine launchers ran the length of the cargo bay ceiling, their silvery struts a makeshift mechanism from the quartermaster. Orna had loaded them up with thirty improvised limpet mines designed to cling to the battle cruiser's hull.

"Orna!" Boots shouted, and the quartermaster swung out from behind the launchers like a grease-stained spider.

Orna plucked a spanner from her mouth and stowed it into a socket on her belt. "What?"

"You heard the call. Ready stations in five." Boots opened a hatch along the far wall and yanked out a flight vest and suit.

"Finally." Orna released the harness and dropped ten feet to the deck like a sledgehammer. "Nilah got the stuff ready?"

"I think so. She's supposed to be at muster." Boots jammed her feet into the suit and pulled it up over her arms before pressing the form button on its belt. It suctioned to her body, granting her freedom of movement, but it pressed her wrinkled clothes against her skin. A puff of body odor shot into her face from the locking collar, and she winced.

Orna nodded at her as she approached. "You ready for this?"

Boots shook her head. "Is that even possible? I wish I had your fire support."

Orna tongued the inside of her mouth, and Boots realized she'd said something stupid, accidentally bringing up Ranger before a battle. "Yeah, well... just stay away from the battle cruiser. I don't want one of these mines sticking to my fighter."

Picking up her helmet off the rack, Boots said, "You and me both."

"Good hunting, Boots."

Orna rushed off to the bridge, leaving Boots to climb up to the Midnight Runner and into the cockpit. She keyed in her access code, and the console rose to life. She eyed the mine launcher rails, perilously close to her fighter's scaffolding, but Orna had assured Boots that the ship would take off just fine.

"Departure, this is Boots, checking in."

"Departure acknowledges, Boots," said Armin. "Stand by for preflight checks."

Boots ran down the list with Armin, her heart thumping every time she said a system was ready. She couldn't help but feel like it was a countdown to their demise.

"Boots," said Armin, "you are cleared for departure on our mark. Stand by."

"Good luck, Prince," she said.

"To both of us."

Aisha boomed through the cargo bay, and the lights flashed red again. "All crew, ten seconds to normal space."

Atmosphere began to drain from the bay. Boots counted down and listened for the familiar thrum of the ship's main thrusters. Right on the dot, she felt the skewing shift into normal space. For a category five zone, there weren't any screeching explosions or searing beams—just the gentle hum of smooth sailing.

"All stations, damage report!" Aisha cried.

The crew ran down the litany of systems in her helmet earpiece, each one coming up nominal. But then, Orna called out, "Scanners offline, Captain. Systems responding, but they can't penetrate whatever... *this* is."

What the hell were they talking about? Boots awaited her turn to report in, hoping they'd pop the bay door and release her. When it came to Boots, she said, "Runner here, ready to deploy."

"All systems... all systems operational, Captain," said Aisha. "Except scanners."

"Then what is this?" asked Cordell. "You're all feeling it, too."

Once more, the crew sounded off, each one confirming that they felt something horrible. Then it came to Boots.

"Sir, I feel fine."

"Standby again, Boots," said Armin. "We're trying to assess the situation."

"Departure, I'd like to request a recon release," said Boots.

"Copy that," said Armin.

"Pop the bay and let her out," said Cordell.

The bay door opened soundlessly, though Boots could feel it grinding through the Runner's mag clamps. As soon as it thunked to a stop, Boots launched, not waiting for orders. If they were in danger, she would do whatever it took to blow the enemy into space dust.

Except once she reached open space, she found nothing—no arcing spells, no enemy warships, just the cool blue orb of Chaparral Two. Sickly light flickered from a nearby star, bathing the azure planet. Boots hadn't expected to find an ocean world, given that the *Harrow* was supposedly secreted away there. Had they hidden it underwater?

"Negative visual contact, but my scanners are down too," said Boots. "What have you got, Boss?"

"It's our opinion," said Cordell, voice labored, "that this place is magically suppressed. It explains why you're the only one not feeling the effects."

"How bad are we talking here? We going to be able to cycle oxygen?"

"Yeah. All the amps and subsystems still work... just a lot of funk out there. I feel certain," he said, and Boots got the impression that he was addressing the entire bridge, "that we can all do our jobs today."

"Copy that," said Boots. "You can still cast?"

"We can, but it's weak," he said. "Don't worry about us."

Before she could say anything else, a streak and a bright flash filled her vision. A battle cruiser sliced across the sky, missile pods bristling. Four fighters shot forth from its bay like angry insects, armed for bear at the *Capricious*.

"Visual contact!" called Boots. "Five bandits: four fighters and a battle cruiser. Echo niner-niner-niner, carom two-zero-one, distance, uh..." she checked her camera's visible spectrum analysis, "twenty thousand. Requesting weapons free."

"Prince here. Weapons free. Prepare for full burn."

Chapter Nineteen

Harmony and Harrow

Boots fired her maneuvering thrusters to center up on the pack of fighters. She'd charge into them on the tail of the *Capricious*, using the marauder's shields for cover.

"Moment of truth, folks. The plan hasn't changed," said Cordell as a pair of shields spun into being around the *Capricious*'s nose. The translucent blue plates aligned, one over the other, hardening the fore defenses. "Execute full burn in three…"

The distant fighters aligned for a strafing run. The marauder's charge would force them to break ranks.

"Two…"

Boots flipped the safeties off all her weapons. They were fighting visual-only in a null-magic field. This was her battle to lose.

"One…"

Her fingers tightened around the throttle.

"Execute."

The *Capricious*'s main drive flared, and the ship raced past Boots. She throttled up, falling in behind its engine wash, and inertia pressed her into her seat. She'd finally started to acclimate to her old settings, and the sporty discomfort gave her an edge in a fight. All the combat actions had resurrected her instincts from the bad old days, and she felt sharp as a knife; a little rusty, but still dangerous.

Ahead of her, the halo of Cordell's shield arced against the silhouette of the *Capricious*—he was taking fire up front from the fighters. Boots got in closer behind him, using the mass for full cover. A missile corkscrewed past the *Capricious* into the blackness beyond, and Boots realized the fight had swung even harder in her favor—no scanners meant that seeker missiles couldn't acquire targets.

"Dispersers at full capacity," called Nilah over the radio.

"Keep them tuned up," said Cordell. "Boots, we're about to bust up that fighter wing. Peel up, because we've got a surprise for them. Missus Jan will call your mark."

"Distance five hundred," said Aisha.

"Copy that," said Boots.

The shield flared brighter as more shots bounced off the front of the *Capricious*, and the engines shone like tiny suns. One of the missiles struck home, sending sparks around the side of the ship in a spray, but it was an indirect hit.

"Mark!" shouted Aisha.

Boots angled her nose up as a pair of fighters streaked overhead. Her cheeks pulled toward her neck as she punched her booster. She clicked the trigger, spraying a burst of slinger fire at them, but they were too far away, and the shots went wide. The fighters spun in place and returned fire, their shots lancing past her as she broke cover to pursue. Her dispersers discharged and whined as they charged again.

Just below her, the *Capricious* rolled and fired its keel gun at one of the bandits shooting at Boots. Aisha's marksman's mark brought the shot home, and the enemy fighter went careening off into space, engines sparking and painting a trail of viscous smoke.

The second fighter charged directly for Boots, slingers blazing. She fired her keel maneuvering thrusters, pushing her fighter out of range of the bolts as she boosted up and over him. Her targeting computer indicated a lock, and she loosed one of her four missiles on instinct—

Only to have it go spiraling off into nowhere, its warhead unable to acquire a target. She'd forgotten about the suppression field's effects already.

"Son of a—" she grumbled, peeling off after the *Capricious*. She should've shredded the enemy's canopy with regular slingers, but a moment of inattentiveness had cost her the opportunity.

"All okay, Boots?" Armin's tinny voice echoed in her comm.

"I finally get some missiles and I can't freaking use them!" said Boots. "Can I get another shot from the keel gun on one of these clowns? It's still three on one out here!"

A spray of spells filled her vision, and Boots flipped the Runner, diving and rolling off-axis with one of the wing thrusters. In the distance, she spied the *Capricious* closing on the battle cruiser, streaks of powerful spells lancing out and shattering on the shields. Two of the fighters had followed, leaving their third member to deal with Boots.

"You're going to have to make do," said Cordell, grunting as a large round blasted his shield. "We're about to engage the battle cruiser."

The Runner shook hard with a deafening strike, and warning alarms filled her ears. The enemy fighter had tattooed a short line down the back of her main drive housing. She'd been lucky—a little to the left, and her eidolon core would've gone up.

"Cheeky little bastard." She spun her fighter to find the enemy entirely too close for comfort, and opened up with her guns. He dodged right, and she slowed her momentum with the main drive, allowing him to pass as she set up a line of fire.

It cut his canopy in half like a chainsaw.

"Two down, two to go!" shouted Boots, laying into her throttle and reorienting toward the *Capricious*.

"Prince here. We could use your help," called Armin. "These other two fighters are chewing up our rear, and the captain needs both shields to fore."

"Copy that." Boots searched open space with her visible light gun cam and found the two fighters. She magnified them onto her console, setting a course. One of the enemy craft glimmered with an arcane shield across its nose.

"Prince, we've got a striker!" she called in, checking her readout. "Echo one-one-three, carom four-zero-nine, distance thirty-two hundred."

"Striker" was their code word for pilots with the shieldmaster's mark and fighter amps: fast spacecraft that could slam into warships while doing little damage to themselves. Boots put a full burn on her throttle, and her warning panel squawked a loud protest.

"Boots," growled Cordell, "I'm taking on the full firepower of a cruiser over here. I can't spare a shield to block. Take him out!"

The striker centered up on the *Capricious*, and Boots rocketed toward it as fast as she could. The Runner would never be as fast as something designed to eviscerate large military ships with its own body.

The striker's scanners didn't work. It wouldn't see her coming, and while a shield protected its front, its rear was open to attack. She punched in auxiliary power to her main drive, and the system positively screeched at her for it. Boots was no mechanist, but she could be reasonably sure her starfighter was upset with her.

Her eyes darted between the heat sensors in her engine cowling, the visual intercept vector, and the view of the unfolding battle in front of her. Her ship made an unfamiliar rattle as it raced for the striker, whose engines flared brightly.

"Go, go, go, baby," muttered Boots, lining up the shot. Fire too soon, and the striker would notice her and peel off. Too late, and she'd be shooting through the enemy—into the open cargo bay of the *Capricious*.

Her warnings reached a fever pitch as Boots loosed a spray of bolts. Enemy dispersers caught the first two hits, but the remaining volley went through. The striker exploded into a glittering eruption of purple eidolon dust and zero-g flames, like smeared orbs. Boots checked the spread of debris—it didn't look like the enemy remains would hit the *Capricious*, so she didn't have to chase them down and put a few shots into them.

"Boss here. You take care of that striker?"

"Yes, sir," said Boots. "Dead as a doornail and one to go."

"Distance to cruiser, one thousand," said Aisha.

"Execute mining maneuver," said Armin. "Boots, you're going to want to stay clear."

The *Capricious*'s main drive angled down, pushing the ship into a forward tumble to point its open cargo bay straight at the battle cruiser. Cordell's shields swung around to protect the back as the ship began to corkscrew.

"Launch mines!" shouted Cordell, parting his shields long enough to let the dozens of discus-shaped charges through. They flew from the spinning cargo bay in a helical pattern, a deadly strand of DNA bound for the battle cruiser.

The remaining enemy fighter made a fast pass over the *Capricious*, slingers perforating the marauder's main drive—the engine it would've used to slow its attack.

It was Laconte all over again. The *Capricious* was going to slam into the battle cruiser, shattering Cordell's amplified shields.

A stray bolt of slinger fire caught the first limpet in a chain, detonating it. The shock wave sent the others off-course, and Cordell had to bat them away with his shields.

"How many more mines you got?" called Boots.

"Zero," said Armin. "Everyone brace for impact!"

Boots was already vectored in to pass the *Capricious* from chasing the striker. She could make a hard run on the cruiser, no targeting computers, no certainty that she could turn in time.

All she had to do was fly through the cruiser's firing solution on the *Capricious* before the two ships collided. Once again she throttled up, and her ship rattled hard.

"I'm going to smash this guy, Boss," said Boots, designating the spot on the battle cruiser where she intended to strike—dead center, where the *Capricious* was going to hit.

"I told you to take out the fighters! You're my only wing, Boots," said Cordell.

She whipped under the *Capricious*, its secondary drives doing everything they could to alter its trajectory. A stray limpet streaked toward her and Boots blew it apart with her slingers, scattering debris and molten metal across the stars.

The battle cruiser came into full view, its bright yellow sides lined with burning hot slingers belching missiles past her cockpit like schools of fish. This was definitely a stupid idea.

"Boots, do you copy?"

"What the hell do you think I'm doing, Captain?"

She depressed the secondary trigger, launching her remaining three missiles. All she needed to do was pierce the cruiser's hull and weaken a central rib, and the *Capricious* might break through. At this range, the missiles wouldn't miss, even without guidance, and since missiles weren't spells, dispersers couldn't stop them, either.

Boots fired her forward maneuvering thrusters and her canopy thrusters, hoping to push her ship down and out of the way before she slammed into the cruiser's hull like an insect.

The first missile struck with the fire of a thousand suns. The cruiser buckled backward as though a god's hand had shoved it. A spinning crescent flash smashed through the cruiser's side, slicing the hull apart and sending both ends spinning outward.

It was a warhead-sized discus round.

"Holy—" came Cordell's voice, but the second two missiles hit their marks, quadrisecting the battle cruiser into exploding chunks.

Boots sailed through the wreckage, her eyes darting across the honeycomb of glowing orange metal. She spied the silhouette of an unsuited body, drifting freely from its former battle station. Lights inside the battle cruiser flickered and went out, leaving only the golden cross-section of decks.

Boots spun her Runner to watch the *Capricious* blast through after her, its shields protecting it from the smaller debris. The marauder continued its corkscrew, planting a shot into the dead center of the last strafing fighter. The small craft went up like a bonfire, pieces of it streaking into a chunk of the battle cruiser.

For a moment, the radio was dead silent.

"So," said Boots, "on my combat record, does that count as one ship, or..."

Cordell's jovial voice came over the comm, laughter erupting behind him. "Okay, okay, let's not get ahead of ourselves, Boots. How many more of those ridiculous warheads you got left?"

She checked her pylon inventory. "Um, zero?"

"Damn," he replied. "We could've used a few of those on Mother's ship."

"Captain Lamarr," said Boots, her heart finally slowing to a human speed, "if you think I'm about to take some lip about saving the crew of your ship—"

"Now, now. Let's talk about that planet. If we don't find somewhere to dock, we aren't even limping home."

Her eyes ran over the debris of the battle cruiser, searching for any survivors, fighters, or pod launches. She found nothing. It disturbed her a little, having sliced through them so cleanly.

"Any landmasses on that planet, Boss?" she called in. "Or is it just ocean?"

Armin chimed in her ear. "This is Prince. According to old surveyor data, that color you're seeing is caused by large deposits of cobalt in the planet's soil. There's no water anywhere on that world."

Boots maneuvered away from the *Capricious* with a few well-placed pulses. "Great. So potential heavy metal poisoning every time you cycle your suit. How hard would it be to colonize?"

"Your reclaimers would have to be one hundred percent efficient. Waste of time. Miss Brio is working on a better survey, but we're still having trouble getting planetary scans."

Boots throttled up, shooting past the *Capricious* as though leading him in for an approach.

"So there's nothing about the planet we can scan?" she asked.

Armin replied, "We can do visual analytics, but that could take some time. And from this angle, we won't get the other side of the planet, or anything in its umbral cone."

Something clicked inside Boots's head, some memory she couldn't quite dredge up.

"Repeat your last, Prince."

"We can't see the dark side of Chaparral Two or anything in the umbral cone—the shadow that the planet casts."

Jean said you would delve the umbra and destroy everything. Do it.

Boots spun her ship to look at the star in the far distance. Her HUD corrected her and showed her two stars, their orbits intertwined in a binary system. "Is the planet tidally locked to those two stars?"

344

Armin made a thoughtful noise. "The survey only shows one star, and the planet shouldn't be locked to it. Our weak predictions based on visual data indicate otherwise. We are detecting a tidal lock."

"The *Harrow* is on the other side, in the planet's umbra. Follow me, and I'll guide you in."

"How do you know that?"

"The widow's diary from Carré."

A pause, then Cordell's voice came over the radio. "Boss here. It's the best we've got. Lead on."

Under basic thrust, the journey to the umbra took two grueling hours. They made a wide arc around the planet, in case the *Harrow* had an automated firing solution. The glass on Boots's ship lit up with a calculation of the light from the binary star system, drawing a long black spike into space where the shadow lay. Green light traced its edges like a coating of acid.

That's where she'd find the *Harrow*.

"Prince to Boots," said Armin. "I'm narrowing down the search a bit."

Her screen flashed, eliminating much of the umbra's sharpness and shortening it considerably. "Interesting…"

"The orbits of the binary stars cause some of these areas to be illuminated from time to time. We want to start with places that remain pitch-black—fully within the umbral shadow. I'm routing data to your Runner. He'll let you know when you're almost out of the star's light."

"Understood. Boots out."

Another hour went by, and Boots's system chirped. She held her breath as the Midnight Runner crossed into the shadow, the star's light disappearing from her canopy. All interference disappeared from her sensors, and proximity alarms rang out as her long-range system detected a massive hulk.

Her stomach dropped. "Contact! Bogey spades, camber zero-niner-zero, carom two-two-four, distance twelve thousand. Please advise."

Armin returned the call. "Visual?"

"Negative, sir. Waiting for my sensors to get a better look at him."

"Solid copy. Take evasive action if necessary. Stand by for orders."

Boots eyed her console, waiting for any warnings, but none came. She glanced back to the *Capricious*, its bulk passing into the shadows behind her.

"Boots, Boss here. Sensors just came back online. We see him."

A half dozen views of a spectacular warship spun into life on Boots's cockpit glass. Her sensors picked up every detail from this range, analyzing them, passing them to her—over a kilometer long with a sleek black hull that melted into the shadows, the ship had a giant spell disc, twenty times larger than anything Boots had ever seen in person. Never had she felt such a strange comingling of exhilaration and dread.

"It's the *Harrow*," said Cordell. "Well done, my friends. Well done, Boots."

She'd known, academically, that it was real from the moment she set foot in Jean Prejean's lair, but hearing those words from her captain sucked the air from her lungs. She never thought she'd actually see another treasure again.

Cordell knocked her out of the moment. "He's not reacting to us, so I doubt anybody is home over there. Automatic defenses will be running full, though. Remember our ADF dreadnoughts? He'll come alive if we take boarding action."

"Prince here. We just got back orienteering, along with the sensors," said Armin. "This is very interesting. It would appear that the light of those binary stars is creating the suppression effect. The star itself is some kind of spell, or at least an arcane phenomenon."

"Incredible. So the magic suppression field has a hole in it, and that's where they parked the ship." Boots's glass gave her a variety of galactic waypoints, including the nearest jump gate—two weeks away. With the *Capricious*'s limping engines, it could take a month.

"Indeed," said Armin. "Like hiding from a harsh storm in the lee of a building."

"We've got to get on board that ship, sir. Mother will be here any moment," said Boots.

"I'm inclined to agree," said Cordell. "You think you can get close? Maybe dismantle some of his anti-air towers?" said Cordell.

"Boss, I don't have any countermeasures except basic dispersers. You know that's not enough for something like this."

"Can you do without?" asked the captain, an edge in his voice.

The fighter's sensors registered a return, showing the *Harrow*'s thousand slingers bristling along its surface. The grainy image she'd seen of it jumping did the ship no justice. Taitutian craftsmanship mingled with strange ship design, giving the vessel the appearance of having rippling muscles under its metal skin.

If she flew in there, she'd be space dust in seconds.

"Negative, Boss. He'd have a firing solution on me before I even got close."

No response came, and she worried that the magical interference had done something to their comms. Or maybe he was mad at her.

"Come in, *Capricious*."

"Stand by, Boots. Our mechanics think they have an idea."

"Copy that. Standing by."

Nilah huffed as she stacked chest after chest next to the cargo bay doors. It was hard work, made harder by the bulky spacesuit she had to wear. "You know, if I'd known we were going to use your new tools to simulate debris, I would've bought cheaper ones."

Orna gave her a sidelong glance through her visor. "And you can afford more. Besides," she grunted, hefting a metal crate, "there'll be better crap on board the *Harrow.*"

"Assuming we make it."

"We'll make it, but it'll be dangerous. Maybe you can get another set of scars to show off." Orna turned away, and Nilah couldn't see her expression. Was she thinking of Ranger?

"I'm not showing off."

"Why not? Scars are cute on you."

It was a simple, stupid plan, but the best one Nilah and Orna could concoct: deactivate all magical items and leap across the twelve-kilometer gap to the *Harrow* while posing as a cloud of debris. The *Harrow* would automatically attack vehicles, so Nilah and Orna would have to make the jump in spacesuits.

Klaxons signaled the venting of atmosphere. Nilah finished having second thoughts right about the time the cargo bay opened up and gave her third thoughts. The planet's surface glimmered far below, phosphorescence from a network of poisonous, ever-burning fires. The black outline of the *Harrow* greeted her, a dark speck on the horizon.

Kin chimed in Nilah's comm. "I'm pleased to be accompanying you on this mission, Miss Brio. I think you'll find my hacking abilities to be an excellent complement to your own."

"Uh, thanks, mate," said Nilah. She didn't like being in charge of Boots's AI. It felt a bit like carrying around someone else's diary.

"I'm concerned the Taitutian infrastructure won't have a socket for me," said Kin. "My model was far more common on Clarkesfall."

"I can figure something out," said Nilah. "Kin, how long will the *Capricious* take to pick us up if Cordell misses and we don't hit the *Harrow*?"

"I'm afraid that won't be possible. You'll enter the planet's gravity well and burn up in the atmosphere long before the *Capricious* can catch up to you."

"Well that's cheery."

"A painless death is more than most humans can hope to get," said Kin.

"Okay, Kin. Thank you for that, uh, perspective. We need you to shut down now. I don't want your energy signature triggering the *Harrow*'s guns."

Orna checked her atmospheric gauges, her voice crackling over Nilah's old comm. "We'll wake you up when we get there, Kin." She gestured Nilah to the pallet of tool chests and braced to push against it. "Can you think of anything else we need to do before we go?"

"Another kiss might be nice if we didn't have these damned helmets on."

"What was that?" Cordell chuckled over the comm.

Orna shot Nilah a murderous glare through the visor. "Nothing, Boss. Hunter One and Two, standing by for orders."

Those were the code names they'd been given. A few months ago, basking in the luxury of a PGRF hospitality suite, Nilah would've thought a code name was cool. Now, it just meant she was doing something stupid. Worse still, she was Hunter Two, and she had a pathological hatred of being second.

"Hunter One and Two, execute in three..."

Nilah activated her mag boots and braced against the deck.

"Two..."

She wrapped her fingers around the pallet's dolly handle, and Orna did the same.

"One..."

Nilah raised her eyes to the *Harrow*, a shadow in the sea of distant fires.

"Execute."

The pair of women shoved as hard as they could. The pallet barely budged at first, but gradually picked up speed. Once they built up enough momentum, they sailed out of the cargo bay and into open space.

"Boss, this is Hunter One. We're floating here. Deactivating oxy scrubbers now."

Nilah followed Orna's lead, shutting down her suit's atmospheric processors. Any energy signatures were dangerous, including the descender discs they'd have to use to land.

"All right, ladies," said Cordell. "I'm about to give you the shove, and it's comms out until you hit home. Hold on to your helmets, and god speed you."

"Hunter One, acknowledged."

"Uh, Hunter Two, acknowledged."

A blue wall of force coalesced behind the pair of spacewalkers, and Nilah's eyes met Orna's. Both women reached up, and in tandem, shut down their communicators. The *Capricious*'s shield gently came to rest against them, matching speed with their slow drift. Nilah could imagine Cordell on the bridge, funneling his magic into the amp, his eyes fixed to the heads-up display.

Boots circled nearby in the Runner, waiting to see them off. She illuminated them with the fighter's searchlight, flashing them three times. Orna waved back.

The shield pulsed once with light before pressing against them and hurling Nilah, Orna, and the tools into the blackness. She was impressed at the crushing force of their acceleration—far stronger than that of the Lang Hyper 8. Her limbs were glued to Cordell's shield. Blood rushed to her head and legs. Then she came free, and her flight had truly begun.

Nilah strained to get her breathing under control; she wouldn't have much air if she panicked. At first, it didn't feel as though they were moving very fast, but then Nilah looked back to see the *Capricious* as a tiny, bright speck.

Minutes stretched on for an eternity. Orna placed her hand over Nilah's as they hurtled through open space. The *Harrow* grew in their vision, and with each closing kilometer, he seemed to double in size. Red running lights burned ominously, like the thousand eyes of a wicked creature.

Halfway through their flight, Orna reached out and grabbed one of the tool chests, gently opening it and shuffling its contents out into the vacuum. They had to create a believable debris field to hamper the sensors from seeing live targets in the middle. Nilah followed suit, never shoving or throwing anything too hard for fear of disrupting her own vector. As long as she kept things pretty equal, she'd stay on course. Her life depended on her slamming straight into the hull at full speed. Soon they inhabited a slowly expanding cloud of metal, rubber, plastic, regraded steel, and fibron. She could only hope the *Harrow*'s sensors would detect them as a shipwreck.

Orna withdrew her descender canister and held on tightly to its girth. Nilah fumbled with her own canister, checking the battery to make certain the radar was disabled. She suppressed her urge to psychically connect to its guts, just in case the automatic defenses could detect a mechanist's magic. Orna nodded at her as they watched the hulking spacecraft draw nearer.

Guns on the ship's surface anxiously followed their progress, but they didn't open fire.

The utter silence of her suit, no atmospheric cycling, unnerved her. Maybe she was only imagining it, but her head felt light. The inside of her visor condensed her breath like the rainforests on her homeworld, and sweat coated her arms. She wondered if incursions like this were the reason the suit had such a unique scent in the first place.

Orna held her descender in front of her as they flew headfirst toward the hull, and Nilah followed suit. Activate too soon, and they'd both be blasted to pieces by the automated defenses seeing an energy signature. Too late, they'd slam into the hull at full speed with no protection. Nilah had no idea how fast they were moving, but it had to be over a hundred kilometers an hour.

They passed through an antenna array, past the con tower and the darkened bridge. Hard armor plates raced toward them, and Nilah thanked her lucky stars that she was an expert at judging distance at high speed. She pulled Orna close to her, just in case the quartermaster wasn't as skilled. Their descender cushions would overlap in the collision, and in a worst-case scenario, Nilah's cushion could catch both of them. She primed herself to flow magic into the canister.

Nilah activated her descender a good twenty meters above the hull, and all guns simultaneously swung toward her. She tried to watch their barrels for the telltale signs of her doom, but tumbled as green phantoplasm enveloped the pair of them. A high-speed collision was never pleasant, but phantoplasm made it survivable. Her limbs tangled with Orna's, and magical ooze jerked them every which way. Orna's descender popped as well, tousling the two women harder as the disparate gelatinous cushions pushed through one another.

They came to rest, and the phantoplasm began to vaporize. Nilah switched on her mag boots before anything else, clamping her heels to the hull and rising to her feet. Orna had landed at an awkward angle, her feet pointing straight up in the air. As the quartermaster struggled to orient herself, she bucked away from the hull, out of arm's reach of any handholds. Nilah snatched her from the air like a wayward child, spun her, and slammed her heels onto the metal. Orna's mag boots suctioned to the surface, and they both activated their comms.

"*Capricious*, this is Hunter One," Orna huffed. "Package delivered. We're intact."

"Yeah. Hunter Two. Same," Nilah breathed, switching on her scrubber. Cool air rolled over her body, and the fog instantly cleared from her vision.

"Good to hear," said Cordell.

"Prince here. We're sending you a waypoint," Armin added. "It's the nearest airlock. Can you confirm visual?"

Nilah glanced around, finding a human-sized circular indention in the hull a few meters away, marked in red on her HUD. "Hunter Two, I see the airlock."

"Great," said Armin. "Proceed to the airlock and...stand by. We're picking up something on the scanner."

Nilah gulped fresh air as they conferred on board the *Capricious*.

"We're picking up countermeasures skimming along the surface of the *Harrow*!" Armin's voice returned, nearly panicked. "Take evasive action, now!"

But to where? They couldn't leap from the ship, or the automatic slingers would shred them. If the countermeasure spells were skimming along the surface, taking cover wouldn't help. Rather than listening to Armin, both women knelt down, traced glyphs, and placed their palms against the intelligent skin of the ship.

The fingers of their gloves held specialized contacts, allowing their magic to flow into machines. Together, they dove into the complex circuitry of the ship's outer skin, quickly locating the nodes that detected the presence of boarders. Cybersecurity on the ship's hull was light, and Nilah quickly pulled apart the protections and locks surrounding the node, while Orna penetrated the core logic.

The spells coming for them couldn't be shut down—not once they'd been launched. However, the spells took their direction from the ship's skin, and that could be fooled. The pair of women managed to access the ship's detectors just in time to see a huge flash of fire explode just a few meters from their position.

"Nice work, Orn—I mean, Hunter One!" Nilah said. "Let's hit that airlock."

But when she turned to Orna, the quartermaster still had her palms to the hull, her face hardened by concentration.

"I'm not going anywhere. This is adaptive logic," she grunted. "Got to keep dismantling it or the skin will repair and it'll detect us. Get to the airlock. You can make it without me."

"Orna, don't be stupid!"

"I'm not. Those spells are going to get loose sooner or later, and when they do, they're taking me out. Get moving. Figured this might happen."

"Hunter Two, this is Prince," said Armin, his voice quiet in Nilah's ears. "Do as she says."

Orna gave her a weak smile, barely visible through the reflection of the sun on her visor. "I shouldn't have survived Carré, but I didn't expect my card to get punched this quickly."

Nilah turned and ran to the airlock. She slapped her palm against the bulkhead and sliced through its security with little effort. "You could distract the spells with a ping across the ship, then run to me!"

"Nilah, I can't!" Orna shouted through gritted teeth. "The ship's code is already adapting to me."

Nilah swallowed. "So this is it?"

The quartermaster's icy eyes were barely visible behind her visor. "For what it's worth, I would've given you that other kiss. Now get in the airlock."

Nilah's connection to the ship's skin was stable; she could still hack the *Harrow*'s sensors. She ducked to the side of the door and began to emulate contacts with the hull—thousands of false boarders tromping across its surface with mag boots, all headed in a line, far across the ship. The defense grid wasn't buying it though, already evolving to account for Nilah's interference. It rejected all her false positives because they were too far away from her—the source of the spell.

If she wanted to get Orna out of this alive, she'd have to trick the *Harrow* with something more believable, something closer. She glanced at the spells circling them—lava-hot balls of flame searching for someone to incinerate. Nilah concentrated and began simulating a dozen boots marching into the open airlock door—a logical boarding scenario. The *Harrow* would feel great multitudes of people swarming into it and, hopefully, react.

Nilah nearly lost her grip on the ship's code as Orna tried to push her out, but she triumphed. Like beads of water sliding across a pane of glass, the spells came rushing toward Nilah, only to fly into the airlock as they chased the thousand phantoms in their computer. Nilah patted the airlock controls, linking with them and shutting the doors on the fire spells, now stuck inside.

The door buckled outward as the spells ruptured inside the enclosed space. A heavy thump traveled up through Nilah's legs, reflected across the hull, and the airlock door went spinning off into the starry blackness. Moisture condensed into icy jets as atmosphere vented into space. The *Harrow* sensed the explosive decompression and slammed down bulkheads inside to seal off the sections around the ruined airlock.

"Come on, Hunter One!" Nilah shouted, but Orna was already charging straight for the open airlock.

Both women tumbled inside to find a corridor large enough to fly a fighter through, sealed on both sides by heavy blast shields. Red lamps pulsed on the ceiling, and wavering magic signs in front of the doors proclaimed: EMERGENCY: SEEK AIR SUPPLY.

"What's the best way to get out of here?" asked Nilah.

Before Orna could respond, gooey spells erupted from the broken airlock, transforming into red-hot metal. Strands of the glowing spells interwove, stretching over and over again until they became a molten web. The ship sealed the corridor and began to pressurize.

"Phase two, let's go," grunted Orna, knocking the cover off a security console and shoving her gloves into the circuits. "Got to take down internal security."

Nilah bounded over to her, tracing her glyph and sinking her fingers into the circuitry of the ship, searching for an opening. She sensed a few hundred springflies closing on their position, and several dozen network crawlers looking to incinerate any hackers. On board the *Capricious*, this incursion had sounded like a good idea, but the reality that faced her was a solid wall of the finest security she'd ever seen.

"It's okay," said Orna, connecting. "We just have to take the network crawlers down one at a time."

"The bulkheads will open up before we've scrambled even one of them." Nilah reconnected, searching for any way out, any way to become an authorized user. "We need universal access now!"

"No one has that."

The atmosphere was thick enough now that Nilah could hear the hiss of onrushing air. The oxygen, their salvation, was the timer for their doom, for when the blast doors opened, their chamber would flood with springflies

Her eyes darted to the base of the blast door, ever fearful that it would begin to rise.

"Wait a minute," said Orna. "Kin. Give him to me."

The quartermaster grinned and held it aloft to activate it, then ripped some wires loose from the circuits, pressing them against Kin's contacts.

A chime echoed through the hallway, and the blast doors shot up with a violent bang, revealing a horde of shivering springflies. The women froze, knowing full well what those scything arms could do to a person in mere fractions of a second. Their spacesuits wouldn't save them.

"Hunters, status," barked Armin. "Hunters, come in."

The swarm of metal death swayed like stalks of wheat. The nearest automaton approached on clicking feet and waved hello with a blade.

Orna began to laugh, slowly at first, before building to an outright cackle. Nilah's eyes darted between the springflies and her disturbed companion, and she wondered if she should back away.

"I knew it!" Orna cried. "Kin has the access codes for the whole damned ship: the ones the mutineers used when they gassed everyone!"

Nilah shook the surprise out of her head. "But how?"

"Boots plugged him into the file system on Carré, and again on Alpha. Of course he downloaded everything. I doubt he even knew he had them."

"That's true," said Kin, his voice now booming through the *Harrow*'s speaker systems. "I only had fragments of programs, but a quick meta-analysis of the ship's open sockets showed how some of them fit. You can remove your helmets, by the way."

"Hunters, status!" shouted Armin. "What the hell is going on over there?"

"*Capricious*, this is Kin. I'm in complete control of all *Harrow* security systems, and you are cleared to dock. Bay fourteen. I'll guide you in."

Nilah had never heard Armin stammer before.

"Well...uh...right, then. Roger that, Marshall."

"Marshall?" asked Nilah.

"It means Kin is the approach authority," said Orna. "Never known Armin to take orders from an AI."

The pair of women slipped off their helmets and glanced anxiously at one another. Only then did it sink in that they were standing aboard the galaxy's most legendary warship, completely alone. There could be a kilometer of serpentine corridors between them and their destination, and they couldn't be certain the derelict was truly abandoned.

"Before I forget," said Orna, wrapping her arms around Nilah's waist, pulling her in close.

Their lips came together in an intimate brush, then a flick of the quartermaster's tongue invited Nilah deeper into the passionate kiss. Even through the thick skin of her spacesuit, she could feel Orna's strong hands roaming up and down her back.

"Excuse me, Hunter One and Hunter Two," said Kin, breaking the moment in two.

Nilah pulled away. The quartermaster let out a goofy chuckle and wiped her mouth on the back of her hand. "What is it, Kin?"

"I've started hacking through some of the *Harrow*'s information systems, and I could use some help. Would you both be so kind as to proceed to the bridge?"

"Sure. Fine," said Orna, never losing her grin.

"Also, I've located the crew," said Kin. "One thousand two hundred souls confirmed deceased on deck fifteen. The storage area has been vented to the vacuum to prevent decomposition."

His words were like ice water on Nilah's heart, the romance dying instantly.

"Cause of death?" asked Nilah.

"Initial scans: asphyxiation and collapsed lungs—neurotoxin," said Kin. "It's not pretty. However, they are dead and I require the assistance of two talented mechanics."

"You want us to plug you in at the bridge or leave you here?" asked Nilah.

"The bridge, please, and hurry. I believe I've subdued the ship's security for now, though I would advise we make haste."

"Plug him into a capital ship and he gets all pushy," muttered Orna. "Lead on, Kin."

Rows of green lights illuminated the way forward, deep into the belly of the *Harrow*.

Chapter Twenty

Requiem

Boots swung around the *Harrow*'s hull, the Runner's engines clanking uncomfortably. Docking took under an hour, and Kin's guidance had been impeccable. She'd never used the AI to pilot anything, so maybe he had always been good. It was more likely that the *Harrow*'s guidance, navigation, and control systems were top of the line. As much as she liked having him connected to the ship, she worried about the experience altering him.

"Just follow my waypoints in, Boots. I'll park you next to the *Capricious* in bay fourteen."

"Copy that, Marshall. Boots inbound."

Boots told herself she wouldn't do this, but her heart thudded a little harder upon hearing his voice from the inside of a fighter. It reminded her too much of his final transmission. She tightened her grip around the Runner's throttle.

Her fighter coasted into the *Harrow*'s massive docking bay alongside the *Capricious*, and she set him down so gently that she barely felt the contact of her skids. The bay doors closed behind her, and status bars filled her view as the enormous room began to repressurize. She couldn't even begin to imagine the arcane atmospheric generators that supported such a beast.

"Lizzie," said Kin, his voice softer than usual.

"Yeah?"

"As you know, your health is of primary concern to me. I'd like to ask you a question for your well-being."

She glanced at the status bars. Fifty-six percent—another minute remaining. "Are you copying the others on this chatter?"

"Just us," said Kin.

She bit her lip. "Okay. Shoot."

"Studies have shown that a promise improves a person's ability to execute difficult actions in stressful times. Six researchers from Hamilton University conducted an experiment—"

"Skip the preamble. What's the deal?"

Kin deliberately took his time. "No matter what lies beyond this bay...no matter what you find out...can you promise to maintain combat readiness?"

Her pulse thumped in her neck. What was he talking about? Boots wondered if his code had been compromised, and took a dry swallow. She'd forever lost Kin the person. If something happened to Kin the computer...

"We're always ready to fight," she said. "The *Harrow* crew here is dead, aren't they?"

"Yes, they are, but you still have other enemies hunting you. Can you promise me that you'll fight when the time comes?"

"What did you find?" she asked. Then, more quietly, "Are you trying to warn me about someone from the *Capricious*?"

"Heavens, no. You must protect them with everything short of your life. Combat statistics have shown that unit cohesion is the single biggest indicator of survival, and—"

"Enough with the stats, Kin. Tell me what you found."

There was a series of chirps. Boots recognized that sound—she'd just asked the computer to do something it couldn't do. "I'm afraid that's not possible. I believe it would impair your survival, and thus, I won't tell you until you promise."

A sigh hissed from between her teeth. "Fine. I promise to be ready to fight, no matter what."

"Good. Please come to the bridge. Nilah and Orna are already there."

The atmospheric status indicators on her glass flashed green, and the canopy opened. Boots yanked off her helmet and hefted herself onto the side step.

She held her helmet to her face and whispered into her microphone, "For a computer, you sure do care a lot."

"I care about you in all the ways a human finds significant, Lizzie," came his voice, tinny and small through her earpiece. "Remember your promise."

They set off from the bay with slingers loaded and drawn. Although they had free run of the ship, Cordell opted to keep the group together. The *Harrow* was double the size of any ship Boots had ever boarded, and they could easily get lost.

They wound their way through the guts of the beast, its hallways dark save for the winking of auxiliary lights and the green running beams Kin laid to direct them. Halfway through the ship, Aisha stopped them.

"Kin, where did you say the crew's bodies were?" asked the pilot. "Isn't that bay near here?"

"Yes," said Kin. "They are all dead, however, so investigation will not be warranted."

Aisha shook her head. "I just want to know what they look like."

"People of all races and origins," said Kin, "clad in various Taitutian military uniforms."

Boots kept her slinger in hand, but finger off the trigger. After all, Kin had told them there was no danger. "Normal military insignia, or the weird ones from Alpha?"

"Normal, Lizzie," said Kin.

Boots chewed her lip. This whole treasure hunt had been one weird thing after another—gods and prophets, culture arks and secret bases, mutineers and secret branches of the Taitutian military. And, of course, there were the racetrack glyphs, too. The boarding party passed the corridor that led to the bay full of corpses, and Boots peered down the hallway, trying to get a better look.

She couldn't stop turning over her promise to Kin in her mind. Why would he ask her to keep it together, no matter what? What psyche-shattering secrets did he think they were going to find?

The *Harrow* conspirators buried their tracks at every turn, killing off anyone who knew anything. That would've been normal for a ridiculous cult, but then they killed off their own members on Alpha, too. What kind of god kills off his own followers?

But what if Henrick Witts wasn't a god?

It struck Boots like an electric shock. What if he was a thief, who'd stolen something important, and killed off all nonessentials to get a bigger share? That made more sense, but what was the treasure—the *Harrow*? No, he would've crewed it and continued sailing open space if that was his plan.

The vision of statues entered Boots's mind, and she recalled the last line of the plaque, dedicated to sacrifices.

THOSE ON CLARKESFALL.

As they rose through the depths of the *Harrow*, Boots could only hope her instincts were wrong.

Boots had only seen the bridge of a capital ship twice before: once as a little girl on a tour, and once in the closing days of the Famine War. Nothing could've prepared her for the bridge of the *Harrow*.

Row after row of stations lined terraced landings, far more than should've been there. A window the size of a city block stretched high overhead, and Boots could see the eerie, crackling surface of the blue planet. A ship this size would've had thirty or forty people on the bridge, but there had to be closer to a hundred seats. Analysis stations rimmed each terrace, and in the center of each landing was a battle planning area. The designers had laid it out as though the *Harrow* was five or six smaller ships combined into one. The commander's chair had ten seats to report status from all the other sections, and an amp system for the commander's magic, whatever it might be. Fire control, near the front, was the largest, and clearly labeled.

This was a superweapon, all right.

The second she set foot onto the bridge, orange light washed over her and an undulating sphere phased into being overhead. Boots and Aisha joined the others by the commander's chair, just as Nilah and Orna took their palms from the consoles, disconnecting.

"Would you like to know what I've found?" Kin's voice boomed over the speakers, bouncing across the wide, open space. "The databanks are redacted, but I think I have a few more clues."

"Enlighten us," Cordell called back to him.

Pictures of a hidden galactic shipyard filled their vision, and Boots squinted to make out the details.

"The *Harrow*, commissioned in 2860, took six years to build in Taitu's most classified shipyards, located in what is now the Gamelan Cluster. He is the brainchild of designer Grand Admiral Henrick Witts and fifteen of Taitu's most powerful banking families, who co-financed construction."

A picture of Taitu's elite, posed in front of a hotel, wafted through the air, flanked by the crests of those families.

"Nilah, tell me these aren't friends of yours," said Boots.

"Those are, um, some of the most important families in the galaxy," said Nilah, "but I wouldn't call them 'friends.'"

"The ship is one of eight brothers, known collectively as the Winnower Fleet."

Boots felt sick. There were nine chairs at Alpha—two for the flagship, one for each of the other commanders. "We already know the names of the fleet commanders, don't we? From Alpha."

"Yes, Lizzie. The other seven ships were scuttled after firing their spell discs and serving their purpose."

Cordell flinched. "I'm sorry, what? There are more of these?"

"Were," corrected Boots. "And each of their commanders got a share of something, didn't they, Kinnard?"

"They did," replied Kin, "in exchange for their worship."

A video feed flickered to life above them depicting a tall, black-robed figure in a gas mask standing in the center of the bridge. The hems of his robes surged with arcane energies, light bleeding off of them in rainbow wisps. His helmet bore a long, inhuman crest of onyx spines across its top, like some terrible lizard from a primordial jungle.

At his feet lay the bodies of slain crew, their faces choked in agony. One by one, more figures in gas masks entered the bridge, surrounding him and throwing themselves prostrate before him. He held out his hands in benediction, and they arose, shaking with zealous elation.

Boots crossed her arms, her stomach in knots. "That's Henrick Witts?"

"Correct," said Kin, highlighting one of the cultists. "And that is Jean Prejean, according to the serial number on his shoulder patch."

Henrick grasped Jean by the face with hands of blue flame, and Jean began to scream. When he released Jean, the man fell to his knees, his eyes glowing with that same fire. The feed switched to a headshot of Prejean, a blond youth with a baby face. Prejean's widow had told the horrifying story of an all-powerful oracle, twisting fate across the galaxy. Could there be someone more powerful than him?

"What did he just do to Prejean?" asked Armin.

Boots closed her eyes. She didn't want to be right. "That's his piece of the spoils. Arcane power."

"And they didn't scuttle the *Harrow* as well, because..." Armin trailed off.

"It's still too valuable. The spell they fired burned out the casting discs of the entire Winnower Fleet, but this is still a technological marvel. If Henrick Witts wishes to go to war, he'll need a ship like the *Harrow* at his disposal."

"That's insane," said Nilah. "If a spell that big had ever been fired, we would've heard about it."

"Not necessarily. With the correct resources and the right cover," said Kin, "one could extract near-limitless arcane energies to bank for later. Human beings are almost perfect batteries and conduits for magic."

Boots's mouth went dry. She didn't want it to be true. "Kin, what was the Winnower Fleet's purpose?"

"Remember your promise, Lizzie."

"Just tell me what you know!" She became acutely aware that the entire crew was watching her.

After a pause, the images overhead reconfigured into the Araujo Arm, Boots's home turf. Eight points of light popped into existence at various points in space, each with a name: *Kingbreaker, Blackstar, Feyhammer, Empyrean, Crow's Quill, Obsidian, Songmaiden*. The *Harrow* was the last to appear, and the view zoomed in close on its exterior, hurtling past star systems. When at last the *Harrow* was the size of Boots's fighter hanging over their heads, the brass disc mounted on its front activated, tracing the largest bloodred glyph Boots had ever seen. The view then rushed back out to the galaxy, showing the other seven ships doing the same, represented by icons of the glyphs they cast.

Boots glanced at Nilah, and the racer's hands began to shake as she watched the simulation. The glyphs formed a conduit, and arcane energies raced through the Araujo Arm, creating a sigil a hundred light-years wide. It then faded from existence, as though fizzling away.

"That's the usurer's mark," said Nilah, her voice quivering. *The mark that exchanges life for power.*

Boots didn't want to know the answer, but she had to ask all the same. "This was...in 2869? They...They actually cast the spell?"

"Yes," said Kin. "The same year everything on Clarkesfall began to die. The year before the Famine War began."

She squinted, taking a step forward as though she could rise into the air to pick apart the visualization with her hands. There, pulsing in the exact center of the fading glyph, was her home planet. She thought of all the friends she'd lost, the children she'd seen starved to death, the choked ball of sand that was once her home.

At the center of it all had been the *Harrow.*

Rage, fear, and shame swept through Boots like a sea of acid, dissolving everything she loved and leaving behind a hollow shell. They'd made a meal of her people, siphoning away all of the life on her home, and all the while, she'd fought like she could make a difference. All the Fallen had. The soldiers who died in service to their country weren't brave—they were prey. They'd been turned from young people into corpses, into tiny components of the most cataclysmic spell ever cast.

"Kin, that's not right," said Cordell. "That can't be right."

Armin sank to the floor, slumping against a wall.

Shut down the pity, Boots. You promised to be battle-ready.

The view switched to a surveillance video of the bridge, Henrick Witts bathing in a sickly pink light as magic suffused his being.

"It is, I'm afraid," said Kin.

Orna pounded the wall hard enough that it would've broken a lesser person's hand. "I say we get this sucker started and send it back where it came from! Give the Taitutians a taste!" She made for the controls.

"Of what? Billions of pointless deaths?" said Aisha.

The quartermaster shoved her away. "Turnabout is fair goddamned play, isn't it?"

"No, it's not! Not when you're talking about innocent lives!" The pilot put a hand on Orna's shoulder, but the quartermaster smacked it away.

"Touch me again and die. Never forget: I was still living in that hell when everyone else fled."

"Stand down, Orna," called the captain, though his voice was only a shadow of its normal majesty. He sounded like he'd been punched in the gut. The quartermaster ignored him, searching for the computer station she could use to jump-start the ship.

Kin interrupted her. "This ship is jump-capable, but its disc is burned out. I suggest you consider an alternate course of action, Miss Sokol."

Battle-ready. The captain ain't going to fix this.

Boots wiped her face clean with a palm and smoothed down her hair. "Don't be stupid, Orna."

"So I'm just, what, acting out?" Orna screamed.

"Yeah," said Boots. "You are. Like a child. And no one can blame you for being so angry and being out of your mind. But you don't want to kill all those people. I can't believe that's how you really feel."

Orna's jaw muscles flexed. "And why not?"

"Because if you did, you'd be just like the monsters who built this ship—and each and every person in this room would put you down like a dog."

That shut everyone up.

Boots turned to address the room. "Orna is right about one thing: we need to bring the *Harrow* back to Taitu. People have to know what happened to Clarkesfall."

Cordell shook his head and gestured to the massive bridge. "I don't even know where to start. I've never captained something like..."

She set her jaw. "We can figure it out, *Captain*." She intoned his rank like a wake-up call and saw the fire reignite behind his eyes.

Nilah had never felt so out of her depth. Like Aisha, she wasn't from Clarkesfall, so she wasn't qualified to comment in any way. The argument rose and fell like a stormy sea around her, and each time it seemed to subside, the whitecaps would rise up and smash the group down again.

Her maybe girlfriend had advocated for the killing of several billion of her people. That, Nilah suspected, was merely a reaction to the worst news Orna had ever heard in her life. She could forgive extreme behavior under the circumstances.

For Nilah, the worst part was seeing the map, with its various glyphs from the Winnower Fleet. She gaped at the glyph cast by the *Obsidian*. She recognized it from somewhere.

"Kin." She nearly choked on the word.

"Yes, Nilah?" he asked through a nearby console, so he didn't get in the way of the ongoing argument.

"Can you cross-reference the Winnower glyphs against the 2894 PGRF championship tracks? Just overlay them and see which ones don't match up."

"Indeed."

Maps of all nineteen races appeared in the air above her, and the Winnower glyphs spun, resized, and mirrored until they locked in place on top of each of them. Of the ten Winnower glyphs, only one fell across a race that had not yet happened—the Voranti Grand Prix.

Around her everyone was still shouting.

"Just because we want revenge on the actual perpetrators, doesn't mean we can be reckless about it!" said Boots. "We're all glad you stopped with the genocide talk, but we've got to think this through."

"Everyone calm down," said Cordell.

"Excuse me." Nilah raised a hand, but no one looked her way.

The vicious squabble between Armin, Orna, and Boots continued unabated. The captain tried to calm them, but he simply wasn't himself. No one particularly cared to listen to him, except Boots.

Nilah dug her nails into her palms. "Listen to me!"

The group stopped fighting long enough to spare her a glance. Even Armin blinked up at her through tearful eyes.

"We *do* have to be somewhat reckless," said Nilah. "They're going to cast the grand glyph again." She jerked her thumb back at the display of sigils overlaid on racetracks. "In five days, they'll have completed another, ah, bigger spell."

"How big?" asked Cordell.

Nilah thought about it, but there wasn't a great expression of scale here. This new one would be millions of times more powerful. "Um...all life in the galaxy big."

Armin rose to his feet. The others gave her their undivided attention.

Kin chimed once. "I've located a set of records using the names you provided from Alpha. They match up with the highest echelons of officers in the Winnower Fleet."

Above the tracks, Kin materialized a hundred disembodied

heads, large enough for everyone to see their features. Underneath each was a glowing nameplate.

"Given the visible light sensor data from the attack in your hotel room on Carré, Boots," said Kin, highlighting one of the heads, "I estimate a 97 percent chance this is Mother, the commander of the *Blackstar*."

The woman in question had a hateful face, already much older in years than the rest of the crew. Her cheeks bore numerous creases from a constant scowl, and her thin nose crooked to one side where it had been broken. "Major Marlisa Gwerder—Developmental Operations Team."

"That explains the godlike power of her glyph," said Boots, jaw muscles flexing.

The rest of the group locked onto Mother's image, staring intently as though their gazes alone could kill her. However, Nilah found herself distracted by two other faces she recognized. The nameplates said Harriet Fulsom, commander of the *Crow's Quill*, and Kendall Hopkins, commander of the *Kingbreaker*, but Nilah knew better: they were Claire Asby, chief of Lang Autosport, and Dwight Mandell, prime minister of Taitu—the two biggest influencers of new track design and placement.

Nilah rubbed her eyebrows. That couldn't be right. She blinked, but they were still there, staring at her in their military identification images. She took a step back, and another, until her back came to rest against one of the battle stations, trapping her with the undeniable truth: her mentors were liars.

If they were using the racetracks as the foundation for their next grand glyph, they'd have to have some support from the inside. She thought back to the press conference she'd watched in the bank lobby on Carré.

"Obviously, I want her to turn herself in so we can move forward. If she could—"

"*Do you believe she's guilty? The police claim they have compelling evidence.*"

"*I've seen the videos, but I'm not a forensic arcanist. I...I don't want to believe she's capable of doing something like that...but I don't know how to disagree with what I've seen.*"

It had been so subtle, Claire's betrayal, and Nilah had loved her like a mother all the while. Claire had played dumb, pandered to Nilah all those years while setting up the biggest heist in the history of the universe: billions of lives' worth of magic. And when Nilah had gotten crossways with her conspiracy, Claire had gone on galactic television and pretended to be disappointed— pretended Nilah was guilty.

How many others were Claire's puppets? Cyril Clowe had been at one point or another. How much did he know about his part before Mother had murdered him? What about Uziah Lesinski and his glyph-casting on Claire's behalf? Was he aware he was participating in genocide? What had they promised him?

Nilah knew one thing for certain: Claire was well aware of what she'd done to Clarkesfall, and she would do it again to another planet, a whole galaxy, given the chance.

The luminous images all vanished, leaving the tiny crew bewildered in the shadows of the bridge.

"Kin!" called Cordell. "What gives?"

A deep red bathed the bridge as klaxons sounded across the ship. "Contact, Captain. Mother's battle cruiser has just jumped into the system."

Chapter Twenty-One

Switchback

Nilah bit her lip. The time had come to face the witch once more.

"How many ships?" shouted the captain.

Kin spun streams of light into images of the one ship with a small wing of fighters barreling toward them, then revealed the craft on a map. "I can see one cruiser, though there may be more."

The captain sat down in the commander's chair and tapped one of the panels. "You're not sure?"

"I can't be. I don't have access to long-range scanners from my current connections."

"What?"

"I can inspect the ship's memory banks and security and operate most of the display technology. Sensors, guidance, navigation, weapons, propulsion, and most other systems are air-gapped; the networks never touch each other. Furthermore, there could be more ships in the antimagic zone outside the umbra."

"We have to get to the *Capricious*!" Armin's voice shook so hard he sounded like he'd start screaming at any second.

Orna yanked him up by his collar. "Don't be stupid! They'd run us down like dogs. We make a go of it here."

"No critical systems, Miss Sokol," said Cordell. "We can't stay on the *Harrow*. We can't steer or shoot."

Boots snatched up her helmet. "I don't want to turn tail, either, but if we're lucky, we can get caught in Mother's spell again, do an automated jump through her magic. It won't be far, but we can lose them in the antimagic field. I'll run escort so we can—"

"Starve to death or run out of oxygen," said Aisha. "Orienteering in that field is a nightmare. We won't make it out of the system."

"I've got it," said Nilah. "I know what to do."

Cordell eyed her from the commander's chair. "All ears, sweetheart."

Nilah took a breath, talking herself into volunteering. There were bound to be hardwired defenses ahead of her. "I'll get Kin connected to the *Harrow*'s main computer core. With our magic and direct access, Orna and I should be able to tear up the main cyber defenses and get him completely integrated. He can get us access to the remaining systems and act as station crew. He'll fly the ship for us."

Cordell scowled. "That's illegal for a reason. If he starts making decisions on his own, we can't stop him."

"Captain," she began, "those people out there erased a whole planet, and they're going to do it again. I'm not sure now is the time to worry about ancient protocols."

"I'll go with her," said Orna. "I need to fight something."

"So when you take Kin, what happens to us?" said Armin. "Are they going to board? Does the mutineers' code still work?"

"They already know you're here," said Kin, new alarms spraying across the bridge like a belt of red stars. "They transmitted unlock codes, and finding me, their AIs are trying to break my hold over the ship. I believe that Miss Brio's plan is the most sound of all our options."

"So we send Nilah and Orna down and keep the bridge clear?" said Boots.

"Yeah. Along with Kin, the only thing keeping Mother from taking over the *Harrow's* security," grumbled Cordell.

A map of the ship appeared, along with several waypoints, before Kin spoke again. "These are the most advantageous choke points if you want to hold the bridge. I've already shut down external data links, but there will be other back doors they can use to attack our information systems. We won't have long. I've installed some malicious code to keep the ship's comms down, but if my viruses aren't connected to me, they can't adapt."

Cordell stood, squaring his shoulders. "All right. Mister Vandevere, you're in charge of overseeing operations from the bridge. You won't get much information here, but start collating everything you can. Find a station and interface with the ship—I want that datamancy working overtime. Missus Jan, Miss Elsworth, you're with me. We're going to take the furthermost choke point and hit them as hard as we can. Then, we fall back in stages. Kin, are you ready to disconnect?"

"Yes." And his crystalline cube slid out of the main console.

Nilah picked him up with her bare hand and, tracing her glyph, forged a psychic link with his memory. She sensed him as a warm star within its structure.

Shall we get started? he asked, his voice an echo in her mind. *I can guide you to the core.*

I suppose we'd better.

The quartermaster slipped from cover to cover ahead of Nilah, checking each corner before allowing her to proceed. Their path to the bridge had been littered with springflies, their clicking talons ready to eviscerate them at a false move. The journey back into the data core was considerably quieter, which did little to quell Nilah's nerves.

Where are all of the countermeasures? she thought to Kin.

I've redeployed them to the rear of the ship. That should give you about sixty-seven seconds to return to the bridge and seal it in case things go wrong.

So we better not mess this up?

No. I recommend not messing anything up.

Orna signaled the all clear as they rounded the bend, coming to the elevators. Nilah punched in the code Kin gave her, calling the car before flattening against one of the walls to wait. Once inside, she stripped off her jacket, exposing her bare arms. She'd suppressed her dermaluxes, but she gave them test pulses of red, green, blue, and white, watching the waves come alive.

"Close your eyes," she said, and Orna turned away, checking her slinger with a scoff.

"What are you going to do? Punch the alarms if we trip them?"

Without answering, Nilah cycled through her intensities, pushing toward ultrabright flares so strong her skin itched. She wanted to be sure her dermaluxes were as optimized and flexible as they could be for whatever might be coming. Orna didn't understand, but there was no point in arguing with someone who'd just found out her planet was deliberately exterminated. Nilah flexed her knuckles before unholstering her slinger and looking down the sights. It wasn't ideal, with Kin in her off-hand.

Orna glanced down at Nilah's grip. "You ever shot one of those before?"

"For a show, once. Had to trade places with a bunch of military blokes for a day. One of them taught me to shoot a bit."

"Stay behind me then."

"Is that the best place for a poor marksman?"

She watched the gears turn in the quartermaster's head. "Take point."

The elevator sounded a note and the doors slid open to reveal darkened corridors. Nilah stepped ahead.

Which way? she asked Kin.

Take the next right.

What kinds of alarms can we expect?

I could disable the acoustic and arcane, but biometric is still an issue. When you come up against locked doors, you must be extra careful. There are bound to be trip sensors I couldn't detect, either.

They made their way deeper into the ship, passing a bank of laboratories wreathed in dim, green light. The shadows of exotic equipment beckoned to the two mechanists. If they survived the day, Nilah vowed to investigate further. Though, given the ship's evil nature, perhaps she didn't want to know what the labs were for.

She signaled to Orna in the direction of the central computer core, and the quartermaster nodded for her to proceed. No sooner had Nilah stepped down than the tile under her foot turned bright red.

I tripped the alarm!

Countermeasures in twenty seconds, was Kin's only reply.

"Run!" she shouted to Orna as they bounded down the hall, bloodred lights following them the whole way.

They reached the door to the main server cluster, its bulk indicating a hermetic seal, hardened against penetrations. They'd never get it open in time.

"Orna! Panel!"

The quartermaster slid onto her knees, coming to a stop in front of the computer panel and slamming a palm against it. She sliced out a glyph, but no matter how fast she was, it couldn't be fast enough—the springflies were coming.

It was with this thought that Nilah slid her slinger over to Orna, along with Kin's cube, then stepped into the dead center of the hallway.

"What are you doing?" Orna bellowed.

"Get the door open."

She was the fastest in the PGRF. Her reflexes were legendary. Her rookie year had shocked even her staunchest critics. Her eyes were quick, able to discern perfect detail at long distances. Her ears were finely tuned to the sounds of machinery. Nilah Brio was a galactic talent, and it was time to prove her mettle.

She signed out her glyph, and magic flowed down her arms, pouring light into her dermaluxes. Springflies had to see, just like everyone else—they had one infrared sensor, and that was it. Infrared was just another wavelength of light. She could fool them. She could stun them.

Or she could get decapitated. Either way, the choice was made.

Metal chittering between klaxons heralded their arrival; a swarm of scything robots zipped along every surface. One springfly would be nearly impossible to stop, and there would be dozens of the shivering bugs. She cleared her mind and channeled her thoughts to her arms.

The dermaluxes began to flicker with invisible light, the strain of it elevating the itching on her arms to an outright burn. She sunk into a fighting pose, though she kept her limbs fluid and her mind clear. She repeated one thought: *I am the fastest.*

The silver blur was almost impossible to see as it bounced around the corner, but Nilah managed to jolt out of the way just in time. Knives whistled past her neck, hauntingly close. Her eyes locked onto the first springfly as it erupted once more in her direction, but this time, she stepped aside and caught its thorax in her bare hand.

Without hesitation, she forged a psychic link to it, finding surprisingly simple software inside. Its core architecture unfolded before her in the span of a heartbeat. There weren't many layers to it, just "go here, kill these two women." Its tick-ticking blade sliced down her arm, but she didn't let go. She only had time to replace one instruction: *KILL* became *PROTECT.* She threw it back down the corridor as the next springfly came bounding toward her, past its brainwashed comrade.

She tried to dodge, but the whirling blades were too quick. It sunk its long fingers into her abdomen, and Nilah gasped. Her dermaluxes went a pale green on reflex, but she forced the infrared light back into their pulse pattern. It tried to withdraw, but she forced her way inside its mind through their skin-to-metal contact.

PROTECT.

She ripped it from her body with a scream and threw it toward the others. A third came whizzing at her so fast she thought her head would roll, but her first convert careened into it, and only the very tip of its blade came across her ear, white and hot. The infrared was clearly having an effect on their targeting, and the hesitation had saved her life for at least the next quarter of a second.

The two springflies scrabbled across the ground, snapping at each other, and Nilah lunged for the newcomer. It made to slice off two of her fingertips, but her tiny ally parried its blow and she was able to slap her palm across its insectoid back.

PROTECT.

This time it was easier, a passing caress across a worthless security system. She ignored the fact that on the ground next to it lay a bloody slice of ear. Another and another whizzed toward her, but between her brainwashed bugs and the infrared reflecting across the blood-slicked floors, they were slow. Nilah smashed her fist into one and brought the heel of her hand across another, implanting her malicious code into their tiny brains.

Orna sucked in a breath as a spark snapped between her and the door panel before erupting in a cloud of acrid smoke. The computer was rejecting her. "I need more time!"

Take all the time you need, Nilah thought, but couldn't speak. A moment's diversion, a stray glance, and she'd be skewered, sliced, or mauled.

Her Flicker began to flow, gracefully transforming from one move to the next, preserving her momentum. Exhilaration flooded her, even as her life's blood poured onto the floor. She didn't waste time attacking—she only needed a glancing block to infect a springfly. Soon, a welter of shrieking metal stoppered the corridor as the tiny war raged. *Pulsar's fire, strobing strike, slingshot*; she deployed every move in her arsenal, always finding her targets where she expected them to be.

Every drive she'd ever taken in her life, every grand prix she'd faced, millions of decisions made in the blink of an eye, couldn't compare with the unbridled thrill of this fight. She was pure force: unstoppable, beautiful, perfect. A glancing blow took a shaving from her elbow. Another notched her skull as it ran a furrow down her hairline.

PROTECT. PROTECT. PROTECT.

The maelstrom of screeching filled what was left of her ears—more devastating than any crash, more transcendent than any crowd's cheers. Her little allies fought bravely, and any enemy who took an injury became Nilah's servitor. Orna screamed at her, but she was only vaguely aware of the quartermaster's voice.

Her wounds began to throb, muscles began to seize, but she

pressed onward. Three springflies remaining. *Accretion's pull, nebula's birth, rising rocket.* Two remaining. *Disrupted orbit, cold star.* One. *Singularity.*

The last pieces of attackers went clattering to the ground at her feet. The pile of killer robots was dozens deep, with much of the ship's security reserves expended by the battle. Nilah reached down and touched her shivering allies, one by one, frying their electronic brains. No reason to risk them turning against her if someone regained control of them.

Her abdomen seared with pain. Hot rivulets of blood ran from cuts on her face, her legs, her arms. Staggering, she turned to look at Orna. The quartermaster had gotten the door open, but instead of going inside, she stared at Nilah, mouth agape. The floors swayed under her feet, and her breath came in shallow rasps. She couldn't lift her arms, could barely keep her eyes open.

"Never doubt it, darling..." said Nilah, struggling to put one foot in front of the other. "I'm the fastest in the whole bloody galaxy."

The cold steel floor rushed toward her face.

Boots held the sticks of her gunnery station steady, looking across the bay to where Cordell stood ready at his own anti-air guns. Mother's hacker crew had stopped them from directing the *Harrow*'s automated defenses to destroy the enemy battle cruiser.

But there was always manual control.

Boots and Cordell could crew two turrets, which wasn't much, but maybe they'd get a lucky shot or two. There were dozens of turret stations across the *Harrow*, but only one atmos-shielded docking bay that could hold Mother's battle cruiser. That was where they'd make their stand.

"Hold, Boots," called Cordell as they watched the cruiser approach. "We get one try here."

The cruiser loomed large in their turret cameras, its fighter wing skimming the surface of the ship like a pack of angry hornets. Under normal circumstances, Boots would've already opened fire, along with a full battery of slinger stations. With just her and the captain, it made more sense to let the cruiser close and try to drill it with heavy spells at close range.

The cruiser filled her entire camera view, and she had to zoom out to reorient. She flexed her fingers, willing herself not to fire.

"Hold!" called Cordell.

The keel of the battle cruiser swelled before them, and Boots peered from behind her gun station to see the battle cruiser less than a thousand kilometers out. She tensed to fire.

"Hold!" called Cordell.

"Range eight-seventy, sir!"

"Copy that!" he replied. "I said hold!"

The battle cruiser's nose was almost touching the docking bay shield when Cordell called, "Fire!"

"Finally!" Boots clicked the trigger, launching dozens of scorching corrosion spells into the hull of the battle cruiser. At such a close range, their dispersers couldn't stop all of the incoming spells, and Boots and Cordell landed more than a few good hits on the cruiser.

The spells began to eat away at the battle cruiser's hull, covering it in creeping rust. The cruiser tried to return fire, but the *Harrow's* turrets had dispersers of their own, easily stopping the incoming spells. Maybe they'd get lucky. Maybe they could actually put Mother down without a fight.

When thick red powder covered the nose of the cruiser, Cordell shouted across to Boots, "Switch to heavies! Let's finish this!"

Boots yanked back the cockbolt and tapped the console buttons to rotate the ammo canister to lancers. With the weakened hull, they could put a bolt of energy straight through the battle cruiser's power plant and finish the fight. The drum thundered into place, and she took aim, trying to imagine shooting through the hull into the central reactor.

She squinted down the sights. "Bye-bye, witch—"

The world flashed gray, and by the time Boots could blink, the battle cruiser was settling onto its landing struts, pieces of its fore hull crumbling with the still-active corrosion spells. The witch had pulled her ship outside of time long enough to land it.

"Captain!" she called, and Cordell hot-footed it toward her, looking back at the ship to make sure they weren't about to mow him down. It'd be foolish for them to use their ship-to-ship slingers inside a docking bay, but these were genocidal maniacs, after all.

Boots and Cordell settled in behind two of the docking cells, taking cover behind the deckhand consoles. They exchanged looks and trained their slingers on the battle cruiser as ramps descended from all sides of its bulk. From here on out, they weren't repelling boarders. They were just buying time for Nilah and Orna.

Boots spotted the first enemy soldier lean out of a hatch to lay down some covering fire. She popped off a shot in his direction, and the opposition erupted from the ship like angry ants.

The magi, clad in vermilion uniforms, poured from the ship in waves, clearly superior fighters to the ragtag crew of the *Capricious*. The open nature of the docking bay allowed Mother's troops to spread out and take up superior positions with little trouble.

Boots ducked behind her console as a barrage of spells crashed against it, melting one side into slag. Cordell popped up to give her cover, but the wall of return fire forced his head down. It had only been ten seconds since the battle started, and they were already pinned, with a strong probability of being exterminated.

"We have to fall back to more controllable ground!" he shouted at her. "Time to get to Aisha!"

"Okay, but—" Another volley dug into Boots's cover. "I can't just start running!"

Cordell traced his glyph, and a glowing blue shield enveloped his forearm, growing as tall as his body. He arose and bolted for Boots's hiding spot, spells arcing across his shield before fizzling into nothing. He almost reached her, but was picked up and thrown fifteen meters into the air by some invisible hand. His shield winked out, and he shouted in surprise; strings of attack spells followed him into the air. He clutched at his chest as though he were being crushed, and Boots poked her head out while all attention was on him.

The telekinetic wasn't hard to spot: she was the big witch with conductor arms and a flashy light show. Boots took careful aim and shot, the spell sailing wide before detonating harmlessly against the hull. It was enough to break the telekinetic's concentration though, and Cordell went plummeting toward the deck. Quick as a wink, he traced out another glyph and his shield coalesced under him. He slammed into the deck shield-first, unharmed, and rolled to his side to deflect a fireball aimed at his back.

The shield was like a beacon for enemy fire, affording Boots the opportunity to dash back into the corridor while Cordell drew attention. She took up a position inside the open blast door as three soldiers rushed Cordell's position. His shield whirled around him, punting one man across the docking bay with a back-snapping crunch. He took another woman's head off with his slinger, and the third soldier peppered his position with fléchettes, only to find Cordell crouched behind his protection.

If Cordell could just get to Boots, she could slam the door and they could beat a hasty retreat. Boots fired into the combat, but her aim was off, and the shot struck Cordell in the side of the leg. He cried out in agony and betrayal. She never had been good with a slinger.

"Sorry!"

"Damn it, Boots!"

The captain made a fist and punched with his spell, breaking every bone in the third soldier's body before hobbling after Boots with all his might. He kept his shield propped behind him, and shot after shot bounced from his back. The telekinetic traced another sigil, and Boots took aim past Cordell.

The captain flinched. "Don't shoot!"

But Boots melted the telekinetic's chest with a well-placed bolt from her slinger. So one for one—not the worst record.

"Let's go, girl! Hit the button!" Though he was ten feet from the docking bay blast door, he rolled under as it slid closed.

The captain lay on his back, panting, and Boots took her finger off the trigger of her slinger. With her free hand, she helped him up and looked at his leg. The wound oozed blood; she'd seen a lot worse in the war. He'd be okay to walk if he didn't put too much pressure on it.

"They're gonna break this door wide open in about fifteen seconds, Captain."

"Yeah. Best we jet."

They ambled down corridor after corridor, Cordell's arm over her shoulder. The plan had been to hold the choke points, but they hadn't been prepared for the sheer number of attackers. At that moment, soldiers were spreading throughout the ship, and Boots felt sure Mother was among them. The plan was to draw the troops back to Aisha's choke point and assault from there, but the pilot would never take out enough of them.

Cordell tapped his comm. "How's the hack coming, Hunter One?"

Orna's voice came back to them, only a whisper. "Hunter Two is down."

The words closed their fingers around Boots's throat, and she had to stop. She stumbled into the wall, shoulder-checking it before sliding to her knees. Had she heard that right? Nilah was down?

"Is she dead?" asked Boots. "Did you see it?"

"I don't know. There's a lot of blood, and I had to...I needed to keep going," said Orna.

Cordell sniffed, his lips a thin line. "I asked how the hack was coming. The rest of our lives depend on it."

A bone-shaking *thwump* reverberated through the corridor, startling Boots to her feet. They were breaking through the blast door.

Cordell placed a hand to his ear. "Orna?"

"Yeah. The hack is coming. I'm on it."

"Good," he said. "Capital ships have all kinds of medical response—"

Spell bolts filled the hallway, sizzling against every surface. The captain traced his sigil while Boots returned fire, trying to buy them time. Troops rushed them, and a discus round came whizzing toward Cordell, its deadly white glow arcing from all sides. He sidestepped and spun, diverting the disc without trying to stop it head-on. The shot shaved flakes of magic from his shield before buzzing through a nearby wall, leaving a long gash.

The captain hit the ground hard, and Boots dragged him backward out of the blistering volleys, a red streak staining the ground behind him. Once they were out of direct fire, she turned him on his back, so she wasn't dragging him on his open wound. She hauled him into a maintenance bay, taking a shorter route back to the next choke point.

"Not much farther, sir," she huffed.

A soldier rounded the corner, and Boots let go of Cordell long enough to pop off two shots, striking the soldier in his hand. He stumbled backward in hysterics, and Cordell tossed a frag grenade after him. Boots hit the deck, covering the captain with her body as the explosion cleared out a few more of the invaders.

She rolled off him and tried to help him up, but he refused. His leg wound had gotten worse with combat action.

"I'm slow. Let me buy you some time," he wheezed.

She glanced down at the leg wound—bad, but not lethal; certainly painful. Then she thought of all the Fallen who were looking for a place to die. The captain had that look about him—of a man giving up, aching for some last-minute heroics. She could never stand men like that.

Boots clocked him across the eyebrow so hard his head hit the deck, then hauled him to his feet. "Sorry, but if you're going to check out..."

"Do as I said, Boots!"

She shoved him toward the far door. "Sorry, no. You're relieved." She jammed the switch and it hissed open.

"On what grounds?"

"Dereliction of duty," she said, hauling him into the next corridor. Only a hundred meters to the main hangar deck where Aisha was. "You're lucky I don't execute you on the spot."

"I forgot what a pain in the ass you are," he grunted, banging the button on the other side of the portal. "Hold up; I'm going to seal this."

Cordell summoned up his shield with a glyph and aligned it to the door. When he opened his hand, the shield rocketed outward and smashed into the thick bulkhead, denting it. It'd take explosives, magic, or a persistent technician to get through, and Boots figured their enemies had all three. Still, it might buy them a critical minute or two.

"Not a lot of juice left," he said. "Too tired."

"You're just a bucket of complaints today."

They hobbled down the hallways together, not resting, and her heart skipped a beat as she spotted the bright lights of the hangar. Cordell slumped against her, even as she quickened her pace. His leg wound had opened up more in all the action, oozing a thick trail of red.

"Almost there, Cordell. Just hang in there."

"Not going to call me Captain anymore?"

"Got to earn that right, sir. You try to die, you ain't my captain."

"All officers are worthless, Boots. Why've you got to pick on me?"

"Because you're better than an officer. You're the bravest—"

A flash of gray—Mother's magic.

Boots's eyes scoured every shadow, searching for her. She remembered the knife appearing through Didier's head, and checked Cordell to make sure he wasn't dead in her arms.

"Boots," he wheezed, "was that what I think it was?"

She hauled him forward. "She hasn't reached us yet. Keep walking."

Their surroundings bled color, yellows shivering away, red warning lights melting into white. Mother's spell closed around them, then subsequently broke, real-world hues socketing into the places they'd fled.

Cordell craned his neck to look behind them. "What happened?"

Boots smirked. "Just like I thought. She can't drag me into her pocket dimension."

They were so close. Just a few more meters to the main hangar.

"Uh, Bootsie..."

They clumsily maneuvered themselves to look back down the corridor and saw Mother, her tattered cloak like fluttering ravens' wings, her brass exoskeleton gleaming in the caution lights. Hundreds of tiny camera irises glittered on her helmet. In her right hand, she held the blade she'd used to end Didier's life. Mother stared them down, waiting for their next move.

"I can't run," whispered Cordell. "We've got to make a stand here."

She looked him over. "You're not that heavy."

"You're pushing fifty. You can't lift my ass," he hissed.

"I'm in my early forties, asshole," said Boots, then waved to the nightmare swordswoman down the hall. "Hey, Marlisa."

The figure in the distance cocked her head. Clearly, she wasn't used to being called by her real name. Her claws clicked.

Boots looked to the captain. Cordell's grip tensed around his slinger. They couldn't stay here. They had to get to the hangar, no matter what.

Grace and power like a murderous cat filled Mother's posture as she sank low and hurtled toward them. Boots spun and hoisted Cordell over one shoulder like an unruly child. Mother's footfalls hammered the deck, drawing ever closer.

"Go! Go! Go!" Cordell cried, his slinger sizzling spell after spell.

Boots couldn't take the time to look back. She didn't want to look back. Her breath sprayed from her puffing cheeks in moist jets, and her heart thudded in her ears.

Twenty meters.

Cordell's slinger clicked, and he ejected the magazine, spent crystals clattering to the ground. He made for the other on his belt, but lost his grip because of Boots's unsteady gait. He snatched Boot's slinger from her hand and resumed firing. Mother's banging steps drew closer.

Ten meters.

The archway to the hangar loomed over her. If she could push a little harder, she'd make it. She'd seen so many corpses in her life—at Laconte, in the black skies over Arca, Didier—and always, Cordell had been there for her. She wouldn't allow him to be taken, too. She'd nearly made it into the wide-open space when Mother slammed into the back of them like a meteorite.

The tip of Mother's sword slipped, white-hot, into Boots's shoulder—the shoulder that bore Cordell. He yowled in pain as the assassin bowled into them, sending all three sprawling into the hangar. The captain skidded to a halt, limp. Boots couldn't see his breath; there wasn't time to watch the rise and fall.

Mother kicked to her feet in a flash, bounding over to Boots with superhuman strength. She seized Boots about the collar, clicking her brass claws inches from Boots's eyes.

"How does it work?" hissed Mother, a hateful sneer white on her lips. "How do you subvert my spells?"

With nothing to lose, Boots took a swing, her forearm crashing into Mother's metallic block like punching a steel pipe. The crone shoved her back against the deck and stomped her fingers, smashing them under brass heels.

"Arcana dystocia," Boots growled through gritted teeth. "No magic."

Mother straightened, looming over her. "A dull-finger? What wonders. Did you know that you're the first person to ever shoot me?"

Somewhere in the rafters, a high-caliber slinger thundered, its potent round sparking against Mother's head and yanking her neck backward. The crone hit the deck with a resounding thud, her hands twisted in agony. Her cloak drifted into place over her like the shadow of death.

"Yeah? Well, Aisha is the second; she never misses," coughed Boots, sitting up to inspect her fallen enemy.

Mother twitched, a demolished face obscured by her cloak, her shattered helmet in bloody pieces across the floor. Boots had seen plenty of kills in her time, and she breathed a sigh of relief when she saw the death rattle reverberate through the crone's frame.

Boots called up to the rafters, "Hit her again, Aisha. I want to make sure this witch is dead."

She could scarcely make out the silhouette of her friend as Aisha cast her pale marksman's sigil in the distance. One more perfectly placed head shot, and it would be case closed for the assassin. Boots lumbered to her feet and took a step back to give the woman some clearance.

Mother's legs and arms whipped her cloak into a frenzy of black tatters as she spun back to life. Her twisting movements brought her to her feet in a tilting leap, as though she could defy gravity through sheer martial prowess. And when the cloak blew aside, Mother seethed at Boots with bright red eyes. A bloody gash marred her temple, but no other serious injuries accompanied it. Boots jumped back as the crone spun once more, her hands whistling through the air.

Except she hadn't attempted to strike Boots—she'd thrown two grenades.

Panicked, Boots glanced back at Aisha as a pair of explosions filled the rafters, ejecting the pilot from their embrace like a smoking comet. Aisha bounced off a wall before smashing into a tower of transit cases, which clattered down around her. It'd been a high-speed, ten-meter drop—extremely bad. Boots couldn't imagine her surviving, but that wasn't the worst of her problems.

Mother washed over Boots in a furious wave of painful blows. "You broke my helmet," she said between punches.

Bloody spittle issued from Boots's lips as she staggered back. "You broke my planet."

Tears filled her eyes as Mother crushed her nose, then tore at her shoulder, ripping it out of socket. "Yes, and no one cared, did they? Did any planet send aid? Evacuate your people? Taitu wouldn't even take your refugees. They were so tired of your squabbling, happy to let you starve out on that ball of sand."

Boots, though barely conscious, raised her one good arm to a fighting pose. She'd be surprised if she got to keep the other—now a horrifying mess of muscle and bone.

"I think we can agree we did the universe a favor," Mother grunted, sinking a foot into Boots's gut like a sledgehammer.

Ribs snapped and Boots went flying across the deck, lighting up with new pain. She forced herself onto her back and stared up at the assassin, unwilling to look away from the killer.

Mother touched the back of a claw to her face, glaring at the blood that came away with it. The crimson syrup glimmered on brass, a regal color palette for a tyrant. In that frozen moment, Boots caught a glimpse of the woman Marlisa Gwerder had been: always cruel, never yielding.

"Oh, but you are animals. Look at you: still glaring at me even though you're bleeding out." Her eagle's gaze flitted to Cordell's still body. "I want to show you...show you just how worthless you are. Would you like that?"

Boots's vision swam and lead filled her hands. *Do it, then, witch. Show me what you've got, but hurry up.*

Mother creaked a smile. "I'm going to bring you your friends' heads."

The assassin turned to Cordell, and her fingertips hissed as she traced her reality-bending glyph. She took it slow, each popping arc reaching a perfect completion.

Colors shimmered and split into prismatic bursts. Mother vanished into her pocket dimension with Cordell.

The indolence gas grenade on Cordell's belt exploded into pearlescent smoke. Mother stumbled out of the cloud, choking and wheezing, her already pallid complexion growing blue as she fell to her knees with a clang.

Boots rolled onto the side with her good arm and tried to stand. Her blood slicked the floor under her. First, she got one knee under her, then a foot. She rose, every nerve in her body crying out. Her feet threatened to leave her, but she widened her eyes, taking deep breaths.

"If... it was just the suit," Boots growled, staggering toward her opponent, "keeping you alive... that would be one thing. A sealed battery won't fall to indolence gas. But I had this thought: What if you had another spell on you?" She tapped her temple. "If I was wrong, you could easily walk over here and kill me. But if I was right..."

Mother squirmed away from the gas, spasming onto her back as her suit failed her.

"What did you need godlike magic for? Because that was the haul you took from my homeworld: all our lives for magic." Another step. "The suit was only to keep you mobile, wasn't it? The godlike magic... that was to keep your failing body alive."

She arrived at her destination: Mother, twitching in terror. The crone raised a hand, and Boots found the strength to kick it away. Mother already looked so much older than she had moments before.

"Don't beg. Let's keep our dignity, Marlisa. After all, your spell will come back when the gas wears off."

With all of her balance, Boots placed the tip of her shoe over Mother's throat and pressed down. The crone struggled against her, but the exosuit lacked the coordination required to knock her off. Boots leaned into it, feeling the meaty crackle of Mother's neck underneath her foot. Boots wouldn't be able to stand much longer. She pulled back and dropped a knee onto the crone's face.

Mother twitched, and then was silent.

Boots crawled off the body, balancing as well as she could on shaky hands and knees. Her comm chimed.

Orna came in loud and breathy. "I got it! Kin is in control of the ship, but you have to get down here! Nilah won't stop bleed-ing and we're pinned do—"

"Lizzie," said Kin, cutting through Orna's communication. His voice was like a blanket: all-encompassing, warm. "Are you conscious?"

"Yeah." Though she sounded distant to her own ears.

"I've been able to seal most of the bulkheads containing Mother's battlegroup."

"Good." She blinked hard. "Scrub the mutineers' code from your memory banks."

"I've already done that."

"Got any neurotoxin left?"

"Two thirds of the supply."

Her body was too heavy; she couldn't hold herself up anymore and sank down onto her ruined shoulder. "Spray it into every room containing the attackers, give them one minute, then vent the toxins into space."

"That's feasible, but I need to get medical robots to you, Cordell, Aisha, and Nilah. Sealing the corridors will impede those first responders. Springflies would be more—"

"Kill every last bastard in the docking bays with the autoturrets."

"You might damage the docking bays or the *Capricious.*"

"Then I want you to jump the ship over the Taitutian capital and start...broadcasting everything." Darkness loomed at the edges of her vision. "Across all frequencies and the Link...I want—I want everyone to know what we know."

"They'll shoot us down."

"God, I hope so. No one needs a ship like this, Kin."

"What about Orna and Armin? They're not critically injured, and jumping will place them in danger."

An eerie stillness fell over the hangar, save for Boots's ragged breathing.

"They'll want to get the truth out there. Execute, Kin."

The ship thrummed with the sounds of autoturrets spinning

up along its bays, reverberating through the hulls. The *Harrow* rocked with explosions. Though the gravity never failed, Boots could feel he was listing to one side. Blood pooled under her cheek as she closed her eyes. She could finally sleep.

"Severe damage to aft impulse thrusters...severe damage to docking bay three...docking bay four...injecting neurotoxin on decks one through six..."

She tried to grumble, but it only came out slurred. "Shut off the warnings, Kin."

"I'm sorry...if you don't wake up, Lizzie, I want you to know that I love you in all the ways you organics value."

"Good night, Kin."

"Good night, Lizzie."

Chapter Twenty-Two

Exfiltration

Pain.
Agonizing explosions across her body. Each moment, another mortar slammed down into a random patch of sinew and bone.

Boots couldn't breathe. She couldn't move more than an inch, and managed that meager effort with shaking muscles.

Piercing beeps. Burning, chemical stenches suffused her, catching in her throat to haunt her lungs. Her breath came in rotted gasps, as though something had died in her mouth.

Then came the nausea—the worst she'd ever felt, like the world pitched her from icy water into baking desert, her head spinning all the way.

Then oily relaxation crept through her body, pushing up through her limbs until all light winked out.

Swear words gurgled from Boots's mouth before full consciousness returned. Coppery syrup coated the inside of her cheeks, and she grimaced. Opening her eyes brought only blurry shades of white, gray, and blue, along with sluggish movements. She rolled on her cot and spat over the side before attempting to sit up.

Big mistake.

She cried out like someone had just taken a hammer to each of her bones. Her left arm throbbed so hard she thought it might rupture.

Then came the deep laughter of a man. Slow and hoarse at first, gaining speed and clarity with each puff of air.

"I knew your ass was going to make it," Cordell croaked from somewhere in the room. "Unkillable."

"Rather be dead than wake to your ugly mug."

"Good evening, Lizzie," came Kin's voice. "Would you like to know the current time?"

"Nah," she replied. "Doesn't much matter. Did we make it to Taitu? Did we broadcast the records?"

"Not yet," said Kin. "We're in transit. I haven't yet sent out the data, since we haven't arrived."

She made to rub her eyes to get the gunk out of them, but her left arm wouldn't move and violently protested the idea. She remembered Mother taking a chunk of her shoulder, the feeling of those brass claws inside her. She'd started feeling sorry for herself when she remembered crushing Mother's throat.

"Can I ask what shape I'm in?" she asked.

"You're alive," he replied.

"I'll take it," said Boots. "We're still in trouble?"

"Sort of," said Cordell. "All of the people hunting us are dead, and we've got a shiny warship, but I don't feel like that's going to last."

Boots's bed gently pressed on her back, sitting her upright in agonizing increments. A medical bot came by and helped her wash her eyes so she could take in the sorry sight of her crewmates. The med bay of the *Harrow* came into focus—thirty cots in rows of five, the ceiling above screened to look like a summer night in Taitu's greenbelt countryside. To her right, Aisha lay sleeping, burn scars covering one of her cheeks and a healing splint glimmering blue around her neck. Her head had been shaved—she must've been resuscitated after her fall.

Nilah lay unconscious on the cot behind her, bloody bandages across her forehead, ear, chest, arm, and hands. Tubes pumped artificial blood into her from a series of yellow tanks, and though her monitored vitals looked weak, they were stable. She'd need a day or two to recover.

Malik rested peacefully beside Aisha, and Boots could've sworn he was just sleeping as usual. She would've thought the *Harrow*'s advanced med bay would be enough to rouse him to consciousness, but it was only enough to prolong his comatose life.

To Boots's left, she found Cordell, his split lips twisted in an insufferable grin. "They all lived, girlie. We all made it through."

"Please don't call me girlie right now, Captain," she groaned.

"Oh, I'm the captain again now?" he laughed.

Boots answered him with a scowl. "Where's Armin?"

"On the bridge, with Orna. It's his watch," said Kin, cutting in. "He is the only uninjured crew member, though I've expressed concern for his emotional well-being."

Why, because his whole planet was murdered and he fought for a sham?

"He's tougher than we think, Kin," said Boots, inspecting her left arm. A full cast covered it, but unlike her crewmates, hers didn't glow with healing light. Either the med bots calculated her dystocia would be in the way, or they figured the arm was no good. She knew she didn't want to see the condition of it.

"I suggest you keep your arm still, Lizzie," said Kin.

"Don't have to tell me twice," she grumbled as a wave of dizziness bowled her over. "I…" She swallowed before speaking, for fear of losing her stomach contents. "I think we need to use the *Harrow* when we get to Taitu."

"We're not opening fire on them, Bootsie," said Cordell. "Besides, the disc is burned out."

Boots smacked her dry mouth. "That's not what I said."

"Well, what did you mean?" Cordell winced as he shifted in his bed.

"Kin, you've got records on the mutineers, right? Like, the prime minister of Taitu is one of those damned gods."

"Yes, Lizzie. Based upon age progression, facial geometry, available footage, and correlated public appearance sensor sweeps, Kendall Hopkins, commander of the *Kingbreaker*, is now Dwight Mandell, Prime Minister."

The head of a pudgy black politician materialized before them, his cheerful grin rendered sickening by the new context.

"We could kill him," said Boots, the rush of venom through her blood the first real pleasure she'd felt since awakening.

Cordell looked at her sidelong, but said nothing.

"What's his spell?" asked Boots.

"According to his military records, Commander Hopkins has the inveigler's mark," said Kin. "Public record states that Dwight Mandell is a falconer, though."

"Someone with mind control, posing as someone with flight," grunted Boots. "Charming."

Cordell chuckled at the accidental pun. "So he probably has machines to help him fly when he needs to show the public his magic. That falconer's mark is him covering up his god-level mind control, which makes him pretty well unbeatable."

"I want to gamble," said Boots, and Cordell's eyes lit. He didn't smile, but she could see him fighting it.

"What are the stakes?"

"The public death of one of the gods who killed our world. We don't just reveal what they did—we put him to death in front of the whole goddamned galaxy and get away with it."

He nodded. "And the odds?"

"That depends on two things: how much video we have of Henrick Witts that we can feed to Kin for analysis..."

"And the other?"

"Whether or not everyone on the crew can still hold a slinger when the time comes."

What remained of the crew of the *Capricious* gathered on the bridge of the *Harrow*, streaking stars passing them by in the darkness. Boots, Cordell, Aisha, Orna, Armin, and Nilah stood in silence, watching the skies with bated breath. Running lights dotted the many terraces and stations, and overheads warmed their view as the ship returned to life.

Aisha's voice echoed across the cavernous space. "Arrival in three...two...one..."

Streaks became pinpricks, and the surface of Taitu rushed to fill their view, its lush greenbelt a beacon of fertility to an entire galaxy. Here was a planet of gardens as far as the eye could see, with great magical wonders and a rich hub of galactic civic activity. It housed politicians and financiers, innovators and artists, its coffers swollen and talent overflowing.

Boots reminded herself that only a few of the Taitutians were genocidal killers.

She wasn't there to kill everyone on the planet—just a major conspirator. But she couldn't help imagining what would become of the Taitutians if that greenbelt started to die, if that water grew stagnant, if the shifting dunes of a rising desert swallowed all of those great works. She knew it was wrong; she felt certain all of these rich folks were innocent of the murder of Clarkesfall, but she wanted to see them suffer.

"I don't think I've ever been more ready for a mission in my life," said Orna, giving Boots a playful hit as she made her way over to the data station.

The quartermaster plunked down next to Nilah, who looked ghastly. Boots wasn't sure if it was the artificial blood or the fact that they were trying to assassinate the prime minister, but she didn't have time to ask. The two mechanists would be thoroughly occupied with information security while the *Harrow* awaited its prey.

"Don't let them hack us," said Boots. "Counting on you girls."

Nilah gave her a mock salute, but she could barely keep her hand up.

"ID codes have been accepted by Taitu's planetary defense grid. They still work," said Aisha.

Cordell ascended the platform of the commander's station as its seat folded into the floor. An armored sling covered much of his arm, and glowing splints still secured his ribs, but he maintained something of his old regal posture. "Perfect. Missus Jan, I think we're done with you for now. Good flying."

Aisha somberly nodded her assent and strode away, disappearing into the bowels of the ship.

Klaxons sounded, red lights flashed, and the image of the *Harrow* swirled into being above the first level of the bridge. Two warships, the *Kaga* and the *Magistrate*, plotted an intercept course, fighters scrambling from their decks. Within minutes, the *Harrow* would be surrounded by an unstoppable army. Between the ship-to-ship engagement and the defense satellites, the legendary *Harrow* wouldn't last thirty minutes in combat with a burned spell disc.

"We've got someone trying to hack ship systems through the comms, Cap," said Orna. "We can hold them off for a few."

"They're hailing us, sir," said Armin. "Telling us to stand down."

Cordell looked to Boots. "Well? Your plan. What do we say?"

Boots smiled. "Tell them we're standing down, sir. They can scan our weapons and see they're offline. Kin, how's your neural analysis of Henrick Witts's speech patterns coming?"

Kin chimed. "I have eighty-six percent of the 171,246 standard language words computed. The most common word I have been unable to interpolate from the Witts video record is 'diaphragm.' I have a ready list of other words that might be signifiers to our enemy, if—"

Boots snorted. "Yeah, yeah, Captain, if you could refrain from discussing breathing with our prey."

"Ain't here to discuss his breathing," said Cordell. "Just here to stop it."

Boots cut a glance to Nilah, who winced, but said nothing. Nilah knew just as well as the rest of them that Dwight Mandell was a mass-murdering planet-killer who intended to destroy everything if given the chance. They'd done the calculations: the grand glyph, if carved with the racetracks, would wipe out all life in the galaxy. The only missing piece of the puzzle was motive. Sure, killing Clarkesfall had scored them more juice than magi of any prior age, but what would they have in a lifeless galaxy? Who was left to rule?

"I've hailed the Green Palace using the private encryption of the conspirators," said Armin. "No response as yet."

Cordell sighed. "Hey, Kin, if they take so much as one shot at us, you need to start broadcasting everything we know. I want every journalist in this sector in possession of unencrypted records. Give them names, dates, schematics, any and all video. I'm not going down without everyone knowing what happened to our world."

"What if he's not here?" asked Nilah. "What if he's offworld?"

"Please concentrate on your duties, Miss Brio," said the captain. "He's here."

"Captain," said Armin, "the Green Palace is responding. They're ready to connect."

"Please ready yourself, Captain Lamarr," said Kin. "It will take me a few moments to prepare the skin."

Boots and the captain exchanged glances, and his throat bobbed with a hard swallow. "Wasn't ever much of an actor. Hope I'm ready for this."

"Don't act, then," said Boots. "Be the authority you are."

Cordell squared his shoulders and assumed a stock-straight posture like the one they'd seen on the videos. He and Boots had spent the past two days reviewing each and every mannerism of Admiral Henrick Witts. She'd come to be intimately familiar with his horrid face: slashes of wrinkles stretched across a severe bone structure. He spoke to his crew without love or compassion, with no sense of familiarity—only ownership. For costumes, they'd selected the robes Witts wore on the night of the mutiny.

So when Cordell answered the call from the Green Palace, Kin overlaid his image with the accursed form of Henrick Witts—speech and body alike.

As Dwight Mandell's face materialized in the cloud of alerts overhead, Boots realized they had no idea how to address him. He was no longer the commander of the *Kingbreaker*, nor would he be considered a prime minister by the all-powerful Henrick Witts. Would Witts speak to him as an equal? Would he call him by his real name? Mandell's jowls waggled as he struggled to find the words to say, and Boots realized that he was panicked.

She glanced down at her outgoing comms image and saw Witts glaring back at her—not a call she'd like to receive.

"My Lord Poet," Mandell stammered, glancing off-camera for a split second.

What the hell is a Lord Poet?

"The time is at hand," said Cordell, each word deliberate and distinct. "Join me at my side, and we will prepare."

Mandell inclined his head, carefully considering his words. "The final glyph isn't for another three days."

Cordell's voice had a seismic rumble to it—the promise of chaos. "I did not misspeak. Either you join me in the spoils, or I depart this system without you. If that happens..."

The Henrick Witts on Boots's screen narrowed his eyes.

"...you will not live to see the coming cataclysm."

Mandell opened his mouth a few times, but no sound emerged.

"You know my power," added Cordell. "These warships are no challenge to me."

It surprised Boots how easily Cordell assumed the role—authority flowed from him. Clothed in Witts, he wasn't a mere smuggler but an unstoppable force, a tidal wave of inexorable will. Though when she remembered his command at Laconte, maybe it wasn't such a stretch; Cordell was charged with life and death, and disobeying him was an unconscionable act.

"I will join you momentarily, my Lord Poet," said Mandell, and awaited some sort of acknowledgment.

Cordell barely cocked an eyebrow, but the effect was immediate. Henrick Witts wasn't the sort of man to be pleased with compliance, only furious with failure. There could be no "very well," or any other happy noises. Mandell, visibly shaken, severed the connection, and the crew turned to one another.

"Well, I feel filthy," said Cordell, shaking his head.

"Don't worry about it, Cap," said Boots. "All in the service of a greater cause."

"What a bastard," Orna added, and Boots noticed Nilah wince once again. It couldn't be easy for the racer, seeing such a close family friend turn out to be the scum of the universe, but she'd be hard-pressed to find sympathy from the survivors of the Famine War.

"The warships are standing down, Captain," said Armin. "Six squadrons have been recalled to base. If they want to scramble against us, they'll take at least fifteen minutes."

"The hacking attempts have stopped," said Nilah. "They're not bothering us anymore."

"Excellent," said Cordell. "I think this might work."

"Let's hope," said Boots.

"Launch detected," said Kin, accompanied by a pulse of red light. "It's from the Green Palace—the minister's personal yacht is inbound."

Cordell smirked. "Phase two, then?"

Waiting in the midship docking bay drained Nilah's wooziness away, replacing it with a cold dread. In mere minutes, she'd be face to face with Dwight Mandell, family friend and monster. Her mind reeled as she tried over and over to reconcile those two truths. She'd played at the Green Palace as a child. He'd been at her first Ultra GP league race. He'd handed her the cup on the podium when she'd won the prior year's Taitu GP at Wilson Fields. He'd always told her they were both champions.

But he'd helped Henrick Witts drain the life from Clarkesfall, relegating its citizens to civil war. In five days, he planned to kill her, and everyone else too, unless they stopped the race.

Nilah chided herself for letting her mind wander. She shouldn't be thinking about this. She never let herself worry about non-sense on the grid—she only thought about how to win. This could be no different. Dwight had the inveigler's mark, giving him the ability to charm his targets. Under the sway of that mark, she would feel a swell of love for him, but she wouldn't necessarily follow orders; that wasn't how love worked, after all. For a short period of time, she'd be consumed with the need to please him.

But there was a second dimension to the problem: Dwight's power would be on a scale heretofore unseen. How would his inveigler's mark change with godlike energy? Perhaps he could detect those who didn't like him and force them into love. Maybe he had an ambient field that caused everyone around him to have vague, pleasant feelings of trust—a useful gift for a prime minister. Then again, he might be able to wipe her personality from her body, forever replacing it with one more amenable to him. Nilah shuddered at that last thought.

She looked to Cordell, Armin, Orna, and Boots. At least her friends were with her.

"Two ships have joined the yacht as escort from the *Kaga*," Kin said, his report echoing through the wide-open docking bay. "They're marauder-class; looks like boarding parties."

"Damn it," Cordell grumbled into his comm. He turned to Boots.

"We have to let them come aboard, Captain," she said, sensing his question.

Orna checked her clip. "We could just have Kin blast the PM's ship and be done with it. Might be the best chance we'll get."

"No!" Nilah interrupted. "I mean, no. We can't do that. I have to see him. The galaxy... needs to see what he is."

Armin nodded. "For what it's worth, our chances of survival improve significantly if we let them board, but we'd best get in position."

"Agreed," said Cordell. "All right, everyone—these men and

women might be soldiers, but they're innocents right now. I don't want to see a single one of them shot. Do I make myself clear?"

"Yes, Captain," the crew replied in unison.

"Kin," called Boots.

"Yes, Lizzie?"

"Start broadcasting video of these events the second Dwight Mandell steps foot onto the *Harrow*, not a moment before. We can't risk him seeing the stream. Get imagery to the *Kaga* and the *Magistrate*. Once the prime minister speaks to us, begin simultaneously broadcasting everything we know on an unencrypted channel as far as it will go. Once the streaming is complete, you're to surrender the ship to Taitutian authorities." Boots turned to Nilah and winked. "And make sure everyone knows that Nilah Brio is on board. That ought to get us some attention from the journos."

Boots's short smile fell away, leaving a hard expression. Nilah started to ask what was wrong, when Boots spoke again.

"And, uh, just in case we all get, you know, brainwashed... I'm deauthorizing all users from your memory banks, myself included."

"Are you sure, Lizzie? I'll carry out my assignments, but you won't be able to ask me anything except the time of day after that."

She wiped her nose. "Yeah. Hey, look, don't make this any worse than it is. I ain't supposed to have a military AI anyway. We're all about to get arrested if we're lucky, and uh..."

Nilah only knew a little about Boots's relationship with her computer; Kin had been her AI for nearly twenty years. She was friends with it. Nilah thought of Orna and Ranger, how he'd carried Orna through the dark times in her life.

"Surely there's another way," said Nilah, but the others shook their heads.

"Forget it, kid," said Boots. "If the PM gets to us, we'll hand him everything we got, Kin included. People have to hear this story. They've got to shut down the last race."

"Authorized user, Elizabeth Elsworth, please state the override code to deauthorize all users."

Boots looked up, as though talking to the dead, and Nilah backed away. She felt like she wasn't supposed to be watching this.

"We've been through a lot, Kin," said Boots.

"Yes, we have, Lizzie."

She pursed her lips. "Authorization code echo-echo-four-three-six-two."

Kin chimed in response, the long reverb of it dying against the steel walls of the docking bay.

"Kin?" asked Boots.

"The time of day is oh-nine-thirty-two, Taitutian standard time," was his reply.

Boots shut her eyes tightly, and Nilah wondered if she would cry. Nilah looked to Cordell, but he was already moving into position with Orna and Armin in tow.

They fanned out, hobbling through the cargo bay, hiding behind anything thick enough to block most scanners. She knew, like the rest of them, that they'd be apprehended in short order. Nilah hid, too, for all the good it would do.

Nilah glanced up into the rafters, where she'd welded the breastplate from Mother's armor, hoping it held when the time came.

It didn't take long for their company to arrive. The pair of Taitutian marauders blasted through the docking shields into the bay, lights flaring, spewing forth two fire teams of marines. Shieldmasters led the soldiers, their blue discs batting any obstructions out of the way. Disorienting balls of light shot through the bay, dazzling anyone who looked directly at them. The marines flowed through the docking stations like water, rousting the crew of the *Capricious* with the constant refrain of, "Drop it! Lay face down and interlace your fingers behind your back!"

The special operations team had stunning efficiency and overwhelming presence. Even if Nilah had been planning to shoot them, the flashing spells and booming voices would've made her think twice. A big man wrestled her to the ground and tore the slinger from her hand, planting a knee on her back as he clapped her hands into steel gloves. She would've screamed in pain if she could've breathed. With the press of a button, the hollow gloves filled with calcifoam, locking her fingers in place.

Blackness crept toward the center of her vision, and Nilah wondered if he'd caused some internal bleeding. He kept his boot on her until, somewhere in the bay, the squad commander called, "Clear!" and everyone visibly relaxed. Her captor hauled her to her feet by her collar, hoisting her toward the center of the room, and when her legs hit the ground, Nilah wondered how much longer she'd be able to stand.

"Thanks, babe," she croaked. "Now I need a doctor."

"Keep your mouth shut!" he screamed into her ear, slamming her against the wall alongside her compatriots, and she nearly fainted.

They hadn't fared much better, given their injuries. Cordell's face was locked in a wince—they'd ripped his arm from the cast, reopening his sword wound. Boots's already bruised nose had a bloody cut across the bridge. Armin's cheek had an extra blush to it from where they'd banged his head against something. Orna was the only halfway healthy-looking person there, and she sneered at the marines as they pulled weapon after weapon from her.

"Sir!" called one of the marines, holding out a comm. "Direct communication from the PM. We're to secure the bay for his landing."

The leader of the group, a squat fellow with beady eyes, spun on his subordinate. "Negative. Advise Minister Mandell that we've not yet swept for explosive devices or magical traps. What's his ETA?"

"Not sure. Let me check."

But he didn't have time. Wind whipped at Nilah's face as Dwight's sleek, silver yacht came barreling through the docking shield to land at one of the open platforms. Landing pincers gripped the clamps as impulse thrusters popped across the hull, and the ship's engines sighed, powering down.

"Guard the prisoners. Hansen, take your folks and secure every entrance to this place," called the squad commander, pointing out two of his fellows. "You and you, with me." He then jogged away toward the yacht, two of his marines trailing behind.

"Continue facing the wall! Do not look at me!" shouted the new woman in charge, and Nilah could feel the aim of the slingers on her back like a hot ray of sun. She kept as still as she could, not eager to be executed by a pack of goons.

Then she heard it—the baritone of Dwight Mandell's voice. Bittersweet feelings raced through her—anger for his betrayal, nostalgia, longing, and loss. She couldn't see him, only the metal wall plate pressed to her cheek, and was glad of it. She didn't want him witnessing the look on her face.

"Well now," rumbled Dwight, his voice full like an opera singer's. It wasn't hard to see how he'd been elected, even without his magic. "What a sorry sight we have here. Couldn't even bother to raid the crew lockers for some new clothes?"

"Sir," said the woman holding them hostage, "we seized these weapons, and—"

The bass thump of Dwight's glyph sapped the strength from

Nilah's knees. A sunny yellow light washed over the bay, warming them, reminding Nilah of everything she ever loved about Dwight. His kind smile, the crow's-feet on his otherwise smooth face, the regal stature of his posture, the salt and pepper of his beard. He'd held her on his lap when he was just a senator, and how had she repaid him? By ignoring his pleas for her to come home; by skulking around the galaxy, undermining his machinations.

He believed the galaxy deserved to die. Who was she to question a god?

Despite the guard's orders, she turned to face Dwight Mandell—the absolute, the inevitable. His smoking glyph hovered in the air, easily four meters across—far beyond his armspan. He hadn't traced it, then; it must've appeared spontaneously in response to his perfection. To see him was to see destiny. To hear him was to hear fate. Compared with Dwight, other charmers were paltry scribblers, only able to exert minor influence on others. She completely, unreservedly loved him, and the majesty of that knowledge thrilled her heart. How had she been allowed to touch him all those years ago, to play in his gardens when she wasn't fit to serve him? Her body felt so cold now at the remembrance of his loving, familial embrace. She glanced at the other crew of the *Capricious*; they, too, were thunderstruck at the foolishness of their plans.

"Hello, Nilah," he said, the twin syllables of her name now a treasured memory to her.

She wept openly at her mistake.

"There's no need to cry, dear," he said, and she nearly choked trying to stifle her sobs.

"I'm so sorry, sir," stammered the guard, her slinger shaking in her hand, gaze casting about between Dwight and Nilah. "I...I told her not to move and I didn't know you knew her, and—"

"Thank you, Major. I hate that you're so well-informed," he

said, and the soldier gasped as he placed a hand on her shoulder. "The public can't know that Nilah Brio and her compatriots brought the *Harrow* here. No one can be allowed to inspect this ship."

She shook her head, tears filling her eyes as well. "Everyone in this bay is cleared at the highest levels, sir. We would never betray your confidences."

He reached out and stroked away a tear from the guard's face. "All magic is fleeting. You'll one day come to hate me."

"I could never!" shouted the guard, biting back a scream.

Nilah felt such pity for her. Betraying Dwight had placed Nilah in her own personal hell—something she'd never wish on anyone.

"I think it's only fitting," said Dwight, "that you and your soldiers kill yourselves."

A split second of slinger fire filled the bay, followed by the sound of two dozen bodies hitting the floor. The silence that followed was a profound testament to the might of a god.

Then Nilah remembered that they were broadcasting a camera feed, and she wailed in agony, collapsing to the ground in a puddle of tears. Dwight rushed to her undeserving side, comforting her, shushing in her ear, rubbing her shoulders with his warm hands to calm her. She forced herself to regain a measure of composure, because her god required it of her.

"What is it, child?" he asked. "Don't cry for them. They died serving me."

She only wished that was why she fought her tears. "No," she sobbed. "I've betrayed you again. The ship is broadcasting all of this to the planet. They've...seen your glory."

A hint of displeasure crossed Dwight's face, and Nilah wished for one of the soldier's slingers so that she could end her worthless existence.

"It is what it is, my dear. You and your crew brought the ship to me, and we'll take it out of here," he said.

Nilah placed her hands to her mouth. "I can't! We can't! There are no authorized users! She set you up and locked you out." With that, Nilah thrust a finger at Boots.

A scream, and Boots slammed her head against the metal bulkhead so hard she fell unconscious—that wicked trickster, that garbage woman. Of course she was dull-fingered; she was born undeserving of the cardioid. No magi could be so vile, so inferior. Boots had evil in her heart, born into a legacy of hateful malice. She'd trapped Dwight aboard the *Harrow*, and when Nilah was done serving her god, she'd gladly cut Boots's throat for him.

How Nilah could've befriended such an unworthy creature was beyond her grasp.

Dwight smiled. Her lord could sense her hatred.

"Nilah," he said, and she shivered, "you're a problem-solver. You can destroy any obstacle that stops us from leaving. Your crew will take me where I need to go."

Of course she could. She'd unravel Kin just like she'd unraveled Ranger, just like the springflies. She could atone. She could give him everything he asked, and she felt as though she might take flight with joy. The machines would serve her, and Dwight in turn.

"One question, my dear," he said, helping her to her feet.

"Anything," she sighed.

He pointed. "Why have you welded that breastplate to the rafters?"

Oh god, no.

Deep in the bowels of the *Harrow*, far away from the beauty of Dwight Mandell's glyph, Aisha fired a discus round from her slinger. It struck the piece of Mother's shoulder pauldron secured

413

to the side of a ventilation shaft, and the round shattered, loosing a single hot shard of energy that traveled up to the mission planning room.

Nilah leapt at Dwight without warning; there was no time.

The shard bounced off one of Mother's greaves and shot through a door, then down a corridor, then across the crew mess, before ricocheting off the inside of Mother's backplate just outside the bay.

She clutched Dwight's head to her bosom, her injuries lighting up like a campfire inside her, but she had to be his shield. She needed to protect him at all costs. His hands flew up to tear her away, and he let out a muffled cry, but she couldn't let him go.

She heard its searing report as the shard struck Mother's breastplate in the docking bay. It slammed into her back as she and Dwight toppled to the ground, and she prayed her body was enough to stop it. They tumbled together, his weight crushing her, until they came to rest a few feet apart. She glanced down at her chest and found blood, frayed fabric, and the sickening white of a cleanly severed rib. Red oozed from her torso, her paltry life given to save true greatness.

Dwight gurgled and sat upright.

"No," she whispered.

A spray of crimson erupted from his throat, and though he tried to stifle the flow, his strength failed him. He fell onto his back, desperately clutching his neck.

"No!" she commanded, then she begged over and over. She clambered to his side, suppressing her own agony to get to him. He reached out to her, letting go of his own grievous injury to wrap his fingers around her neck.

Yes, take me as payment.

The warmth of his presence began to fade, even as darkness

pressed into Nilah's vision. Reverence became pity. The spell came free of her bones. Pity became horror. She scrabbled at his slick hands, trying to pry them free. Horror became fury. She smashed a fist into his nose. His eyes rolled back in his head, and the last of his lifeblood spluttered to the deck as his hands went slack around her throat.

As unconsciousness swept in on her, swift and black, Nilah realized that this was how a god dies—

Like a rabid dog put down.

Chapter Twenty-Three

Finish Line

S oft sheets, a cool breeze.

Nilah stirred and felt not a single twinge of pain within her lithe body—though she wasn't accustomed to feeling so weak. A single pump whispered peacefully beside her bed, its well-tuned mechanism fading into the murmur of water.

Her eyes creaked open to find a shady room, its ceiling a canopy of swaying palm fronds in the fresh sea air. She raised her head above the cocoon of pillows and clean linens to find billowing curtains, and through them, an impossibly bright emerald sea. She turned the other way to find her father, his dark, full cheeks shining with jeweled tears.

"Oh, thank god, my Nilah," he whimpered, running his fingers over her hair. "My little girl. I'm so sorry."

"Hi, Dad," she sighed, then drowsiness oozed into her like a sweet liquor, and she closed her eyes again. "Don't let them take off the scars on my face, okay? I want those. Don't..."

"Okay, baby. We'll discuss it later." Her father's soft touch stroked away layer after layer of consciousness until she melted into dreams.

When she opened her eyes again, she could swear she saw Malik's silhouette. She blinked a few times, unsure of how much time had passed. She rubbed away the sleep gunk, trying to get a better look at him, trying to see if this was just a drug-induced hallucination or a dream.

But his warm smile was altogether real.

"I hear you're in the wrong sport, Miss Brio. You should've been a ballplayer," he said, in that silken voice she thought she'd never hear again.

She smacked her dry lips together and sat up. "Malik, what?"

He arched an eyebrow and laughed. "The captain told me how you caught me."

She rose from the bed and threw her arms around him, squeezing as tightly as she could. "Where are the others?"

"They're down a few floors, in the cheap beds," he said. "That's where I was until an hour ago. I wanted to see you as soon as I could, so I could thank you for saving my life."

"It was nothing," said Nilah, looking around her projected hospital room, taking in the scent of sand and sea. Then she winked at Malik. "I mean, other than the greatest catch of all time."

He gave her a toothy grin. "I see your injuries haven't changed you. I'm so glad."

"Shouldn't you be getting some rest?"

He shook his head. "I don't think I'll be sleeping again for days. Now that I've gotten the antidote, I intend to stretch my poor legs a bit."

Malik stood, smoothing down his trousers. Now that she was more awake, she took in his outfit—linen robes and soft shoes. He looked as though he might head to bed at any second.

"I have to be getting back," he said. "Aisha is coming out of surgery soon, and I'd like to pop in."

"May I come with you?" she asked, rising from the bed. Her

ribs burned, and her eyes watered, but she forced herself to stand up straight. "Maybe I've been asleep too long, too."

When Boots awoke this time, she found a usurer mage tending to her wounds, his hands the green of a forest as he pulled bruises from her skin on her right arm. He traced bare fingers along her stitches, and they knit together into angry, pink scars. Her left arm killed her, but the right positively vibrated with pleasure from the spell—his expensive spell.

"Take it easy, Elizabeth," he said, his voice practiced and courteous, like an actor.

Boots craned her neck to look behind him. She found a spacious, well-appointed room with a window out onto the Mirror—one of the most famous lakes in the entire galaxy, nestled in Taitu's capital of Aior. The gravity had the authentic feel of a planet, not synthetic space fakery. The usurer, the view, the furniture—Boots knew a poor woman like her shouldn't be there.

"Doc, I can't afford this." She sat up despite his protestations, and the sheets fell away, revealing only a hospital gown.

"Easy, Miss Elsworth. We're here to help you."

It was then she saw the dozens of containers of brown algae beside his feet, their life force drained to repair hers. Biobatteries like those weren't cheap, and she knew she was already in over her head. A nurse wheeled a cart into the room with a fresh supply of the verdant bio gel, but Boots waved him off.

"No, no, I'm well enough," she coughed. "I can't pay for any of this. So, uh, if you still want to help me, you can help me find my clothes. Let's settle up and get done here."

"Miss Elsworth," said the doctor, "you can't leave now. You're risking a blood infection from your new—"

"What can I say? I'm a risk taker," she said, planting her palms on the railing of the bed to let herself down.

But one of her hands wouldn't touch. It only clanged.

"Your medical expenses will be covered by the state," protested the doctor, but his words passed by like distant clouds.

Boots's left arm wasn't an arm by any definition she could appreciate. Wires and tubes twisted through pistons and around steel scaffolding before terminating in a graceless manipulator. It encircled the railing in a loose robotic grip, its palm nothing more than the required association of cams and springs. Silicone pads covered the tips of phalanges, and when one of the pads touched the rail, she felt a small electric shock in her shoulder—not painful, just enough to let her know she was touching something.

It ached. She could see her left arm was missing, but it still throbbed with her racing heart.

"We'll…leave you alone," said the doctor, ushering the nurse out with him.

Boots thought of Henrick Witts, and his corrupt, withering touch. He'd desiccated her planet, sparked the civil war that took so many of her friends, robbed Orna of her childhood, taken Malik, taken Didier…taken Kin. Henrick had invaded every part of her life; now he'd taken a piece of her body. She might've been suicidal once or twice, but she'd always been Boots: plump, short, and magicless, but healthy.

And now part of her wasn't Boots.

She swallowed, the tightness in her throat the only warning of onrushing tears. Her cries came in stuttering sobs.

She tried to bury her face in her hands by instinct, but the cold metal jarred her out of it. With her good hand, she stroked her cheek and wiped away wetness. She held the other hand at bay, an alien invader. Her eyes followed the steel's length to her bare shoulder, ringed with itchy, red scars where her body met the prosthesis. She located the clips and gingerly removed the bolts holding her arm in place.

When she pulled it away, she found only a machined screw as thick as her thumb. She flexed the ball of her shoulder and the screw pin changed orientation, pointing this way and that. Then she threw the arm to the floor without a second thought. With her good hand, she pinched the pin, then gave it a light tug. It felt as though she'd pulled every muscle connected to her shoulder.

Boots yanked the sheets up over her torso and rolled onto her side, curling up in the tightest ball she could. Without her other arm, the bedclothes slipped from her, leaving her cold, exposed, and ashamed in a way she couldn't understand. She'd seen wounds like hers in the Famine War, but nothing so ugly as that arm.

Hospital staffers' shoes squeaked against the bare floor, but she didn't turn to see them. Someone picked up the arm; she heard it click as they turned it over, inspecting it for damage. Her table rattled as the arm was laid upon it.

"I'm fine," she whispered. "Get the hell out."

And they did, for a while.

Then the door opened again, and a voice said, "They told me you didn't even ask about me. That's cold, Bootsie."

She turned to see Cordell, her face swerving violently between anger at the disturbance, grief over the arm, and outright laughter. Cordell stood in her doorway, his abdomen wrapped in a glowing duraplex cast. The moron still wore his bloody captain's rags, like he didn't have more Clarkesfall crap in his closet on the ship. Armin helped him through, wearing the first genuine smile she'd seen on the first mate.

A thousand quips came to her mind, but instead, Boots said, "So if we're here, Aisha took the shot. How is she?"

Armin helped Cordell take a seat by the bed, then pulled up a chair for himself. "She's resting. Spinal grafts. Full recovery in a week or two. She sends her regards."

Boots scratched her nose with her remaining hand. "Tougher than she looks."

"One god down," said Cordell.

"Three," corrected Boots. "Prejean, Mother, and Mandell."

Cordell smirked. "They were a little shocked when they found her body. Maybe we should've moved the old woman with the crushed throat to the morgue."

"Maybe we should've jettisoned her corpse into the Taitutian atmosphere," Boots spat. "Crone doesn't deserve a grave."

"That's hard, Bootsie," said Cordell.

She shrugged, and they chewed on the silence for a moment.

"And Orna and Nilah?" asked Boots.

"A few floors up. A lot nicer up there than down here."

Boots found that hard to believe, but she let it slide.

"It was a strange feeling," said Armin, "getting a rescue party after assassinating the PM."

"That's it? They just... came and got us?"

Armin scratched his nose. "Yeah. Simple as that. Kin negotiated the surrender of the ship, and they took it over, well, amicably. I mean, we were still under arrest, but, you know, within a couple of hours, the Taitutians had all our data and cleared our names. Though, I suspect the ensuing lawsuits will take a few decades to sort out."

She sat upright. "What's going to happen to Kin? Can I get him back? Can they help me unlock him?"

The men exchanged uncomfortable glances, and Cordell was the first to speak. "Look, he's been connected to at least two of the most classified systems in the galaxy—the bunker on Carré and the *Harrow* itself. It's simple data contamination—they have to lock him up now. In addition to that, you weren't really licensed to have a military AI, were you?"

She glared at him. "Don't you try to rationalize taking him away. The evidence is out in the open, and I deserve that computer."

Cordell held up his hands. "That's fair. I'm just telling you what they're going to tell you. But there's good news in the bad."

Armin leaned forward, grinning. "Kin was able to modify the *Harrow's* broadcast equipment to overpower all radio comms on the planet. The data packets hit the Link, and they've been snatched up by the Galactic Transparency Initiative. Every journalist out there is picking it over now."

"We've got all of the conspirators dead to rights, and they've gone underground," said Cordell. "The gods can probably hide for a while, but just like the prime minister, they can't stay in power. Law enforcement everywhere is on high alert, and they've been purging anyone who's tied to the conspiracy. Folks like Uziah Lesinski are going to jail forever... or they've been taken out by strike teams. There's been a pretty serious shift in power here on Taitu, as well..."

She couldn't believe what she was hearing. Galactic news? Was she safe? Could they really stop running?

"What do you mean, 'shift in power'?"

"Sweetheart, you slept through a coup." Cordell pointed to her metal arm, which lay limp on the table. "So put your arm back on, because some important people owe you favors. The new PM wants to thank you personally for exposing the conspiracy. Not only that, but the Clarkesfall Veterans Restitution Fund wants to build a memorial in our honor."

It was like the bed dropped out from under Boots; she could hardly tell if she was floating or falling with that news. "I'd rather not see anyone."

Cordell shrugged. "Either you meet them on their terms and give them the interviews they want, or you get stalked. That's the deal.

Play nice, pose for pictures, and the PM's security detail might run interference with the press at large."

Armin picked up the robotic limb and offered to help her socket it to her shoulder. Boots recoiled as though the metal was red-hot.

Eventually, she succumbed to his sour gaze and let him snap the arm onto her. "Why'd they give me such a trash prosthesis, anyway? This thing looks like it's freaking ancient."

"That's because it is," said Armin. "Modern prostheses use magic to transmit data. They haven't made models for people like you yet."

"A lot of research went into that 'trash prosthesis,'" said Cordell. "It may not look like it, but that arm took a team of geniuses the week to build, so you ought to be grateful you've got it. Probably cost a fortune."

She shook her head. "That's what someone tells me every time I get to be even remotely normal: 'You ought to be grateful.' Is it too much to ask that I get to do the same crap as you scribblers?"

Cordell leaned forward, close enough that she could smell the sweet cologne on his skin. "We survived because of you. You gave all the final orders. You killed Mother when everyone buckled. You came up with the plan that exposed and killed Mandell. You may have saved an entire galaxy..."

Armin beamed, a bad look for him.

Cordell cuffed her on the piston where her bicep should've been. "So cheer the hell up. You seem to manage to get things done... better than any scribbler I know, for sure."

The first mate winked. "Besides, if you don't like it, you can pay them to design a new one."

She frowned. "Awfully cavalier with my cash, aren't you? I can't even afford this place without state assistance."

He sniffed. "Now seems like a good time to tell you we got salvage rights to the *Harrow*. You've got one hundred sixty million argents in a Taitutian bank account right now. Each one of us does."

His words drained the blood from her face as surely as if he'd opened a vein.

"Are you serious?"

The officers started with giggles, boiling over into laughter.

"You're not serious, right?"

They slapped each other on the backs and shook her shoulders so much it hurt.

She grimaced. "You boys know that ship was worth four and a half billion, right? Our shares don't even make up half of that. They're worth... thirty-two plus seventy... just over one billion. Did you already sign as the executive, Captain?"

Cordell's eyes rolled. "Oh, you call me Captain when we're divvying up the shares?"

"If I think I'm getting cheated, I do."

"You just got a hundred and sixty million, woman!"

She did some quick calculations. "And, by my count, it should've been six hundred forty million! What happened to the other three quarters of my cash?"

He scowled. "First off, galactic salvage lawyers got half."

"I hope they earned it," she said, crossing her arms. The scratchy wiring harnesses of her metallic claw unnerved her.

"You got paid, didn't you?"

"And where's the other half?"

Armin bit his lip. "That part is dicey. The Taitutian state only allowed us to take half the salvage fee."

"What? That was our ship!"

"Technically, some members of Mother's battlegroup were still in the Taitutian military, so we committed piracy when we commandeered the *Harrow*," said Armin.

424

"They were goddamned spies!"

"Then, we put a warship directly over their capital and broadcast state secrets to everyone with ears."

"That was to make sure the conspiracy came to light!"

The first mate stood and shoved his hands in his pockets. "Oh, I'm with you. And I think, with your recent popularity, we could've eventually won the court case...sometime within the decade."

She sat back. "So we caved for a quick coin."

Armin pursed his lips. "As a datamancer, I'd be remiss if I didn't tell you that a hundred sixty million today is worth a lot more than a billion in a decade. Investments and—"

Cordell held up a finger. "You factor in the dozens of interview fees, speaking engagements, fictional rights, and on and on, you'll have a tiny little empire with your name on it. On the social side alone, you could easily double or triple your money if you play those cards right. And you know, I think I'm starting to see the appeal of fame. You could probably go back on the Link, get your show back together. How about, *In Search of the* Harrow, or *Harrowing Horizons*?"

"Those names are terrible. Stick to captaining starships."

"So figure out our next adventure. We could get to the top of the Link ratings together. Help me find a producer."

His eyes gleamed in that all-too-familiar way: he wanted to gamble again.

"And all I have to do is talk to people?" she asked.

"Basically."

Boots looked out the window and took a deep breath. That plot of land on Hopper's Hope was going to have a distillery sooner, rather than later.

"I think I'll just take my cash and skip the media deals, thanks," she said. "One show was enough for me."

* * *

A few days later when Boots left the hospital, she found Nilah waiting for her in the glassy lobby. The racer wore a sensible black suit, her sunglasses reflecting the orange light of a perfect dusk.

"Checked ourselves out, did we?" asked Nilah.

Boots gave her a pained smile, peering past her companion into the road beyond, where a few reporters gathered like vultures. "Probably for the best. The press thinks I'm here for another two days, so I may as well get while the getting is good."

Nilah narrowed her eyes and repeated, " 'While the getting is good.' "

"Listen, kid, this ain't my scene and you know it." Boots's cheeks reddened. "If you want someone to blow something up, I'm your gal. But, uh, the press and stuff..."

Nilah laughed. "So, what, you're going to hide out in some hotel? Boots, you don't know the journos like I do. They'll find—"

"Not staying on Taitu," Boots interrupted, and Nilah's shocked expression nearly broke her heart. Boots stared down at her feet, unable to look Nilah in the eye. "Look, I...I don't know how to say this. The mission is over, and I had to head out at some point. It was fun to be back with the old gang for a bit, but I'm not a soldier anymore. I did what I was supposed to—gave the government my firsthand account and all. Not that it was required, since Kin recorded everything." The stab of losing her AI hit her all over again, and she mustered an awkward grin. "Besides, I'm rich now. I got what I wanted, you know."

The press had gotten wise to their conversation. A gaggle of silhouettes gathered outside the hospital doors, imagers in their hands, and the Taitutian State Guards rushed to clear them off and secure the entryway.

"I see." Nilah blinked, then recovered her composure. "Well, that's all right, mate! We'd be happy to have you at my father's

426

estate, or you can lodge for a bit in my house up on Morrison Station. Please, you simply must."

"Ah, hell. I don't think you get it." Boots scratched the back of her head. She'd never been one for talking about feelings. "I don't particularly want to hang around Taitu with, well...with what those people did to my home. And I know it was only a few bad eggs, but those bad eggs were running the damned government."

It wasn't the kind of wound Boots could recover from in a lifetime, much less the course of a few days. The Taitutian authorities had treated her with kid gloves, like they'd all done something wrong. If Nilah hadn't fought by her side, Boots's view would've been even dimmer. It wasn't logical, but logic would take some time to catch up to what she'd just lived.

"We were so naive when the war broke out, and then...we fought for nothing." Boots's eyes burned.

Nilah's mask of cheer began to crack. "But you made a difference this time."

"I don't want to be a hero, Nilah. I want my country back."

They stood together in silence for a minute, the journalistic cacophony growing outside.

"You're the greatest, kid. When we met, I totally hated you—with your bragging and posturing. Thought you were full of it, but..." Boots jammed her hands in her pockets and forced herself to look Nilah in the eye. "You're everything you said you were and more."

"And you acted like a washed-up nobody, so..." Nilah wiped a tear from her scarred cheek, her tattoos flooding with blue light. "I guess you're nothing like you said you were. One of a kind, that's you."

The press had worked themselves into a frenzy, trying every angle to capture this touching moment—so they could sell it as part of a package, turning the worst tragedy in galactic history into a couple of argents. Boots had been happy for them to disseminate the records from the *Harrow*, but now they were just a bunch of hyenas.

"I've got to get out of here," said Boots, sniffing. "They're about to start eating each other out there."

"Yeah." Nilah wasn't even bothering to cover her tears. "Stay in touch."

Boots smirked. "Keep your nose clean. Try not to murder the other drivers this time."

Nilah sputtered a laugh and threw her arms around Boots in a tight hug. Boots's chest felt as though it would split open, but she kept it together and patted Nilah a few times on the back.

She couldn't stay—not right now.

There were rolling fields of barley waiting for her.

The next three weeks were total mayhem for Nilah. Though her public persona had never been great—her publicist had to sprint to keep up with her trash-talking—she became the darling of her homeworld. Teenagers approached her with fresh dermalux tattoos, modeled precisely upon hers. Every media outlet in the galaxy flocked to Aior to speak with her as soon as possible.

They treated her like a queen, like the leader of the gritty crew of the *Capricious*. Everyone wanted to make her a perfect hero because she came from the right planet and had the right name, but it made her uncomfortable. At every group interview, she corrected history to point out that Boots and Orna had saved them all.

Nilah spent her wild nights with Orna, who quickly became an obsession for the press. They followed the pair around incessantly, and unlike Boots, Orna seemed to relish the attention. The quartermaster's icy eyes and bravado captivated the public, and soon, offers of representation came rolling in. They wanted her in dramas, clothes, and fighting competitions.

Nilah's merchandise sold out of every store, and the outlets on the Link couldn't keep up. That was excellent, except for the fact that Claire Asby was in hiding, the league commissioner had been taken out by a military strike, and the government had frozen all of Lang Autosport's assets along with much of the PGRF. And so, there was no one to resupply the retail outlets, creating instant collectors' classics. Nilah didn't mind too terribly—her salvage share alone was worth three years of her contract with Lang—but it was a shame to let all that advertising go to waste.

For obvious reasons, the final race at Vorlanti had been canceled, and the points remained tied between her and Kristof. This fact rattled around in her head as she ascended to the rooftop garden of Ubaxa, an exclusive restaurant on the Emerald Road River. Kristof pulled out her chair for her, then sat down across the table. Luminous drink options tumbled through the air before them, and they selected some libations before the projections faded away.

She looked Kristof over in the glow of the restaurant, his blond hair tousled by a river breeze. Despite losing his job, he looked well enough—hale and happy to see her.

"You didn't return my calls," she said.

"I haven't been allowed to call you since you got back," he replied, wiping his hands with a steaming towel. "Since Claire disappeared, they had to make sure I was...well, wasn't going to kill you."

"Please. If you murder people as well as you drive, I've got nothing to fear."

"Ah, there's the Nilah I know. I worried the added fame would change you."

Their drinks arrived, along with the chef, who made it patently clear that this meal was on the house for the great Nilah Brio.

Kristof smirked and added a magnum of 2860 Drapeau Rouge to their tab in response, and the chef retreated.

"I don't think I've ever been comped a meal here," said Kristof, folding his hands in his lap.

"Oh, now. They would've comped me if I were the galactic racing champion too," she said, her eyes taking in the ten thousand magically suspended lanterns over the garden. "With the PGRF half dismantled and all the tracks banned from use, I guess we'll never know who would've been champion, will we, darling?"

"Not so. The rules are clear, I'm afraid," said Kristof. "I'm the champion. I held the pole position nine times to your seven."

"What?" It was the first time anyone had given her bad news in the past few weeks.

He held up a hand. "However, I believe you would've taken Vorlanti. This was your year. You were everything a great driver should be... and then some."

"Yeah, but that's all over now. Lost the momentum of the winning streak. Lost my car. Lost my team."

Kristof took a sip of his gin while they waited for the sparkling wine to arrive. When he set the glass down, his eyes glittered conspiratorially. "You still have a teammate, you know."

"Two drivers can't form a team, Kristof."

"Why not? According to the press, you have the money."

"Sure, but if I'm hiring the drivers, I need top talent. You can be a reserve driver, maybe." She gave him a wink.

The sparkling wine arrived, and they uncorked it to great fanfare. Their waiter filled two long-stemmed flutes with the golden liquid, trails of bubbles snaking through it like strings of pearls. Nilah held up her glass in salute to Kristof.

"To the finish line," she said.

"To the finish line."

She'd had Drapeau Rouge a dozen times on the podium, but

the dry wine took on a far sweeter character, given the trials that had brought her to this place. Her dermaluxes shone cool blue under her suit sleeves, making halos around her hands.

Kristof pointed to her cold light. "Why so sad?"

Nilah took a large gulp of her wine and set the glass on the table. She straightened her napkin to align it with her place setting, then looked out over the valley. She couldn't look at Kristof as she spoke.

"I wanted to say thank you for defending me...you know... in the interviews. After Claire rolled over on me, everyone was so sure I was guilty."

He plopped his own glass on the table. "I've never been so furious as I was listening to those journalists. I don't like you all the time, but I know you wouldn't murder someone."

A flash of gold from her tattoos. "You do like me, though."

"Don't tell anyone."

She glanced at him, then tapped the table absentmindedly. She wasn't used to feeling nervous. "I'm going to miss this. Going to miss racing."

He laughed. "What are you talking about? You'll get your edge back!"

But she didn't laugh.

"What, you're done?" His smile disappeared. "You're serious?"

She locked eyes with him, willing him to understand.

"No. You are not quitting. That's out of the question. You're one of the greats, Nilah! This was your year!"

"My year came and went, Kristof."

"You see, this is what I hate about you! On the track, you're perfect, but in your life, you're impetuous, arrogant, reactionary!" He rubbed his eyebrows, his jaw tensing. "Dramatic."

She cocked an eyebrow. "Who's being dramatic?"

He held his hands out to her, almost begging. "Nilah, we've

been together since the karting days. You're a sister to me. You've been here to push me every step of the way, and you—you're probably the reason I'm a champion now. At the beginning of the season, I was ready to throttle you, but you know...that made me fight harder, drive better."

Her blue faded to white. "Other champions will come, Kristof. There's a lot of young talent in the under leagues—"

But he stopped her with a look.

"Okay," she said. "I'll admit it—we're a good match. Without me in your way, you're going to be galactic champion over and over, and no one can stop you. Is that what you want to hear?"

He rested his chin against a palm. "I want you to say you'll be coming back. I want to see you next season. They're building all-new tracks! There's new management, new rules, and—"

"I can't do that, Kristof. I have other matters to attend to."

The first course arrived: gabbar confit, with a Norlan crema sauce and sprinkled smoked sugar. The plates were tiny works of art, with the bloodred gabbar fruit swirling against the chartreuse crema. It was the perfect vegetarian cuisine, ideally suited to Nilah's tastes, yet neither of them lifted a utensil.

"That's not right," he said. "You should be making your place in racing history. You're being stupid."

She gestured to the rest of the restaurant. "I'm the one getting comped for saving civilization. I think you're forgetting that I've already made my place in history."

He picked up his fork, contemplated his food, then tossed the fork onto the plate. "Goddamn it. This is because some of those bastards got away, isn't it?"

"Could you rest, knowing they were out there?"

"Yes! I mean, no, but look at you! You show up sliced to ribbons, scars on your face! You're going to get killed, Nilah. Why can't you let the professionals handle this?"

She ran her fingers along the puffy slashes on her cheek—the souvenir given to her by Ranger in his last moments. They almost looked like cat's whiskers. She'd let the surgeons and healers take all the springfly scars away from her, even replacing the missing bit of her ear, but she wondered if she'd regret it. She'd earned those marks facing down some of the deadliest bots out there, and she'd miss them.

She wasn't sure Kristof could understand. Racers loved to tackle ridiculous challenges, but between safety equipment and ironclad standards, real injuries were rare. Any amount of risk to the body was deemed unacceptable. How could someone from that world comprehend the choice to face danger?

"Because," she began, "I've been close to real perfection."

"Oh, come on."

"Racing is all about repetition. Yeah, you can have a good line on a lap, but it's impossible to have it on all sixty or seventy. The weather changes, the track changes, they change the tire compounds, there's too much clag on the tarmac, a wreck leaves a piece of broken fibron. You can try to adapt, but face it: what we do is memorization."

"That's not true. We have to improvise."

She smiled. "Kristof, we get the track plan a year in advance. Our engineers pick it over with a fine-tooth comb. We drive it for five hundred hours in the simulator. Mages stream it into our dreams when we sleep. By the time we get to race day, all we care about is a mechanical failure and making sure that the other buffoons don't crash into us."

He tapped his chest. "That's because you drive with your head and not your heart."

"The heart takes pole position. The head wins races."

"Is that right? Pole position won me the championship."

"My track record speaks for itself, but you don't have to listen to me. You're the most talented driver I've ever met," she said, raising her glass in mock salute. "But when I was out in the wild, facing down threats we'd never seen, I couldn't rehearse. I just had to do what was inside. If I flinched, I died. If I made a mistake, I died. To drive a perfect lap, that's easy. What I felt on the *Harrow*... it was the next level."

"I think the blood loss may have scrambled your brains." He picked up his fork again and scooped some of the red fruit flesh into his mouth.

She pushed the food around her plate, but didn't take a bite. "For the past few nights, I've been waking up with nightmares."

He looked her over thoughtfully.

"I dream of being an old woman, safe and sound, tucked away in the edge of the galaxy. In the dream, Henrick Witts never came after me, and I never went after him... and I never got to feel what I felt with the *Capricious* ever again. I'm just... old."

"Are your dusty cabinets covered with Galactic Champion trophies? Because then it sounds like a great dream."

She sighed. "How can I care about racing when I just helped determine the fate of worlds? I just... can't anymore."

"You're going to get killed."

She looked across at him, stars in her eyes.

"But what a grand way to die."

The next morning, a dour-looking gentleman from the Ministry of Security showed up at Nilah's hotel bearing an intercepted video transmission from Claire. They'd tracked it to Clarkesfall's dusty husk, but lost the trail there. It said simply, "Don't follow us. I'd hate to have to kill you myself." Nilah spent the rest of the day trying to shake off the fury and scorn she felt, throwing herself into interviews and advertisements.

Anything to forget Claire's profound betrayal for a moment.

When Nilah went home that night, she didn't adjourn to her

well-furnished apartments on Morrison Station. Her driver took her to the state spaceport. Hot wind and a low rumble from distant engines forced their way into the transport as she opened the door—the passing whispers of ships launching in the distance. She'd once loathed this place, only coming here to board the Lang shuttle to the next race. She had no love of the journey, only longing for the arrival.

But now, she watched ships launch, rising columns of smoke like the pillars of some divine palace, and a calm fell upon her heart. As she walked toward the civilian docks, her boots felt ten kilograms lighter; she could almost leap offworld by herself. Ahead of her, surrounded by a cadre of heavily armed state guards, stood the *Capricious*, and in its wide-open cargo bay, Orna.

Nilah strode purposefully toward the quartermaster, and the guards parted for her. Her arms entangled with Orna's, and they kissed, Nilah's dermaluxes fluttering pink.

Orna didn't let go. "The captain is almost ready to launch. Said your goodbyes to everyone?"

"Yeah. Dad wasn't excited, to say the least. He took it better than Kristof. The fans will be barmy, of course."

"They'll have to get over it," said Orna. "I want you with us."

Nilah hooked a finger under Orna's collar and felt the silky texture of her shirt. It was Camden Cross—expensive, and one of Nilah's former sponsors. "You've certainly upgraded your wardrobe here on Taitu. You're not going to miss the luxury?"

"I've enjoyed the attention," she sighed. "The crowds, the cameras. They like me for a change, and they're not asking me to… They're not like the fighting pits. And yeah, the new clothes are dumb I guess, but they're cool, too. They remind me of you." Orna scratched the back of her head, smiling. "I want to be stylish, like you. I love the effect you have on me."

"I love you, too."

Orna actually blushed, her many scars becoming white slashes on red-hot cheeks.

"Oh my god! You're blushing!"

Orna looked away. "Shut up."

"Your cheeks are like ruddy little apples! Oh, I love you!" She pinched Orna's face, laughing, and the quartermaster tried to duck away. "Can you get any redder?"

"Stop it!" Orna tried to duck away, but Nilah jumped on the tall woman's back.

"Never forget that I'm the fastest!" She leaned down and gingerly bit Orna's ear, and Orna froze. "Tell me you love me, too."

"I... love you."

"Good." And with hot breath, Nilah whispered, "Carry me inside."

They tromped up the cargo ramp into the bay and found Cordell leaning against a pallet, a lit cigarette in his hand. His solemn expression curled into amusement at the sight of them.

"I'm glad to see you two are having fun."

"About to have a lot more fun, Cap," Nilah chuckled.

"I see," he said. "Y'all ready to get underway? We can leave whenever you want."

"Give us thirty minutes," said Orna.

Nilah slipped down off her companion's back. "An hour, sir."

"Maybe two," added Orna.

Cordell snorted. "We're firing boosters in thirty. If you haven't moved the earth by then, the *Capricious* is going to move it for you."

"I think I'll manage," said Nilah, taking Orna's hand and leading her away.

Chapter Twenty-Four

Extraction

12 November, 2895
One year after the Harrow *returned to Taitu.*

B oots hefted the sack of millet over her shoulder, grunting as it slapped across her back. Dust sifted through shafts of sunlight. The shimmering motes would've been pretty if she hadn't been so sweaty, but the particulates clung to every inch of her exposed shoulders.

She flopped the sack over the mill and snapped her left hand, revealing a short blade inside the index finger. She sliced down the bag and picked up its tails, allowing the millet to spill over. Golden grains streamed into the hopper, and Boots shook the bag out, getting every last bit. Boots flipped the switch on the mill, instantly creating buckets of powdery grain. The deafening grind of the machine filled her warehouse, reflecting off the concrete floors and aluminum walls.

When she pounded the shutoff, the hum continued. At first, she thought the motor was stuck. Then she realized it was coming from outside the warehouse, low and thick, like a tractor engine. Her itinerant employees had already gone back to the colony for the day, so it couldn't have been them.

Boots wiped a glove across her forehead to clear away the sweat, only to leave a dirty streak. She pulled a handkerchief from her back pocket, but it was filthier than her glove. She shook it out and mopped her brow as best she could, then pulled one of the many slingers in her warehouse from its hiding place, checking the clip; she never felt truly safe, given that Witts and much of his cult were still out there. Cautiously, she headed out the door in search of the sound.

Wind swept her green valley in waves, flattening the long grasses of Hopper's Hope. She spied Twickenham Colony in the distance, its structural lights only starting to flicker awake in the setting sun. Warm engine wash filled the air, and she looked up to see the dark belly of the *Capricious* looming over her, the source of the heavy thrum. The ship settled down in her staging area, nearly knocking over a stack of corn crates. She swore as one of her imported barrels went rolling down the hill.

Boots waved her hands and gestured to the ongoing damage with the universal symbol for "What do you think you're doing?" But the ship continued its landing sequence.

When he'd settled onto his pylons, she counted at least three grand worth of damage. That landing area was for skimmers hauling small supplies, not marauders. The rear cargo doors began to open up, the slow whine considerably smoother than she remembered. He'd had some restoration work done.

"Hey!" she shouted the second she spotted a silhouette. "You can't park that junk heap here!"

Cordell came ambling down the newly ejected ramp in a sparkling-white captain's jacket, a lit cigarette hanging from his lips.

He glanced over his shoulder at the damage. "Oh, don't you worry about it. I'll pay for that."

"Great. So you're going to get me another order of Herschelite sherry casks before we go to maturation tomorrow?"

He smirked. "It's good to see you, Boots."

"You couldn't call ahead?"

"I was worried you'd disappear again."

"Nah. I would've just put out a closed sign and locked up."

"So you got your distillery all set up?"

"That I did. Making whiskey in the ancient style—no magic, just hard work. Calling it 'Kinnard's Way.'"

"I like it. The no-magic thing is a good angle. I'm sure you got folks lined up around the corner for the stuff."

"Sure," she said, "except the first casks won't be ready for the next decade. I can't use accelerators like most of the other distilleries."

He shook his head. "I hear you. Always got to do things the hard way, Boots."

"Maybe that's how I like it."

The engines shut off behind him, their whine steadily falling in pitch.

"What are you doing?" she asked. "I said you couldn't park here."

He took a long drag. "Just wondering if we could come rest planet-side for a while. Have a nice relaxing visit with an old friend."

"Got in some trouble, did you?"

"Maybe."

"Pissed off a few more gods?"

"Maybe." A long cloud of his cigarette smoke spiraled away on the wind. "So...can we come in?"

Armin appeared beside his captain, hands in his pockets. He hadn't changed a day, save for the welcoming smile on his face. "Hey, Boots. We can make it worth your while."

Boots craned her neck to look behind him, and her heart leapt at the sight of Nilah, looking stronger than ever. She'd thickened up, grown more muscular, and she stood with sure feet spread wide. Nilah's ocean wave tattoos beamed golden light across the bay, illuminating Orna, as well as a suit of bloodred tactical armor lurking behind her. It wandered to the edge of the ramp and sampled the air. Aisha stood behind them with Malik, his arm around her. And there were two others Boots didn't recognize—a pair of gingers that had to be brother and sister.

When Boots squinted, she spied the Midnight Runner, his hull brightly painted with the shades of Arca, his cockpit empty and calling to her. In that direction lay her home, and she felt its pull like gravity had failed her.

She knew why they'd come. If she let Cordell into her house, they'd spend all night drinking out of the stills and swapping stories until she followed him into the great darkness beyond.

She could stop it, though. She could tell him to clear off, that she didn't want any part of it—that she finally had everything she wanted. She could claim peace for the rest of her life.

Boots grunted and waved them onward.

"Ah, come on. You look like you could use a drink."

The story continues in . . .

A BAD DEAL FOR THE WHOLE GALAXY

Coming in December 2018!

Acknowledgments

The rules for crafting compelling salvage maps were a key part of this narrative, so maybe I can come up with some rules for crafting compelling fiction. Let's see...

Rule number one: A great book starts with great beta readers.
I was lucky to have several canaries in the coal mines of this story, and though none of my beta readers dropped dead, the news wasn't always good. These are the people who told me what I had to hear, not what I wanted to hear: Sharyn Hamilton, Maggie Rider, Joseph Johnston, Chris Bupp, and Stephen Granade.

Rule number two: A killer agent makes a killer manuscript.
Connor Goldsmith of Fuse Literary helped me get the *Capricious* up and sailing before an editor ever touched it. He upped our quality and our game, giving us our best chances of success in the strange world of publishing. It's always nice when you find someone who both grasps your subtext and won't put up with your crap. I've always wanted to be a series author, and he opened those doors for me.

Rule number three: You're only as good as your editor.

Acknowledgments

At World Fantasy Con, I asked for a sit-down with Brit Hvide, since she'd read the manuscript, and she proceeded to give me a blow-by-blow of all my mistakes. After a few minutes, she said, "I feel like I'm just tearing up your manuscript, and you're not saying anything!" So I turned around my notebook and showed her where I'd written all of the captivating advice I'd received. Even when she hadn't yet bought the book, she shared her wisdom with me for free. Any author who gets to work with her should count themselves lucky.

And just when I thought things couldn't get better, Nivia Evans came along and added a layer of polish I hadn't realized was missing. It must be both a blessing and a curse to have such a detailed eye, and I count myself lucky to have benefited from it.

Rule number four: Smart writers spend their days around smarter people.

I want to thank the alumni of Smoky Writers 2015, where I started this project, for listening to my ramblings about spaceships and race cars. We may have all gotten stuck atop a peak in the blistering cold, with a car literally careening down the mountainside at one point, but at least we had each other. Also, there was that murky hot tub, because someone left a moonshine peach in the skimmer. I guess what I'm really saying is: I love you folks.

And, like so many authors, I'd be nothing without my beloved, so here's to you, Renee Chantel White.

extras

orbit

meet the author

Photo Credit: Rebecca Winks

ALEX WHITE was born and raised in the American South. They take photos, write music, and spend hours on YouTube watching other people blacksmith. They value challenging and subversive writing, but they'll settle for a good time.

In the shadow of rockets in Huntsville, Alabama, Alex lives and works as an experience designer with their spouse, son, two dogs, and a cat named Grim. Favored pastimes include Legos and race cars. They take their whiskey neat and their espresso black.

if you enjoyed
A BIG SHIP AT THE EDGE OF THE UNIVERSE

look out for

A BAD DEAL FOR THE WHOLE GALAXY

by

Alex White

The crew of the legendary Capricious *are rich enough to retire in comfort for the rest of their days, but none of it matters if the galaxy is still in danger.*

Nilah and Boots, the ship's newest crew members, hear the word of a mysterious cult that may have links back to an ancient and all-powerful magic. To find it, hotheaded Nilah will have to go undercover and find the source of their power without revealing her true identity. Meanwhile, Boots is forced to confront the one person she'd hoped never to see again: her old, turncoat, treasure-hunting partner.

CHAPTER ONE

Polyphony

They writhed and swayed, bodies in motion to a blistering-hot beat.

Wisps of arcane fireworks drifted through the crowd—glimmering wireframe dragons and murmurations of cormorants spraying cool flakes of magic as they passed. Every stare that wasn't trained on the light show overhead rested on the singer Indira Panjala, whose silvered hair flowed in time with the kick drum.

Impossibly, Aaron Forscythe's eyes met Nilah Brio's.

This was the premier concert event in the galaxy. No reasonable person would have their eyes anywhere but the stage. But Nilah Brio's target was looking right at her, recognition in his expression.

She'd taken every precaution. She wore a purple wig over her now-famous mohawk. She'd done up her face, accenting different contours, flowing lines of neon makeup covering most of her features. She'd worn the sort of short party dress she hated. Her dermaluxes were covered in translucent sleeves, obscuring the patterns—even though every hundredth person in the crowd had copied her tattoos.

Confirming her fears, he spun and began shouldering through the crowd away from her.

"I've been made!" Nilah shouted into her comm, taking off after him.

"Hunter Two, hit him with a sleeper, say he's drunk, and bring him back to the ship." Cordell Lamarr's deep voice entered her ear, overpowering Indira's crescendo.

Nilah's target shoved a woman so hard she went sprawling to the floor. He plowed through the bystanders with an unnatural strength, creating a rising chorus of protestations.

"I'm bloody trying," snapped Nilah, vaulting over a stumbling drunk before juking past another. Her dermalux tattoos flared to life with strobing white light, temporarily blinding anyone unfortunate enough to look directly at them. The crowd parted before her, people eager to cover their eyes and look away.

If Aaron hadn't been smacking everyone around, he might've disappeared into the crowd with little difficulty. The shifting light show of the Panjala concert made him tough to track across a sea of bobbing heads. A few meters away, hands flailed as someone shoved another concertgoer; Nilah's eyes snapped onto Aaron as the culprit. He'd almost made it to the edge of the arena.

"Planetwise exit! Hunter One, block him off," she called out into her comm.

"Damn." Orna Sokol's voice enjoined the radio chatter. "I'm too far away. There are a lot of tunnels down there. Don't lose him. ETA two minutes."

"I'm not going to lose him," said Nilah, dodging a spilling drink. "I'm the one that found him."

"You're also the one that got spotted," said Orna, chuckling.

"We'll talk about this on the ship," hissed Nilah.

"Focus up," said Cordell, "We're hearing a lot of chatter from concert security. You might want to shut those tattoos off."

"Blast it," Nilah grumbled, suppressing her dermaluxes as her target made it to the arena's emergency exit.

Aaron kicked the door open and stormed out onto the balconies above Goldsmith Park, leaving Nilah to wrestle through the remainder of the crowd. By the time she stumbled outside, the only sign of him was a stomping sprint on the stairwell below. Cool, night-cycle air tickled her bare skin, and this high up, wind whipped at her dress. She leaned over the railing to see if she could spot him, and was rewarded by the sizzle of a lancer bolt passing by her head.

"He shot at me!" she said, ducking away from the edge.

"Getting a lot of police chatter," said Cordell. "That slinger fire triggered the detectors. Cops are on the way."

"Hang back, babe," said Orna. "This is turning into a cluster."

Nilah quickly leaned out twice more to catch a view of her quarry nearly to the base of the stairs and the lush greenery of Goldsmith Park. If she didn't stop him now, he'd get into the Morrison Station superstructure and vanish. All the hunting they'd done would be worthless if he went to ground. She eyed the emergency descender box and swallowed. It was only sixteen floors or so to sidewalk.

"Not the stupidest thing I've done," she muttered.

"Wait. ETA eighty seconds," said Orna.

Nilah pulled open the emergency box, finding ten shiny descenders inside. She took one of the clear discs and shook it, just to make sure the binary spells inside were still good.

She was an ex-racer, and an expert at judging speeds and distances. Forty-eight meters to the ground would make for a pretty quick fall. She spied Forscythe's shadow as he rounded the final corner and burst out into the open.

Now or never. She swung her legs over the railing. The bass beat of the arena thumped in her ears.

Nilah leapt into the neon haze of Morrison Station's downtown, the descender clutched tightly in her hand. Wind roared in her ears. The shadowy figure of her target grew exponentially in size.

She snapped the descender mere feet away from Aaron's head, gelatinous phantoplasm instantly enveloping the both of them, blunting the kinetic energy of her fall. Their limbs interlocked as they bounced across the park grounds, the world free-spinning.

Eventually, the bubble of goo burst, spitting them out onto the summery grass beneath the statue of Carrie Morrison. The pair arose, dripping with smoky gelatin, and came to regard one another. Nilah brought her fists to a fighting posture, and her dermaluxes began to pulse in time with the distant music underneath frosted armbands.

Aaron was boring for a trust-fund child. Given his heritage of extreme wealth, she'd expected better—perhaps some sort of cosmetic modifications. Either Aaron had never been modified, or the person who'd done his nose had no taste.

"Nilah Brio," said Aaron, smirking. "The little racer who never did."

"'Never did' what?"

"Won the Driver's Crown," he said, a tremor entering his voice. "He'll be pleased when I bring him your body."

She rolled her eyes. "Oh, my god. You cannot be serious right now. I saved the universe from your lot and literally punched out a horde of springflies. It was all over the Link."

"The news always lies," he said, whipping his slinger level with her face and blasting off a few lancers.

She tumbled away from his wavering aim with little difficulty, rolling to her feet and bolting forward. Nilah's flashing arms made wide, pulsing arcs, the tattoos leaving only the afterimage of waves upon the eyes of her target. Two more shots erupted in her direction, but Aaron didn't have the military precision required to make them land. His grip on the slinger was too tight, too amateur.

Nilah whipped her arms toward him, momentarily blinding Aaron with the spray of light, then sent a dark kick straight into his jaw, lifting him up off the ground. He came down hard on the small of his back, then slackened.

"ETA thirty seconds," said Orna, her voice almost panicked. "What's going on over there, babe?"

"I just took him down. Glass jaw, as they say—"

Two figures emerged from the shadows around the Morrison monument, glinting knives twirling in their hands. Both male, clad in fine suits, their postures spoke of expertise. Perhaps they were bodyguards for Aaron. Perhaps they were assassins come to cut her limb from limb. Either way, she'd have to deal with them alone. Her stomach churned at the thought of engaging trained killers.

"Forscythe has friends," said Nilah. She squared herself to the newcomers, her dermaluxes gently pulsing like lightning in a storm cloud. "Hello, boys."

They spread out to flank her, silent as ghosts. Aaron began to stir. His beady eyes flew open, and he scrambled to his feet, dashing away between the two newcomers. In two seconds, he'd be into the access corridors.

"Why don't we skip all of this?" Nilah asked of the closest one. "You can just walk aw—"

They slashed glyphs from the air with their fingers—one elemental sigil of ice, the other of wind. Together, the spells could form a flash-freeze that would kill her instantly. Her eyes darted from spell to spell, searching for the more powerful of the two casters.

Nilah dashed for the wind caster, falling upon him in a hail of flashing blows. He tried to ward her off with the knife, but she kicked it away; his spell fizzled in the jolt. With his guard softened, she leapt for him like a great cat, latching on and attacking. The man shouted in pain as she wrapped her legs around his chest, boxing his ears and eyes with punishing fists. She kicked off of him, knocking him backward against a rock, where he lay still.

She rose to her feet to find the frost caster's glyph engorged with power. The fellow moved with surprising alacrity, ripping arcane ligatures from the night. She'd misjudged their skill, taking out the wrong target first. The ice caster's fingers smeared closed the last throbbing line of the glyph, and the air crackled with frost.

It was like being thrust into the raw vacuum of space. Every inch of her overexposed skin seared with pain as frigid air wicked moisture away from the surface. Her eyes stung, and she shut them on reflex. Nilah wanted to shout, but when she opened her mouth, the freezing air bit her throat. Orna had been right, Nilah shouldn't have engaged them alone. The spell howled, wrapped around the distant sounds of Panjala.

Then came another noise: a familiar, mechanical galloping.

A metallic screech erupted from above them, and a suit of bloodred mechanical battle armor landed upon the ice caster, folding him in half. As soon as Nilah could move a muscle, she looked away, shivering. She was glad to see Charger, but would've preferred a less lethal resolution.

Charger's cockpit hissed, popping open to reveal Orna strapped inside, a smile on her face. "Told you to wait, babe."

"And how were you supposed to come to my rescue if I did?"

"Hunters, enough cute banter," interrupted Cordell. "Have we got eyes on Forscythe?"

Nilah bounded up to Charger and mounted his back plate, sinking her feet into his vents like stirrups. "In pursuit, Boss."

Orna shut herself back inside the cockpit, and the battle armor rocketed in the direction of the Morrison Station access corridor. Nilah held on for dear life as the creature beneath her loped along.

Nilah wrapped her arms around Charger's metal neck. "We really should put some handholds on the big guy for this! Some up top and footholds on the side."

"I'm not putting love handles on my killbot."

They reached the superstructure access hatch, which poked out from between a pair of bushes. Charger's claws left long ruts in the grass as the pair skidded to a halt. Caution flashers blinked around the thick door frame, indicating the lack of gravity beyond. The drive range didn't extend to the outer hull. Charger stepped inside, and Nilah's stomach flipped as she adjusted to weightlessness.

The superstructure was a mesh of translucent tunnels with running lights, punctuated every now and again by a viewport. From the city streets inside Morrison Station, the tunnels above appeared as a glowing, glassy web across open space. During racing seasons, Nilah had enjoyed using the tunnels for fitness training, doing speed runs between the various observation decks dotting Morrison's expansive hull. She could do a hundred kilometers of low-grav kicks easily.

The bright corridor extended before them, splitting into three offshoots. They kicked off to the end of the corridor, and Charger sampled the air as they flew. His neck snapped to the right, polychroic lenses flashing green with excitement.

"Good boy," Orna murmured through his speakers, and they bounded down the right side of the split.

They raced through the superstructure, Charger scenting out their prey with little trouble. Each of the bot's powerful kicks left an unfortunate red stain on the pristine walls, and Nilah wondered what they'd tell the police. When they reached the first observation deck, they found Aaron Forscythe trembling and red-faced, his slinger placed against his temple. He stood before the a wide cupola window, and Taitu was in planetrise behind him.

Charger's high-cal slingers swung out from their hip holsters before Nilah could even blink, but Orna stayed her hand.

"This isn't how it was supposed to happen," said Aaron, his voice cracking. Upon hearing him, Nilah guessed that he couldn't have been much older than eighteen. "You shouldn't have been there!"

Nilah pushed off Charger's back, grabbing on to one of the floor's many handrails. If he decided to fire at her, it'd be tricky to get out of the way. She couldn't maneuver as unpredictably in zero gravity—it'd just be a straight line. "We tracked your message. We know someone was here to recruit you. What have you gotten into?"

"They're going to kill me," he said, gritting his teeth.

"If you don't drop it," said Orna, locking back the hammers on Charger's massive slingers, "I don't think they'll get the chance. Now tell us who you were meeting."

"That's open space behind that window," Nilah warned, placing a hand atop one of Charger's slingers.

"Yeah, well, I'm sick of going after these newbies," said Orna. "Bunch of rich idiots with almost no intel."

Aaron sneered. "You think we can't end you and everyone you love?"

Orna's laugh came out tinny through Charger's speakers. "The only thing you're doing is boring me to death."

"Stop, darling." Nilah tensed her legs, preparing to leap away in case he took a shot at her. "I'm sure he thinks he's very important."

"You ruined this for me!" screamed Aaron. "I was chosen!"

Nilah and Charger exchanged glances.

"I mean," Nilah began, "not really. I've met the chosen ones. They're stonking powerful, and you can't even shoot straight. Just give up."

A glint of sunlight warmed the window as their star crested Taitu's horizon. Nilah prayed no civilians would come around for a morning constitutional.

"Look, let's work something out," said Nilah. "I want to get back to my comfy clothes."

"'Work something out'?" He laughed, a tear rolling down his cheek. "You've robbed me of my place among the gods."

"Believe me," Nilah said, inching closer. "I've met your gods before, and they're as mortal as you and me. You know what we can do. You've seen the shows on the Link. You've read the news stories."

"You got lucky once," said Aaron. "This is different."

"Can I shoot him yet?" growled Orna through Charger's speakers. "He's getting annoying."

"What did your recruiter want you to do? What was the price of entry?" asked Nilah, motioning for Orna to lower her weapons. "We might be able to arrange protection."

"Indira Panjala spoke up against the Children of the Singularity," said Aaron, shaking his head. Tears rolled down his cheeks, and his face twisted with something like shame. "Anyone who stands in the way of their plans has to die. Just like me."

Nilah raised a hand and tentatively floated closer. Maybe she could talk him down and compel him to help her.

His face darkened and he pointed his slinger at Nilah. "Just like you."

"Down!" Orna shouted, and Charger knocked her flat against the floor, where she bounced into the air. The bot placed a single devastating shot through Aaron's chest—and melted the window behind him.

The world went red. Charger held Nilah flat against the sudden decompression, pinning her to the deck with prehensile toes. Klaxons screeched in her ears. Her wig was sucked away, tearing to purple strands as it caught a jagged outcropping. Through the crack into the stars beyond, she saw Aaron Forscythe clutching his chest and struggling against the inevitable. Then, glowing nanotubes healed over the station's wound, and the crying wind grew higher in pitch before winking out.

It would be a few minutes before the cops got there. By then, Nilah and Orna would be long gone from Morrison station.

The air pressure returned to normal.

"*Capricious,* this is Hunter Two," huffed Nilah, "Mission failed. We need a pickup."

if you enjoyed
A BIG SHIP AT THE EDGE OF THE UNIVERSE

look out for

ADRIFT

by

Rob Boffard

In the far reaches of space, a tour group embarks on what will be the trip of a lifetime—in more ways than one...

At Sigma Station, a remote mining facility and luxury hotel in deep space, a group of tourists boards a small vessel to take in the stunning views of the Horsehead Nebula.

But while they're out there, a mysterious ship with devastating advanced technology attacks the station. Their pilot's quick thinking means that the tourists escape with their lives—but as the dust settles, they realize they may be the only survivors...

Adrift in outer space on a vastly under-equipped ship, they've got no experience, no weapons, no contact with civilization.

They are way out of their depth, and if they can't figure out how to work together, they're never getting home alive.

Because the ship that destroyed the station is still out there. And it's looking for them.

CHAPTER 1

Rainmaker's heads-up display is a nightmare.

The alerts are coming faster than she can dismiss them. Lock indicators. Proximity warnings. Fuel signals. Created by her neurochip, appearing directly in front of her.

The world outside her fighter's cockpit is alive, torn with streaking missiles and twisting ships. In the distance, a nuke detonates against a frigate, a baby sun tearing its way into life. The Horsehead Nebula glitters behind it.

Rainmaker twists her ship away from the heatwave, making it dance with precise, controlled thoughts. As she does so, she gets a full view of the battle: a thousand Frontier Scorpion fighters, flipping and turning and destroying each other in an arena bordered by the hulking frigates.

The Colony forces thought they could hold the area around Sigma Orionis—they thought they could take control of the jump gate and shut down all movement into this sector. They didn't bank on an early victory at Proxima freeing up a third of the Frontier Navy, and now they're backed into a corner, fighting like hell to stay alive.

Maybe this'll be the battle that does it. Maybe this is the one that finally stops the Colonies for good.

Rainmaker's path has taken her away from the main thrust of

the battle, out towards the edge of the sector. Her targeting systems find a lone enemy: a black Colony fighter, streaking towards her. She's about to fire when she stops, cutting off the thought.

Something's not right.

"Control, this is Rainmaker." Despite the chaos, her voice is calm. "I have locked on incoming. Why's he alone? Over."

The reply is clipped and urgent. "Rainmaker, this is Frontier Control: evade, evade, evade. *Do not engage.* You have multiple bogies closing in on your six. They're trying to lock the door on you, over."

Rainmaker doesn't bother to respond. Her radar systems were damaged earlier in the fight, and she has to rely on Control for the bandits she can't see. She breaks her lock, twisting her craft away as more warnings bloom on her console. "Twin, Blackbird, anybody. I've got multiples inbound, need a pickup, over."

The sarcastic voice of one of her wingmen comes over the comms. "Can't handle 'em yourself? I'm disappointed."

"Not a good time, Omen," she replies, burning her thrusters. "Can you help me or not? Over."

"Negative. Got three customers to deal with over here. Get in line."

A second, older voice comes over her comms. "Rainmaker, this is Blackbird. What's your twenty? Over."

Her neurochip recognises the words, both flashing up the info on her display and automatically sending it to Blackbird's. "Quadrant thirty-one," she says anyway, speaking through gritted teeth.

"Roger," says Blackbird. "I got 'em. Just sit tight. I'll handle it for y— Shit, I'm hit! I—"

"Eric!" Rainmaker shouts Blackbird's real name, her voice so loud it distorts the channel. But he's already gone. An impactor streaks past her, close enough for her to see the launch burns on its surface.

"Control, Rainmaker," she says. "Confirm Blackbird's position, I've lost contact!"

Control doesn't reply. Why would they? They're fighting a thousand fires at once, advising hundreds of Scorpion fighters. Forget the callsigns that command makes them use: Blackbird is a number to them, and so is she, and unless she does something right now, she's going to join him.

She twists her ship, forcing the two chasing Colony fighters to face her head-on. They're a bigger threat than the lone one ahead. Now, they're coming in from her eleven and one o'clock, curving towards her, already opening fire. She guns the ship, aiming for the tiny space in the middle, racing to make the gap before their impactors close her out.

"Thread the needle," she whispers. "Come on, thread the needle, thr—"

Everything freezes.

The battle falls silent.

And a blinking-red error box appears above one of the missiles.

"Oh. Um." Hannah Elliott's voice cuts through the silence. "Sorry, ladies and gentlemen. One second."

The box goes away—only to reappear a split second later, like a fly buzzing back to the place it was swatted. This time, the simulation gives a muted *ding*, as if annoyed that Hannah can't grasp the point.

She rips the slim goggles from her head. She's not used to them— she forgot to put her lens in after she woke up, which meant she had to rely on the VR room's antiquated backup system. A strand of her long red hair catches on the strap, and she has to yank it loose, looking down at the ancient console in front of her.

"Sorry, ladies and gentlemen," she says again. "Won't be a minute."

Her worried face is reflected on the dark screen, her freckles making her look even younger than she is. She uses her finger this time, stabbing at the box's confirm button on the small access terminal on the desk. It comes back with a friend, a second, identical error box superimposed over the first. Beyond it, an impactor sits frozen in Rainmaker's viewport.

"Sorry." *Stop saying sorry.* She tries again, still failing to bring up the main menu. "It's my first day."

Stony silence. The twenty tourists in the darkened room before her are strapped into reclining motion seats with frayed belts. Most have their eyes closed, their personal lenses still displaying the frozen sim. A few are blinking, looking faintly annoyed. One of them, an older man with a salt-and-pepper beard, catches Hannah's eye with a scowl.

She looks down, back at the error boxes. She can barely make out the writing on them—the VR's depth of field has made the letters as tiny as the ones on the bottom line of an eye chart.

She should reset the sim. But how? Does that mean it will start from scratch? Can she fast-forward? The supervisor who showed it to her that morning was trying to wrangle about fifteen new tour guides, and the instructions she gave amounted to watching the volume levels and making sure none of the tourists threw up when Rainmaker turned too hard.

Hannah gives the screen an experimental tap, and breathes a sigh of relief when a menu pops up: a list of files. There. Now she just has to—

But which one is it? The supervisor turned the sim on, and Hannah doesn't know which file she used. Their names are meaningless.

She taps the first one. Bouncy music explodes from the room's speakers, loud enough to make a couple of the tourists jump. She pulls the goggles back on, to be greeted by an animated, space-suited lizard firing lasers at a huge, tentacled alien. A booming

465

voice echoes across the music. "Adventurers! Enter the world of Reptar as he saves the galaxy from—"

Hannah stops Reptar saving the galaxy. In the silence that follows, she can feel her cheeks turning red.

She gives the screen a final, helpless look, and leaps to her feet. She'll figure this out. Somehow. They wouldn't have given her this job if they didn't think she could deal with the unexpected.

"OK!" She claps her hands together. "Sorry for the mix-up. I think there's a bit of a glitch in the old sim there."

Her laugh gets precisely zero reaction. Swallowing, she soldiers on.

"So, as you saw, that was the Battle of Sigma Orionis, which took place fifteen years ago, which would be . . ." She thinks hard. "2157, in the space around the hotel we're now in. Hopefully our historical sim gave you a good idea of the conditions our pilots faced—it was taken directly from one of their neurochip feeds.

"Coincidentally, the battle took place almost exactly a hundred years after we first managed to send a probe through a wormhole, which, as you . . . which fuelled the Great Expansion, and led to the permanent, long-range gates, like the one you came in on."

"We know," says the man with the salt-and-pepper beard. He reminds Hannah of a particularly grumpy high school teacher she once had. "It was in the intro you played us."

"Right." Hannah nods, like he's made an excellent point. She'd forgotten about the damn intro video, her jump-lag from the day before fuzzing her memory. All she can remember is a voiceover that was way, way too perky for someone discussing a battle as brutal as Sigma Orionis.

She decides to keep going. "So, the . . . the Colonies lost that particular fight, but the war actually kept going for five years after the Frontier captured the space around Sigma."

They know this already, too. Why is she telling them? Heat creeps up her cheeks, a sensation she does her best to ignore.

"Anyway, if you've got any questions about the early days of the Expansion, while we were still constructing the jump gates, then I'm your girl. I actually did my dissertation on—"

Movement, behind her. She turns to see one of the other tour guides, a big dude with a tribal tattoo poking out of the collar of his red company shirt.

"Oh, thank God," Hannah hisses at him. "Do you know how to fix the sim?"

He ignores her. "OK, folks," he says to the room, smooth and loud. "That concludes our VR demonstration. Hope you enjoyed it, and if you have any questions, I'll be happy to answer them while our next group of guests are getting set up."

Before Hannah can say anything, he turns to her, his smile melting away. "Your sim slot was over five minutes ago. Get out of here."

He bends down, and with an effortless series of commands, resets the simulator. As the tourists file out, the bearded man glances at her, shaking his head.

Hannah digs in her back pocket, her face still hot and prickly. "Sorry. The sim's really good, and I got kind of wrapped up in it, so..." She says the words with a smile, which fades as the other guide continues to ignore her.

She doesn't even know what she's doing—the sim wasn't good. It was creepy. Learning about a battle was one thing—actually being there, watching people get blown to pieces...

Sighing, she pulls her crumpled tab out of her pocket and unfolds it. Her schedule is faithfully written out on it, copied off her lens—a habit she picked up when she was a kid, after her mom's lens glitched and they missed a swimming trial. "Can you tell me how to get to the dock?"

The other guide glances at the outdated tab, his mouth forming a moue of distaste. "There should be a map on your lens."

"Haven't synced it to the station yet." She's a little too embarrassed to tell him that it's still in its solution above the tiny sink in her quarters, and she forgot to go back for it before her shift started.

She would give a kidney to go back now, and not just for the lens. Her staff cabin might be small enough for her to touch all four walls at once without stretching, but it has a bed in it. With *sheets*. They might be scratchy and thin and smell of bleach, but the thought of pulling them over her head and drifting off is intoxicating.

The next group is pushing inside the VR room, clustered in twos and threes, eyeing the somewhat threadbare motion seats. The guide has already forgotten Hannah, striding towards the incoming tourists, booming a welcome.

"Thanks for your help," Hannah mutters, as she slips out of the room.

The dock. She was there yesterday, wasn't she? Coming off the intake shuttle. How hard could it be to find a second time? She turns right out of the VR room, heading for where she thinks the main station atrium is. According to her tab, she isn't late, but she picks up her pace all the same.

The wide, gently curved walkway is bordered by a floor-to-ceiling window taller than the house Hannah grew up in. The space is packed with more tourists. Most of them are clustered at the apex, admiring the view dominated by the Horsehead Nebula.

Hannah barely caught a glimpse when they arrived last night, which was filled with safety briefings and room assignments and roster changes and staff canteen conversations that were way too loud. She had sat at a table to one side, both hoping that someone would come and talk to her, and hoping they wouldn't.

In the end, with something like relief, she'd managed to slink off for a few hours of disturbed sleep.

The station she's on used to be plain old Sigma XV—a big, boring, industrial mining outpost that the Colony and the Frontier fought over during the war. They still did mining here—helium-3, mostly, for fusion reactors—but it was now also known as the Sigma Hotel and Luxury Resort.

It always amazed Hannah just how quickly it had all happened. It felt like the second the war ended, the tour operators were lobbying the Frontier Senate for franchise rights. Now, Sigma held ten thousand tourists, who streamed in through the big jump gate from a dozen different worlds and moons, excited to finally be able to travel, hoping for a glimpse of the Neb.

Like the war never happened. Like there weren't a hundred different small conflicts and breakaway factions still dotted across both Frontier *and* Colonies. The aftershocks of war, making themselves known.

Not that Sigma Station was the only one in on the action. It was happening everywhere—apparently there was even a tour company out Phobos way that took people inside a wrecked Colony frigate which hadn't been hauled back for salvage yet.

As much as Hannah feels uncomfortable with the idea of setting up a hotel here, so soon after the fighting, she needs this job. It's the only one her useless history degree would get her, and at least it means that she doesn't have to sit at the table at her parents' house on Titan, listening to her sister talk about how fast her company is growing.

The walkway she's on takes a sharp right, away from the windows, opening up into an airy plaza. The space is enormous, climbing up ten whole levels. A glittering light fixture the size of a truck hangs from the ceiling, and in the centre of the floor there's a large fountain, fake marble cherubs and dragons spouting water streams that crisscross in midair.

The plaza is packed with more tourists, milling around the

fountain or chatting on benches or meandering in and out of the shops and restaurants that line the edges. Hannah has to slow down, sorry-ing and excuse-me-ing her way through.

The wash of sensations almost overwhelms her, and she can't help thinking about the sheets again. White. Cool. Light enough to slide under and—

No. Come on. Be professional.

Does she go left from here, or is it on the other side of the fountain? Recalling the station map she looked at while they were jumping is like trying to decipher something in Sanskrit. Then she sees a sign above one of the paths leading off the plaza. *Ship Dock B.* That's the one.

Three minutes later, she's there. The dock is small, a spartan mustering area with four gangways leading out from the station to the airlock berths. There aren't many people around, although there are still a few sitting on benches. One of them, a little girl, is asleep: curled up with her hands tucked between shoulder and cheek, legs pulled up to her chest. Her mom—or the person Hannah thinks is her mom—sits next to her, blinking at something on her lens.

There are four tour ships visible through the glass, brightly lit against the inky black. Hannah's been on plenty of tours, and she still can't help thinking that every ship she's ever been on is ugly as hell. She's seen these ones before: they look like flattened, upside-down elephant droppings, a bulbous protrusion sticking out over each of the cockpits.

Hannah jams her hand in her jeans pocket for the tab. She wrote the ship's name for the shift in tiny capitals next to the start time: RED PANDA. Her gaze flicks between the four ships, but it takes her a second to find the right one. The name is printed on the side in big, stencilled letters, with a numbered designation in smaller script underneath.

She looks from the *Panda* to its gangway. Another guide is

making his way onto it. He's wearing the same red shirt as her, and he has the most fantastic hair: a spiked purple mohawk at least a foot high.

Her tab still in hand, she springs onto the gangway. "Hey!" she says, forcing a confidence she doesn't feel into her voice. "I'm on for this one. Anything I need to know?"

Mohawk guy glances over his shoulder, an expression of bored contempt on his face. He keeps walking, his thick black boots booming on the metal plating.

"Um. Hi?" Hannah catches up to him. "I think this one's mine?"

She tries to slip past him, but he puts up a meaty hand, blocking her path. "Nice try, rook," he says, that bored look still on his face. "You're late. Shift's mine."

"What are you talking about?" She swipes a finger across her tab, hunting for the little clock.

"Don't you have a lens?"

This time it takes Hannah a lot more effort to stay calm. "There," she says, pointing at her schedule. "I'm not late. I'm supposed to be on at eleven, and it's..." she finds the clock in the corner of her tab. "Eleven-o-two."

"My *lens* says eleven-o-six. Anyway, you're still late. I get the shift."

"What? No. Are you serious?"

He ignores her, resuming his walk towards the airlock. As he does, Hannah remembers the words from the handbook the company sent her before she left Titan: *Guides who are late for their shift will lose it. Please try not to be late!!!*

He can't do this. He can't. But who are the crew chiefs going to believe? The new girl? She'll lose a shift on her first day, which means she's already in the red, which means that maybe they don't keep her past her probation. A free shuttle ride back to Titan, and we wish you all the best in your future endeavours.

Anger replaces panic. This might not be her dream job, but it's work, and at the very least it means she's going *somewhere* with her life. She can already see the faces of her parents when she tells them she lost her job, and that is not going to happen. Not ever.

"Is that hair growing out of your ears, too?" she says, more furious than she's been in a long time. "I said I'm *here*. It's *my shift*."

He turns to look at her, dumbfounded. "What did you just say?"

Hannah opens her mouth to return fire, but nothing comes out.

Her mom and dad would know. Callista definitely would. Her older sister would understand exactly how to smooth things over, make this asshole see things her way. Then again, there's no way either her parents or Callie would ever have taken a job like this, so they wouldn't be in this situation. They're not here now, and they can't help her.

"It's all right, Donnie," says a voice.

Hannah and Mohawk guy—Donnie—turn to see the supervisor walking up. She's a young woman, barely older than Hannah, with a neat bob of black hair and a pristine red shirt. Hannah remembers meeting her last night, for about two seconds, but she's totally blanking on her name. Her gaze automatically goes to the woman's breast pocket, and she's relieved to see a badge: *Atsuke*.

"Come on, boss," Donnie says. "She was late." He glances at Hannah, and the expression on his face clearly says that he's just getting started.

"I seem to remember you being late on *your* first day." Atsuke's voice is pleasant and even, like a newsreader's.

"*And*," Donnie says, as if Atsuke hadn't spoken. "She was talking bakwas about my hawk. Mad disrespectful. I've been here a lot longer than she has, and I don't see why—"

"Well, to be fair, Donnie, your hair *is* pretty stupid. Not to mention against regs. I've told you that, like, ten times."

Donnie stares at her, shoulders tight. In response, Atsuke raises a perfectly shaped eyebrow.

He lets out a disgusted sigh, then shoves past them. "You got lucky, rook," he mutters, as he passes Hannah.

Her chest is tight, like she's just run a marathon, and she exhales hard. "Thank you *so* much," she says to Atsuke. "I'm really sorry I was late—I thought I had enough time to—"

"Hey." Atsuke puts a hand on her shoulder. "Take a breath. It's fine."

Hannah manages a weak smile. Later, she is going to buy Atsuke a drink. Multiple drinks.

"It's an easy one today," Atsuke says. "Eight passengers. Barely a third of capacity. Little bit about the station, talk about the war, the treaty, what we got, what the Colonies got, the role Sigma played in everything, get them gawking at the Neb… twenty minutes, in and out. Square?"

She looks down at Hannah's tab, then glances up with a raised eyebrow.

"My lens is glitching," Hannah says.

"Right." This time, Atsuke looks a little less sure. She reaches in her shirt pocket, and hands Hannah a tiny clip-on mic. "Here. Links to the ship automatically. You can pretty much just start talking. And listen: just be cool. Go do this one, and then there'll be a coffee waiting for you when you get back."

Forget the drink. She should take out another loan, buy Atsuke shares in the touring company. "I will. I mean, yeah. You got it."

Atsuke gestures to the airlock at the far end of the gangway. "Get going. And if Volkova gives you any shit, just ignore her. Have fun."

Hannah wants to ask who Volkova is, but Atsuke is already heading back, and Hannah doesn't dare follow. She turns, and marches as fast she can towards the *Red Panda*'s airlock.

Follow us:

f **/orbitbooksUS**

𝕏 **/orbitbooks**

▶ **/orbitbooks**

Join our mailing list
to receive alerts on our
latest releases and deals.

orbitbooks.net

Enter our monthly
giveaway for the chance
to win some epic prizes.

orbitloot.com